To mike From

Linda

KIPLING STORIES

PLATT & MUNK
GREAT WRITERS
COLLECTION

KIPLING STORIES

Twenty-eight Exciting Tales
by the Master Storyteller

RUDYARD KIPLING

PLATT & MUNK, *Publishers*
NEW YORK

THE DRUMS OF THE FORE AND AFT

"And a little child shall lead them."

IN the Army List they still stand as "The Fore and Fit Princess Hohenzollern-Sigmaringen-Auspach's Merther-Tydfilshire Own Royal Loyal Light Infantry, Regimental District 329A," but the Army through all its barracks and canteens knows them now as the "Fore and Aft." They may in time do something that shall make their new title honorable, but at present they are bitterly ashamed, and the man who calls them "Fore and Aft" does so at the risk of the head which is on his shoulders.

Two words breathed into the stables of a certain Cavalry Regiment will bring the men out into the streets with belts and mops and bad language; but a whisper of "Fore and Aft" will bring out this regiment with rifles.

Their one excuse is that they came again and did their best to finish the job in style. But for a time all their world knows that they were openly beaten, whipped, dumb-cowed, shaking and afraid. The men know it; their officers know it; the Horse Guards know it, and when the next war comes the enemy will know it also. There are two or three regiments of the Line that have a black mark against their names which they will then wipe out, and it will be excessively inconvenient for the troops upon whom they do their wiping.

The courage of the British soldier is officially supposed to be above proof, and, as a general rule, it is so. The exceptions are decently shoveled out of sight, only to be referred to in the freshet of unguarded talk that occasionally swamps a Mess-table at midnight. Then one hears strange and horrible stories of men not following their officers, of orders being given by those who had no right to give them, and of disgrace that, but for the standing luck of the British Army, might have ended in brilliant disaster. These are unpleasant stories to listen to, and the Messes tell them under their breath, sitting by the big wood fires, and the young officer bows his head and thinks to himself, please God, his men shall never behave unhandily.

The British soldier is not altogether to be blamed for occasional lapses; but this verdict he should not know. A moderately intelligent General will waste six months in mastering the craft of the particular war that he may be waging; a Colonel may utterly misunderstand the capacity of his regiment for three months after it has taken the field; and even a Company Commander may err and be deceived as to the temper and temperament of his own handful: wherefore the soldier, and the soldier of to-day more particularly, should not be blamed for falling back. He should be shot or hanged afterward—*pour encourager les autres;* but he should not be vilified in newspapers, for that is want of tact and waste of space.

He has, let us say, been in the service of the Empress

for, perhaps, four years. He will leave in another two years. He has no inherited morals, and four years are not sufficient to drive toughness into his fibre, or to teach him how holy a thing is his Regiment. He wants to drink, he wants to enjoy himself—in India he wants to save money—and he does not in the least like getting hurt. He has received just sufficient education to make him understand half the purport of the orders he receives, and to speculate on the nature of clean, incised, and shattering wounds. Thus, if he is told to deploy under fire preparatory to an attack, he knows that he runs a very great risk of being killed while he is deploying, and suspects that he is being thrown away to gain ten minutes' time. He may either deploy with desperate swiftness, or he may shuffle, or bunch, or break, according to the discipline under which he has lain for four years.

Armed with imperfect knowledge, cursed with the rudiments of an imagination, hampered by the intense selfishness of the lower classes, and unsupported by any regimental associations, this young man is suddenly introduced to an enemy who in eastern lands is always ugly, generally tall and hairy, and frequently noisy. If he looks to the right and the left and sees old soldiers —men of twelve years' service, who, he knows, know what they are about—taking a charge, rush, or demonstration without embarrassment, he is consoled and applies his shoulder to the butt of his rifle with a stout heart. His peace is the greater if he hears a senior, who has taught him his soldiering and broken his head on occasion, whispering:—"They'll shout and carry on like this for five minutes. Then they'll rush in, and then we've got 'em by the short hairs!"

But, on the other hand, if he sees only men of his own term of service, turning white and playing with their triggers and saying:—"What the Hell's up now?" while the Company Commanders are sweating into their sword-hilts and shouting:—"Front-rank, fix bayonets. Steady there—steady! Sight for three hundred— no, for five! Lie down, all! Steady! Front-rank, kneel!" and so forth, he becomes unhappy; and grows acutely miserable when he hears a comrade turn over with the rattle of fire-irons falling into the fender, and the grunt of a pole-axed ox. If he can be moved about a little and allowed to watch the effect of his own fire on the enemy he feels merrier, and may be then worked up to the blind passion of fighting, which is, contrary to general belief, controlled by a chilly Devil and shakes men like ague. If he is not moved about, and begins to feel cold at the pit of the stomach, and in that crises is badly mauled and hears orders that were never given, he will break, and he will break badly; and of all things under the sight of the Sun there is nothing more terrible than a broken British regiment. When the worst comes to the worst and the panic is really epidemic, the men must be e'en let go, and the Company Commanders had better escape to the enemy and stay there for safety's sake. If they can be made to come again they are not pleasant men to meet, because they will not break twice.

About thirty years from this date, when we have succeeded in half-educating everything that wears trousers, our Army will be a beautifully unreliable machine. It will know too much and it will do too little. Later still, when all men are at the mental level of the officer of to-day it will sweep the earth. Speaking roughly, you must employ either blackguards or gentlemen, or, best of all, blackguards commanded by gentlemen, to do butcher's work with efficiency and despatch. The ideal soldier should, of course, think for himself—the *Pocket-book* says so. Unfortunately, to attain this virtue, he has to pass through the phase of thinking of himself, and that is misdirected genius. A blackguard may be slow to think for himself, but he is genuinely anxious to kill, and a little punishment teaches him how to guard his own skin and perforate another's. A power-fully prayerful Highland Regiment, officered by rank Presbyterians, is, perhaps, one degree more terrible in action than a hard-bitten thousand of irresponsible Irish ruffians led by most improper young unbelievers. But these things prove the rule—which is that the midway men are not to be trusted alone. They have ideas about the value of life and an upbringing that has not taught them to go on and take the chances. They are care-fully unprovided with a backing of comrades who have been shot over, and until that backing is re-introduced, as a great many Regimental Commanders intend it shall be, they are more liable to disgrace themselves than the size of the Empire or the dignity of the Army allows. Their officers are as good as good can be, be-cause their training begins early, and God has arranged that a clean-run youth of the British middle classes shall, in the matter of backbone, brains, and bowels, surpass all other youths. For this reason a child of eighteen will stand up, doing nothing, with a tin sword in his hand and joy in his heart until he is dropped. If he dies, he dies like a gentleman. If he lives, he writes Home that he has been "potted," "sniped," "chipped" or "cut over," and sits down to besiege Government for a wound-gratuity until the next little war breaks out, when he perjures himself before a Medical Board, blarneys his Colonel, burns incense round his Adjutant, and is allowed to go to the Front once more.

Which homily brings me directly to a brace of the most finished little fiends that ever banged drum or tootled fife in the Band of a British Regiment. They ended their sinful career by open and flagrant mutiny and were shot for it. Their names were Jakin and Lew —Piggy Lew—and they were bold, bad drummer-boys, both of them frequently birched by the Drum-Major of the Fore and Aft.

Jakin was a stunted child of fourteen, and Lew was about the same age. When not looked after, they smoked and drank. They swore habitually after the manner of the Barrack-room, which is cold-swearing and comes from between clinched teeth; and they fought religiously once a week. Jakin had sprung from some London gutter and may or may not have passed through Dr. Barnado's hands ere he arrived at the dignity of drummer-boy. Lew could remember nothing except the regiment and the delight of listening to the Band from his earliest years. He hid somewhere in his grimy little soul a genuine love for music, and was most mistakenly furnished with the head of a cherub: insomuch that beautiful ladies who watched the Regiment in church were wont to speak of him as a "darling." They never heard his vitriolic comments on their manners and morals, as he walked back to barracks with the Band and matured fresh causes of offence against Jakin.

The other drummer-boys hated both lads on account of their illogical conduct. Jakin might be pounding Lew, or Lew might be rubbing Jakin's head in the dirt, but any attempt at aggression on the part of an outsider was met by the combined forces of Lew and Jakin; and the consequences were painful. The boys were the Ishmaels of the corps, but wealthy Ishmaels, for they sold battles in alternate weeks for the sport of the barracks when they were not pitted against other boys; and thus amassed money.

On this particular day there was dissension in the camp. They had just been convicted afresh of smoking, which is bad for little boys who use plug-tobacco, and Lew's contention was that Jakin had "stunk so 'orrid bad from keepin' the pipe in pocket," that he and he alone was responsible for the birching they were both tingling under.

"I tell you I 'd the pipe back o' barricks," said Jakin, pacifically.

"You're a bloomin' liar," said Lew, without heat.

"You're a bloomin' little barstard," said Jakin, strong in the knowledge that his own ancestry was unknown.

Now there is one word in the extended vocabulary of barrack-room abuse that cannot pass without comment. You may call a man a thief and risk nothing. You may even call him a coward without finding more than a boot whiz past your ear, but you must not call a man a bastard unless you are prepared to prove it on his front teeth.

"You might ha' kep' that till I wasn't so sore," said Lew, sorrowfully, dodging round Jakin's guard.

"I'll make you sorer," said Jakin, genially, and got home on Lew's alabaster forehead. All would have gone well and this story, as the books say, would never have been written, had not his evil fate prompted the Bazar-Sergeant's son, a long, employless man of five and twenty, to put in an appearance after the first round. He was eternally in need of money, and knew that the boys had silver.

"Fighting again," said he. "I'll report you to my father, and he'll report you to the Color-Sergeant."

"What's that to you?" said Jakin, with an unpleasant dilation of the nostrils.

"Oh! nothing to *me*. You'll get into trouble and you've been up too often to afford that."

"What the Hell do you know about what we've done?" asked Lew the Seraph. *"You* aren't in the Army, you lousy, cadging civilian."

He closed in on the man's left flank.

"Jes' 'cause you find two gentlemen settlin' their dif-f'rences with their fistes you stick in your ugly nose where you aren't wanted. Run 'ome to your 'arf-caste slut of a Ma—or we'll give you what-for," said Jakin.

The man attempted reprisals by knocking the boys' heads together. The scheme would have succeeded had not Jakin punched him vehemently in the stomach, or had Lew refrained from kicking his shins. They fought together, bleeding and breathless, for half an hour, and after heavy punishment, triumphantly pulled down their opponent as terriers pull down a jackal.

"Now," gasped Jakin, "I'll give you whatfor." He proceeded to pound the man's features while Lew stamped on the outlying portions of his anatomy. Chivalry is not a strong point in the composition of the average drummer-boy. He fights, as do his betters, to make his mark.

Ghastly was the ruin that escaped, and awful was the wrath of the Bazar-Sergeant. Awful too was the scene in Orderly-room when the two reprobates appeared to answer the charge of half-murdering a "civilian." The Bazar-Sergeant thirsted for a criminal action, and his son lied. The boys stood to attention while the black clouds of evidence accumulated.

"You little devils are more trouble than the rest of the Regiment put together," said the Colonel, angrily. "One might as well admonish thistledown, and I can't well put you in cells or under stoppages. You must be flogged again."

"Beg y' pardon, Sir. Can't we say nothin' in our own defence, Sir?" shrilled Jakin.

"Hey! What? Are you going to argue with me?" said the Colonel.

"No, Sir," said Lew. "But if a man come to you, Sir, and said he was going to report you, Sir, for 'aving a bit of a turn-up with a friend, Sir, an' wanted to get money out o' *you*, Sir"—

The Orderly-room exploded in a roar of laughter. "Well?" said the Colonel.

"That was what that measly *Jarnwar* there did, Sir, and 'e'd 'a' *done* it, Sir, if we 'adn't prevented 'im. We didn't 'it 'im much, Sir. 'E 'adn't no manner o' right to interfere with us, Sir. I don't mind bein' flogged by the Drum-Major, Sir, nor yet reported by *any* Corp'ral, but I'm—but I don't think it's fair, Sir, for a civilian to come an' talk over a man in the Army."

A second shout of laughter shook the Orderly-room, but the Colonel was grave.

"What sort of characters have these boys?" he asked of the Regimental Sergeant-Major.

"Accordin' to the Bandmaster, Sir," returned that revered official—the only soul in the regiment whom the boys feared—"they do everything *but* lie, Sir."

"Is it like we'd go for that man for fun, Sir?" said Lew, pointing to the plaintiff.

"Oh, admonished,—admonished!" said the Colonel, testily, and when the boys had gone he read the Bazar-Sergeant's son a lecture on the sin of unprofitable meddling, and gave orders that the Bandmaster should keep the Drums in better discipline.

"If either of you come to practice again with so much as a scratch on your two ugly little faces," thundered the Bandmaster, "I'll tell the Drum-Major to take the skin off your backs. Understand that, you young devils."

Then he repented of his speech for just the length of time that Lew, looking like a Seraph in red worsted embellishments, took the place of one of the trumpets

—in hospital—and rendered the echo of a battle-piece. Lew certainly was a musician, and had often in his more exalted moments expressed a yearning to master every instrument of the Band.

"There's nothing to prevent your becoming a Band-master, Lew," said the Bandmaster, who had composed waltzes of his own, and worked day and night in the interests of the Band.

"What did he say?" demand Jakin, after practice.

"'Said I might be a bloomin' Bandmaster, an' be asked in to 'ave a glass o' sherry-wine on Mess-nights."

"Ho! 'Said you might be a bloomin' non-combatant, did 'e! That's just about wot 'e would say. When I've put in my boy's service—it's a bloomin' shame that doesn't count for pension—I'll take on a privit. Then I'll be a Lance in a year—knowin' what I know about the ins an' outs o' things. In three years I'll be a bloomin' Sergeant. I won't marry then, not I! I'll 'old on and learn the orf'cers' ways an' apply for exchange into a reg'ment that doesn't know all about me. Then I'll be a bloomin' orf'cer. Then I'll ask you to 'ave a glass o' sherry-wine, *Mister* Lew, an' you'll bloomin' well 'ave to stay in the hanty-room while the Mess-Sergeant brings it to your dirty 'ands."

"'S'pose *I'm* going to be a Bandmaster? Not I, quite. I'll be a orf'cer too. There's nothin' like taking to a thing an' stickin' to it, the Schoolmaster says. The reg'ment don't go 'ome for another seven years. I'll be a Lance then or near to."

Thus the boys discussed their futures, and conducted themselves with exemplary piety for a week. That is to say, Lew started a flirtation with the Color-Sergeant's daughter, aged thirteen,—"not," as he explained to Jakin, "with any intention o' matrimony, but by way o' keepin' my 'and in." And the black-haired Cris Delighan enjoyed that flirtation more than previous ones, and the other drummer-boys raged furiously together, and Jakin preached sermons on the dangers of "bein' tangled along o' petticoats."

But neither love nor virtue would have held Lew long in the paths of propriety had not the rumor gone abroad that the Regiment was to be sent on active service, to take part in a war which, for the sake of brevity, we will call "The War of the Lost Tribes."

The barracks had the rumor almost before the Mess-room, and of all the nine hundred men in barracks not ten had seen a shot fired in anger. The Colonel had, twenty years ago, assisted at a Frontier expedition; one of the Majors had seen service at the Cape; a confirmed deserter in E Company had helped to clear streets in Ireland; but that was all. The Regiment had been put by for many years. The overwhelming mass of its rank and file had from three to four years' service; the non-commissioned officers were under thirty years old; and men and sergeants alike had forgotten to speak of the stories written in brief upon the Colors—the New Colors that had been formally blessed by an Archbishop in England ere the Regiment came away.

They wanted to go to the Front—they were enthusiastically anxious to go—but they had no knowledge of what war meant, and there was none to tell them. They were an educated regiment, the percentage of

school-certificates in their ranks was high, and most of
the men could do more than read and write. They had
been recruited in loyal observance of the territorial idea;
but they themselves had no notion of that idea. They
were made up of drafts from an overpopulated manu-
facturing district. The system had put flesh and muscle
upon their small bones, but it could not put heart into
the sons of those who for generations had done overmuch work for overscanty pay, had sweated in drying-
rooms, stooped over looms, coughed among white-lead
and shivered on lime-barges. The men had found food
and rest in the Army, and now they were going to
fight "niggers"—people who ran away if you shook a
stick at them. Wherefore they cheered lustily when the
rumor ran, and the shrewd, clerkly non-commissioned
officers speculated on the chances of batta and of saving
their pay. At Headquarters, men said:—"The Fore
and Fit have never been under fire within the last generation. Let us, therefore, break them in easily by setting them to guard lines of communication." And this
would have been done but for the fact that British
Regiments were wanted—badly wanted—at the Front,
and there were doubtful Native Regiments that could
fill the minor duties. "Brigade 'em with two strong
Regiments," said Headquarters. "They may be
knocked about a bit, but they'll learn their business before they come through. Nothing like a night-alarm
and a little cutting-up of stragglers to make a Regiment
smart in the field. Wait till they've had half a dozen
sentries' throats cut."
The Colonel wrote with delight that the temper of

his men was excellent, that the Regiment was all that could be wished and as sound as a bell. The Majors smiled with a sober joy, and the subalterns waltzed in pairs down the Mess-room after dinner and nearly shot themselves at revolver practice. But there was consternation in the hearts of Jakin and Lew. What was to be done with the drums? Would the Band go to the Front? How many of the drums would accompany the Regiment?

They took council together, sitting in a tree and smoking.

"It's more than a bloomin' toss-up they'll leave us be'ind at the Depôt with the women. You'll like that," said Jakin, sarcastically.

" 'Cause o' Cris, y' mean? Wot's a woman, or a 'ole bloomin' depôt o' women, 'longside o' the chanst of field-service? You know I'm as keen on goin' as you," said Lew.

" 'Wish I was a bloomin' bugler," said Jakin, sadly. "They'll take Tom Kidd along, that I can plaster a wall with, an' like as not they won't take us."

"Then let's go an' make Tom Kidd so bloomin' sick 'e can't bugle no more. You 'old 'is 'ands an' I'll kick him," said Lew, wriggling on the branch.

"That ain't no good neither. We ain't the sort o' characters to presoon on our rep'tations—they're bad. If they had the Band at the Depôt we don't go, and no error *there*. If they take the Band we may get cast for medical unfitness. Are you medical fit, Piggy?" said Jakin, digging Lew in the ribs with force.

"Yus," said Lew, with an oath. "The Doctor says

your 'eart's weak through smokin' on an empty stummick. Throw a chest an' I'll try yer."

Jakin threw out his chest, which Lew smote with all
his might. Jakin turned very pale, gasped, crowed,
screwed up his eyes and said,—"That's all right."

"You'll do," said Lew. "I've 'eard o' men dyin' when
you 'it 'em fair on the breast-bone."

" 'Don't bring us no nearer goin', though," said Jakin.
"Do you know where we're ordered?"

"Gawd knows, an' 'e won't split on a pal. Somewheres up to the Front to kill Paythans—hairy big
beggars that turn you inside out if they get 'old o' you.
They say their women are good-looking, too."

"Any loot?" asked the abandoned Jakin.

"Not a bloomin' ana, they say, unless you dig up the
ground an' see what the niggers 'ave 'id. They're a
poor lot." Jakin stood upright on the branch and
gazed across the plain.

"Lew," said he, "there's the Colonel coming. 'Colonel's a good old beggar. Let's go an' talk to 'im."

Lew nearly fell out of the tree at the audacity of the
suggestion. Like Jakin he feared not God neither regarded he Man, but there are limits even to the audacity
of drummer-boy, and to speak to a Colonel was . . .

But Jakin had slid down the trunk and doubled in
the direction of the Colonel. That officer was walking
wrapped in thought and visions of a C. B.—yes, even a
K. C. B., for had he not at command one of the best
Regiments of the Line—the Fore and Fit? And he
was aware of two small boys charging down upon him.
Once before it had been solemnly reported to him that

"the Drums were in a state of mutiny"; Jakin and Lew being the ringleaders. This looked like an organized conspiracy.

The boys halted at twenty yards, walked to the regulation four paces, and saluted together as well set-up as a ramrod and little taller.

The Colonel was in a genial mood; the boys appeared very forlorn and unprotected on the desolate plain, and one of them was handsome.

"Well!" said the Colonel, recognizing them. "Are you going to pull me down in the open? I'm sure I never interfere with you, even though"—he sniffed suspiciously—"you have been smoking."

It was time to strike while the iron was hot. Their hearts beat tumultuously.

"Beg y' pardon, Sir," began Jakin. "The Reg'ment's ordered on active service, Sir?"

"So I believe," said the Colonel, courteously.

"Is the Band goin', Sir?" said both together. Then, without pause, "We're goin', Sir, ain't we?"

"You!" said the Colonel, stepping back the more fully to take in the two small figures. "You! You'd die in the first march."

"No, we wouldn't, Sir. We can march with the Regiment anywheres—p'rade an' anywhere else," said Jakin.

"If Tom Kidd goes 'e'll shut up like a claspknife," said Lew. "Tom 'as very close veins in both 'is legs, Sir."

"Very how much?"

"Very close veins, Sir. That's why they swells after long p'rade, Sir. If 'e can go, we can go, Sir."

Again the Colonel looked at them long and intently.

"Yes, the Band is going," he said, as gravely as though he had been addressing a brother officer. "Have you any parents, either of you two?"

"No, Sir," rejoicingly from Lew and Jakin. "We're both orphans, Sir. There's no one to be considered of on our account, Sir."

"You poor little sprats, and you want to go up to the Front with the Regiment, do you? Why?"

"I've wore the Queen's Uniform for two years," said Jakin. "It's very 'ard, Sir, that a man don't get no recompense for doin' 'is dooty, Sir."

"An'—an' if I don't go, Sir," interrupted Lew, "the Bandmaster 'e says 'e'll catch an' make a bloo—a blessed musician o' me, Sir. Before I've seen any service, Sir."

The Colonel made no answer for a long time. Then he said quietly:—"If you're passed by the Doctor I dare say you can go. I shouldn't smoke if I were you."

The boys saluted and disappeared. The Colonel walked home and told the story to his wife, who nearly cried over it. The Colonel was well pleased. If that was the temper of the children, what would not the men do?

Jakin and Lew entered the boys' barrack-room with great stateliness, and refused to hold any conversation with their comrades for at least ten minutes. Then, bursting with pride, Jakin drawled:—"I've bin intervooin' the Colonel. Good old beggar is the Colonel. Says I to 'im, 'Colonel,' says I, 'let me go the Front,

along o' the Reg'ment.' 'To the Front you shall go,'
says 'e, 'an' I only wish there was more like you among
the dirty little devils that bang the bloomin' drums.'
Kidd, if you throw your 'coutrements at me for tellin'
you the truth to your own advantage, your legs 'll
swell."

None the less there was a Battle-Royal in the barrack-
room, for the boys were consumed with envy and hate,
and neither Jakin nor Lew behaved in conciliatory
wise.

"I'm goin' out to say adoo to my girl," said Lew, to
cap the climax. "Don't none o' you touch my kit because it's wanted for active service, me bein' specially
invited to go by the Colonel."

He strolled forth and whistled in the clump of trees
at the back of the Married Quarters till Cris came to
him, and, the preliminary kisses being given and taken,
Lew began to explain the situation.

"I'm goin' to the Front with the Reg'ment," he said,
valiantly.

"Piggy, you're a little liar," said Cris, but her heart
misgave her, for Lew was not in the habit of lying.

"Liar yourself, Cris," said Lew, slipping an arm
round her. "I'm goin'. When the Reg'ment marches
out you'll see me with 'em, all galliant and gay. Give
us another kiss, Cris, on the strength of it."

"If you'd on'y a-stayed at the Depôt—where you
ought to ha' bin—you could get as many of 'em as—as
you dam please," whimpered Cris, putting up her
mouth.

"It's 'ard, Cris. I grant you it's 'ard. But what's a

man to do? If I'd a-stayed at the Depôt, you wouldn't think anything of me."

"Like as not, but I'd 'ave you with me, Piggy. An' all the thinkin' in the world isn't like kissin'.'"

"An' all the kissin' in the world isn't like 'avin' a medal to wear on the front o' your coat."

"*You* won't get no medal."

"Oh, yus, I shall though. Me an' Jakin are the only acting-drummers that'll be took along. All the rest is full men, an' we'll get our medals with them."

"They might ha' taken anybody but you, Piggy. You'll get killed—you're so venturesome. Stay with me, Piggy, darlin', down at the Depôt, an' I'll love you true forever."

"Ain't you goin' to do that *now,* Cris? You said you was."

"O' course I am, but th' other's more comfortable. Wait till you've growed a bit, Piggy. You aren't no taller than me now."

"I've bin in the army for two years an' I'm not goin' to get out of a chanst o' seein' service an' don't you try to make me do so. I'll come back, Cris, an' when I take on as a man I'll marry you—marry you when I'm a Lance."

"Promise, Piggy?"

Lew reflected on the future as arranged by Jakin a short time previously, but Cris's mouth was very near to his own.

"I promise, s'elp me Gawd!" said he.

Cris slid an arm round his neck.

"I won't 'old you back no more, Piggy. Go away an'

get your medal, an' I'll make you a new button-bag as nice as I know how," she whispered.

"Put some o' your 'air into it, Cris, an' I'll keep it in my pocket so long's I'm alive."

Then Cris wept anew, and the interveiw ended. Public feeling among the drummer-boys rose to fever pitch and the lives of Jakin and Lew became unenviable. Not only had they been permitted to enlist two years before the regulation boy's age—fourteen—but, by virtue, it seemed, of their extreme youth, they were allowed to go to the Front—which thing had not happened to acting-drummers within the knowledge of boy. The Band which was to accompany the Regiment had been cut down to the regulation twenty men, the surplus returning to the ranks. Jakin and Lew were attached to the Band as supernumeraries, though they would much have preferred being Company buglers.

" 'Don't matter much," said Jakin, after the medical inspection. "Be thankful that we're 'lowed to go at all. The Doctor 'e said that if we could stand what we took from the Bazar-Sergeant's son we'd stand pretty nigh anything."

"Which we will," said Lew, looking tenderly at the ragged and ill-made housewife that Cris had given him, with a lock of her hair worked into a sprawling "L" upon the cover.

"It was the best I could," she sobbed. "I wouldn't let mother nor the Sergeant's tailor 'elp me. Keep it always, Piggy, an' remember I love you true."

They marched to the railway station, nine hundred and sixty strong, and every soul in cantonments turned out to see them go. The drummers gnashed their teeth at Jakin and Lew marching with the Band, the married women wept upon the platform, and the Regiment cheered its noble self black in the face.

"A nice level lot," said the Colonel to the Second-in-Command, as they watched the first four companies entraining.

"Fit to do anything," said the Second-in-Command, enthusiastically. "But it seems to me they're a thought too young and tender for the work in hand. It's bitter cold up at the Front now."

"They're sound enough," said the Colonel. "We must take our chance of sick casualties."

So they went northward, ever northward, past droves and droves of camels, armies of camp followers, and legions of laden mules, the throng thickening day by day, till with a shriek the train pulled up at a hopelessly congested junction where six lines of temporary track accommodated six forty-wagon trains; where whistles blew, Babus sweated and Commissariat officers swore from dawn till far into the night amid the wind-driven chaff of the fodder-bales and the lowing of a thousand steers.

"Hurry up—you're badly wanted at the Front," was the message that greeted the Fore and Aft, and the occupants of the Red Cross carriages told the same tale.

" 'Tisn't so much the bloomin' fightin'," gasped a headbound trooper of Hussars to a knot of admiring Fore and Afts. " 'Tisn't so much the bloomin' fightin', though there's enough o' that. It's the bloomin' food an' the bloomin' climate. Frost all night 'cept when it hails, and biling sun all day, and the water stinks fit to knock you down. I got my 'ead chipped like a egg; I've got pneumonia too, an' my guts is all out o' order. 'Tain't no bloomin' picnic in those parts, I can tell you."

"Wot are the niggers like?" demanded a private.

"There's some prisoners in that train yonder. Go on look at 'em. They're the aristocracy o' the country. The common folk are a dashed sight uglier. If you want to know what they fight with, reach under my seat an' pull out the long knife that's there."

They dragged out and beheld for the first time the grim, bone-handled, triangular Afghan knife. It was almost as long as Lew.

"That's the thing to jint ye," said the trooper, feebly.

"It can take off a man's arm at the shoulder as easy as slicing butter. I halved the beggar that used that 'un, but there's more of his likes up above. They don't understand thrustin', but they're devils to slice."

The men strolled across the tracks to inspect the Afghan prisoners. They were unlike any "niggers" that the Fore and Aft had ever met—these huge, black-haired, scowling sons of the Beni-Israel. As the men stared the Afghans spat freely and muttered one to another with lowered eyes.

"My eyes! Wot awful swine!" said Jakin, who was in the rear of the procession. "Say, old man, how you got *packrowed,* eh? *Kiswasti* you wasn't hanged for your ugly face, hey?"

The tallest of the company turned, his leg-irons, clanking at the movement, and stared at the boy. "See!"

he cried to his fellows in Pushto. "They send children against us. What a people, and what fools!"

"*Hya!*" said Jakin, nodding his head cheerily. "You go down-country. *Khana* get, *peenikapanee* get—live like a bloomin' Raja *ke marfik*. That's a better *bando-bust* than baynit get it in your innards. Good-bye, ole man. Take care o' your beautiful figure-'ed, an' try to look *kushy.*"

The men laughed and fell in for their first march when they began to realize that a soldier's life was not all beer and skittles. They were much impressed with the size and bestial ferocity of the niggers whom they had now learned to call "Paythans," and more with the exceeding discomfort of their own surroundings. Twenty old soldiers in the corps would have taught them how to make themselves moderately snug at night, but they had no old soldiers, and, as the troops on the line of march said, "they lived like pigs." They learned the heart-breaking cussedness of camp-kitchens and camels and the depravity of an E. P. tent and a wither-wrung mule. They studied animalculæ in water, and developed a few cases of dysentery in their study.

At the end of their third march they were disagreeably surprised by the arrival in their camp of a hammered iron slug which, fired from a steadyrest at seven hundred yards, flicked out the brains of a private seated by the fire. This robbed them of their peace for a night, and was the beginning of a long-range fire carefully calculated to that end. In the daytime they saw nothing except an occasional puff of smoke from a crag above the line of march. At night there were distant spurts of flame and occasional casualties, which set the whole camp blazing into the gloom, and, occasionally, into opposite tents. Then they swore vehemently and vowed that this was magnificent but not war.

Indeed it was not. The Regiment could not halt for reprisals against the *franctireurs* of the countryside. Its duty was to go forward and make connection with the Scotch and Gurkha troops with which it was brigaded. The Afghans knew this, and knew too, after their first tentative shots, that they were dealing with a raw regiment. Thereafter they devoted themselves to the task of keeping the Fore and Aft on the strain. Not for anything would they have taken equal liberties with a seasoned corps—with the wicked little Gurkhas, whose delight it was to lie out in the open on a dark night and stalk their stalkers—with the terrible, big men dressed in women's clothes, who could be heard praying to their God in the night-watches, and whose peace of mind no amount of "sniping" could shake— or with those vile Sikhs, who marched so ostentatiously unprepared and who dealt out such grim reward to those who tried to profit by that unpreparedness. This white regiment was different—quite different. It slept like a hog, and, like a hog, charged in every direction when it was roused. Its sentries walked with a footfall that could be heard for a quarter of a mile; would fire at anything that moved—even a driven donkey—and when they had once fired, could be scientifically "rushed" and laid out a horror and an offence against the morning sun. Then there were camp-followers who straggled and could be cut up without fear. Their shrieks would disturb the white boys, and the loss of their services would inconvenience them sorely.

Thus, at every march, the hidden enemy became bolder and the regiment writhed and twisted under attacks it could not avenge. The crowning triumph was a sudden night-rush ending in the cutting of many tent-ropes, the collapse of the sodden canvas and a glorious knifing of the men who struggled and kicked below. It was a great deed, neatly carried out, and it shook the already shaken nerves of the Fore and Aft. All the courage that they had been required to exercise up to this point was the "two o'clock in the morning courage": and they, so far, had only succeeded in shooting their comrades and losing their sleep.

Sullen, discontented, cold, savage, sick, with their uniforms dulled and unclean, the "Fore and Aft" joined their Brigade.

"I hear you had a tough time of it coming up," said the Brigadier. But when he saw the hospital-sheets his face fell.

"This is bad," said he to himself. "They're as rotten as sheep." And aloud to the Colonel,—"I'm afraid we can't spare you just yet. We want all we have, else I should have given you ten days to recruit in."

The Colonel winced. "On my honor, Sir," he returned, "there is not the least necessity to think of sparing us. My men have been rather mauled and upset without a fair return. They only want to go in somewhere where they can see what's before them."

" 'Can't say I think much of the Fore and Fit," said the Brigadier, in confidence, to his Brigade-Major. "They've lost all their soldiering, and, by the trim of them, might have marched through the country from the other side. A more fagged-out set of men I never put eyes on."

"Oh, they'll improve as the work goes on. The parade gloss has been rubbed off a little, but they'll put on field polish before long," said the Brigade-Major. "They've been mauled, and they quite don't understand it."

They did not. All the hitting was on one side, and it was cruelly hard hitting with accessories that made them sick. There was also the real sickness that laid hold of a strong man and dragged him howling to the grave. Worst of all, their officers knew just as little of the country as the men themselves, and looked as if they did. The Fore and Aft were in a thoroughly unsatisfactory condition, but they believed that all would be well if they could once get a fair go-in at the enemy. Pot-shots up and down the valleys were unsatisfactory, and the bayonet never seemed to get a chance. Perhaps it was as well, for a long-limbed Afghan with a knife had a reach of eight feet, and could carry away enough lead to disable three Englishmen. The Fore and Fit would like some rifle-practice at the enemy—all seven hundred rifles blazing together. That wish showed the mood of the men.

The Gurkhas walked into their camp, and in broken, barrack-room English strove to fraternize with them; offered them pipes of tobacco and stood them treat at the canteen. But the Fore and Aft, not knowing much of the nature of the Gurkhas, treated them as they would treat any other "niggers," and the little men in green trotted back to their firm friends the Highlanders, and with many grins confided to them:—"That dam white regiment no dam use. Sulky—ugh! Dirty —ugh! Hya, any tot for Johnny?" Whereat the Highlanders smote the Gurkhas as to the head, and told them not to vilify a British Regiment, and the Gurkhas grinned cavernously, for the Highlanders were their elder brothers and entitled to the privileges of kinship. The common soldier who touches a Gurkha is more than likely to have his head sliced open.

Three days later the Brigadier arranged a battle according to the rules of war and the peculiarity of the Afghan temperament. The enemy were massing in inconvenient strength among the hills, and the moving or many green standards warned him that the tribes were "up" in aid of the Afghan regular troops. A squadron and a half of Bengal Lancers represented the available Cavalry, and two screw-guns borrowed from a column thirty miles away, the Artillery at the General's disposal.

"If they stand, as I've a very strong notion that they will, I fancy we shall see an infantry fight that will be worth watching," said the Brigadier. "We'll do it in style. Each regiment shall be played into action by its Band, and we'll hold the Cavalry in reserve."

"For *all* the reserve?" somebody asked.

"For all the reserve; because we're going to crumple them up," said the Brigadier, who was an extraordinary

Brigadier, and did not believe in the value of a reserve when dealing with Asiatics. And, indeed, when you come to think of it, had the British Army consistently waited for reserves in all its little affairs, the boundaries of Our Empire would have stopped at Brighton beach.

That battle was to be a glorious battle.

The three regiments debouching from three separate gorges, after duly crowning the heights above, were to converge from the centre, left and right upon what we will call the Afghan army, then stationed toward the lower extremity of a flat-bottomed valley. Thus it will be seen that three sides of the valley practically belonged to the English, while the fourth was strictly Afghan property. In the event of defeat the Afghans had the rocky hills to fly to, where the fire from the guerilla tribes in aid would cover their retreat. In the event of victory these same tribes would rush down and lend their weight to the rout of the British.

The screw-guns were to shell the head of each Afghan rush that was made in close formation, and the Cavalry, held in reserve in the right valley, were to gently stimulate the break-up which would follow on the combined attack. The Brigadier, sitting upon a rock overlooking the valley, would watch the battle unrolled at his feet. The Fore and Aft would debouch from the central gorge, the Gurkhas from the left, and the Highlanders from the right, for the reason that the left flank of the enemy seemed as though it required the most hammering. It was not every day that an Afghan force would take ground in the open, and the Brigadier was resolved to make the most of it.

"If we only had a few more men," he said, plain-
tively, "we could surround the creatures and crumble
'em up thoroughly. As it is, I'm afraid we can only
cut them up as they run. It's a great pity."

The Fore and Aft had enjoyed unbroken peace for
five days, and were beginning, in spite of dysentery,
to recover their nerve. But they were not happy, for
they did not know the work in hand, and had they
known, would not have known how to do it.
Throughout those five days in which old soldiers might
have taught them the craft of the game, they discussed
together their misadventures in the past—how such an
one was alive at dawn and dead ere the dusk, and with
what shrieks and struggles such another had given up
his soul under the Afghan knife. Death was a new and
horrible thing to the sons of mechanics who were used
to die decently of zymotic disease; and their careful
conservation in barracks had done nothing to make
them look upon it with less dread.

Very early in the dawn the bugles began to blow, and
the Fore and Aft, filled with a misguided enthusiasm,
turned out without waiting for a cup of coffee and a
biscuit; and were rewarded by being kept under arms
in the cold while the other regiments leisurely prepared
for the fray. All the world knows that it is ill taking
the breeks off a Highlander. It is much iller to try to
make him stir unless he is convinced of the necessity
for haste.

The Fore and Aft awaited, leaning upon their rifles
and listening to the protests of their empty stomachs.
The Colonel did his best to remedy the default of lin-

ing as soon as it was borne in upon him that the affair would not begin at once, and so well did he succeed that the coffee was just ready when—the men moved off, their Band leading. Even then there had been a mistake in time, and the Fore and Aft came out into the valley ten minutes before the proper hour. Their Band wheeled to the right after reaching the open, and retired behind a little rocky knoll still playing while the regiment went past.

It was not a pleasant sight that opened on the unobstructed view, for the lower end of the valley appeared to be filled by an army in position—real and actual regiments attired in red coats, and—of this there was no doubt—firing Martini-Henry bullets which cup up the ground a hundred yards in front of the leading company. Over that pock-marked ground the regiment had to pass, and it opened the ball with a general and profound courtesy to the piping pickets; ducking in perfect time, as though it had been brazed on a rod. Being half-capable of thinking for itself, it fired a volley by the simple process of pitching its rifle into its shoulder and pulling the trigger. The bullets may have accounted for some of the watchers on the hillside, but they certainly did not affect the mass of enemy in front, while the noise of the rifles drowned any orders that might have been given.

"Good God!" said the Brigadier, sitting on the rock high above all. "That regiment has spoiled the whole show. Hurry up the others, and let the screw-guns get off."

But the screw-guns, in working round the heights,

had stumbled upon a wasp's nest of a small mud fort which they incontinently shelled at eight hundred yards, to the huge discomfort of the occupants, who were unaccustomed to weapons of such devilish precision.

The Fore and Aft continued to go forward but with shortened stride. Where were the other regiments, and why did these niggers use Martinis? They took open order instinctively, lying down and firing at random, rushing a few paces forward and lying down again, according to the regulations. Once in this formation, each man felt himself desperately alone, and edged in toward his fellow for comfort's sake.

Then the crack of his neighbor's rifle at his ear led him to fire as rapidly as he could—again for the sake of the comfort of the noise. The reward was not long delayed. Five volleys plunged the files in banked smoke impenetrable to the eye, and the bullets began to take ground twenty or thirty yards in front of the firers, as the weight of the bayonet dragged down, and to the right arms wearied with holding the kick of the leaping Martini. The Company Commanders peered helplessly through the smoke, the more nervous mechanically trying to fan it away with their helmets.

"High and to the left!" bawled a Captain till he was hoarse. "No good! Cease firing, and let it drift away a bit."

Three and four times the bugles shrieked the order, and when it was obeyed the Fore and Aft looked that their foe should be lying before them in mown swaths of men. A light wind drove the smoke to leeward, and showed the enemy still in position and apparently unaffected. A quarter of a ton of lead had been buried a furlong in front of them, as the ragged earth attested.

That was not demoralizing. They were waiting for the mad riot to die down, and were firing quietly into the heart of the smoke. A private of the Fore and Aft spun up his company shrieking with agony, and another was kicking the earth and gasping, and a third, ripped through the lower intestines by a jagged bullet, was calling aloud on his comrades to put him out of his pain. These were the casualties, and they were not soothing to hear or see. The smoke cleared to a dull haze.

Then the foe began to shout with a great shouting and a mass—a black mass—detached itself from the main body, and rolled over the ground at horrid speed. It was composed of, perhaps, three hundred men, who would shout and fire and slash if the rush of their fifty comrades who were determined to die carried home. The fifty were Ghazis, half-maddened with drugs and wholly mad with religious fanaticism. When they rushed the British fire ceased, and in the lull the order was given to close ranks and meet them with the bayonet.

Any one who knew the business could have told the Fore and Aft that the only way of dealing with a Ghazi rush is by volleys at long ranges; because a man who means to die, who desires to die, who will gain heaven by dying, must, in nine cases out of ten, kill a man who has a lingering prejudice in favor of life if he can close with the latter. Where they should have closed and

gone forward, the Fore and Aft opened out and skir-
mished, and where they should have opened out and
fired, they closed and waited.

A man dragged from his blankets half awake and
unfed is never in a pleasant frame of mind. Nor does
his happiness increase when he watches the whites of
the eyes of three hundred six-foot fiends upon whose
beards the foam is lying, upon whose tongues is a roar
of wrath, and in whose hands are three-foot knives.

The Fore and Aft heard the Gurkha bugles bringing
that regiment forward at the double, while the neigh-
ing of the Highland pipes came from the left. They
strove to stay where they were, though the bayonets
wavered down the line like the oars of a ragged boat.
Then they felt body to body the amazing physical
strength of their foes; a shriek of pain ended the rush,
and the knives fell amid scenes not to be told. The
men clubbed together and smote blindly—as often as
not at their own fellows. Their front crumpled like
paper, and the fifty Ghazis passed on; their backers,
now drunk with success, fighting as madly as they.

Then the rear-ranks were bidden to close up, and the
subalterns dashed into the stew—alone. For the rear-
rank had heard the clamor in front, the yells and the
howls of pain, and had seen the dark stale blood that
makes afraid. They were not going to stay. It was the
rushing of the camps over again. Let their officers go
to Hell, if they chose; they would get away from the
knives.

"Come on!" shrieked the subalterns, and their men,

cursing them, drew back, each closing into his neighbor and wheeling round.

Charteris and Devlin, subalterns of the last company, faced their death alone in the belief that their men would follow.

"You've killed me, you cowards," sobbed Devlin and dropped, cut from the shoulder-strap to the centre of the chest, and a fresh detachment of his men retreating, always retreating, trampled him under foot as they made for the pass whence they had emerged.

> I kissed her in the kitchen and I kissed her in the hall.
> Child'un, child'un, follow me!
> Oh Golly, said the cook, is he gwine to kiss us all?
> Halla—Halla—Halla Halleujah!

The Gurkhas were pouring through the left gorge and over the heights at the double to the invitation of their regimental Quickstep. The black rocks were crowned with dark green spiders as the bugles gave tongue jubilantly:

> In the morning! In the morning by the bright light!
> When Gabriel blows his trumpet in the morning!

The Gurkha rear-companies tripped and blundered over loose stones. The front-files halted for a moment to take stock of the valley and to settle stray boot-laces. Then a happy little sigh of contentment soughed down the ranks, and it was as though the land smiled, for behold there below was the enemy, and it was to meet them that the Gurkhas had doubled so hastily. There was much enemy. There would be amusement. The little men hitched their *kukris* well to hand, and gaped

expectantly at their officers as terriers grin ere the stone
is cast for them to fetch. The Gurkhas' ground sloped
downward to the valley, and they enjoyed a fair view
of the proceedings. They sat upon the bowlders to
watch, for their officers were not going to waste their
wind in assisting to repulse a Ghazi rush more than
half a mile away. Let the white men look to their own
front.

"Hi! yi!" said the Subadar-Major, who was sweating
profusely. "Dam fools yonder, stand close-order! This
is no time for close order, it's the time for volleys.
Ugh!"

Horrified, amused, and indignant, the Gurkhas beheld the retirement—let us be gentle—of the Fore and
Aft with a running chorus of oaths and commentaries.
"They run! The white men run! Colonel Sahib, may
we also do a little running?" murmured Runbir Thap-
pa, the Senior Jemadar.

But the Colonel would have none of it. "Let the
beggars be cut up a little," said he wrathfully. "Serves
'em right. They'll be prodded into facing round in a
minute." He looked through his field-glasses, and
caught the glint of an officer's sword.

"Beating 'em with the flat—damned conscripts!
How the Ghazis are walking into them!" said he.

The Fore and Aft, heading back, bore with their officers. The narrowness of the pass forced the mob into
solid formation, and the rear-rank delivered some sort
of a wavering volley. The Ghazis drew off, for they
did not know what reserves the gorge might hide.
Moreover, it was never wise to chase white men too far.

They returned as wolves return to cover, satisfied with the slaughter that they had done, and only stopping to slash at the wounded on the ground. A quarter of a mile had the Fore and Aft retreated, and now, jammed in the pass, was quivering with pain, shaken and demoralized with fear, while the officers, maddened beyond control, smote the men with the hilts and the flats of their swords.

"Get back! Get back, you cowards—you women! Right about face—column of companies, form—you hounds!" shouted the Colonel, and the subalterns swore aloud. But the Regiment wanted to go—to go anywhere out of the range of those merciless knives. It swayed to and fro irresolutely with shouts and outcries, while from the right the Gurkhas dropped volley after volley of cripple-stopper Snider bullets at long range into the mob of the Ghazis returning to their own troops.

The Fore and Aft Band, though protected from direct fire by the rocky knoll under which it had sat down, fled at the first rush. Jakin and Lew would have fled also, but their short legs left them fifty yards in the rear, and by the time the Band had mixed with the regiment, they were painfully aware that they would have to close in alone and unsupported.

"Get back to that rock," gasped Jakin. "They won't see us there."

And they returned to the scattered instruments of the Band; their hearts nearly bursting their ribs.

"Here's a nice show for *us*," said Jakin, throwing himself full length on the ground. "A bloomin' fine

show for British Infantry! Oh, the devils! They've
gone an' left us alone here! Wot'll we do?"

Lew took possession of a cast-off water bottle, which
naturally was full of canteen rum, and drank till he
coughed again.

"Drink," said he, shortly. "They'll come back in a
minute or two—you see."

Jakin drank, but there was no sign of the regiment's
return. They could hear a dull clamor from the head
of the valley of retreat, and saw the Ghazis slink back,
quickening their pace as the Gurkhas fired at them.

"We're all that's left of the Band, an' we'll be cut up
as sure as death," said Jakin.

"I'll die game, then," said Lew, thickly, fumbling
with his tiny drummer's sword. The drink was working on his brain as it was on Jakin's.

" 'Old on! I know something better than fightin',"
said Jakin, "stung by the splendor of a sudden
thought" due chiefly to rum. "Tip our bloomin' cowards to come back. The Paythan beggars are well
away. Come on, Lew! We won't get hurt. Take the
fife an' give me the drum. The Old Step for all your
bloomin' guts are worth! There's a few of our men
coming back now. Stand up, ye drunken little de-
faulter. By your right—quick march!"

He slipped the drum-sling over his shoulder, thrust
the fife into Lew's hand, and the two boys marched out
of the cover of the rock into the open, making a hideous hash of the first bars of the "British Grenadiers."

As Lew had said, a few of the Fore and Aft were

coming back sullenly and shamefacedly under the
stimulus of blows and abuse; their red coats shone at
the head of the valley, and behind them were wavering bayonets. But between this shattered line and the
enemy, who with Afghan suspicion feared that the hasty
retreat meant an ambush, and had not moved therefore,
lay half a mile of a level ground dotted only by the
wounded.

The tune settled into full swing and the boys kept
shoulder to shoulder, Jakin banging the drum as one
possessed. The one fife made a thin and pitiful squeak-
ing, but the tune carried far, even to the Gurkhas.

"Come on, you dogs!" muttered Jakin, to himself.
"Are we to play forhever?" Lew was staring straight in
front of him and marching more stiffly than ever he
had done on parade.

And in bitter mockery of the distant mob, the old
tune of the Old Line shrilled and rattled:

> Some talk of Alexander,
> And some of Hercules;
> Of Hector and Lysander,
> And such great names as these!

There was a far-off clapping of hands from the Gurkhas, and a roar from the Highlanders in the distance,
but never a shot was fired by British or Afghan. The
two little red dots moved forward in the open parallel
to the enemy's front.

> But of all the world's great heroes
> There's none that can compare,
> With a tow-row-row-row-row-row,
> To the British Grenadier!

The men of the Fore and Aft were gathering thick at the entrance into the plain. The Brigadier on the heights far above was speechless with rage. Still no movement from the enemy. The day stayed to watch the children.

Jakin halted and beat the long roll of the Assembly, while the fife squealed despairingly.

"Right about face! Hold up, Lew, you're drunk," said Jakin. They wheeled and marched back:

> Those heroes of antiquity
> Ne'er saw a cannon-ball,
> Nor knew the force o' powder,

"Here they come!" said Jakin. "Go on, Lew:"

> To scare their foes withal!

The Fore and Aft were pouring out of the valley. What officers had said to men in that time of shame and humiliation will never be known; for neither officers nor men speak of it now.

"They are coming anew!" shouted a priest among the Afghans. "Do not kill the boys! Take them alive, and they shall be of our faith."

But the first volley had been fired, and Lew dropped on his face. Jakin stood for a minute, spun around and collapsed, as the Fore and Aft came forward, the maledictions of their officers in their ears, and in their hearts the shame of open shame.

Half the men had seen the drummers die, and they made no sign. They did not even shout. They doubled out straight across the plain in open order, and they did not fire.

"This," said the Colonel of the Gurkhas, softly, "is the real attack, as it ought to have been delivered. Come on, my children."

"Ulu-lu-lu-lu!" squealed the Gurkhas, and came down with a joyful clicking of *kukris*—those vicious Gurkha knives.

On the right there was no rush. The Highlanders, cannily commending their souls to God (for it matters as much to a dead man whether he has been shot in a Border scuffle or at Waterloo) opened out and fired according to their custom, that is to say without heat and without intervals, while the screw-guns, having disposed of the impertinent mud fort aforementioned, dropped shell after shell into the clusters round the flickering green standards on the heights.

"Charrging is an unfortunate necessity," murmured the Color-Sergeant of the right company of the Highlanders.

"It makes the men sweer so, but I am thinkin' that it will come to a charrge if these black devils stand much longer. Stewarrt, man, you're firing into the eye of the sun, and he'll not take any harm for Government ammuneetion. A foot lower and a great deal slower! What are the English doing? They're very quiet there in the centre. Running again?"

The English were not running. They were hacking and hewing and stabbing, for though one white man is seldom physically a match for an Afghan in a sheep-skin or wadded coat, yet, through the pressure of many white men behind, and a certain thirst for revenge in his heart, he becomes capable of doing much with both

ends of his rifle. The Fore and Aft held their fire till
one bullet could drive through five or six men, and
the front of the Afghan force gave on the volley. They
then selected their men, and slew them with deep gasps
and short hacking coughs, and groanings of leather
belts against strained bodies, and realized for the first
time that an Afghan attacked is far less formidable than
an Afghan attacking; which fact old soldiers might
have told them.

But they had no old soldiers in their ranks.

The Gurkhas' stall at the bazar was the noisiest, for
the men were engaged—to a nasty noise as of beef being
cut on the block—with the *kukri,* which they preferred
to the bayonet; well knowing how the Afghan hates
the half-moon blade.

As the Afghans wavered, the green standards on the
mountain moved down to assist them in a last rally.
Which was unwise. The Lancers chafing in the right
gorge had thrice despatched their only subaltern as
galloper to report on the progress of affairs. On the
third occasion he returned, with a bullet-graze on his
knee, swearing strange oaths in Hindoostani, and saying that all things were ready. So that Squadron
swung round the right of the Highlanders with a
wicked whistling of wind in the pennons of its lances,
and fell upon the remnant just when, according to all
the rules of war, it should have waited for the foe to
show more signs of wavering.

But it was a dainty charge, deftly delivered, and it
ended by the Cavalry finding itself at the head of the
pass by which the Afghans intended to retreat; and

down the track that the lances had made streamed two companies of the Highlanders, which was never intended by the Brigadier. The new development was successful. It detached the enemy from his base as a sponge is torn from a rock, and left him ringed about with fire in that pitiless plain. And as a sponge is chased around the bath-tub by the hand of the bather, so were the Afghans chased till they broke into little detachments much more difficult to dispose of than large masses.

"See!" quoth the Brigadier. "Everything has come as I arranged. We've cut their base, and now we'll bucket 'em to pieces."

A direct hammering was all that the Brigadier had dared hope for, considering the size of the force at his disposal; but men who stand or fall by the errors of their opponents may be forgiven for turning Chance into Design. The bucketing went forward merrily. The Afghan forces were upon the run—the run of wearied wolves who snarl and bite over their shoulders. The red lances dipped by twos and threes, and, with a shriek, up rose the lance-butt, like a spar on a stormy sea, as the trooper cantering forward cleared his point. The Lancers kept between their prey and the steep hills, for all who could were trying to escape from the valley of death. The Highlanders gave the fugitives two hundred yards' law, and then brought them down, gasping and choking ere they could reach the protection of the bowlders above. The Gurkhas followed suit; but the Fore and Aft were killing on their own account, for they had penned a mass of men between their bayonets and a wall of rock, and the flash of the rifles was lighting the wadded coats.

"We cannot hold them, Captain Sahib!" panted a Ressaidar of Lancers. "Let us try the carbine. The lance is good, but it wastes time."

They tried the carbine, and still the enemy melted away—fled up the hills by hundreds when there were only twenty bullets to stop them. On the heights the screw-guns ceased firing—they had run out of ammunition—and the Brigadier groaned, for the musketry fire could not sufficiently smash the retreat. Long before the last volleys were fired, the litters were out in force looking for the wounded. The battle was over, and, but for want of fresh troops, the Afghans would have been wiped off the earth. As it was they counted their dead by hundreds, and nowhere were the dead thicker than in the track of the Fore and Aft.

But the Regiment did not cheer with the Highlanders, nor did they dance uncouth dances with the Gurkhas among the dead. They looked under their brows at the Colonel as they leaned upon their rifles and panted.

"Get back to camp, you. Haven't you disgraced yourself enough for one day! Go and look to the wounded. It's all you're fit for," said the Colonel. Yet for the past hour the Fore and Aft had been doing all that mortal commander could expect. They had lost heavily because they did not know how to set about their business with proper skill, but they had borne themselves gallantly, and this was their reward.

A young and sprightly Color-Sergeant, who had be-

gun to imagine himself a hero, offered his water-bottle
to a Highlander, whose tongue was black with thirst.
"I drink with no cowards," answered the youngster,
huskily, and, turning to a Gurkha, said, "Hya, Johnny!
Drink water got it?" The Gurkha grinned and passed
his bottle. The Fore and Aft said no word.

They went back to camp when the field of strife
had been a little mopped up and made presentable,
and the Brigadier, who saw himself a Knight in three
months, was the only soul who was complimentary to
them. The Colonel was heart-broken and the officers
were savage and sullen.

"Well," said the Brigadier, "they are young troops
of course, and it was not unnatural that they should
retire in disorder for a bit."

"Oh, my only Aunt Maria!" murmured a junior
Staff Officer. "Retire in disorder! It was a bally run!"

"But they came again as we all know," cooed the
Brigadier, the Colonel's ashy-white face before him,
"and they behaved as well as could possibly be expected. Behaved beautifully, indeed. I was watching
them. It's not a matter to take to heart, Colonel. As
some German General said of his men, they wanted
to be shooted over a little, that was all." To himself he
said: "Now they're blooded I can give 'em responsible
work. It's as well that they got what they did. 'Teach
'em more than half a dozen rifle flirtations, that will—
later—run alone and bite. Poor old Colonel, though."

All that afternoon the heliograph winked and flick-
ered on the hills, striving to tell the good news to a
mountain forty miles away. And in the evening there

arrived, dusty, sweating, and sore, a misguided Correspondent who had gone out to assist at a trumpery
village-burning and who had read off the message from
afar, cursing his luck the while.

"Let's have the details somehow—as full as ever you
can, please. It's the first time I've ever been left this
campaign," said the Correspondent to the Brigadier;
and the Brigadier, nothing loath, told him how an
Army of Communication had been crumpled up, destroyed, and all but annihilated by the craft, strategy,
wisdom, and foresight of the Brigadier.

But some say, and among these be the Gurkhas who
watched on the hillside, that that battle was won by
Jakin and Lew, whose little bodies were borne up just
in time to fit two gaps at the head of the big ditch-grave
for the dead under the heights of Jagai.

WEE WILLIE WINKIE

"An officer and a gentleman."

H IS full name was Percival William Williams, but he picked up the other name in a nursery-book, and that was the end of the christened titles. His mother's *ayah* called him Willie-*Baba,* but as he never paid the faintest attention to anything that the *ayah* said, her wisdom did not help matters.

His father was the Colonel of the 195th, and as soon as Wee Willie Winkie was old enough to understand what Military Discipline meant, Colonel Williams put him under it. There was no other way of managing the child. When he was good for a week, he drew good-conduct pay; and when he was bad, he was deprived of his good-conduct stripe. Generally he was bad, for India offers so many chances to little six-year-olds of going wrong.

Children resent familiarity from strangers, and Wee Willie Winkie was a very particular child. Once he accepted an acquaintance, he was graciously pleased to thaw. He accepted Brandis, a subaltern of the 195th, on sight. Brandis was having tea at the Colonel's, and Wee Willie Winkie entered strong in the possession of a good-conduct badge won for not chasing the hens round the compound. He regarded Brandis with grav-

ity for at least ten minutes, and then delivered himself
of his opinion.

"I like you," said he, slowly, getting off his chair
and coming over to Brandis. "I like you. I shall call
you Coppy, because of your hair. Do you *mind* being
called Coppy? it is because of ve hair, you know."

Here was one of the most embarrassing of Wee Willie Winkie's peculiarities. He would look at a stranger
for some time, and then, without warning or explanation, would give him a name. And the name stuck.
No regimental penalties could break Wee Willie Winkie of this habit. He lost his good-conduct badge for
christening the Commissioner's wife "Pobs"; but
nothing that the Colonel could do made the Station
forego the nickname, and Mrs. Collen remained Mrs.
"Pobs" till the end of her stay. So Brandis was christened "Coppy," and rose, therefore, in the estimation
of the regiment.

If Wee Willie Winkie took an interest in any one,
the fortunate man was envied alike by the mess and the
rank and file. And in their envy lay no suspicion of
self-interest. "The Colonel's son" was idolized on his
own merits entirely. Yet Wee Willie Winkie was not
lovely. His face was permanently freckled, as his legs
were permanently scratched, and in spite of his
mother's almost tearful remonstrances he had insisted
upon having his long yellow locks cut short in the military fashion. "I want my hair like Sergeant Tum-
mil's," said Wee Willie Winkie, and, his father
abetting, the sacrifice was accomplished.

Three weeks after the bestowal of his youthful affections on Lieutenant Brandis—henceforward to be called "Coppy" for the sake of brevity—Wee Willie Winkie was destined to behold strange things and far beyond his comprehension.

Coppy returned his liking with interest. Coppy had let him wear for five rapturous minutes his own big sword—just as tall as Wee Willie Winkie. Coppy had promised him a terrier pup; and Coppy had permitted him to witness the miraculous operation of shaving. Nay, more—Coppy had said that even he, Wee Willie Winkie, would rise in time to the ownership of a box of shiny knives, a silver soap-box and a silver-handled "sputter-brush," as Wee Willie Winkie called it. Decidedly, there was no one except his father, who could give or take away good-conduct badges at pleasure, half so wise, strong, and valiant as Coppy with the Afghan and Egyptian medals on his breast. Why, then, should Coppy be guilty of the unmanly weakness of kissing—vehemently kissing—a "big girl," Miss Allardyce to wit? In the course of a morning ride, Wee Willie Winkie had seen Coppy so doing, and, like the gentleman he was, had promptly wheeled round and cantered back to his groom, lest the groom should also see.

Under ordinary circumstances he would have spoken to his father, but he felt instinctively that this was a matter on which Coppy ought first to be consulted.

"Coppy," shouted Wee Willie Winkie, reining up outside that subaltern's bungalow early one morning— "I want to see you, Coppy!"

"Come in, youn' 'un," returned Coppy, who was at

early breakfast in the midst of his dogs. "What mischief have you been getting into now?"

Wee Willie Winkie had done nothing notoriously bad for three days, and so stood on a pinnacle of virtue.

"I've been doing nothing bad," said he, curling himself into a long chair with a studious affectation of the Colonel's languor after a hot parade. He buried his freckled nose in a tea-cup and, with eyes staring roundly over the rim, asked:—"I say, Coppy, is it pwoper to kiss big girls?"

"By Jove! You're beginning early. Who do you want to kiss?"

"No one. My muvver's always kissing me if I don't stop her. If it isn't pwoper, how was you kissing Major Allardyce's big girl last morning, by ve canal?"

Coppy's brow wrinkled. He and Miss Allardyce had with great craft managed to keep their engagement secret for a fortnight. There were urgent and imperative reasons why Major Allardyce should not know how matters stood for at least another month, and this small marplot had discovered a great deal too much.

"I saw you," said Wee Willie Winkie, calmly. "But ve groom didn't see. I said, '*Hut jao.*'"

"Oh, you had that much sense, you young Rip," groaned poor Coppy half amused and half angry. "And how many people may have you told about it?"

"Only me myself. You didn't tell when I twied to wide ve buffalo ven my pony was lame; and I fought you wouldn't like."

"Winkie," said Coppy, enthusiastically, shaking the small hand, "you're the best of good fellows. Look

here, you can't understand all these things. One of
these days—hang it, how can I make you see it!—I'm
going to marry Miss Allardyce, and then she'll be Mrs.
Coppy, as you say. If your young mind is so scandalized at the idea of kissing big girls, go and tell your
father."

"What will happen?" said Wee Willie Winkie, who
firmly believed that his father was omnipotent.

"I shall get into trouble," said Coppy, playing his
trump card with an appealing look at the holder of the
ace.

"Ven I won't," said Wee Willie Winkie, briefly.
"But my faver says it's un-man-ly to be always kissing,
and I didn't fink *you'd* do vat, Coppy."

"I'm not always kissing, old chap. It's only now
and then, and when you're bigger you'll do it too.
Your father meant it's not good for little boys."

"Ah!" said Wee Willie Winkie, now fully enlightened. "It's like ve sputter-brush?"

"Exactly," said Coppy, gravely.

"But I don't fink I'll ever want to kiss big girls, nor
no one, 'cept my muvver. And I *must* vat, you know."

There was a long pause, broken by Wee Willie Winkie.

"Are you fond of vis big girl, Coppy?"

"Awfully!" said Coppy.

"Fonder van you are of Bell or ve Butcha—or me?"

"It's in a different way," said Coppy. "You see, one
of these days Miss Allardyce will belong to me, but
you'll grow up and command the Regiment and—all
sorts of things. It's quite different, you see."

"Very well," said Wee Willie Winkie, rising. "If you're fond of ve big girl, I won't tell any one. I must go now."

Coppy rose and escorted his small guest to the door, adding: "You're the best of little fellows, Winkie. I tell you what. In thirty days from now you can tell if you like—tell any one you like."

Thus the secret of the Brandis-Allardyce engagement was dependent on a little child's word. Coppy, who knew Wee Willie Winkie's idea of truth, was at ease, for he felt that he would not break promises. Wee Willie Winkie betrayed a special and unusual interest in Miss Allardyce, and, slowly revolving round that embarrassed young lady, was used to regard her gravely with unwinking eye. He was trying to discover why Coppy should have kissed her. She was not half so nice as his own mother. On the other hand, she was Coppy's property, and would in time belong to him. Therefore it behooved him to treat her with as much respect as Coppy's big sword or shiny pistol.

The idea that he shared a great secret in common with Coppy kept Wee Willie Winkie unusually virtuous for three weeks. Then the Old Adam broke out, and he made what he called a "camp-fire" at the bottom of the garden. How could he have foreseen that the flying sparks would have lighted the Colonel's little hayrick and consumed a week's store for the horses? Sudden and swift was the punishment—deprivation of the good-conduct badge and, most sorrowful of all, two-days' confinement to barracks—the house and veranda—coupled with the withdrawal of the light of his father's countenance.

He took the sentence like the man he strove to be, drew himself up with a quivering under-lip, saluted, and, once clear of the room, ran to weep bitterly in his nursery—called by him "my quarters." Coppy came in the afternoon and attempted to console the culprit.

"I'm under awwest," said Wee Willie Winkie, mournfully, "and I didn't ought to speak to you."

Very early the next morning he climbed on to the roof of the house—that was not forbidden—and beheld Miss Allardyce going for a ride.

"Where are you going?" cried Wee Willie Winkie.

"Across the river," she answered, and trotted forward.

Now the cantonment in which the 195th lay was bounded on the north by a river—dry in the winter. From his earliest years, Wee Willie Winkie had been forbidden to go across the river, and had noted that even Coppy—the almost almighty Coppy—had never set foot beyond it. Wee Willie Winkie had once been read to, out of a big blue book, the history of the Princess and the Goblins—a most wonderful tale of a land where the Goblins were always warring with the children of men until they were defeated by one Curdie. Ever since that date it seemed to him that the bare black and purple hills across the river were inhabited by Goblins, and, in truth, every one had said that there lived the Bad Men. Even in his own house the lower halves of the windows were covered with green paper

on account of the Bad Men who might, if allowed
clear view, fire into peaceful drawing-rooms and comfortable bedrooms. Certainly, beyond the river, which
was the end of all the Earth, lived the Bad Men. And
here was Major Allardyce's big girl, Coppy's property,
preparing to venture into their borders! What would
Coppy say if anything happened to her? If the Goblins ran off with her as they did with Curdie's Princess?
She must at all hazards be turned back.

The house was still. Wee Willie Winkie reflected
for a moment on the very terrible wrath of his father;
and then—broke his arrest! It was a crime unspeakable. The low sun threw his shadow, very large and
very black, on the trim garden-paths, as he went down
to the stables and ordered his pony. It seemed to him
in the hush of the dawn that all the big world had been
bidden to stand still and look at Wee Willie Winkie
guilty of mutiny. The drowsy groom handed him
his mount, and, since the one great sin made all others
insignificant, Wee Willie Winkie said that he was going to ride over to Coppy Sahib, and went out at a foot-
pace, stepping on the soft mould of the flower-borders.

The devastating track of the pony's feet was the last
misdeed that cut him off from all sympathy of Humanity. He turned into the road, leaned forward, and
rode as fast as the pony could put foot to the ground
in the direction of the river.

But the liveliest of twelve-two ponies can do little
against the long canter of a Waler. Miss Allardyce
was far ahead, and passed through the crops beyond,
the Police-post, when all the guards were asleep, and

her mount was scattering the pebbles of the river bed
as Wee Willie Winkie left the cantonment and British
India behind him. Bowed forward and still flogging,
Wee Willie Winkie shot into Afghan territory, and
could just see Miss Allardyce a black speck, flickering
across the stony plain. The reason of her wandering
was simple enough. Coppy, in a tone of too-hastily-
assumed authority, had told her over night that she
must not ride out by the river. And she had gone to
prove her own spirit and teach Coppy a lesson.

Almost at the foot of the inhospitable hills, Wee
Willie Winkie saw the Waler blunder and come down
heavily. Miss Allardyce struggled clear, but her ankle
had been severely twisted, and she could not stand.
Having thus demonstrated her spirit, she wept copi-
ously, and was surprised by the apparition of a white,
wide-eyed child in khaki, on a nearly spent pony.

"Are you badly, badly hurted?" shouted Wee Willie
Winkie, as soon as he was within range. "You didn't
ought to be here."

"I don't know," said Miss Allardyce, ruefully ignor-
ing the reproof. "Good gracious, child, what are *you*
doing here?"

"You said you was going acwoss ve wiver," panted
Wee Willie Winkie, throwing himself off his pony.
"And nobody—not even Coppy—must go acwoss ve
wiver, and I came after you ever so hard, but you
wouldn't stop, and now you've hurted yourself, and
Coppy will be angwy wiv me, and—I've bwoken my
awwest! I've bwoken my awwest!"

The future Colonel of the 195th sat down and

sobbed. In spite of the pain in her ankle the girl was moved.

"Have you ridden all the way from cantonments, little man? What for?"

"You belonged to Coppy. Coppy told me so!" wailed Wee Willie Winkie, disconsolately. "I saw him kissing you, and he said he was fonder of you van Bell or ve Butcha or me. And so I came. You must get up and come back. You didn't ought to be here. Vis is a bad place, and I've bwoken my awwest."

"I can't move, Winkie," said Miss Allardyce, with a groan. "I've hurt my foot. What shall I do?"

She showed a readiness to weep afresh, which steadied Wee Willie Winkie, who had been brought up to believe that tears were the depth of unmanliness. Still, when one is as great a sinner as Wee Willie Winkie, even a man may be permitted to break down.

"Winkie," said Miss Allardyce, "when you've rested a little, ride back and tell them to send out something to carry me back in. It hurts fearfully."

The child sat still for a little time and Miss Allardyce closed her eyes; the pain was nearly making her faint. She was roused by Wee Willie Winkie tying up the reins on his pony's neck and setting it free with the vicious cut of his whip that made it whicker. The little animal headed toward the cantonments.

"Oh, Winkie! What are you doing?"

"Hush!" said Wee Willie Winkie. "Vere's a man coming—one of ve Bad Men. I must stay wiv you. My faver says a man must *always* look after a girl.

Jack will go home, and ven vey'll come and look for us. Vat's why I let him go."

Not one man but two or three had appeared from behind the rocks of the hills, and the heart of Wee Willie Winkie sank within him, for just in this manner were the Goblins wont to steal out and vex Curdie's soul. Thus had they played in Curdie's garden, he had seen the picture, and thus had they frightened the Princess's nurse. He heard them talking to each other, and recognized with joy the bastard Pushto that he had picked up from one of his father's grooms lately dismissed. People who spoke that tongue could not be the Bad Men. They were only natives after all.

They came up to the bowlders on which Miss Allardyce's horse had blundered.

Then rose from the rock Wee Willie Winkie, child of the Dominant Race, aged six and three-quarters, and said briefly and emphatically *"Jao!"* The pony had crossed the river-bed.

The men laughed, and laughter from natives was the one thing Wee Willie Winkie could not tolerate. He asked them what they wanted and why they did not depart. Other men with most evil faces and crooked-stocked guns crept out of the shadows of the hills, till, soon, Wee Willie Winkie was face to face with an audience some twenty strong. Miss Allardyce screamed.

"Who are you?" said one of the men.

"I am the Colonel Sahib's son, and my order is that you go at once. You black men are frightening the Miss Sahib. One of you must run to cantonments and take the news that Miss Sahib has hurt herself, and that the Colonel's son is here with her."

"Put our feet into the trap?" was the laughing reply. "Hear this boy's speech!"

"Say that I sent you—I, the Colonel's son. They will give you money."

"What is the use of this talk? Take up the child and the girl, and we can at least ask for the ransom. Ours are the villages on the heights," said a voice in the background.

These *were* the Bad Men—worse than Goblins—and it needed all Wee Willie Winkie's training to prevent him from bursting into tears. But he felt that to cry before a native, excepting only his mother's *ayah,* would be an infamy greater than any mutiny. Moreover, he, as future Colonel of the 195th, had that grim regiment at his back.

"Are you going to carry us away?" said Wee Willie Winkie, very blanched and uncomfortable.

"Yes, my little *Sahib Bahadur,*" said the tallest of the men, "and eat you afterward."

"That is child's talk," said Wee Willie Winkie. "Men do not eat men."

A yell of laughter interrupted him, but he went on firmly,—"And if you do carry us away, I tell you that all my regiment will come up in a day and kill you all without leaving one. Who will take my message to the Colonel Sahib?"

Speech in any vernacular—and Wee Willie Winkie had a colloquial acquaintance with three—was easy to the boy who could not yet manage his "r's" and "th's" aright.

Another man joined the conference, crying:—"O foolish men! What this babe says is true. He is the heart's heart of those white troops. For the sake of peace let them go both, for if he be taken, the regiment will break loose and gut the valley. *Our* villages are in the valley, and we shall not escape. That regiment are devils. They broke Khoda Yar's breast-bone with kicks when he tried to take the rifles; and if we touch this child they will fire and rape and plunder for a month, till nothing remains. Better to send a man back to take the message and get a reward. I say that this child is their God, and that they will spare none of us, nor our women, if we harm him."

It was Din Mahommed, the dismissed groom of the Colonel, who made the diversion, and an angry and heated discussion followed. Wee Willie Winkie, standing over Miss Allardyce, waited the upshot. Surely his "wegiment," his own "wegiment," would not desert him if they knew of his extremity.

*   *   *   *   *   *   *

The riderless pony brought the news to the 195th, though there had been consternation in the Colonel's household for an hour before. The little beast came in through the parade ground in front of the main barracks, where the men were settling down to play Spoil-five till the afternoon. Devlin, the Color Sergeant of E Company, glanced at the empty saddle and tumbled through the barrack-rooms, kicking up each Room

Corporal as he passed. "Up, ye beggars! There's something happened to the Colonel's son," he shouted.

"He couldn't fall off! S'elp me, *'e couldn't* fall off,"
blubbered a drummer-boy. "Go an' hunt acrost the
river. He's over there if he's anywhere, an' maybe
those Pathans have got 'im. For the love o' Gawd don't
look for 'im in the nullahs! Let's go over the river."

"There's sense in Mott yet," said Devlin. "E Company, double out to the river—sharp!"

So E Company, in its shirt-sleeves mainly, doubled
for the dear life, and in the rear toiled the perspiring
Sergeant, adjuring it to double yet faster. The cantonment was alive with the men of the 195th hunting for
Wee Willie Winkie, and the Colonel finally overtook
E Company, far too exhausted to swear, struggling in
the pebbles of the river-bed.

Up the hill under which Wee Willie Winkie's Bad
Men were discussing the wisdom of carrying off the
child and the girl, a look-out fired two shots.

"What have I said?" shouted Din Mahommed.
"There is the warning! The *pulton* are out already
and are coming across the plain! Get away! Let us
not be seen with the boy!"

The men waited for an instant, and then, as another
shot was fired, withdrew into the hills, silently as they
had appeared.

"The wegiment is coming," said Wee Willie Winkie,
confidently, to Miss Allardyce, "and it's all wight.
Don't cwy!"

He needed the advice himself, for ten minutes later,

when his father came up, he was weeping bitterly with his head in Miss Allardyce's lap.

And the men of the 195th carried him home with shouts and rejoicings; and Coppy, who had ridden a horse into a lather, met him, and, to his intense disgust, kissed him openly in the presence of the men.

But there was balm for his dignity. His father assured him that not only would the breaking of arrest be condoned, but that the good-conduct badge would be restored as soon as his mother could sew it on his blouse-sleeve. Miss Allardyce had told the Colonel a story that made him proud of his son.

"She belonged to you, Coppy," said Wee Willie Winkie, indicating Miss Allardyce with a grimy forefinger. "I *knew* she didn't ought to go acwoss de wiver, and I knew ve wegiment would come to me if I sent Jack home."

"You're a hero, Winkie," said Coppy—"a *pukka* hero!"

"I don't know what vat means," said Wee Willie Winkie, "but you mustn't call me Winkie any no more. I'm Percival Will'am Will'ams."

And in this manner did Wee Willie Winkie enter into his manhood.

MY OWN TRUE GHOST STORY

As I came through the Desert thus it was—
As I came through the Desert.
                    —*The City of Dreadful Night.*

SOMEWHERE in the Other World, where there
are books and pictures and plays and shop-win-
dows to look at, and thousands of men who spend
their lives in building up all four, lives a gentleman
who writes real stories about the real insides of people;
and his name is Mr. Walter Besant. But he will insist
upon treating his ghosts—he has published half a work-
shopful of them—with levity. He makes his ghost-
seers talk familiarly, and, in some cases, flirt outrage-
ously, with the phantoms. You may treat anything,
from a Viceroy to a Vernacular Paper, with levity; but
you must behave reverently toward a ghost, and particularly an Indian one.

There are, in this land, ghosts who take the form of
fat, cold, pobby corpses, and hide in trees near the roadside till a traveler passes. Then they drop upon his
neck and remain. There are also terrible ghosts of
women who have died in child-bed. These wander
along the pathways at dusk, or hide in the crops near a
village, and call seductively. But to answer their call
is death in this world and the next. Their feet are

turned backward that all sober men may recognize
them. There are ghosts of little children who have
been thrown into wells. These haunt well-curbs and
the fringes of jungles, and wail under the stars, or catch
women by the wrist and beg to be taken up and carried. These and the corpse-ghosts, however, are only
vernacular articles and do not attack Sahibs. No native
ghost has yet been authentically reported to have frightened an Englishman; but many English ghosts have
scared the life out of both white and black.

Nearly every other Station owns a ghost. There are
said to be two at Simla, not counting the woman who
blows the bellows at Syree dâk-bungalow on the Old
Road; Mussoorie has a house haunted of a very lively
Thing; a White Lady is supposed to do night-watch-
man round a house in Lahore; Dalhousie says that one
of her houses "repeats" on autumn evenings all the incidents of a horrible horse-and-precipice accident; Mur-
ree has a merry ghost, and, now that she has been
swept by cholera, will have room for a sorrowful one;
there are Officers' Quarters in Mian Mir whose doors
open without reason, and whose furniture is guaranteed
to creak, not with the heat of June but with the weight
of Invisibles who come to lounge in the chair; Peshawur possesses houses that none will willingly rent; and
there is something—not fever—wrong with a big bungalow in Allahabad. The older Provinces simply bristle
with haunted houses, and march phantom armies along
their main thoroughfares.

Some of the dâk-bungalows on the Grand Trunk
Road have handy little cemeteries in their compound—

witnesses to the "changes and chances of this mortal life" in the days when men drove from Calcutta to the Northwest. These bungalows are objectionable places to put up in. They are generally very old, always dirty, while the *khansamah* is as ancient as the bungalow. He either chatters senilely, or falls into the long trances of age. In both moods he is useless. If you get angry with him, he refers to some Sahib dead and buried these thirty years, and says that when he was in that Sahib's service not a *khansamah* in the Province could touch him. Then he jabbers and mows and trembles and fidgets among the dishes, and you repent of your irritation.

In these dâk-bungalows, ghosts are most likely to be found, and when found, they should be made a note of. Not long ago it was my business to live in dâk-bungalows. I never inhabited the same house for three nights running, and grew to be learned in the breed. I lived in Government-built ones with red brick walls and rail ceilings, an inventory of the furniture posted in every room, and an excited snake at the threshold to give welcome. I lived in "converted" ones—old houses officiating as dâk-bungalows--where nothing was in its proper place and there wasn't even a fowl for dinner. I lived in second-hand palaces where the wind blew through open-work marble tracery just as uncomfortably as through a broken pane. I lived in dâk-bungalows where the last entry in the visitors' book was fifteen months old, and where they slashed off the curry-kid's head with a sword. It was my good-luck to meet all sorts of men, from sober traveling missionaries and deserters flying from British Regiments, to drunken loafers who threw whiskey bottles at all who passed; and my still greater good-fortune just to escape a maternity case. Seeing that a fair proportion of the tragedy of our lives out here acted itself in dâk-bungalows, I wondered that I had met no ghosts. A ghost that would voluntarily hang about a dâk-bungalow would be mad of course; but so many men have died mad in dâk-bungalows that there must be a fair percentage of lunatic ghosts.

In due time I found my ghost, or ghosts rather, for there were two of them. Up till that hour I had sympathized with Mr. Besant's method of handling them, as shown in *"The Strange Case of Mr. Lucraft and Other Stories."* I am now in the Opposition.

We will call the bungalow Katmal dâk-bungalow. But *that* was the smallest part of the horror. A man with a sensitive hide has no right to sleep in dâk-bungalows. He should marry. Katmal dâk-bungalow was old and rotten and unrepaired. The floor was of worn brick, the walls were filthy, and the windows were nearly black with grime. It stood on a bypath largely used by native Sub-Deputy Assistants of all kinds, from Finance to Forests; but real Sahibs were rare. The *khansamah,* who was nearly bent double with old age, said so.

When I arrived, there was a fitful, undecided rain on the face of the land, accompanied by a restless wind, and every gust made a noise like the rattling of dry bones in the stiff toddy-palms outside. The *khansamah* completely lost his head on my arrival. He had served

a Sahib once. Did I know that Sahib. He gave me
the name of a well-known man who has been buried
for more than a quarter of a century, and showed me
an ancient daguerreotype of that man in his prehistoric
youth. I had seen a steel engraving of him at the head
of a double volume of Memoirs a month before, and I
felt ancient beyond telling.

The day shut in and the *khansamah* went to get me
food. He did not go through the pretence of calling
it *"khana"*—man's victuals. He said *"ratub,"* and that
means, among other things, "grub"—dog's rations.
There was no insult in his choice of the term. He had
forgotten the other word, I suppose.

While he was cutting up the dead bodies of animals,
I settled myself down, after exploring the dâk-bungalow. There were three rooms, beside my own, which
was a corner kennel, each giving into the other through
dingy white doors fastened with long iron bars. The
bungalow was a very solid one, but the partition-walls
of the rooms were almost jerry-built in their flimsiness.
Every step or bang of a trunk echoed from my room
down the other three, and every footfall came back
tremulously from the far walls. For this reason I shut
the door. There were no lamps—only candles in long
glass shades. An oil wick was set in the bath-room.

For bleak, unadulterated misery that dâk-bungalow
was the worst of the many that I had ever set foot in.
There was no fireplace, and the windows would not
open; so a brazier of charcoal would have been useless.
The rain and the wind splashed and gurgled and
moaned round the house, and the toddy-palms rattled

and roared. Half a dozen jackals went through the compound singing, and a hyena stood afar off and mocked them. A hyena would convince a Sadducee of the Resurrection of the Dead—the worst sort of Dead. Then came the *ratub*—a curious meal, half native and half English in composition—with the old *khansamah* babbling behind my chair about dead and gone English people, and the wind-blown candles playing shadow-bo-peep with the bed and the mosquito-curtains. It was just the sort of dinner and evening to make a man think of every single one of his past sins, and of all the others that he intended to commit if he lived.

Sleep, for several hundred reasons, was not easy. The lamp in the bath-room threw the most absurd shadows into the room, and the wind was beginning to talk nonsense.

Just when the reasons were drowsy with blood-sucking I heard the regular—"Let-us-take-and-heave-him-over" grunt of doolie-bearers in the compound. First one doolie came in, then a second, and then a third. I heard the doolies dumped on the ground, and the shutter in front of my door shook. "That's some one trying to come in," I said. But no one spoke, and I persuaded myself that it was the gusty wind. The shutter of the room next to mine was attacked, flung back, and the inner door opened. "That's some Sub-Deputy Assistant," I said, "and he has brought his friends with him. Now they'll talk and spit and smoke for an hour."

But there were no voices and no footsteps. No one was putting his luggage into the next room. The door shut, and I thanked Providence that I was to be left in peace. But I was curious to know where the doolies had gone. I got out of bed and looked into the darkness. There was never a sign of a doolie. Just as I was getting into bed again, I heard, in the next room, the sound that no man in his senses can possibly mistake—the whir of a billiard ball down the length of the slates when the striker is stringing for break. No other sound is like it. A minute afterward there was another whir, and I got into bed. I was not frightened—indeed I was not. I was very curious to know what had become of the doolies. I jumped into bed for that reason.

Next minute I heard the double click of a cannon and my hair sat up. It is a mistake to say that hair stands up. The skin of the head tightens and you can feel a faint, prickly bristling all over the scalp. That is the hair sitting up.

There was a whir and a click, and both sounds could only have been made by one thing—a billiard ball. I argued the matter out at great length with myself; and the more I argued the less probable it seemed that one bed, one table, and two chairs—all the furniture of the room next to mine—could so exactly duplicate the sounds of a game of billiards. After another cannon, a three-cushion one to judge by the whir, I argued no more. I had found my ghost and would have given worlds to have escaped from that dâk-bungalow. I listened, and with each listen the game grew clearer. There was whir on whir and click on click. Sometimes there was a double click and a whir and another click. Beyond any sort of doubt, people were playing billiards in the next room. And the next room was not big enough to hold a billiard table!

Between the pauses of the wind I heard the game go forward—stroke after stroke. I tried to believe that I could not. hear voices; but that attempt was a failure.

Do you know what fear is? Not ordinary fear of insult, injury or death, but abject, quivering dread of something that you cannot see—fear that dries the inside of the mouth and half of the throat—fear that makes you sweat on the palms of the hands, and gulp in order to keep the uvula at work? This is a fine Fear—a great cowardice, and must be felt to be appreciated. The very improbability of billiards in a dâk-bungalow proved the reality of the thing. No man—drunk or sober—could imagine a game at billiards, or invent the splitting crack of a "screw-cannon."

A severe course of dâk-bungalows has this disadvantage—it breeds infinite credulity. If a man said to a confirmed dâk-bungalow-haunter:—"There is a corpse in the next room, and there's a mad girl in the next but one, and the woman and man on that camel have just eloped from a place sixty miles away," the hearer would not disbelieve because he would know that nothing is too wild, grotesque, or horrible to happen in a dâk-bungalow.

This credulity, unfortunately, extends to ghosts. A rational person fresh from his own house would have turned on his side and slept. I did not. So surely as I was given up as a bad carcass by the scores of things in the bed because the bulk of my blood was in my heart, so surely did I hear every stroke of a long game at billiards played in the echoing room behind the iron-barred door. My dominant fear was that the players might want a maker. It was an absurd fear; because creatures who could play in the dark would be above such superfluities. I only know that that was my terror; and it was real.

After a long long while, the game stopped, and the door banged. I slept because I was dead tired. Otherwise I should have preferred to have kept awake. Not for everything in Asia would I have dropped the door-bar and peered into the dark of the next room.

When the morning came, I considered that I had done well and wisely, and inquired for the means of departure.

"By the way, *khansamah*," I said, "what were those three doolies doing in my compound in the night?"

"There were no doolies," said the *khansamah*.

I went into the next room and the daylight streamed through the open door. I was immensely brave. I would, at that hour, have played Black Pool with the owner of the big Black Pool down below.

"Has this place always been a dâk-bungalow?" I asked.

"No," said the *khansamah*. "Ten or twenty years ago, I have forgotten how long, it was a billiard-room."

"A how much?"

"A billiard-room for the Sahibs who built the Railway. I was *khansamah* then in the big house where all the Railway-Sahibs lived, and I used to come across with brandy-*shrab*. These three rooms were all one, and they held a big table on which the Sahibs played every evening. But the Sahibs are all dead now, and the Railway runs, you say, nearly to Kabul."

"Do you remember anything about the Sahibs?"

"It is long ago, but I remember that one Sahib, a fat man and always angry, was playing here one night, and he said to me:—'Mangal Khan, brandy-*pani do*,' and I filled the glass, and he bent over the table to strike, and his head fell lower and lower till it hit the table, and his spectacles came off, and when we—the Sahibs and I myself—ran to lift him he was dead. I helped to carry him out. Aha, he was a strong Sahib! But he is dead and I, old Mangal Khan, am still living, by your favor."

That was more than enough! I had my ghost—a first-hand, authenticated article. I would write to the Society for Psychical Research—I would paralyze the Empire with the news! But I would, first of all, put eighty miles of assessed crop-land between myself and that dâk-bungalow before nightfall. The Society might send their regular agent to investigate later on.

I went into my own room and prepared to pack after noting down the facts of the case. As I smoked I heard the game begin again—with a miss in balk this time, for the whir was a short one.

The door was open and I could see into the room. *Click—click!* That was a cannon. I entered the room without fear, for there was sunlight within and a fresh breeze without. The unseen game was going on at a tremendous rate. And well it might, when a restless little rat was running to and fro inside the dingy ceiling-cloth, and a piece of loose window-sash was making fifty breaks off the window-bolt as it shook in the breeze!

Impossible to mistake the sound of billiard balls! Impossible to mistake the whir of a ball over the slate! But I was to be excused. Even when I shut my enlightened eyes the sound was marvelously like that of a fast game.

Entered angrily the faithful partner of my sorrows, Kadir Baksh.

"This bungalow is very bad and low-caste! No wonder the Presence was disturbed and is speckled. Three sets of doolie-bearers came to the bungalow late last night when I was sleeping outside, and said that it was their custom to rest in the rooms set apart for the English people! What honor has the *khansamah?* They tried to enter, but I told them to go. No wonder, if these *Oorias* have been here, that the Presence is sorely spotted. It is shame, and the work of a dirty man!"

Kadir Baksh did not say that he had taken from each gang two annas for rent in advance, and then, beyond my earshot, had beaten them with the big green umbrella whose use I could never before divine. But Kadir Baksh has no notions of morality.

There was an interview with the *khansamah,* but as he promptly lost his head, wrath gave place to pity, and pity led to a long conversation, in the course of which he put the fat Engineer-Sahib's tragic death in three separate stations—two of them fifty miles away. The third shift was to Calcutta, and there the Sahib died while driving a dog-cart.

If I had encouraged him the *khansamah* would have wandered all through Bengal with his corpse.

I did not go away as soon as I intended. I stayed for the night, while the wind and the rat and the sash and the window-bolt played a ding-dong "hundred and fifty up." Then the wind ran out and the billiards stopped, and I felt that I had ruined my one genuine, hall-marked ghost story.

Had I only stopped at the proper time, I could have made *anything* out of it.

That was the bitterest thought of all!

"THE FINEST STORY IN THE WORLD"

> "Or ever the knightly years were gone
> With the old world to the grave,
> I was a king in Babylon
> And you were a Christian slave."
>   —*W. E. Henley.*

HIS name was Charlie Mears; he was the only
son of his mother who was a widow, and he
lived in the north of London, coming into the
City every day to work in a bank. He was twenty
years old and suffered from aspirations. I met him in
a public billiard-saloon where the marker called him
by his given name, and he called the marker "Bulls-
eyes." Charlie explained, a little nervously, that he had
only come to the place to look on, and since looking on
at games of skill is not a cheap amusement for the
young, I suggested that Charlie should go back to his
mother.

That was our first step toward better acquaintance.
He would call on me sometimes in the evenings instead of running about London with his fellow-clerks;
and before long, speaking of himself as a young man
must, he told me of his aspirations, which were all literary. He desired to make himself an undying name,
chiefly through verse, though he was not above sending

73

stories of love and death to the drop-a-penny-in-the-slot journals. It was my fate to sit still while Charlie read me poems of many hundred lines, and bulky fragments of plays that would surely shake the world. My reward was his unreserved confidence, and the self-revelations and troubles of a young man are almost as holy as those of a maiden. Charlie had never fallen in love, but was anxious to do so on the first opportunity; he believed in all things good and all things honorable, but, at the same time, was curiously careful to let me see that he knew his way about the world as befitted a bank clerk on twenty-five shillings a week. He rhymed "dove" with "love" and "moon" with "June," and devoutly believed that they had never so been rhymed before. The long lame gaps in his plays he filled up with hasty words of apology and description and swept on, seeing all that he intended to do so clearly that he esteemed it already done, and turned to me for applause.

I fancy that his mother did not encourage his aspirations, and I know that his writing-table at home was the edge of his washstand. This he told me almost at the outset of our acquaintance; when he was ravaging my bookshelves, and a little before I was implored to speak the truth as to his chances of "writing something really great, you know." Maybe I encouraged him too much, for, one night, he called on me, his eyes flaming with excitement, and said breathlessly:

"Do you mind—can you let me stay here and write all this evening? I won't interrupt you, I won't really. There's no place for me to write in at my mother's."

"What's the trouble?" I said, knowing well what that trouble was.

"I've a notion in my head that would make the most splendid story that was ever written. Do let me write it out here. It's *such* a notion!"

There was no resisting the appeal. I set him a table; he hardly thanked me, but plunged into the work at once. For half an hour the pen scratched without stopping. Then Charlie sighed and tugged his hair. The scratching grew slower, there were more erasures, and at last ceased. The finest story in the world would not come forth.

"It looks such awful rot now," he said, mournfully. "And yet it seemed so good when I was thinking about it. What's wrong?"

I could not dishearten him by saying the truth. So I answered: "Perhaps you don't feel in the mood for writing."

"Yes I do—except when I look at this stuff. Ugh!"

"Read me what you've done," I said.

He read, and it was wondrous bad, and he paused at all the specially turgid sentences, expecting a little approval; for he was proud of those sentences, as I knew he would be.

"It needs compression," I suggested, cautiously.

"I hate cutting my things down. I don't think you could alter a word here without spoiling the sense. It reads better aloud than when I was writing it."

"Charlie, you're suffering from an alarming disease afflicting a numerous class. Put the thing by, and tackle it again in a week."

"I want to do it at once. What do you think of it?"

"How can I judge from a half-written tale? Tell me the story as it lies in your head."

Charlie told, and in the telling there was everything that his ignorance had so carefully prevented from escaping into the written word. I looked at him, and wondering whether it were possible that he did not know the originality, the power of the notion that had come in his way? It was distinctly a Notion among notions. Men had been puffed up with pride by notions not a tithe as excellent and practicable. But Charlie babbled on serenely, interrupting the current of pure fancy with samples of horrible sentences that he purposed to use. I heard him out to the end. It would be folly to allow his idea to remain in his own inept hands, when I could do so much with it. Not all that could be done indeed; but, oh so much!

"What do you think?" he said, at last. "I fancy I shall call it 'The Story of a Ship.'"

"I think the idea's pretty good; but you won't be able to handle it for ever so long. Now I"—

"Would it be of any use to you? Would you care to take it? I should be proud," said Charlie promptly.

There are few things sweeter in this world than the guileless, hot-headed, intemperate, open admiration of a junior. Even a woman in her blindest devotion does not fall into the gait of the man she adores, tilt her bonnet to the angle at which he wears his hat, or interlard her speech with his pet oaths. And Charlie did all these things. Still it was necessary to salve my conscience before I possessed myself of Charlie's thoughts.

"Let's make a bargain. I'll give you a fiver for the notion," I said.

Charlie became a bank-clerk at once.

"Oh, that's impossible. Between two pals, you know, if I may call you so, and speaking as a man of the world, I couldn't. Take the notion if it's any use to you. I've heaps more."

He had—none knew this better than I—but they were the notions of other men.

"Look at it as a matter of business—between men of the world," I returned. "Five pounds will buy you any number of poetry-books. Business is business, and you may be sure I shouldn't give that price unless"—

"Oh, if you put it *that* way," said Charlie, visibly moved by the thought of the books. The bargain was clinched with an agreement that he should at unstated intervals come to me with all the notions that he possessed, should have a table of his own to write at, and unquestioned right to inflict upon me all his poems and fragments of poems. Then I said, "Now tell me how you came by this idea."

"It came by itself." Charlie's eyes opened a little.

"Yes, but you told me a great deal about the hero that you must have read before somewhere."

"I haven't any time for reading, except when you let me sit here, and on Sundays I'm on my bicycle or down the river all day. There's nothing wrong about the hero, is there?"

"Tell me again and I shall understand clearly. You say that your hero went pirating. How did he live?"

"He was on the lower deck of this ship-thing that I was telling you about."

"What sort of ship?"

"It was the kind rowed with oars, and the sea spurts through the oar-holes and the men row sitting up to their knees in water. Then there's a bench running down between the two lines of oars and an overseer with a whip walks up and down the bench to make the men work."

"How do you know that?"

"It's in the tale. There's a rope running overhead, looped to the upper deck, for the overseer to catch hold of when the ship rolls. When the overseer misses the rope once and falls among the rowers, remember the hero laughs at him and gets licked for it. He's chained to his oar of course—the hero."

"How is he chained?"

"With an iron band round his waist fixed to the bench he sits on, and a sort of handcuff on his left wrist chaining him to the oar. He's on the lower deck where the worst men are sent, and the only light comes from the hatchways and through the oar-holes. Can't you imagine the sunlight just squeezing through between the handle and the hole and wobbling about as the ship moves?"

"I can, but I can't imagine your imagining it."

"How could it be any other way? Now you listen to me. The long oars on the upper deck are managed by four men to each bench, the lower ones by three, and the lowest of all by two. Remember it's quite dark on the lowest deck and all the men there go mad.

When a man dies at his oar on that deck he isn't thrown overboard, but cut up in his chains and stuffed through the oar-hole in little pieces."

"Why?" I demanded, amazed, not so much at the information as the tone of command in which it was flung out.

"To save trouble and to frighten the others. It needs two overseers to drag a man's body up to the top deck; and if the men at the lower deck oars were left alone, of course they'd stop rowing and try to pull up the benches by all standing up together in their chains."

"You've a most provident imagination. Where have you been reading about galleys and galley-slaves?"

"Nowhere that I remember. I row a little when I get the chance. But, perhaps, if you say so, I may have read something."

He went away shortly afterward to deal with book-sellers, and I wondered how a bank clerk aged twenty could put into my hands with a profligate abundance of detail, all given with absolute assurance, the story of extravagant and bloodthirsty adventure, riot, piracy, and death in unnamed seas. He had led his hero a desperate dance through revolt against the overseers, to command of a ship of his own, and ultimate establishment of a kingdom on an island "somewhere in the sea, you know"; and, delighted with my paltry five pounds, had gone out to buy the notions of other men, that these might teach him how to write. I had the consolation of knowing that this notion was mine by right of purchase, and I thought that I could make something of it.

When next he came to me he was drunk—royally
drunk on many poets for the first time revealed to him.
His pupils were dilated, his words tumbled over each
other, and he wrapped himself in quotations. Most of
all was he drunk with Longfellow.

"Isn't it splendid? Isn't it superb?" he cried, after
hasty greetings. "Listen to this—

> " 'Wouldst thou,'—so the helmsman answered,
>   'Know the secret of the sea?
>   Only those who brave its dangers
>   Comprehend its mystery.'

By gum!

> " 'Only those who brave its dangers
>   Comprehend its mystery,' "

he repeated twenty times, walking up and down the
room and forgetting me. "But *I* can understand it too,"
he said to himself. "I don't know how to thank you
for that fiver. And this; listen—

> " 'I remember the black wharves and the ships
>   And the sea-tides tossing free,
>   And the Spanish sailors with bearded lips,
>   And the beauty and mystery of the ships,
>   And the magic of the sea.'

I haven't braved any dangers, but I feel as if I knew all
about it."

"You certainly seem to have a grip of the sea. Have
you ever seen it?"

"When I was a little chap I went to Brighton once;
we used to live in Coventry, though, before we came to
London. I never saw it,

" 'When descends on the Atlantic
The gigantic
Storm-wind of the Equinox.' "

He shook me by the shoulder to make me understand the passion that was shaking himself.

"When that storm comes," he continued, "I think
that all the oars in the ship that I was talking about get
broken, and the rowers have their chests smashed in by
the bucking oar-heads. By the way, have you done
anything with that notion of mine yet?"

"No. I was waiting to hear more of it from you.
Tell me how in the world you're so certain about the
fittings of the ship. You know nothing of ships."

"I don't know. It's as real as anything to me until I
try to write it down. I was thinking about it only last
night in bed, after you had loaned me 'Treasure Island';
and I made up a whole lot of new things to go into the
story."

"What sort of things?"

"About the food the men ate; rotten figs and black
beans and wine in a skin bag, passed from bench to
bench."

"Was the ship built so long ago as *that?*"

"As what? I don't know whether it was long ago or
not. It's only a notion, but sometimes it seems just as
real as if it was true. Do I bother you with talking
about it?"

"Not in the least. Did you make up anything else?"

"Yes, but it's nonsense." Charlie flushed a little.

"Never mind; let's hear about it."

"Well, I was thinking over the story, and after awhile

I got out of bed and wrote down on a piece of paper the sort of stuff the men might be supposed to scratch on their oars with the edges of their handcuffs. It seemed to make the thing more lifelike. It *is* so real to me, y'know."

"Have you the paper on you?"

"Ye-es, but what's the use of showing it? It's only a lot of scratches. All the same, we might have 'em reproduced in the book on the front page."

"I'll attend to those details. Show me what your men wrote."

He pulled out of his pocket a sheet of notepaper, with a single line of scratches upon it, and I put this carefully away.

"What is it supposed to mean in English?" I said.

"Oh, I don't know. Perhaps it means 'I'm beastly tired.' It's great nonsense," he repeated, "but all those men in the ship seem as real as people to me. Do do something to the notion soon; I should like to see it written and printed."

"But all you've told me would make a long book."

"Make it then. You've only to sit down and write it out."

"Give me a little time. Have you any more notions?"

"Not just now. I'm reading all the books I've bought. They're splendid."

When he had left I looked at the sheet of notepaper with the inscription upon it. Then I took my head tenderly between both hands, to make certain that it was not coming off or turning round. Then . . . but there seemed to be no interval between quitting my rooms and finding myself arguing with a policeman outside a door marked *Private* in a corridor of the British Museum. All I demanded, as politely as possible, was "the Greek antiquity man." The policeman knew nothing except the rules of the Museum, and it became necessary to forage through all the houses and offices inside the gates. An elderly gentleman called away from his lunch put an end to my search by holding the notepaper between finger and thumb and sniffing at it scornfully.

"What does this mean? H'mm," said he. "So far as I can ascertain it is an attempt to write extremely corrupt Greek on the part"—here he glared at me with intention—"of an extremely illiterate—ah—person." He read slowly from the paper, *"Pollock, Erckmann, Tauchnitz, Henniker"*—four names familiar to me.

"Can you tell me what the corruption is supposed to mean—the gist of the thing?" I asked.

"I have been—many times—overcome with weariness in this particular employment. That is the meaning." He returned me the paper, and I fled without a word of thanks, explanation, or apology.

I might have been excused for forgetting much. To me of all men had been given the chance to write the most marvelous tale in the world, nothing less than the story of a Greek galley-slave, as told by himself. Small wonder that his dreaming had seemed real to Charlie. The Fates that are so careful to shut the doors of each successive life behind us had, in this case, been neglectful, and Charlie was looking, though that he did not know, where never man had been permitted to look with full knowledge since Time began. Above all, he was absolutely ignorant of the knowledge sold to me for five pounds; and he would retain that ignorance, for bank-clerks do not understand metempsychosis, and a sound commercial education does not include Greek. He would supply me—here I capered among the dumb gods of Egypt and laughed in their battered faces— with material to make my tale sure—so sure that the world would hail it as an impudent and vamped fiction. And I—I alone would know that it was absolutely and literally true. I,—I alone held this jewel to my hand for the cutting and polishing. Therefore I danced again among the gods till a policeman saw me and took steps in my direction.

It remained now only to encourage Charlie to talk, and here there was no difficulty. But I had forgotten those accursed books of poetry. He came to me time after time, as useless as a surcharged phonograph— drunk on Byron, Shelley, or Keats. Knowing now what the boy had been in his past lives, and desperately anxious not to lose one word of his babble, I could not hide from him my respect and interest. He misconstrued both into respect for the present soul of Charlie Mears, to whom life was as new as it was to Adam, and interest in his readings; and stretched my patience to breaking point by reciting poetry—not his own now, but that of others. I wished every English poet blotted out of the memory of mankind. I blasphemed the mightiest names of song because they had drawn Charlie from the path of direct narrative, and would, later, spur him to imitate them; but I choked down my impatience until the first flood of enthusiasm should have spent itself and the boy returned to his dreams.

"What's the use of my telling you what *I* think, when these chaps wrote things for the angels to read?" he growled, one evening. "Why don't you write something like theirs?"

"I don't think you're treating me quite fairly," I said, speaking under strong restraint.

"I've given you the story," he said, shortly, replunging into "Lara."

"But I want the details."

"The things I make up about the damned ship that you call a galley? They're quite easy. You can just make 'em up yourself. Turn up the gas a little, I want to go on reading."

I could have broken the gas globe over his head for his amazing stupidity. I could indeed make up things for myself did I only know what Charlie did not know that he knew. But since the doors were shut behind me I could only wait his youthful pleasure and strive to keep him in good temper. One minute's want of guard might spoil a priceless revelation; now and again he would toss his books aside—he kept them in my rooms, for his mother would have been shocked at the waste of good money had she seen them—and launched into his sea dreams. Again I cursed all the poets of England. The plastic mind of the bank-clerk had been overlaid, colored and distorted by that which he had read, and the result as delivered was a confused tangle of other voices most like the muttered song through a City telephone in the busiest part of the day.

He talked of the galley—his own galley had he but known it—with illustrations borrowed from the "Bride of Abydos." He pointed the experiences of his hero with quotations from "The Corsair," and threw in deep and desperate moral reflections from "Cain" and "Manfred," expecting me to use them all. Only when the talk turned on Longfellow were the jarring cross-currents dumb, and I knew that Charlie was speaking the truth as he remembered it.

"What do you think of this?" I said one evening, as soon as I understood the medium in which his memory worked best, and, before he could expostulate, read him the whole of "The Saga of King Olaf!"

He listened open-mouthed, flushed, his hands drumming on the back of the sofa where he lay, till I came to the Song of Einar Tamberskelver and the verse:

> "Einar then, the arrow taking
> From the loosened string,
> Answered: 'That was Norway breaking
> 'Neath thy hand, O King.'"

He gasped with pure delight of sound.

"That's better than Byron, a little," I ventured.

"Better? Why it's *true*! How could he have known?"

I went back and repeated:

> "'What was that?' said Olaf, standing
> On the quarter-deck,
> 'Something heard I like the stranding
> Of a shattered wreck?'"

"How could he have known how the ships crash and the oars rip out and go *z-zzp* all along the line? Why

only the other night. . . . But go back please and read
'The Skerry of Shrieks' again."

"No, I'm tired. Let's talk. What happened the
other night?"

"I had an awful nightmare about that galley of ours.
I dreamed I was drowned in a fight. You see we ran
alongside another ship in harbor. The water was dead
still except where our oars whipped it up. You know
where I always sit in the galley?" He spoke haltingly
at first, under a fine English fear of being laughed at.

"No. That's news to me," I answered, meekly, my
heart beginning to beat.

"On the fourth oar from the bow on the right side
on the upper deck. There were four of us at that oar,
all chained. I remember watching the water and trying to get my handcuffs off before the row began.
Then we closed up on the other ship, and all their
fighting men jumped over our bulwarks, and my bench
broke and I was pinned down with the three other
fellows on top of me, and the big oar jammed across
our backs."

"Well?" Charlie's eyes were alive and alight. He
was looking at the wall behind my chair.

"I don't know how we fought. The men were
trampling all over my back, and I lay low. Then our
rowers on the left side—tied to their oars, you know—
began to yell and back water. I could hear the water
sizzle, and we spun round like a cockchafer and I
knew, lying where I was, that there was a galley coming up bow-on, to ram us on the left side. I could just
lift up my head and see her sail over the bulwarks. We

wanted to meet her bow to bow, but it was too late.
We could only turn a little bit because the galley on our
right had hooked herself on to us and stopped our
moving. Then, by gum! there was a crash! Our left
oars began to break as the other galley, the moving one
y'know, stuck her nose into them. Then the lower-
deck oars shot up through the deck planking, butt first,
and one of them jumped clean up into the air and came
down again close to my head."

"How was that managed?"

"The moving galley's bow was plunking them back
through their own oar-holes, and I could hear the devil
of a shindy in the decks below. Then her nose caught
us nearly in the middle, and we tilted sideways, and
the fellows in the right-hand galley unhitched their
hooks and ropes, and threw things on to our upper deck
—arrows, and hot pitch or something that stung, and
we went up and up and up on the left side, and the
right side dipped, and I twisted my head round and
saw the water stand still as it topped the right bulwarks, and then it curled over and crashed down on
the whole lot of us on the right side, and I felt it hit my
back, and I woke."

"One minute, Charlie. When the sea topped the
bulwarks, what did it look like?" I had my reasons
for asking. A man of my acquaintance had once gone
down with a leaking ship in a still sea, and had seen
the water-level pause for an instant ere it fell on the
deck.

"It looked just like a banjo-string drawn tight, and
it seemed to stay there for years," said Charlie.

Exactly! The other man had said: "It looked like a silver wire laid down the bulwarks, and I thought it was never going to break." He had paid everything except the bare life for this little valueless piece of knowledge, and I had traveled ten thousand weary miles to meet him and take his knowledge at second hand. But Charlie, the bank-clerk on twenty-five shillings a week, he who had never been out of sight of a London omnibus, knew it all. It was no consolation to me that once in his lives he had been forced to die for his gains. I also must have died scores of times, but behind me, because I could have used my knowledge, the doors were shut.

"And then?" I said, trying to put away the devil of envy.

"The funny thing was, though, in all the mess I didn't feel a bit astonished or frightened. It seemed as if I'd been in a good many fights, because I told my next man so when the row began. But that cad of an overseer on my deck wouldn't unloose our chains and give us a chance. He always said that we'd all be set free after a battle, but we never were; we never were." Charlie shook his head mournfully.

"What a scoundrel!"

"I should say he was. He never gave us enough to eat, and sometimes we were so thirsty that we used to drink salt-water. I can taste that salt-water still."

"Now tell me something about the harbor where the fight was fought."

"I didn't dream about that. I know it was a harbor, though; because we were tied up to a ring on a white wall and all the face of the stone under water was covered with wood to prevent our ram getting chipped when the tide made us rock."

"That's curious. Our hero commanded the galley, didn't he?"

"Didn't he just! He stood by the bows and shouted like a good 'un. He was the man who killed the overseer."

"But you were all drowned together, Charlie, weren't you?"

"I can't make that fit quite," he said, with a puzzled look. "The galley must have gone down with all hands, and yet I fancy that the hero went on living afterward. Perhaps he climbed into the attacking ship. I wouldn't see that, of course. I was dead, you know."

He shivered slightly and protested that he could remember no more.

I did not press him further, but to satisfy myself that he lay in ignorance of the workings of his own mind, deliberately introduced him to Mortimer Collins's "Transmigration," and gave him a sketch of the plot before he opened the pages.

"What rot it all is!" he said, frankly, at the end of an hour. "I don't understand his nonsense about the Red Planet Mars and the King, and the rest of it. Chuck me the Longfellow again."

I handed him the book and wrote out as much as I could remember of his description of the sea-fight, appealing to him from time to time for confirmation of fact or detail. He would answer without raising his eyes from the book, as assuredly as though all his knowledge lay before him on the printed page. I spoke under the normal key of my voice that the current might not be broken, and I know that he was not aware of what he was saying, for his thoughts were out on the sea with Longfellow.

"Charlie," I asked, "when the rowers on the galleys mutinied how did they kill their overseers?"

"Tore up the benches and brained 'em. That happened when a heavy sea was running. An overseer on the lower deck slipped from the centre plank and fell among the rowers. They choked him to death against the side of the ship with their chained hands quite quietly, and it was too dark for the other overseer to see what had happened. When he asked, he was pulled down too and choked, and the lower deck fought their way up deck by deck, with the pieces of the broken benches banging behind 'em. How they howled!"

"And what happened after that?"

"I don't know. The hero went away—red hair and red beard and all. That was after he had captured our galley, I think."

The sound of my voice irritated him, and he motioned slightly with his left hand as a man does when interruption jars.

"You never told me he was red-headed before, or that he captured your galley," I said, after a discreet interval.

Charlie did not raise his eyes.

"He was as red as a red bear," said he, abstractedly. "He came from the north; they said so in the galley when he looked for rowers—not slaves, but free men.

Afterward—years and years afterward—news came from another ship, or else he came back"—

His lips moved in silence. He was rapturously re-tasting some poem before him.

"Where had he been, then?" I was almost whispering that the sentence might come gentle to whichever section of Charlie's brain was working on my behalf.

"To the Beaches—the Long and Wonderful Beaches!" was the reply, after a minute of silence.

"To Furdurstrandi?" I asked, tingling from head to foot.

"Yes, to Furdurstrandi," he pronounced the word in a new fashion. "And I too saw"— The voice failed.

"Do you know what you have said?" I shouted, incautiously.

He lifted his eyes, fully roused now. "No!" he snapped. "I wish you'd let a chap go on reading. Hark to this:

" 'But Othere, the old sea captain,
　He neither paused nor stirred
　　Till the king listened, and then
　　Once more took up his pen
　And wrote down every word.

" 'And to the King of the Saxons
　In witness of the truth,
　　Raising his noble head,
　　He stretched his brown hand and said,
　"Behold this walrus tooth." ' "

By Jove, what chaps those must have been, to go sailing all over the shop never knowing where they'd fetch the land! Hah!"

"Charlie," I pleaded, "if you'll only be sensible for a minute or two I'll make our hero in our tale every inch as good as Othere."

"Umph! Longfellow wrote that poem. I don't care about writing things any more. I want to read." He was thoroughly out of tune now, and raging over my own ill-luck, I left him.

Conceive yourself at the door of the world's treasure-house guarded by a child—an idle irresponsible child playing knuckle-bones—on whose favor depends the gift of the key, and you will imagine one half my torment. Till that evening Charlie had spoken nothing that might not lie within the experiences of a Greek galley-slave. But now, or there was no virtue in books, he had talked of some desperate adventure of the Vikings, of Thorfin Karlsefne's sailing to Wineland, which is America, in the ninth or tenth century. The battle in the harbor he had seen; and his own death he had described. But this was a much more startling plunge into the past. Was it possible that he had skipped half a dozen lives and was then dimly remembering some episode of a thousand years later? It was a maddening jumble, and the worst of it was that Charlie Mears in his normal condition was the last person in the world to clear it up. I could only wait and watch, but I went to bed that night full of the wildest imaginings. There was nothing that was not possible if Charlie's detestable memory only held good.

I might rewrite the Saga of Thorfin Karlsefne as it had never been written before, might tell the story of the first discovery of America, myself the discoverer.

But I was entirely at Charlie's mercy, and so long as there was a three-and-six-penny Bohn volume within his reach Charlie would not tell. I dared not curse him openly; I hardly dared jog his memory, for I was dealing with the experiences of a thousand years ago, told through the mouth of a boy of to-day; and a boy of to-day is affected by every change of tone and gust of opinion, so that he lies even where he desires to speak the truth.

I saw no more of him for nearly a week. When next I met him it was in Gracechurch Street with a billbook chained to his waist. Business took him over London Bridge and I accompanied him. He was very full of the importance of that book and magnified it. As we passed over the Thames we paused to look at a steamer unloading great slabs of white and brown marble. A barge drifted under the steamer's stern and a lonely cow in that barge bellowed. Charlie's face changed from the face of the bank-clerk to that of an unknown and—though he would not have believed this—a much shrewder man. He flung out his arms across the parapet of the bridge and laughing very loudly, said:

"When they heard *our* bulls bellow the Skrœlings ran away!"

I waited only for an instant, but the barge and the cow had disappeared under the bows of the steamer before I answered.

"Charlie, what do you suppose are Skrœlings?"

"Never heard of 'em before. They sound like a new kind of seagull. What a chap you are for asking questions!" he replied. "I have to go to the cashier of

the Omnibus Company yonder. Will you wait for me
and we can lunch somewhere together? I've a notion
for a poem."

"No, thanks. I'm off. You're sure you know nothing about Skrœlings?"

"Not unless he's been entered for the Liverpool
Handicap." He nodded and disappeared in the crowd.

Now it is written in the Saga of Eric the Red or that
of Thorfin Karlsefne, that nine hundred years ago
when Karlsefne's galleys came to Leif's booths, which
Leif had erected in the unknown land called Markland, which may or may not have been Rhode Island,
the Skrœlings—and the Lord He knows who these may
or may not have been—came to trade with the Vikings,
and ran away because they were frightened at the
bellowing of the cattle which Thorfin had brought
with him in the ships. But what in the world could a
Greek slave know of that affair? I wandered up and
down among the streets trying to unravel the mystery,
and the more I considered it, the more baffling it grew.
One thing only seemed certain, and that certainty took
away my breath for the moment. If I came to full
knowledge of anything at all, it would not be one life
of the soul in Charlie Mears's body, but half a dozen—
half a dozen several and separate existences spent on
blue water in the morning of the world!

Then I walked round the situation.

Obviously if I used my knowledge I should stand
alone and unapproachable until all men were as wise
as myself. That would be something, but manlike I
was ungrateful. It seemed bitterly unfair that Charlie's

memory should fail me when I needed it most. Great
Powers above—I looked up at them through the fog
smoke—did the Lords of Life and Death know what
this meant to me? Nothing less than eternal fame of
the best kind, that comes from One, and is shared by
one alone. I would be content—remembering Clive, I
stood astounded at my own moderation,—with the
mere right to tell one story, to work out one little con-
tribution to the light literature of the day. If Charlie
were permitted full recollection for one hour—for sixty
short minutes—of existences that had extended over a
thousand years—I would forego all profit and honor
from all that I should make of his speech. I would
take no share in the commotion that would follow
throughout the particular corner of the earth that calls
itself "the world." The thing should be put forth
anonymously. Nay, I would make other men believe
that they had written it. They would hire bull-hided
self-advertising Englishmen to bellow it abroad. Preach-
ers would found a fresh conduct of life upon it, swearing that it was new and that they had lifted the fear of
death from all mankind. Every Orientalist in Europe
would patronize it discursively with Sanskrit and Pali
texts. Terrible women would invent unclean variants
of the men's belief for the elevation of their sisters.
Churches and religions would war over it. Between
the hailing and re-starting of an omnibus I foresaw the
scuffles that would arise among half a dozen denomi-
nations all professing "the doctrine of the True Metempsychosis as applied to the world and the New Era";
and saw, too, the respectable English newspapers shy-

ing, like frightened kine, over the beautiful simplicity of the tale. The mind leaped forward a hundred— two hundred—a thousand years. I saw with sorrow that men would mutilate and garble the story; that rival creeds would turn it upside down till, at last, the western world which clings to the dread of death more closely than the hope of life, would set it aside as an interesting superstition and stampede after some faith so long forgotten that it seemed altogether new. Upon this I changed the terms of the bargain that I would make with the Lords of Life and Death. Only let me know, let me write, the story with sure knowledge that I wrote the truth, and I would burn the manuscript as a solemn sacrifice. Five minutes after the last line was written I would destroy it all. But I must be allowed to write it with absolute certainty.

There was no answer. The flaming colors of an Aquarium poster caught my eye and I wondered whether it would be wise or prudent to lure Charlie into the hands of the professional mesmerist, and whether, if he were under his power, he would speak of his past lives. If he did, and if people believed him . . . but Charlie would be frightened and flustered, or made conceited by the interviews. In either case he would begin to lie, through fear or vanity. He was safest in my own hands.

"They are very funny fools, your English," said a voice at my elbow, and turning round I recognized a casual acquaintance, a young Bengali law student, called Grish Chunder, whose father had sent him to England to become civilized. The old man was a retired native official, and on an income of five pounds a month contrived to allow his son two hundred pounds a year, and the run of his teeth in a city where he could pretend to be the cadet of a royal house, and tell stories of the brutal Indian bureaucrats who ground the faces of the poor.

Grish Chunder was a young, fat, full-bodied Bengali dressed with scrupulous care in frock coat, tall hat, light trousers and tan gloves. But I had known him in the days when the brutal Indian Government paid for his university education, and he contributed cheap sedition to *Sachi Durpan,* and intrigued with the wives of his schoolmates.

"That is very funny and very foolish," he said, nodding at the poster. "I am going down to the Northbrook Club. Will you come too?"

I walked with him for some time. "You are not well," he said. "What is there in your mind? You do not talk."

"Grish Chunder, you've been too well educated to believe in a God, haven't you?"

"Oah, yes, *here!* But when I go home I must conciliate popular superstition, and make ceremonies of purification, and my women will anoint idols."

"And hang up *tulsi* and feast the *purohit,* and take you back into caste again and make a good *khuttri* of you again, you advanced social Free-thinker. And you'll eat *desi* food, and like it all, from the smell in the courtyard to the mustard oil over you."

"I shall very much like it," said Grish Chunder, unguardedly. "Once a Hindu—always a Hindu. But I like to know what the English think they know."

"I'll tell you something that one Englishman knows. It's an old tale to you."

I began to tell the story of Charlie in English, but Grish Chunder put a question in the vernacular, and the history went forward naturally in the tongue best suited for its telling. After all it could never have been told in English. Grish Chunder heard me, nodding from time to time, and then came up to my rooms where I finished the tale.

"*Beshak,*" he said, philosophically. "*Lekin darwaza band hai.*. (Without doubt, but the door is shut.) I have heard of this remembering of previous existences among my people. It is of course an old tale with us, but, to happen to an Englishman—a cow-fed *Malechh* —an outcast. By Jove, that is most peculiar!"

"Outcast yourself, Grish Chunder! You eat cow-beef every day. Let's think the thing over. The boy remembers his incarnations."

"Does he know that?" said Grish Chunder, quietly, swinging his legs as he sat on my table. He was speaking in English now.

"He does not know anything. Would I speak to you if he did? Go on!"

"There is no going on at all. If you tell that to your friends they will say you are mad and put it in the papers. Suppose, now, you prosecute for libel."

"Let's leave that out of the question entirely. Is there any chance of his being made to speak?"

"There is a chance. Oah, yess! But *if* he spoke it

would mean that all this world would end now—
instanto—fall down on your head. These things are
not allowed, you know. As I said, the door is shut."

"Not a ghost of a chance?"

"How can there be? You are a Christi-án, and it is
forbidden to eat, in your books, of the Tree of Life, or
else you would never die. How shall you all fear death
if you all know what your friend does not know that
he knows? I am afraid to be kicked, but am not afraid
to die, because I know what I know. You are not
afraid to be kicked, but you are afraid to die. If you
were not, by God! you English would be all over the
shop in an hour, upsetting the balances of power, and
making commotions. It would not be good. But no
fear. He will remember a little and a little less, and he
will call it dreams. Then he will forget altogether.
When I passed my First Arms Examination in Calcutta that was all in the cram-book on Wordsworth.
Trailing clouds of glory, you know."

"This seems to be an exception to the rule."

"There are no exceptions to rules. Some are not so
hard-looking as others, but they are all the same when
you touch. If this friend of yours said so-and-so and
so-and-so, indicating that he remembered all his lost
lives, or one piece of a lost life, he would not be in the
bank another hour. He would be what you called sack
because he was mad, and they would send him to an
asylum for lunatics. You can see that, my friend."

"Of course I can, but I wasn't thinking of him. His
name need never appear in the story."

"Ah! I see. That story will never be written. You can try."

"I am going to."

"For your own credit and for the sake of money, *of course?*"

"No. For the sake of writing the story. On my honor that will be all."

"Even then there is no chance. You cannot play with the Gods. It is a very pretty story now. As they say, Let it go on that—I mean at that. Be quick; he will not last long."

"How do you mean?"

"What I say. He has never, so far, thought about a woman."

"Hasn't he, though!" I remembered some of Charlie's confidences.

"I mean no woman has thought about him. When that comes; *bus—hogya*—all up! I know. There are millions of women here. Housemaids, for instance."

I winced at the thought of my story being ruined by a housemaid. And yet nothing was more probable.

Grish Chunder grinned.

"Yes—also pretty girls—cousins of his house, and perhaps *not* of his house. One kiss that he gives back again and remembers will cure all this nonsense, or else"—

"Or else what? Remember he does not know that he knows."

"I know that. Or else, if nothing happens he will become immersed in the trade and the financial speculations like the rest. It must be so. You can see that it must be so. But the woman will come first, *I* think."

There was a rap at the door, and Charlie charged in impetuously. He had been released from office, and by the look in his eyes I could see that he had come over for a long talk; most probably with poems in his pockets. Charlie's poems were very wearying, but sometimes they led him to talk about the galley.

Grish Chunder looked at him keenly for a minute.

"I beg your pardon," Charlie said, uneasily; "I didn't know you had any one with you."

"I am going," said Grish Chunder.

He drew me into the lobby as he departed.

"That is your man," he said, quickly. "I tell you he will never speak all you wish. That is rot—bosh. But he would be most good to make to see things. Suppose now we pretend that it was only play"—I had never seen Grish Chunder so excited—"and pour the ink-pool into his hand. Eh, what do you think? I tell you that he could see *anything* that a man could see. Let me get the ink and the camphor. He is a seer and he will tell us very many things."

"He may be all you say, but I'm not going to trust him to your gods and devils."

"It will not hurt him. He will only feel a little stupid and dull when he wakes up. You have seen boys look into the ink-pool before."

"That is the reason why I am not going to see it any more. You'd better go, Grish Chunder."

He went, declaring far down the staircase that it was throwing away my only chance of looking into the future.

This left me unmoved, for I was concerned for the past, and no peering of hypnotized boys into mirrors and ink-pools would help me to that. But I recognized Grish Chunder's point of view and sympathized with it.

"What a big black brute that was!" said Charlie, when I returned to him. "Well, look here, I've just done a poem; did it instead of playing dominoes after lunch. May I read it?"

"Let me read it to myself."

"Then you miss the proper expression. Besides, you always make my things sound as if the rhymes were all wrong."

"Read it aloud, then. You're like the rest of 'em."

Charlie mouthed me his poem, and it was not much worse than the average of his verses. He had been reading his books faithfully, but he was not pleased when I told him that I preferred my Longfellow undiluted with Charlie.

Then we began to go through the MS. line by line; Charlie parrying every objection and correction with:

"Yes, that may be better, but you don't catch what I'm driving at."

Charles was, in one way at least, very like one kind of poet.

There was a pencil scrawl at the back of the paper and "What's that?" I said.

"Oh that's not poetry at all. It's some rot I wrote last night before I went to bed and it was too much bother to hunt for rhymes; so I made it a sort of blank verse instead."

Here is Charlie's "blank verse":

"We pulled for you when the wind was against us and the
sails were low.
Will you never let us go?
We ate bread and onions when you took towns or ran aboard
quickly when you were beaten back by the foe,
The captains walked up and down the deck in fair weather
singing songs, but we were below,
We fainted with our chins on the oars and you did not see
that we were idle for we still swung to and fro.
Will you never let us go?
The salt made the oar handles like sharkskin; our knees
were cut to the bone with salt cracks; our hair was stuck to
our foreheads; and our lips were cut to our gums and you
whipped us because we could not row.
Will you never let us go?
But in a little time we shall run out of the portholes as the
water runs along the oarblade, and though you tell the others
to row after us you will never catch us till you catch the oar-
thresh and tie up the winds in the belly of the sail. Aho!
Will you never let us go?

"H'm. What's oar-thresh, Charlie?"

"The water washed up by the oars. That's the sort
of song they might sing in the galley, y' know. Aren't
you ever going to finish that story and give me some
of the profits?"

"It depends on yourself. If you had only told me
more about your hero in the first instance it might
have been finished by now. You're so hazy in your
notions."

"I only want to give you the general notion of it—
the knocking about from place to place and the fighting and all that. Can't you fill in the rest yourself?

Make the hero have a girl on a pirate-galley and marry her or do something."

"You're a really helpful collaborator. I suppose the hero went through some few adventures before he married."

"Well then, make him a very artful cad—a low sort of man—a sort of political man who went about making treaties and breaking them—a black-haired chap who hid behind the mast when the fighting began."

"But you said the other day that he was red-haired."

"I couldn't have. Make him black-haired of course. You've no imagination."

Seeing that I had just discovered the entire principles upon which the half-memory falsely called imagination is based, I felt entitled to laugh, but forbore, for the sake of the tale.

"You're right. *You're* the man with imagination. A black-haired chap in a decked ship," I said.

"No, an open ship—like a big boat."

This was maddening.

"Your ship has been built and designed, closed and decked in; you said so yourself," I protested.

"No, no, not that ship. That was open, or half decked because— By Jove you're right. You made me think of the hero as a red-haired chap. Of course if he were red, the ship would be an open one with painted sails."

Surely, I thought, he would remember now that he had served in two galleys at least—in a three-decked Greek one under the black-haired "political man," and

again in a Viking's open sea-serpent under the man
"red as a red bear" who went to Markland. The devil
prompted me to speak.

"Why, 'of course,' Charlie?" said I.

"I don't know. Are you making fun of me?"

The current was broken for the time being. I took
up a notebook and pretended to make many entries
in it.

"It's a pleasure to work with an imaginative chap
like yourself," I said, after a pause. "The way that
you've brought out the character of the hero is simply
wonderful."

"Do you think so?" he answered, with a pleased
flush. "I often tell myself that there's more in me than
my mo— than people think."

"There's an enormous amount in you."

"Then, won't you let me send an essay on The Ways
of Bank Clerks to *Tit-Bits,* and get the guinea prize?"

"That wasn't exactly what I meant, old fellow: perhaps it would be better to wait a little and go ahead
with the galley-story."

"Ah, but I sha'n't get the credit of that. *Tit-Bits*
would publish my name and address if I win. What
are you grinning at? They *would.*"

"I know it. Suppose you go for a walk. I want to
look through my notes about our story."

Now this reprehensible youth who left me, a little
hurt and put back, might for aught he or I knew have
been one of the crew of the Argo—had been certainly
slave or comrade to Thorfin Karlsefne. Therefore he
was deeply interested in guinea competitions. Remem-

bering what Grish Chunder had said I laughed aloud. The Lords of Life and Death would never allow Charlie Mears to speak with full knowledge of his pasts, and I must even piece out what he had told me with my own poor inventions while Charlie wrote of the ways of bank-clerks.

I got together and placed on one file all my notes; and the net result was not cheering. I read them a second time. There was nothing that might not have been compiled at second-hand from other people's books—except, perhaps, the story of the fight in the harbor. The adventures of a Viking had been written many times before; the history of a Greek galley-slave was no new thing, and though I wrote both, who could challenge or confirm the accuracy of my details? I might as well tell a tale of two thousand years hence. The Lords of Life and Death were as cunning as Grish Chunder had hinted. They would allow nothing to escape that might trouble or make easy the minds of men. Though I was convinced of this, yet I could not leave the tale alone. Exaltation followed reaction, not once but twenty times in the next few weeks. My moods varied with the March sunlight and flying clouds. By night or in the beauty of a spring morning I perceived that I could write that tale and shift continents thereby. In the wet, windy afternoons, I saw that the tale might indeed be written, but would be nothing more than a faked, false-varnished, sham-rusted piece of Wardour Street work at the end. Then I blessed Charlie in many ways—though it was no fault of his. He seemed to be busy with prize competitions, and I saw less and less of him as the weeks went by and the earth cracked and grew ripe to spring, and the buds swelled in their sheaths. He did not care to read or talk of what he had read, and there was a new ring of self-assertion in his voice. I hardly cared to remind him of the galley when we met; but Charlie alluded to it on every occasion, always as a story from which money was to be made.

"I think I deserve twenty-five per cent, don't I, at least," he said, with beautiful frankness. "I supplied all the ideas, didn't I?"

This greediness for silver was a new side in his nature. I assumed that it had been developed in the City, where Charlie was picking up the curious nasal drawl of the underbed City man.

"When the thing's done we'll talk about it. I can't make anything of it at present. Red-haired or black-haired heros are equally difficult."

He was sitting by the fire staring at the red coals. "I can't understand what you find so difficult. It's all as clear as mud to me," he replied. A jet of gas puffed out between the bars, took light and whistled softly. "Suppose we take the red-haired hero's adventures first, from the time that he came south to my galley and captured it and sailed to the Beaches."

I knew better now than to interrupt Charlie. I was out of reach of pen and paper, and dared not move to get them lest I should break the current. The gas-jet puffed and whinnied, Charlie's voice dropped almost to a whisper, and he told a tale of the sailing of an open galley to Furdurstrandi, of sunsets on the open sea, seen under the curve of the one sail evening after evening when the galley's beak was notched into the centre of the sinking disc, and "we sailed by that for we had no other guide," quoth Charlie. He spoke of a landing on an island and explorations in its woods, where the crew killed three men whom they found asleep under the pines. Their ghosts, Charlie said, followed the galley, swimming and choking in the water, and the crew cast lots and threw one of their number overboard as a sacrifice to the strange gods whom they had offended. Then they ate sea-weed when their provisions failed, and their legs swelled, and their leader, the red-haired man, killed two rowers who mutinied, and after a year spent among the woods they set sail for their own country, and a wind that never failed carried them back so safely that they all slept at night. This, and much more Charlie told. Sometimes the voice fell so low that I could not catch the words, though every nerve was on the strain. He spoke of their leader, the red-haired man, as a pagan speaks of his God; for it was he who cheered them and slew them impartially as he thought best for their needs; and it was he who steered them for three days among floating ice, each floe crowded with strange beasts that "tried to sail with us," said Charlie, "and we beat them back with the handles of the oars."

The gas-jet went out, a burned coal gave way, and the fire settled down with a tiny crash to the bottom of the grate. Charlie ceased speaking, and I said no word.

"By Jove!" he said, at last, shaking his head. "I've

been staring at the fire till I'm dizzy. What was I going to say?"

"Something about the galley."

"I remember now. It's 25 per cent of the profits, isn't it?"

"It's anything you like when I've done the tale."

"I wanted to be sure of that. I must go now. I've —I've an appointment." And he left me.

Had my eyes not been held I might have known that that broken muttering over the fire was the swan-song of Charlie Mears. But I thought it the prelude to fuller revelation. At last and at last I should cheat the Lords of Life and Death!

When next Charlie came to me I received him with rapture. He was nervous and embarrassed, but his eyes were very full of light, and his lips a little parted.

"I've done a poem," he said; and then, quickly: "it's the best I've ever done. Read it." He thrust it into my hand and retreated to the window.

I groaned inwardly. It would be the work of half an hour to criticise—that is to say praise—the poem sufficiently to please Charlie. Then I had good reason to groan, for Charlie, discarding his favorite centipede metres, had launched into shorter and choppier verse, and verse with a motive at the back of it. This is what I read:

> "The day is most fair, the cheery wind
>   Halloos behind the hill,
> Where he bends the wood as seemeth good,
>   And the sapling to his will!
> Riot O wind; there is that in my blood
>   That would not have thee still!

"She gave me herself, O Earth, O Sky;
    Grey sea, she is mine alone!
Let the sullen boulders hear my cry,
    And rejoice tho' they be but stone!

"Mine! I have won her O good brown earth,
    Make merry! 'Tis hard on Spring;
Make merry; my love is doubly worth
    All worship your fields can bring!
Let the hind that tills you feel my mirth
    At the early harrowing."

"Yes, it's the early harrowing, past a doubt," I said, with a dread at my heart. Charlie smiled. but did not answer.

"Red cloud of the sunset, tell it abroad;
    I am victor. Greet me O Sun,
Dominant master and absolute lord
    Over the soul of one!"

"Well?" said Charlie, looking over my shoulder.

I thought it far from well, and very evil indeed, when he silently laid a photograph on the paper—the photograph of a girl with a curly head, and a foolish slack mouth.

"Isn't it—isn't it wonderful?" he whispered, pink to the tips of his ears, wrapped in the rosy mystery of first love. "I didn't know; I didn't think—it came like a thunderclap."

"Yes. It comes like a thunderclap. Are you very happy, Charlie?"

"My God—she—she loves me!" He sat down repeating the last words to himself. I looked at the hairless face, the narrow shoulders already bowed by deskwork, and wondered when, where, and how he had loved in his past lives.

"What will your mother say?" I asked, cheerfully.

"I don't care a damn what she says."

At twenty the things for which one does not care a damn should, properly, be many, but one must not include mothers in the list. I told him this gently; and he described Her, even as Adam must have described to the newly named beasts the glory and tenderness and beauty of Eve. Incidentally I learned that She was a tobacconist's assistant with a weakness for pretty dress, and had told him four or five times already that She had never been kissed by a man before.

Charlie spoke on and on, and on; while I, separated from him by thousands of years, was considering the beginnings of things. Now I understood why the Lords of Life and Death shut the doors so carefully behind us. It is that we may not remember our first wooings. Were it not so, our world would be without inhabitants in a hundred years.

"Now, about that galley-story," I said, still more cheerfully, in a pause in the rush of the speech.

Charlie looked up as though he had been hit. "The galley—what galley? Good heavens, don't joke, man! This is serious! You don't know how serious it is!"

Grish Chunder was right. Charlie had tasted the love of woman that kills remembrance, and the finest story in the world would never be written.

THE SOLID MULDOON

Did ye see John Malone, wid his shinin', brand-new hat?
Did ye see how he walked like a grand aristocrat?
There was flags an' banners wavin' high, an' dhress and shtyle
    were shown,
But the best av all the company was Misther John Malone.
                       —John Malone.

THERE had been a royal dog-fight in the ravine at the back of the rifle-butts, between Learoyd's *Jock* and Ortheris's *Blue Rot*—both mongrel Rampur hounds, chiefly ribs and teeth. It lasted for twenty happy, howling minutes, and then *Blue Rot* collapsed and Ortheris paid Learoyd three rupees, and we were all very thirsty. A dog-fight is a most heating entertainment, quite apart from the shouting, because Rampurs fight over a couple of acres of ground. Later, when the sound of belt-badges clicking against the necks of beer-bottles had died away, conversation drifted from dog to man-fights of all kinds. Humans resemble red-deer in some respects. Any talk of fighting seems to wake up a sort of imp in their breasts, and they bell one to the other, exactly like challenging bucks. This is noticeable even in men who consider themselves superior to Privates of the Line: it shows the Refining Influence of Civilization and the March of Progress.

Tale provoked tale, and each tale more beer. Even dreamy Learoyd's eyes began to brighten, and he unburdened himself of a long history in which a trip to Malham Cove, a girl at Pateley Brigg, a ganger, himself and a pair of clogs were mixed in drawling tangle.

"An' so Ah coot's yead oppen from t' chin to t' hair, an' he was abed for t' matter o' a month," concluded Learoyd, pensively.

Mulvaney came out a revery—he was lying down—and flourished his heels in the air. "You're a man, Learoyd," said he, critically, "but you've only fought wid men, an' that's an ivry-day expayrience; but I've stud up to a ghost, an' that was *not* an ivry-day expayrience."

"No?" said Ortheris, throwing a cork at him. "You git up an' address the 'ouse—you an' yer expayriences. Is it a bigger one nor usual?"

" 'Twas the livin' trut'!" answered Mulvaney, stretching out a huge arm and catching Ortheris by the collar. "Now where are ye, me son? Will ye take the wurrud av the Lorrd out av my mouth another time?" He shook him to emphasize the question.

"No, somethin' else, though," said Ortheris, making a dash at Mulvaney's pipe, capturing it and holding it at arm's length; "I'll chuck it acrost the ditch if you don't let me go!"

"You maraudin' hathen! 'Tis the only cutty I iver loved. Handle her tinder or I'll chuck *you* acrost the nullah. If that poipe was bruk—Ah! Give her back to me, sorr!"

Ortheris had passed the treasure to my hand. It

was an absolutely perfect clay, as shiny as the black ball at Pool. I took it reverently, but I was firm.

"Will you tell us about the ghost-fight if I do?" I said.

"Is ut the shtory that's troublin' you? Av course I will. I mint to all along. I was only gettin' at ut my own way, as Popp Doggle said whin they found him thrying to ram a cartridge down the muzzle. Orth'ris, fall away!"

He released the little Londoner, took back his pipe, filled it, and his eyes twinkled. He has the most eloquent eyes of any one that I know.

"Did I iver tell you," he began, "that I was wanst the divil of a man?"

"You did," said Learoyd, with a childish gravity that made Ortheris yell with laughter, for Mulvaney was always impressing upon us his great merits in the old days.

"Did I iver tell you," Mulvaney continued, calmly, "that I was wanst more av a divil than I am now?"

"Mer—ria! You don't mean it?" said Ortheris.

"Whin I was Corp'ril—I was rejuced afterward— but, as I say, *whin* I was Corp'ril, I was a divil of a man."

He was silent for nearly a minute, while his mind rummaged among old memories and his eye glowed. He bit upon the pipe-stem and charged into his tale.

"Eyah! They was great times. I'm ould now; me hide's wore off in patches; sinthrygo has disconceited me, an' I'm a married man tu. But I've had my day— I've had my day, an' nothin' can take away the taste av

that! Oh my time past, whin I put me fut through
ivry livin' wan av the Tin Commandmints between
Revelly and Lights Out, blew the froth off a pewter,
wiped me moustache wid the back av me hand, an'
slept on ut all as quiet as a little child! But ut's over—
ut's over, an' 'twill niver come back to me; not though
I prayed for a week av Sundays. Was there *any* wan in
the Ould Rig'mint to touch Corp'ril Terence Mulvaney
whin that same was turned out for sedukshin? I niver
met him. Ivry woman that was not a witch was worth
the runnin' afther in those days, an' ivry man was my
dearest frind or—I had stripped to him an' we knew
which was the betther av the tu.

"Whin I was Corp'ril I wud not ha' changed wid the
Colonel—no, nor yet the Commandher-in-Chief. I
wud be a Sargint. There was nothin' I wud not be!
Mother av Hivin, look at me! Fwhat am I *now?*

"We was quartered in a big cantonmint—'tis no
manner av use namin' names, for ut might give the
barricks disrepitation—an' I was the Imperor av the
Earth to my own mind, an' wan or tu women thought
the same. Small blame to thim. Afther we had lain
there a year, Bragin, the Color Sargint av E Comp'ny,
wint an' took a wife that was lady's maid to some big
lady in the Station. She's dead now is Annie Bragin—
died in child-bed at Kirpa Tal, or ut may ha' been Al-
morah—seven—nine years gone, an' Bragin he married agin. But she was a pretty woman whin Bragin
inthrojuced her to cantonmint society. She had eyes
like the brown av a buttherfly's wing whin the sun
catches ut, an' a waist no thicker than my arm, an' a

little sof' button av a mouth I would ha' gone through all Asia bristlin' wid bay'nits to get the kiss av. An' her hair was as long as the tail av the Colonel's charger —forgive me mentionin' that blunderin' baste in the same mouthful with Annie Bragin—but 'twas all shpun gold, an' time was when ut was more than di'monds to me. There was niver pretty woman yet, an' I've had thruck wid a few, cud open the door to Annie Bragin.

" 'Twas in the Cath'lic Chapel I saw her first, me oi rolling round as usual to see fwhat was to be seen. 'You're too good for Bragin, my love,' thinks I to me- silf, 'but that's a mistake I can put straight, or my name is not Terence Mulvaney.'

"Now take my wurrd for ut, you Orth'ris there an' Learoyd, an' kape out av the Married Quarters—as I did not. No good iver comes av ut, an' there's always the chance av your bein' found wid your face in the dirt, a long picket in the back av your head, an' your hands playing the fifes on the tread av another man's doorstep. 'Twas so we found O'Hara, he that Rafferty killed six years gone, when he wint to his death wid his hair oiled, whistlin' *Larry O'Rourke* betune his teeth. Kape out av the Married Quarters, I say, as I did not. 'Tis onwholesim, 'tis dangerous, an' 'tis ivrything else that's bad, but—O my sowl, 'tis swate while ut lasts!

"I was always hangin' about there whin I was off duty an' Bragin wasn't, but niver a sweet word beyon' ordinar' did I get from Annie Bragin. ' 'Tis the per- varsity av the sect,' sez I to mesilf, an' gave my cap an- other cock on my head an' straightened my back— 'twas the back av a Dhrum Major in those days—an' wint off as tho' I did not care, wid all the women in the Married Quarters laughin'. I was pershuaded—most bhoys *are* I'm thinkin'—that no women born av woman cud stand against me av I hild up my little finger. I had reason fer thinkin' that way—till I met Annie Bragin.

"Time an' agin whin I was blandandherin' in the dusk a man wud go past me as quiet as a cat. 'That's quare,' thinks I, 'for I am, or I should be, the only man in these parts. Now what divilment can Annie be up to?' Thin I called myself a blayguard for thinkin' such things; but I thought thim all the same. An' that, mark you, is the way av a man.

"Wan evenin' I said:—'Mrs. Bragin, manin' no disrespect to you, who is that Corp'ril man'—I had seen the stripes though I cud niver get sight av his face— '*who* is that Corp'ril man that comes in always whin I'm goin' away?'

"'Mother av God!' sez she, turnin' as white as my belt; 'have *you* seen him too?'

"'Seen him!' sez I; 'av coorse I have. Did ye want me not to see him, for'—we were standin' talkin' in the dhark, outside the veranda av Bragin's quarters—'you'd betther tell me to shut me eyes. Onless I'm mistaken, he's come now.'

"An', sure enough, the Corp'ril man was walkin' to us, hangin' his head down as though he was ashamed av hin.silf.

"'Good-night, Mrs. Bragin,' sez I, very cool; ''tis not for me to interfere wid your *a-moors;* but you might

manage some things wid more dacincy. I'm off to canteen,' I sez.

"I turned on my heel an' wint away, swearin' I wud
give that man a dhressin' that wud shtop him messin'
about the Married Quarters for a month an' a week. I
had not tuk ten paces before Annie Bragin was hangin'
on to my arm, an' I cud feel that she was shakin' all
over.

" 'Stay wid me, Mister Mulvaney,' sez she; 'you're
flesh an' blood, at the least—are ye not?'

" 'I'm *all* that,' sez I, an' my anger wint away in a
flash. 'Will I want to be asked twice, Annie?'

"Wid that I slipped my arm round her waist, for,
begad, I fancied she had surrindered at discretion, an'
the honors av war were mine.

" 'Fwhat nonsinse is this?' sez she, dhrawin' hersilf
up on the tips av her dear little toes. 'Wid the mother's
milk not dhry on your impident mouth? Let go!' she
sez.

" 'Did ye not say just now that I was flesh and
blood?' sez I. 'I have not changed since,' I sez; an' I
kep' my arm where ut was.

" 'Your arms to yourself!' sez she, an' her eyes
sparkild.

" 'Sure, 'tis only human nature,' sez I, an' I kep' my
arm where ut was.

" 'Nature or no nature,' sez she, 'you take your arm
away or I'll tell Bragin, an' he'll alter the nature av your
head. Fwhat d'you take me for?' she sez.

" 'A woman,' sez I; 'the prettiest in barricks.'

" 'A *wife*,' sez she; 'the straightest in cantonmints!'

"Wid that I dropped my arm, fell back tu paces, an' saluted, for I saw that she mint fwhat she said."

"Then you know something that some men would give a good deal to be certain of. How could you tell?" I demanded in the interests of Science.

"Watch the hand," said Mulvaney; "av she shut her hand tight, thumb down over the knuckle, take up your hat an' go. You'll only make a fool av yoursilf av you shtay. But av the hand lies opin on the lap, or av you see her thryin' to shut ut, an' she can't,—go on! She's not past reasonin' wid.

"Well, as I was sayin', I fell back, saluted, an' was goin' away.

" 'Shtay wid me,' she sez. 'Look! He's comin' again.' "She pointed to the veranda, an' by the Hoight av Impart'nince, the Corp'ril man was comin' out av Bragin's quarters.

" 'He's done that these five evenin's past,' sez Annie Bragin. 'Oh, fwhat will I do!'

" 'He'll not do ut again,' sez I, for I was fightin' mad.

"Kape way from a man that has been a thrifle crossed in love till the fever's died down. He rages like a brute beast. I wint up to the man in the veranda, manin', as sure as I sit, to knock the life out av him. He slipped into the open. 'Fwhat are you doin' philanderin' about here, ye scum av the gutter?' sez I polite, to give him his warnin', for I wanted him ready.

"He niver lifted his head, but sez, all mournful an' melancolius, as if he thought I wud be sorry for him: 'I can't find her,' sez he.

"'My troth,' sez I, 'you've lived too long—you an' your seekin's an' findin's in a dacint married woman's quarters! Hould up your head, ye frozen thief av Genesis,' sez I, 'an' you'll find all you want an' more!'

"But he niver hild up, an' I let go from the shoulder to where the hair is short over the eyebrows.

"'That'll do your business,' sez I, but it nearly did mine instid. I put my bodyweight behind the blow, but I hit nothing at all, an' near put my shoulther out. The Corp'ril man was not there, an' Annie Bragin, who had been watchin' from the veranda, throws up her heels, an' carries on like a cock whin his neck's wrung by the dhrummer-bhoy. I wint back to her, for a livin' woman, an' a woman like Annie Bragin, is more than a p'rade-groun' full av ghosts. I'd never seen a woman faint before, an' I stud like a shtuck calf, askin' her whether she was dead, an' prayin' her for the love av me, an' the love av her husband, an' the love av the Virgin, to opin her blessed eyes again, an' callin' mesilf all the names undher the canopy av Hivin for plaguin' her wid my miserable *a-moors* whin I ought to ha' stud betune her an' this Corp'ril man that had lost the number av his mess.

"I misremimber fwhat nonsinse I said, but I was not so far gone that I cud not hear a fut on the dirt outside. 'Twas Bragin comin' in, an' by the same token Annie was comin' to. I jumped to the far end av the veranda an' looked as if butter wudn't melt in my mouth. But Mrs. Quinn, the Quarter-Master's wife that was, had tould Bragin about my hangin' round Annie.

" 'I'm not pleased wid you, Mulvaney,' sez Bragin, unbucklin' his sword, for he had been on duty.

" 'That's bad hearin',' I sez, an' I knew that the pickets were dhriven in. 'What for, Sargint?' sez I.

" 'Come outside,' sez he, 'an' I'll show you why.'

" 'I'm willin',' I sez; 'but my stripes are none so ould that I can afford to lose thim. Tell me now, *who* do I go out wid?' sez I.

"He was a quick man an' a just, an' saw fwhat I wud be afther. 'Wid Mrs. Bragin's husband,' sez he. He might ha' known by me askin' that favor that I had done him no wrong.

"We wint to the back av the arsenal an' I stripped to him, an' for ten minutes 'twas all I cud do to prevent him killin' himself against my fistes. He was mad as a dumb dog—just frothing wid rage; but he had no chanst wid me in reach, or learnin', or anything else.

" 'Will ye hear reason?' sez I, whin his first wind was run out.

" 'Not whoile I can see,' sez he. Wid that I gave him both, one after the other, smash through the low gyard that he'd been taught whin he was a boy, an' the eyebrow shut down on the cheek-bone like the wing av a sick crow.

" 'Will you hear reason now, ye brave man?' sez I.

" 'Not whoile I can speak,' sez he, staggerin' up blind as a stump. I was loath to do ut, but I wint round an' swung into the jaw side-on an' shifted ut a half pace to the lef'.

" 'Will ye hear reason now?' sez I; 'I can't keep my timper much longer, an' 'tis like I will hurt you.'

" 'Not whoile I can stand,' he mumbles out av one corner av his mouth. So I closed an' threw him—blind, dumb, an' sick, an' jammed the jaw straight.

" 'You're an ould fool, *Mister* Bragin,' sez I.

" 'You're a young thief,' sez he, 'an' you've bruk my heart, you an' Annie betune you!'

"Thin he began cryin' like a child as he lay. I was sorry as I had niver been before. 'Tis an awful thing to see a strong man cry.

" 'I'll swear on the Cross!' sez I.

" 'I care for none av your oaths,' sez he.

" 'Come back to your quarters,' sez I, 'an' if you don't believe the livin', begad, you shall listen to the dead,' I sez.

"I hoisted him an' tuk him back to his quarters. 'Mrs. Bragin,' sez I, 'here's a man that you can cure quicker than me.'

" 'You've shamed me before my wife,' he whimpers.

" 'Have I so?' sez I. 'By the look on Mrs. Bragin's face I think I'm for a dhressin'-down worse than I gave you.'

"An' I was! Annie Bragin was woild wid indigna. tion. There was not a name that a dacint woman cud use that was not given my way. I've had my Colonel walk roun' me like a cooper roun' a cask for fifteen minutes in Ord'ly Room, bekaze I wint into the Corner Shop an unstrapped lewnatic; but all that I iver tuk from his rasp av a tongue was ginger-pop to fwhat Annie tould me. An' that, mark you, is the way av a woman.

"Whin ut was done for want av breath, an' Annie

was bendin' over her husband, I sez: ' 'Tis all thrue, an' I'm a blayguard an' you're an honest woman; but will you tell him of wan service that I did you?'

"As I finished speakin' the Corp'ril man came up to the veranda, an' Annie Bragin shqualed. The moon was up, an' we cud see his face.

" 'I can't find her,' sez the Corp'ril man, an' wint out like the puff av a candle.

" 'Saints stand betune us an' evil!' sez Bragin, crossin' himself; 'that's Flahy av the Tyrone.'

" 'Who was he?' I sez, 'for he has given me a dale av fightin' this day.'

"Bragin tould us that Flahy was a Corp'ril who lost his wife av cholera in those quarters three years gone, an' wint mad, an' *walked* afther they buried him, huntin' for her.

" 'Well,' sez I to Bragin, 'he's been hookin' out av Purgathory to kape company wid Mrs. Bragin ivry evenin' for the last fortnight. You may tell Mrs. Quinn, wid my love, for I know that she's been talkin' to you, an' you've been listenin', that she ought to ondherstand the differ 'twixt a man an' a ghost. She's had three husbands,' sez I, 'an' *you*'ve got a wife too good for you. Instid av which you lave her to be boddered by ghosts an'—an' all manner av evil spirruts. I'll niver go talkin' in the way av politeness to a man's wife again Good-night to you both,' sez I; an' wid that I wint away, havin' fought wid woman, man and Divil all in the heart av an hour. By the same token I gave Father Victor wan rupee to say a mass for Flahy's soul, me havin' discommoded him by shticking my fist into his systim."

"Your ideas of politeness seem rather large, Mulvaney," I said.

"That's as you look at ut," said Mulvaney, calmly; "Annie Bragin niver cared for me. For all that, I did not want to leave anything behin' me that Bragin could take hould av to be angry wid her about—whin an honust wurrd cud ha' cleared all up. There's nothing like opin-speakin'. Orth'ris, ye scutt, let me put me oi to that bottle, for my throat's as dhry as whin I thought I wud get a kiss from Annie Bragin. An' that's fourteen years gone! Eyah! Cork's own city an' the blue sky above ut—an' the times that was—the times that was!"

THE THREE MUSKETEERS

An' when the war began, we chased the bold Afghan,
An' we made the bloomin' Ghazi for to flee, boys O!
An' we marched into Kabul, an' we tuk the Balar 'Issar
An' we taught 'em to respec' the British Soldier.
                                    —Barrack Room Ballad.

MULVANEY, Ortheris and Learoyd are Privates in B Company of a Line Regiment, and personal friends of mine. Collectively I think, but am not certain, they are the worst men in the regiment so far as genial blackguardism goes.

They told me this story, in the Umballa Refreshment Room while we were waiting for an up-train. I supplied the beer. The tale was cheap at a gallon and a half.

All men know Lord Benira Trig. He is a Duke, or an Earl, or something unofficial; also a Peer; also a Globe-trotter. On all three counts, as Ortheris says, " 'e didn't deserve no consideration." He was out in India for three months collecting materials for a book on "Our Eastern Impedimenta," and quartering himself upon everybody, like a Cossack in evening-dress.

His particular vice—because he was a Radical, men said—was having garrisons turned out for his inspection. He would then dine with the Officer Commanding, and insult him, across the Mess table, about the

appearance of the troops. That was Benira's way.
He turned out troops once too often. He came to
Helanthami Cantonment on a Tuesday. He wished to
go shopping in the bazars on Wednesday, and he "desired" the troops to be turned out on a Thursday. *On
—a—Thursday.* The Officer Commanding could not
well refuse; for Benira was a Lord. There was an in-
dignation-meeting of subalterns in the Mess Room, to
call the Colonel pet names.

"But the rale dimonstrashin," said Mulvaney, "was
in B Comp'ny barrick; we three headin' it."

Mulvaney climbed on to the refreshment-bar, settled
himself comfortably by the beer, and went on, "Whin
the row was at ut's foinest an' B Comp'ny was fur goin'
out to murther this man Thrigg on the p'rade-groun',
Learoyd here takes up his helmut an' sez—fwhat was
ut ye said?"

"Ah said," said Learoyd, "gie us t' brass. Tak oop a
subscripshun, lads, for to put off t' p'rade, an' if t'
p'rade's not put off, ah'll gie t' brass back agean. Thot's
wot ah said. All B Coomp'ny knawed me. Ah took
oop a big subscripshun—fower rupees eight annas 'twas
—an' ah went oot to turn t' job over. Mulvaney an'
Orth'ris coom with me."

"We three raises the Divil in couples gin'rally," explained Mulvaney.

Here Ortheris interrupted. "'Ave you read the papers?" said he.

"Sometimes," I said.

"We 'ad read the papers, an' we put hup a faked
decoity, a—a sedukshun."

"*Ab*dukshin, ye cockney," said Mulvaney.

"*Ab*dukshun or *se*dukshun—no great odds. Any'ow, we arranged to taik an' put Mister Benhira out o' the way till Thursday was hover, or 'e too busy to rux 'isself about p'raids. *Hi* was the man wot said, 'We'll make a few rupees off o' the business.' "

"We hild a Council av War," continued Mulvaney, "walkin' roun' by the Artill'ry Lines. I was Prisidint, Learoyd was Minister av Finance, an' little Orth'ris here was"—

"A bloomin' Bismarck! *Hi* made the 'ole show pay."

"This interferin' bit av a Benira man," said Mulvaney, "did the thrick for us himself; for, on me sowl, we hadn't a notion av what was to come afther the next minut. He was shoppin' in the bazar on fut. 'Twas dhrawin' dusk thin, an' we stud watchin' the little man hoppin' in an' out av the shops, thryin' to injuce the navgurs to *mallum* his *bat*. Prisintly, he sthrols up, his arrums full av thruck, an' he sez in a consiquinshal way, shticking out his little belly, 'Me good men,' sez he, 'have ye seen the Kernel's b'roosh?' —'B'roosh?' says Learoyd. 'There's no b'roosh here— nobbut a *hekka*.'—'Fwhat's that?' sez Thrigg. Learoyd shows him wan down the sthreet, an' he sez, 'How thruly Orientil! I will ride on a *hekka*.' I saw thin that our Rigimintal Saint was for givin' Thrigg over to us neck an' brisket. I purshued a *hekka*, an' I sez to the dhriver-divil, I sez, 'Ye black limb, there's a *Sahib* comin' for this *hekka*. He wants to go *jildi* to the Padsahi Jhil'—'twas about tu moiles away—'to shoot snipe—*chirria*. You dhrive *Jehannum ke marfik, mal-*

lum—like Hell? 'Tis no manner av use *bukkin'* to the *Sahib,* bekaze he doesn't *samjao* your talk. Av he *bolos* anything, just you *choop* and *chel. Dekker?* Go *arsty* for the first *arder*-mile from cantonmints. Thin *chel, Shaitan ke marfik,* an' the *chooper* you *choops* an' the *jilder* you *chels* the better *kooshy* will that *Sahib* be; an' here's a rupee for ye?'

"The *hekka*-man knew there was somethin' out av the common in the air. He grinned an' sez, *'Bote achee!* I goin' damn fast.' I prayed that the Kernel's b'roosh wudn't arrive till me darlin' Benira by the grace av God was undher weigh. The little man puts his thruck into the *hekka* an' scuttles in like a fat guinea-pig; niver offerin' us the price av a dhrink for our services in helpin' him home. 'He's off to the Padsahi *jhil.*' sez I to the others."

Ortheris took up the tale—

"Jist then, little Buldoo kim up, 'oo was the son of one of the Artillery grooms—'e would 'av made a 'evinly newspaper-boy in London, bein' sharp an' fly to all manner o' games. 'E 'ad bin watchin' us puttin' Mister Benhira into 'is temporary baroush, an' 'e sez, 'What *'ave* you been a doin' of, *Sahibs?'* sez 'e. Learoyd 'e caught 'im by the ear an 'e sez"—

"Ah says," went on Learoyd, "'Young mon, that mon's gooin' to have t' goons out o' Thursday—to-morrow—an' thot's more work for you, young mon. Now, sitha, tak' a *tat* an' a *lookri,* an' ride tha domdest to t' Padsahi Jhil. Cotch thot there *hekka,* and tell t' driver iv your lingo thot you've coom to tak' his place. T' *Sahib* doesn't speak t' *bat,* an' he's a little mon. Drive t' *hekka* into t' Padsahi Jhil into t' watter. Leave t' Sahib there an' roon hoam; an' here's a rupee for tha.'"

Then Mulvaney and Ortheris spoke together in alternate fragments: Mulvaney leading [You must pick out the two speakers as best you can]:—"He was a knowin' little divil was Bhuldoo,—'e sez *bote achee* an' cuts—wid a wink in his oi—but *Hi* sez there's money to be made—an' I wanted to see the ind av the campaign—so *Hi* says we'll double hout to the Padsahi Jhil—an' save the little man from bein' dacoited by the murtherin' Bhuldoo—an' turn hup like reskooers in a Vic'oria Melodrama—so we doubled for the *jhil,* an' prisintly there was the divil av a hurroosh behind us an' three bhoys on grasscuts' ponies come by, poundin' along for the dear life—s'elp me Bob, hif Bhuldoo 'adn't raised a rig'lar *harmy* of decoits—to do the job in shtile. An' we ran, an' they ran, shplittin' with laughin', till we gets near the *jhil*—and 'ears sounds of distress floatin' molloncolly on the hevenin' hair." [Ortheris was growing poetical under the influence of the beer. The duet recommenced: Mulvaney leading again.]

"Thin we heard Bhuldoo, the dacoit, shoutin' to the *hekka* man, an' wan of the young divils brought his stick down on the top av the *hekka*-cover, an' Benira Thrigg inside howled 'Murther an' Death.' Bhuldoo takes the reins and dhrives like mad for the *jhil,* havin' dishpersed the *hekka*-dhriver—'oo cum up to us an' 'e sez, sez 'e, 'That *Sahib's* nigh mad with funk! Wot devil's work 'ave you led me into?'—'Hall right,' sez we, 'you catch that there pony an' come along. This *Sahib's* been decoited, an' we're going to resky 'im!'

Says the driver, 'Decoits! Wot decoits? That's Bhuldoo
the *budmash*'—'Bhuldoo be shot!' sez we. 'Tis a woild
dissolute Pathan frum the hills. There's about eight av
thim coercin' the *Sahib*. You remimber that an' you'll
get another rupee!' Thin we heard the *whop-whop-*
whop av the *hekka* turnin' over, an' a splash av water
an' the voice av Benira Thrigg callin' upon God to forgive his sins—an' Bhuldoo an' 'is friends squotterin' in
the water like boys in the Serpentine."

Here the Three Musketeers retired simultaneously
into the beer.

"Well? What came next?" said I.

"Fwhat nex'?" answered Mulvaney, wiping his
mouth. "Wud ye let three bould sodger-bhoys lave the
ornamint av the House av Lords to be dhrowned an'
dacoited in a *jhil*? We formed line av quarther-column
an' we discinded upon the inimy. For the better
part av tin minutes you could not hear yerself spake.
The *tattoo* was screamin' in chune wid Benira Thrigg
an' Bhuldoo's army, an' the shticks was whistlin' roun'
the *hekka,* an' Orth'ris was beatin' the *hekka*-cover wid
his fistes, an' Learoyd yellin', 'Look out for their
knives!' an' me cuttin' into the dark, right an' lef', dish-
persin' army corps av Pathans. Holy Mother av Moses!
'twas more disp'rit than Ahmid Kheyl wid Maiwund
thrown in. Afther a while Bhuldoo an' his bhoys flees.
Have ye iver seen a rale live Lord thryin' to hide his
nobility undher a fut an' a half av brown swamp-
wather? 'Tis the livin' image av a water-carrier's goat-
skin wid the shivers. It tuk toime to pershuade me
frind Benira he was not disimbowilled: an' more toime

to get out the *hekka*. The dhriver come up afther the battle, swearin' he tuk a hand in repulsin' the inimy. Benira was sick wid the fear. We escorted him back, very slow, to cantonmints, for that an' the chill to soak into him. It suk! Glory be to the Rigimintil Saint, but it suk to the marrow av Lord Benira Thrigg!"

Here Ortheris, slowly, with immense pride—" 'E sez, 'You har my noble preservers,' sez 'e. 'You har a *h*onor to the British Harmy,' sez 'e. With that 'e describes the hawful band of dacoits wot set on 'im. There was about forty of 'em an' 'e was hoverpowered by numbers, so 'e was; but 'e never lorst 'is presence of mind, so 'e didn't. 'E guv the *hekka*-driver five rupees for 'is noble assistance, an' 'e said 'e would see to us after 'e 'ad spoken to the Kernul. For we was a *h*onor to the Regiment, we was."

"An' we three," said Mulvaney, with a seraphic smile, "have dhrawn the par-ti-cu-lar attinshin av Bobs Bahadur more than wanst. But he's a rale good little man is Bobs. Go on, Orth'ris, my son."

"Then we leaves 'im at the Kernul's 'ouse, werry sick, an' we cuts hover to B Comp'ny barrick an' we sez we 'ave saved Benira from a bloody doom, an' the chances was agin there bein' p'raid on Thursday. About ten minutes later come three envelicks, one for each of us. S'elp me Bob, if the old bloke 'adn't guv us a fiver apiece—sixty-four rupees in the bazar! On Thursday 'e was in 'orspital recoverin' from 'is sanguinary encounter with a gang of Pathans, an' B Comp'ny was drinkin' 'emselves into Clink by squads. So there never was no Thursday p'raid. But the Kernul, when 'e 'eard of our galliant conduct, 'e sez, 'Hi know there's been some devilry somewheres,' sez 'e, 'but I can't bring it 'ome to you three.'"

"An' my privit imprisshin is," said Mulvaney, getting off the bar and turning his glass upside down, "that, av they had known they wudn't have brought ut home. 'Tis flyin' in the face, firstly av Nature, secon' av the Rig-lations, an' third the will av Terence Mulvaney, to hold p'rades av Thursdays."

"Good, ma son!" said Learoyd; "but, young mon, what's t' notebook for?"

"Let be," said Mulvaney; "this time next month we're in the *Sherapis*. 'Tis immortial fame the gentleman's goin' to give us. But kape it dhark till we're out av the range av me little frind Bobs Bahadur."

And I have obeyed Mulvaney's order.

BAA BAA, BLACK SHEEP

Baa baa, black sheep,
Have you any wool?
Yes, sir; yes, sir; three bags full.
One for the master, one for the dame—
None for the little boy that cries down the lane.

—Nursery Rhyme

THE FIRST BAG

"When I was in my father's house I was in a better place."

THEY were putting Punch to bed—the *ayah* and the *hamal* and Meeta, the big *Surti* boy with *the* red-and-gold turban. Judy, already tucked inside her mosquito-curtains, was nearly asleep. Punch had been allowed to stay up for dinner. Many privileges had been accorded to Punch within the last ten days, and a greater kindness from the people of his world had encompassed his ways and works, which were mostly obstreperous. He sat on the edge of his bed and swung his bare legs defiantly.

"Punch-*baba* going to bye-lo?" said the *ayah*, suggestively.

"No," said Punch. "Punch-*baba* wants the story about the Ranee that was turned into a tiger. Meeta must tell it, and the *hamal* shall hide behind the door and make tiger-noises at the proper time."

"But Judy-*baba* will wake up," said the *ayah*.

"Judy-*baba* is waking," piped a small voice from the mosquito-curtains. "There was a Ranee that lived at Delhi. Go on, Meeta," and she fell fast asleep again while Meeta began the story.

Never had Punch secured the telling of that tale with so little opposition. He reflected for a long time. The *hamal* made the tiger-noises in twenty different keys.

"Top!" said Punch, authoritatively. "Why doesn't papa come in and say he is going to give me *put-put?*"

"Punch-*baba* is going away," said the *ayah*. "In another week there will be no Punch-*baba* to pull my hair any more." She sighed softly, for the boy of the household was very dear to her heart.

"Up the Ghauts in a train?" said Punch, standing on his bed. "All the way to Nassick, where the Ranee tiger lives?"

"Not to Nassick this year, little sahib," said Meeta, lifting him on his shoulder. "Down to the sea, where the cocoanuts are thrown, and across the sea in a big ship. Will you take Meeta with you to *Belait?*"

"You shall all come," said Punch, from the height of Meeta's strong arms. "Meeta, and the *ayah,* and the *hamal,* and Bhini-in-the-garden, and the salaam-captain-sahib-snake-man."

There was no mockery in Meeta's voice when he replied: "Great is the sahib's favor," and laid the little man down in the bed, while the *ayah,* sitting in the moonlight at the doorway, lulled him to sleep with an interminable canticle such as they sing in the Roman

Catholic Church at Parel. Punch curled himself into
a ball and slept.

Next morning, Judy shouted that there was a rat in
the nursery; and thus he forgot to tell her the wonderful news. It did not much matter, for Judy was only
three and she would not have understood. But Punch
was five, and he knew that going to England would
be much more nicer than a trip to Nassick.

.   .   .   .

And papa and mamma sold the brougham and the
piano, and stripped the house, and curtailed the allowance of crockery for the daily meals, and took long
counsel together over a bundle of letters bearing the
Rocklington postmark.

"The worst of it is that one can't be certain of anything," said papa, pulling his mustache. "The letters
in themselves are excellent, and the terms are moder-
ate enough."

"The worst of it is that the children will grow up
away from me," thought mamma; but she did not say
it aloud.

"We are only one case among hundreds," said papa,
bitterly. "You shall go home again in five years, dear."

"Punch will be ten then—and Judy eight. Oh, how
long and long and long the time will be! And we have
to leave them among strangers."

"Punch is a cheery little chap. He's sure to make
friends wherever he goes."

"And who could help loving my Ju?"

They were standing over the cots in the nursery late

at night, and I think that mamma was crying softly.
After papa had gone away she knelt down by the side
of Judy's cot. The *ayah* saw her and put up a prayer
that the *memsahib* might never find the love of her
children taken away from her and given to a stranger.

Mamma's own prayer was a slightly illogical one.
Summarized it ran: "Let strangers love my children,
and be as good to them as I should be; but let *me* preserve their love and their confidence forever and ever.
Amen." Punch scratched himself in his sleep, and Judy
moaned a little. That seems to be the only answer to
the prayer; and, next day, they all went down to the
sea, and there was a scene at the Apollo Bunder when
Punch discovered that Meeta could not come, too, and
Judy learned that the *ayah* must be left behind. But
Punch found a thousand fascinating things in the rope,
block, and steam-pipe line on the big P. and O. steamer
long before Meeta and the *ayah* had dried their tears.

"Come back, Punch-*baba*," said the *ayah*.

"Come back," said Meeta, "and be a *Burra sahib*."

"Yes," said Punch, lifted up in his father's arms to
wave good-bye. "Yes, I will come back, and I will be
a *Burra sahib Baha dur!*"

At the end of the first day, Punch demanded to be
set down in England, which he was certain must be
close at hand. Next day, there was a merry breeze, and
Punch was very sick. "When I come back to Bombay,"
said Punch, on his recovery, "I will come by the road—
in a broom-*gharri*. This is a very naughty ship."

The Swedish boatswain consoled him, and he modified his opinions as the voyage went on. There was so

much to see, and to handle, and ask questions about that Punch nearly forgot the *ayah,* and Meeta, and the *hamal,* and with difficulty remembered a few words of the Hindoostanee, once his second speech.

But Judy was much worse. The day before the steamer reached Southampton, mamma asked her if she would not like to see the *ayah* again. Judy's blue eyes turned to the stretch of sea that had swallowed all her tiny past, and she said: *"Ayah!* What *ayah?"*

Mamma cried over her and Punch marveled. It was then that he heard, for the first time, mamma's passionate appeal to him never to let Judy forget mamma. Seeing that Judy was young, ridiculously young, and that mamma, every evening for four weeks past, had come into the cabin to sing her and Punch to sleep with a mysterious tune that he called "Sonny, my soul," Punch could not understand what mamma meant. But he strove to do his duty; for, the moment mamma left the cabin, he said to Judy:

"Ju, you remember mamma?"

" 'Torse I do," said Judy.

"Then *always* remember mamma, else I won't give you the paper ducks that the red-haired Captain Sahib cut out for me."

So Judy promised always to "bemember mamma."

Many and many a time was mamma's command laid upon Punch, and papa would say the same thing with an insistence that awed the child.

"You must make haste and learn to write, Punch," said papa, "and then you'll be able to write letters to us in Bombay."

"I'll come into your room," said Punch, and papa choked.

Papa and mamma were always choking in those days. If Punch took Judy to task for not "bemembering," they choked. If Punch sprawled on the sofa in the Southampton lodging-house and sketched his future in purple and gold, they choked; and so they did if Judy put up her mouth for a kiss.

Through many days all four were vagabonds on the face of the earth—Punch with no one to give orders to, Judy too young for anything, and papa and mamma grave, distracted, and choking.

"Where," demanded Punch, wearied of a loathsome contrivance on four wheels with a mound of luggage atop—"*where* is our broom-*gharri*? This thing talks so much that *I* can't talk. Where is our *own* broom-*gharri*? When I was at Bandstand, before we comed away, I asked Inverarity Sahib why he was sitting in it, and he said it was his own. And I said, 'I will *give* it you'—I like Inverarity Sahib—and I said, 'Can you put your legs through the pully-wag loops by the windows?' And Inverarity Sahib said 'No,' and laughed. *I* can put my legs through the pully-wag loops. I can put my legs through *these* pully-wag loops. Look! Oh, mamma's crying again! I didn't know. I wasn't not to do *so*."

Punch drew his legs out of the loops of the four-wheeler; the door opened and he slid to the earth, in a cascade of parcels, at the door of an austere little villa whose gates bore the legend, "Downe Lodge." Punch gathered himself together and eyed the house with disfavor. It stood on a sandy road, and a cold wind tickled his knickerbockered legs.

"Let us go away," said Punch. "This is not a pretty place."

But mamma and papa and Judy had quitted the cab, and all the luggage was being taken into the house. At the door-step stood a woman in black, and she smiled largely, with dry, chapped lips. Behind her was a man —big, bony, gray, and lame as to one leg—behind him a boy of twelve, black-haired and oily in appearance. Punch surveyed the trio, and advanced without fear, as he had been accustomed to do in Bombay when callers came and he happened to be playing in the veranda.

"How do you do?" said he. "I am Punch." But they were all looking at the luggage—all except the gray man, who shook hands with Punch and said he was "a smart little fellow." There was much running about and banging of boxes, and Punch curled himself up on the sofa in the dining-room and considered things.

"I don't like these people," said Punch. "But never mind. We'll go away soon. We have always went away soon from everywhere. I wish we was gone back to Bombay *soon*."

The wish bore no fruit. For six days mamma wept at intervals, and showed the woman in black all Punch's clothes—a liberty which Punch resented. "But p'r'aps she's a new white *ayah*," he thought. "I'm to call her Antirosa, but she doesn't call *me* sahib. She says just Punch," he confided to Judy. "What is Antirosa?"

Judy didn't know. Neither she nor Punch had heard

anything of an animal called an aunt. Their world
had been papa and mamma, who knew everything,
permitted everything, and loved everybody—even
Punch when he used to go into the garden at Bombay
and fill his nails with mold after the weekly nail-cut-
ting, because, as he explained, between two strokes of
the slipper, to his sorely tried father, his fingers "felt so
new at the ends."

In an undefined way, Punch judged it advisable to
keep both parents between himself and the woman in
black and the boy in black hair. He did not approve
of them. He liked the gray man, who had expressed
a wish to be called "Uncleharri." They nodded at
each other when they met, and the gray man showed
him a little ship with rigging that took up and down.

"She is a model of the *Brisk*—the little *Brisk* that
was sore exposed that day at Navarino." The gray
man hummed the last words and fell into a reverie.
"I'll tell you about Navarino, Punch, when we go for
walks together; and you mustn't touch the ship, because she's the *Brisk*."

Long before that walk, the first of many, was taken,
they roused Punch and Judy in the chill dawn of a
February morning to say good-bye, and of all people
in the wide earth, to papa and mamma—both crying
this time. Punch was very sleepy, and Judy was cross.

"Don't forget us," pleaded mamma. "Oh, my little
son, don't forget us, and see that Judy remembers us,
too."

"I've told Judy to bemember," said Punch, wriggling,
for his father's beard tickled his neck. "I've told Judy

--ten—forty—'leven thousand times. But Ju's so young
—quite a baby—isn't she?"

"Yes," said papa, "quite a baby, and you must be
good to Judy, and make haste to learn to write and—
and—and—"

Punch was back in his bed again. Judy was fast
asleep, and there was the rattle of a cab below. Papa
and mamma had gone away. Not to Nassick; that was
across the sea. To some place much nearer, of course,
and equally of course they would return. They came
back after dinner-parties, and papa had come back
after he had been to a place called "The Snows," and
mamma with him, to Punch and Judy at Mrs. Inverarity's house in Marine Lines. Assuredly they would
come back again. So Punch fell asleep till the true
morning, when the black-haired boy met him with the
information that papa and mamma had gone to Bombay, and that he and Judy were to stay at Downe Lodge
"forever." Antirosa, tearfully appealed to for a con-
tradiction, said that Harry had spoken the truth, and
that it behooved Punch to fold up his clothes neatly
on going to bed. Punch went out and wept bitterly
with Judy, into whose fair head he had driven some
ideas of the meaning of separation.

When a matured man discovers that he has been deserted by Providence, deprived of his God, and cast
without help, comfort, or sympathy, upon a world
which is new and strange to him, his despair, which
may find expression in evil-living, the writing of his
experiences, or the more satisfactory diversion of sui-
cide, is generally supposed to be impressive. A child,

under exactly similar circumstances, as far as its knowledge goes, can not very well curse God and die. It
howls till its nose is red, its eyes are sore, and its head
aches. Punch and Judy, through no fault of their own,
had lost all their world. They sat in the hall and cried;
the black-haired boy looking on from afar.

The model of the ship availed nothing, though the
gray man assured Punch that he might pull the rigging up and down as much as he pleased; and Judy
was promised free entry into the kitchen. They wanted
papa and mamma, gone to Bombay beyond the seas,
and their grief, while it lasted, was without remedy.

When the tears ceased, the house was very still. Antirosa had decided it was much better to let the children
"have their cry out," and the boy had gone to school.
Punch raised his head from the floor and sniffled
mournfully. Judy was nearly asleep. Three short years
had not taught her how to bear sorrow with full knowledge. There was a distant dull boom in the air—a repeated heavy thud. Punch knew that sound in Bombay in the monsoon. It was the sea—the sea that must
be traversed before any one could get to Bombay.

"Quick, Ju!" he cried, "we're close to the sea. I can
hear it! Listen! That's where they've went. P'r'aps
we can catch them, if we was in time. They didn't
mean to go without us. They've only forgot."

"Iss," said Judy. "They've only forgotted. Less go
to the sea."

The hall door was opened and so was the garden
gate.

"It's very, very big, this place," he said, looking cautiously down the road, "and we will get lost; but I will find a man and order him to take me back to my house —like I did in Bombay."

He took Judy by the hand, and the two fled hatless in the direction of the sound of the sea. Downe Villa was almost the last of a range of newly built houses running out, through a chaos of brick-mounds, to a heath where gypsies occasionally camped, and where the Garrison Artillery of Rocklington practiced. There were few people to be seen, and the children might have been taken for those of the soldiery who ranged far. Half an hour the wearied little legs tramped across heath, potato-field, and sand-dune.

"I'se so tired," said Judy, "and mamma will be angry."

"Mamma's *never* angry. I suppose she is waiting at the sea now while papa gets tickets. We'll find them and go along with. Ju, you mustn't sit down. Only a little more and we'll come to the sea. Ju, if you sit down I'll *thmack* you!" said Punch.

They climbed another dune, and came upon the great gray sea at low tide. Hundreds of crabs were scuttling about the beach, but there was no trace of papa and mamma, not even of a ship upon the waters—nothing but sand and mud for miles and miles.

And "Uncleharri" found them by chance—very muddy and very forlorn—Punch dissolved in tears, but trying to divert Judy with an "ickle trab," and Judy wailing to the pitiless horizon for "mamma, mamma!" and again "mamma!"

THE SECOND BAG

Ah, well-a-day, for we are souls bereaved!
Of all the creatures under heaven's wide scope
We are most hopeless, who had once most hope,
And most beliefless, who had most believed.
            —*The City of Dreadful Night.*

All this time not a word about Black Sheep. He came later, and Harry, the black-haired boy, was mainly responsible for his coming.

Judy—who could help loving little Judy?—passed, by special permit, into the kitchen and thence straight to Aunty Rosa's heart. Harry was Aunty Rosa's one child, and Punch was the extra boy about the house. There was no special place for him or his little affairs, and he was forbidden to sprawl on sofas and explain his ideas about the manufacture of this world and his hopes for his future. Sprawling was lazy and wore out sofas, and little boys were not expected to talk. They were talked to, and the talking to was intended for the benefit of their morals. As the unquestioned despot of the house at Bombay, Punch could not quite understand how he came to be of no account in this his new life.

Harry might reach across the table and take what he wanted; Judy might point and get what she wanted. Punch was forbidden to do either. The gray man was his great hope and stand-by for many months after papa left, and he had forgotten to tell Judy to "bemember mamma."

This lapse was excusable, because, in the interval, he

had been introduced by Aunty Rosa to two very impressive things—an abstraction called God, the intimate friend and ally of Aunty Rosa, generally believed to live behind the kitchen-range, because it was hot there —and a dirty brown book filled with unintelligible dots and marks. Punch was always anxious to oblige everybody. He, therefore, welded the story of the Creation on to what he could recollect of his Indian fairy tales, and scandalized Aunty Rosa by repeating the result to Judy. It was a sin, a grievous sin, and Punch was talked to for a quarter of an hour. He could not understand where the iniquity came in, but was careful not to repeat the offense, because Aunty Rosa told him that God had heard every word he had said and was very angry. If this were true, why didn't God come and say so, thought Punch, and dismissed the matter from his mind. Afterward he learned to know the Lord as the only thing in the world more awful than Aunty Rosa—as a creature that stood in the background and counted the strokes of the cane.

But the reading was, just then, a much more serious matter than any creed. Aunty Rosa sat him upon a table and told him that A B meant ab.

"Why?" said Punch. "A is a and B is bee. *Why* does A B mean ab?"

"Because I tell you it does," said Aunty Rosa, "and you've got to say it."

Punch said it accordingly, and for a month hugely against his will, stumbled through the brown book, not in the least comprehending what it meant. But Uncle Harry, who walked much, and generally alone, was

wont to come into the nursery and suggest to Aunty
Rosa that Punch should walk with him. He seldom
spoke, but he showed Punch all Rocklington, from the
mud-banks and the sand of the back-bay to the great
harbors where ships lay at anchor, and the dockyards
where the hammers are never still, and the marine-
store shops, and the shiny brass counters in the offices
where Uncle Harry went once every three months with
a slip of blue paper and received sovereigns in exchange; for he held a wound-pension. Punch heard,
too, from his lips, the story of the Battle of Navarino,
where the sailors of the fleet, for three days afterward,
were deaf as posts and could only sign to each other.
"That was because of the noise of the guns," said Uncle
Harry, "and I have got the wadding of a bullet somewhere inside me now."

Punch regarded him with curiosity. He had not the
least idea what wadding was, and his notion of a bullet
was a dock-yard cannon-ball bigger than his own head.
How could Uncle Harry keep a cannon-ball inside
him? He was ashamed to ask, for fear Uncle Harry
might be angry.

Punch had never known what anger—real anger—
meant until one terrible day when Harry had taken his
paint-box to paint a boat with, and Punch had protested
with a loud and lamentable voice. Then Uncle Harry
had appeared on the scene, and, muttering something
about "strangers' children," had, with a stick, smitten
the black-haired boy across the shoulders till he wept
and yelled, and Aunty Rosa came in and abused Uncle
Harry for cruelty to his own flesh and blood, and Punch

shuddered to the tips of his shoes. "It wasn't my fault," he explained to the boy, but both Harry and Aunty Rosa said that it was, and that Punch had told tales, and for a week there were no more walks with Uncle Harry.

But that week brought a great joy to Punch.

He had repeated, till he was thrice weary, the statement that "the cat lay on the mat and the rat came in."

"Now I can truly read," said Punch, "and now I will never read anything in the world."

He put the brown book in the cupboard where his school-books lived, and accidently tumbled out a venerable volume, without covers, labeled "Sharpe's Magazine." There was the most portentous picture of a griffin on the first page, with verses below. The griffin carried off one sheep a day from a German village, till a man came with a "falchion" and split the griffin open. Goodness only knew what a falchion was, but there was the griffin, and his history was an improvement upon the eternal cat.

"This," said Punch, "means things, and now I will know all about everything in all the world." He read till the light failed, not understanding a tithe of the meaning, but tantalized by glimpses of new worlds hereafter to be revealed.

"What is a 'falchion?' What is a 'wee lamb?' What is a 'base *us*urper?' What is a 'verdant me-ad?'" he demanded, with flushed cheeks, at bed-time of the astonished Aunt Rosa.

"Say your prayers and go to sleep," she replied, and that was all the help Punch then or afterward found at her hands in the new and delightful exercise of reading.

"Aunt Rosa only knows about God and things like that," argued Punch. "Uncle Harry will tell me."

The next walk proved that Uncle Harry could not help either; but he allowed Punch to talk, and even sat down on a bench to hear about the griffin. Other walks brought other stories as Punch ranged farther afield, for the house held a large store of old books that no one ever opened—from Frank Fairlegh, in serial numbers, and the earlier poems of Tennyson, contributed anonymously to "Sharpe's Magazine," to '62 Exhibition Catalogues, gay with colors and delightfully incomprehensible, and odd leaves of "Gulliver's Travels."

As soon as Punch could string a few pot-books together he wrote to Bombay, demanding by return of post "all the books in all the world." Papa could not comply with this modest indent, but sent "Grimm's Fairy Tales" and a "Hans Andersen." That was enough. If he were only left alone Punch could pass, at any hour he chose, into a land of his own, beyond reach of Aunty Rosa and her God, Harry and his teasements, and Judy's claims to be played with.

"Don't disturve me, I'm reading. Go and play in the kitchen," grunted Punch. "Aunty Rosa lets *you* go there." Judy was cutting her second teeth and was fretful. She appealed to Aunty Rosa, who descended on Punch.

"I was reading," he explained, "reading a book. I *want* to read."

"You're only doing that to show off," said Aunty Rosa. "But we'll see. Play with Judy now, and don't open a book for a week."

Judy did not pass a very enjoyable playtime with Punch, who was consumed with indignation. There was a pettiness at the bottom of the prohibition which puzzled him.

"It's what I like to do," he said, "and she's found out that and stopped me. Don't cry, Ju—it wasn't your fault—*please* don't cry, or she'll say I made you."

Ju loyally mopped up her tears, and the two played in their nursery, a room in the basement and half underground, to which they were regularly sent after the midday dinner while Aunty Rosa slept. She drank wine—that is to say, something from a bottle in the cellaret—for her stomach's sake; but if she did not fall asleep she would sometimes come into the nursery to see that the children were really playing. Now, bricks, wooden hoops, nine-pins, and china-ware can not amuse forever, especially when all fairyland is to be won by the mere opening of a book, and, as often as not, Punch would be discovered reading to Judy or telling her interminable tales. That was an offense in the eyes of the law, and Judy would be whisked off by Aunty Rosa, while Punch was left to play alone, "and be sure that I hear you doing it."

It was not a cheering employ, for he had to make a playful noise. At last, with infinite craft, he devised an arrangement whereby the table could be supported as to three legs on toy bricks, leaving the fourth clear to bring down on the floor. He could work the table

with one hand and hold a book with the other. This
he did till an evil day when Aunty Rosa pounced upon
him unawares and told him that he was "acting a lie."

"If you're old enough to do that," she said—her temper was always worst after dinner—"you're old enough
to be beaten."

"But—I'm—I'm not a animal!" said Punch, aghast.
He remembered Uncle Harry and the stick, and turned
white. Aunty Rosa had hidden a light cane behind
her, and Punch was beaten then and there over the
shoulders. It was a revelation to him. The room-door
was shut, and he was left to weep himself into repentance and work out his own gospel of life.

Aunty Rosa, he argued, had the power to beat him
with many stripes. It was unjust and cruel, and
mamma and papa would never have allowed it. Unless, perhaps, as Aunty Rosa seemed to imply, they had
sent secret orders, in which case he was abandoned, indeed. It would be discreet in the future to propitiate
Aunty Rosa; but, then, again, even in matters in which
he was innocent, he had been accused of wishing to
"show off." He had "shown off" before visitors when
he had attacked a strange gentleman—Harry's uncle,
not his own—with requests for information about the
griffin and the falchion, and the precise nature of the
tilbury in which Frank Fairlegh rode; all points of
paramount interest which he was bursting to understand. Clearly it would not do to pretend to care for
Aunty Rosa.

At this point Harry entered and stood afar off. eyeing Punch, a disheveled heap in the corner of the room, with disgust.

"You're a liar—a young liar," said Harry, with great unction, "and you're to have tea down here because you're not fit to speak to us. And you're not to speak to Judy again till mother gives you leave. You'll corrupt her. You're only fit to associate with the servant. Mother says so."

Having reduced Punch to a second agony of tears, Harry departed downstairs with the news that Punch was still rebellious.

Uncle Harry sat uneasily in the dining-room. "Rosa," said he, at last, "can't you leave the child alone? He's a good enough little chap when I met him."

"He puts on his best manners with you, Henry," said Aunty Rosa, "but I'm afraid, I'm very much afraid, that he is the black sheep of the family."

Harry heard and stored up the name for future use. Judy cried till she was bidden to stop, her brother not being worth tears; and the evening concluded with the return of Punch to the upper regions and a private sitting at which all the blinding horrors of hell were revealed to Punch with such store of imagery as Aunty Rosa's narrow mind possessed.

Most grievous of all was Judy's round-eyed reproach, and Punch went to bed in the depths of the Valley of Humiliation. He shared his room with Harry and knew the torture in store. For an hour and a half he had to answer that young gentleman's question as to his motives for telling a lie, and a grievous lie, the precise quantity of punishment inflicted by Aunty Rosa,

and had also to profess his deep gratitude for such religious instruction as Harry thought fit to impart.

From that day began the downfall of Punch, now
Black Sheep.

"Untrustworthy in one thing, untrustworthy in all,"
said Aunty Rosa, and Harry felt that Black Sheep was
delivered into his hands. He would wake him up in
the night to ask him why he was such a liar.

"I don't know," Punch would reply.

"Then don't you think you ought to get up and pray
to God for a new heart?"

"Y-yess."

"Get out and pray, then!"   And Punch would get
out of bed with raging hate in his heart against all the
world, seen and unseen. He was always tumbling into
trouble. Harry had a knack of cross-examining him
as to his day's doings, which seldom failed to lead him,
sleepy and savage, into half-a-dozen contradictions—all
duly reported to Aunty Rosa next morning.

"But it *wasn't* a lie," Punch would begin, charging
into a labored explanation that landed him more hopelessly in the mire. "I said that I didn't say my prayers
twice over in the day, and *that* was on Tuesday. *Once*
I did. I *know* I did, but Harry said I didn't," and so
forth, till the tension brought tears, and he was dismissed from the table in disgrace.

"You usen't to be as bad as this!" said Judy, awe-
stricken at the catalogue of Black Sheep's crimes.
"Why are you so bad now?"

"I don't know," Black Sheep would reply. "I'm not,
if I only wasn't bothered upside down. I knew what

I *did,* and I want to say so; but Harry always makes it out different somehow, and Aunty Rosa doesn't believe a word I say. Oh, Ju! don't you say I'm bad, too."

"Aunty Rosa says you are," said Judy. "She told the vicar so when he came yesterday."

"Why does she tell all the people outside the house about me? It isn't fair," said Black Sheep. "When I was in Bombay, and was bad—*doing* bad, not made-up bad like this—mamma told papa, and papa told me he knew, and that was all. *Outside* people didn't know, too—even Meeta didn't know."

"I don't remember," said Judy, wistfully. "I was all little then. Mamma was just as fond of you as she was of me, wasn't she?"

"'Course she was. So was papa. So was everybody."

"Aunty Rosa likes me more than she does you. She says that you are a trial and a black sheep, and I'm not to speak to you more than I can help."

"Always? Not outside of the times when you mustn't speak to me at all?"

Judy nodded her head mournfully. Black Sheep turned away in despair, but Judy's arms were round his neck.

"Never mind, Punch," she whispered. "I *will* speak to you just the same as ever and ever. You're my own, own brother, though you are—though Aunty Rosa says you're bad, and Harry says you're a little coward. He says that if I pulled your hair hard, you'd cry."

"Pull, then," said Punch.

Judy pulled gingerly.

"Pull harder—as hard as you can! There! I don't

mind how much you pull it *now*. If you'll speak to
me the same as ever, I'll let you pull it as much as you
like—pull it out if you like. But I know if Harry came
and stood by and made you do it, I'd cry."

So the two children sealed the compact with a kiss,
and Black Sheep's heart was cheered within him, and
by extreme caution and careful avoidance of Harry, he
acquired virtue, and was allowed to read undisturbed
for a week. Uncle Harry took him for walks and consoled him with rough tenderness, never calling him
Black Sheep. "It's good for you, I suppose, Punch," he
used to say. "Let us sit down. I'm getting tired." His
steps led him now, not to the beach, but to the ceme-
tery of Rocklington, amid the potato fields. For hours
the gray man would sit on a tombstone, while Black
Sheep read epitaphs, and then, with a sigh would stump
home again.

"I shall lie there soon," said he to Black Sheep, one
winter evening, when his face showed white as a worn
silver coin under the lights of the chapel lodge. "You
needn't tell Aunty Rosa."

A month later, he turned sharp round, ere half a
morning walk was completed, and stumped back to the
house. "Put me to bed, Rosa," he muttered. "I've
walked my last. The wadding has found me out."

They put him to bed, and for a fortnight the shadow
of his sickness lay upon the house, and Black Sheep
went to and fro unobserved. Papa had sent him some
new books, and he was told to keep quiet. He retired
into his own world, and was perfectly happy. Even at
night his felicity was unbroken. He could lie in bed

and string himself tales of travel and adventure while Harry was down-stairs.

"Uncle Harry's going to die," said Judy, who now lived almost entirely with Aunty Rosa.

"I'm very sorry," said Black Sheep, soberly. "He told me that a long time ago."

Aunty Rosa heard the conversation. "Will nothing check your wicked tongue?" she said, angrily. There were blue circles round her eyes.

Black Sheep retreated to the nursery and read "Cometh Up as a Flower" with deep and uncomprehending interest. He had been forbidden to read it on account of its "sinfulness," but the bonds of the universe were crumbling, and Aunty Rosa was in great grief.

"I'm glad," said Black Sheep. "She's unhappy now. It wasn't a lie, though. *I* knew. He told me not to tell."

That night Black Sheep woke with a start. Harry was not in the room, and there was a sound of sobbing on the next floor. Then the voice of Uncle Harry, singing the song of the Battle of Navarino, cut through the darkness:

> " 'Our vanship was the Asia—
> The Albion and Genoa!' "

"He's getting well," thought Black Sheep, who knew the song through all its seventeen verses. But the blood froze at his little heart as he thought. The voice leaped an octave and rang shrill as a boatswain's pipe:

> " 'And next came on the lovely Rose,
> The Philomel, her fire-ship, closed,

And the little Brisk was sore exposed
That day at Navarino.' "

"That day at Navarino, Uncle Harry!" shouted Black
Sheep, half wild with excitement and fear of he knew
not what.

A door opened, and Aunty Rosa screamed up the
stair-case: "Hush! For God's sake, hush, you little
devil! Uncle Harry is *dead!*"

THE THIRD BAG

"Journeys end in lovers' meeting,
Every wise man's son doth know."

"I wonder what will happen to me now," thought
Black Sheep, when the semi-pagan rites, peculiar to the
burial of the dead in middle-class houses, had been accomplished, and Aunty Rosa, awful in black crape,
had returned to this life. "I don't think I've done anything bad that she knows of. I suppose I will soon.
She will be very cross after Uncle Harry's dying, and
Harry will be cross, too. I'll keep in the nursery."

Unfortunately for Punch's plans, it was decided that
he should be sent to a day-school which Harry attended. This meant a morning walk with Harry, and,
perhaps, an evening one; but the prospect of freedom
in the interval was refreshing. "Harry'll tell everything I do, but I won't do anything," said Black Sheep.
Fortified with this virtuous resolution, he went to
school, only to find that Harry's version of his character
had preceded him, and that life was a burden in conse-

quence. He took stock of his associates. Some of them were unclean, some of them talked in dialect, many dropped their *h's,* and there were two Jews and a negro, or someone quite as dark, in the assembly. "That's a *hubshi,*" said Black Sheep to himself. "Even Meeta used to laugh at a *hubshi.* I don't think this is a proper place." He was indignant for at least an hour, till he reflected that any expostulation on his part would be by Aunty Rosa construed into "showing off," and that Harry would tell the boys.

"How do you like school?" said Aunty Rosa at the end of the day.

"I think it is a very nice place," said Punch, quietly.

"I suppose you warned the boys of Black Sheep's character?" said Aunty Rosa to Harry.

"Oh, yes," said the censor of Black Sheep's morals. "They all know about him."

"If I was with my father," said Black Sheep, stung to the quick, "I shouldn't *speak* to those boys. He wouldn't let me. They live in shops. I saw them go into shops—where their fathers live and sell things."

"You're too good for that school, are you?" said Aunty Rosa, with a bitter smile. "You ought to be grateful, Black Sheep, that those boys speak to you at all. It isn't every school that takes little liars."

Harry did not fail to make much capital out of Black Sheep's ill-considered remark, with the result that several boys, including the *hubshi,* demonstrated to Black Sheep the eternal equality of the human race by smacking his head, and his consolation from Aunty Rosa was that it "served him right for being vain." He learned,

however, to keep his opinions to himself, and by propi-
tiating Harry in carrying books and the like to secure
a little peace. His existence was not too joyful. From
nine till twelve he was at school, and from two to four,
except on Saturdays. In the evenings he was sent down
into the nursery to prepare his lessons for the next day,
and every night came the dreaded cross-questionings at
Harry's hand. Of Judy he saw but little. She was
deeply religious—at six years of age religion is easy to
come by—and sorely divided between her natural love
for Black Sheep and her love for Aunty Rosa, who
could do no wrong.

The lean woman returned that love with interest,
and Judy, when she dared, took advantage of this for
the remission of Black Sheep's penalties. Failures in
lessons at school were punished at home by a week
without reading other than school books, and Harry
brought the news of such a failure with glee. Further,
Black Sheep was then bound to repeat his lessons at
bed-time to Harry, who generally succeeded in making
him break down, and consoled him by gloomiest fore-
bodings for the morrow. Harry was at once spy, practical joker, inquisitor, and Aunty Rosa's deputy execu-
tioner. He filled his many posts to admiration. From
his actions, now that Uncle Harry was dead, there was
no appeal. Black Sheep had not been permitted to
keep any self-respect at school; at home he was of course
utterly discredited, and grateful for any pity that the
servant-girls—they changed frequently at Downe Lodge
because they, too, were liars—might show. "You're
just fit to row in the same boat with Black Sheep," was

a sentiment that each new Jane or Eliza might expect to hear, before a month was over, from Aunty Rosa's lips; and Black Sheep was used to ask new girls whether they had yet been compared to him. Harry was "Master Harry" in their mouths; Judy was officially "Miss Judy;" but Black Sheep was never anything more than Black Sheep *tout court*.

As time went on and the memory of papa and mamma became wholly overlaid by the unpleasant task of writing them letters, under Aunty Rosa's eye, each Sunday, Black Sheep forgot what manner of life he had led in the beginning of things. Even Judy's appeals to "try and remember about Bombay" failed to quicken him.

"I can't remember," he said. "I know I used to give orders and mamma kissed me."

"Aunty Rosa will kiss you if you are good," pleaded Judy.

"Ugh! I don't want to be kissed by Aunty Rosa. She'd say I was doing it to get something more to eat."

The weeks lengthened into months, and the holidays came; but just before the holidays Black Sheep fell into deadly sin.

Among the many boys whom Harry had incited to "punch Black Sheep's head because he daren't hit back," was one more aggravating than the rest, who, in an unlucky moment, fell upon Black Sheep when Harry was not near. The blows stung, and Black Sheep struck back at random with all the power at his command. The boy dropped and whimpered. Black Sheep was astounded at his own act, but, feeling the

unresisting body under him, shook it with both his
hands in blind fury, and then began to throttle his
enemy, meaning honestly to slay him.   There was a
scuffle, and Black Sheep was torn off the body by Harry
and some colleagues, and cuffed home, tingling but ex-
ultant.   Aunty Rosa was out; pending her arrival,
Harry set himself to lecture Black Sheep on the sin of
murder—which he described as the offense of Cain.

"Why didn't you fight him fair?   What did you hit
him when he was down for, you little cur?"

Black Sheep looked up at Harry's throat, and then at
a knife on the dinner-table.

"I don't understand," he said, wearily.   "You always
set him on me, and told me I was a coward when I
blubbered.   Will you leave me alone until Aunty Rosa
comes in?   She'll beat me if you tell her I ought to be
beaten; so it's all right."

"It's all wrong," said Harry, magisterially.   "You
nearly killed him, and I shouldn't wonder if he dies."

"Will he die?" said Black Sheep.

"I dare say," said Harry, "and then you'll be hanged."

"All right," said Black Sheep, possessing himself of
the table-knife.   "Then I'll kill you now.   You say
things and do things, and . . . and *I* don't know how
things happen, and you never leave me alone—and I
don't care *what* happens!"

He ran at the boy with the knife, and Harry fled upstairs to his room, promising Black Sheep the finest
thrashing in the world when Aunty Rosa returned.
Black Sheep sat at the bottom of the stairs, the table-
knife in his hand, and wept for that he had not killed

Harry. The servant-girl came up from the kitchen, took the knife away, and consoled him. But Black Sheep was beyond consolation. He would be badly beaten by Aunty Rosa; then there would be another beating at Harry's hands; then Judy would not be allowed to speak to him; then the tale would be told at school, and then. . . .

There was no one to help and no one to care, and the best way out of the business was by death. A knife would hurt; but Aunty Rosa had told him, a year ago, that if he sucked paint he would die. He went into the nursery, unearthed the now disused Noah's Ark, and sucked the paint off as many animals as remained. It tasted abominable, but he had licked Noah's dove clean by the time Aunty Rosa and Judy returned. He went upstairs and greeted them with: "Please, Aunty Rosa, I believe I've nearly killed a boy at school, and I've tried to kill Harry, and when you've done all about God and hell, will you beat me and get it over?"

The tale of the assault as told by Harry could only be explained on the ground of possession by the devil. Wherefore Black Sheep was not only most excellently beaten, once by Aunty Rosa, and once, when thoroughly cowed down, by Harry, but he was further prayed for at family prayers, together with Jane, who had stolen a cold *rissole* from the pantry and snuffled audibly as her enormity was brought before the Throne of Grace. Black Sheep was sore and stiff, but triumphant. He would die that very night and be rid of them all. No, he would ask for no forgiveness from Harry, and at bed-time would stand no questioning at

Harry's hands, even though addressed as "Young Cain."

"I've been beaten," said he, "and I've done other things. I don't care what I do. If you speak to me to-night, Harry, I'll get out and try to kill you. Now, you can kill me if you like."

Harry took his bed into the spare room, and Black Sheep lay down to die.

It may be that the makers of Noah's arks know that their animals are likely to find their way into young mouths, and paint them accordingly. Certain it is that the common, weary next morning broke through the windows and found Black Sheep quite well and a good deal ashamed of himself, but richer by the knowledge that he could, in extremity, secure himself against Harry for the future.

When he descended to breakfast on the first day of the holidays, he was greeted with the news that Harry, Aunty Rosa, and Judy were going away to Brighton, while Black Sheep was to stay in the house with the servant. His latter outbreak suited Aunty Rosa's plans admirably. It gave her good excuse for leaving the extra boy behind. Papa in Bombay, who really seemed to know a young sinner's wants to the hour, sent, that week, a package of new books. And with these, and the society of Jane on board-wages, Black Sheep was left alone for a month.

The books lasted for ten days. They were eaten too quickly, in long gulps of four-and-twenty hours at a time. Then came days of doing absolutely nothing, of dreaming dreams and marching imaginary armies up and down stairs, of counting the number of banisters,

and of measuring the length and breadth of every room
in hand-spans—fifty down the side, thirty across, and
fifty back again. Jane made many friends, and, after
receiving Black Sheep's assurance that he would not tell
of her absences, went out daily for long hours. Black
Sheep would follow the rays of the sinking sun from
the kitchen to the dining-room, and thence upward to
his own bed-room, until all was gray dark, and he ran
down to the kitchen fire and read by its light. He was
happy in that he was left alone and could read as much
as he pleased. But, later, he grew afraid of the shadows
of window-curtains and the flapping of doors and the
creaking of shutters. He went out into the garden, and
the rustling of the laurel bushes frightened him.

He was glad when they all returned—Aunty Rosa,
Harry, and Judy—full of news, and Judy laden with
gifts. Who could help loving loyal little Judy. In return for all her merry babblement, Black Sheep confided to her that the distance from the hall door to the
top of the first landing was exactly one hundred and
eighty-four hand-spans. He had found it out himself.

Then the old life recommenced; but with a difference, and a new sin. To his other iniquities Black
Sheep had now added a phenomenal clumsiness—was
as unfit to trust in action as he was in word. He himself could not account for spilling everything he
touched, upsetting glasses as he put his hand out, and
bumping his head against doors that were manifestly
shut. There was a gray haze upon all his world, and it
narrowed month by month, until at last it left Black
Sheep almost alone with the flapping curtains that

were so like ghosts, and the nameless terrors of broad
daylight that were only coats on pegs, after all.

Holidays came and holidays went, and Black Sheep
was taken to see many people whose faces were all
exactly alike; was beaten when occasion demanded,
and tortured by Harry on all possible occasions; but
defended by Judy through good and evil report, though
she thereby drew upon herself the wrath of Aunty
Rosa.

The weeks were interminable, and papa and mamma
were clean forgotten. Harry had left school and was a
clerk in a banking-office. Freed from his presence,
Black Sheep resolved that he should no longer be deprived of his allowance of pleasure-reading. Consequently when he failed at school he reported that all
was well, and conceived a large contempt for Aunty
Rosa as he saw how easy it was to deceive her. "She
says I'm a little liar when I don't tell lies, and now I
do, she doesn't know," thought Black Sheep. Aunty
Rosa had credited him in the past with petty cunning
and stratagem that had never entered into his head.
By the light of the sordid knowledge that she had revealed to him, he paid her back full tale. In a household where the most innocent of his motives—his natural yearning for a little affection—had been interpreted
into a desire for more bread and jam, or to ingratiate
himself with strangers and so put Harry into the background, his work was easy. Aunty Rosa could pene-
trate certain kinds of hypocrisy, but not all. He set his
child's wits against hers and was no more beaten. It
grew monthly more and more of a trouble to read the

school-books, and even the pages of the open-print
story-books danced and were dim. So Black Sheep
brooded in the shadows that fell about him and cut
him off from the world, inventing horrible punishments for "dear Harry," or plotting another line of the
tangled web of deception that he wrapped round Aunty
Rosa. Then the crash came and the cobwebs were
broken. It was impossible to foresee everything. Aunty
Rosa made personal inquiries as to Black Sheep's progress and received information that startled her. Step
by step, with a delight as keen as when she convicted
an under-fed house-maid of the theft of cold meats,
she followed the trail of Black Sheep's delinquencies.
For weeks and weeks, in order to escape banishment
from the book-shelves, he had made a fool of Aunty
Rosa, of Harry, of God, of all the world! Horrible,
most horrible, and evidence of an utterly depraved
mind.

Black Sheep counted the cost. "It will only be one
big beating and then she'll put a card with 'Liar' on my
back, same as she did before. Harry will whack me
at prayers and tell me I'm a child of the devil, and give
me hymns to learn. But I've done all my reading and
she never knew. She'll say she knew all along. She's
an old liar, too," said he.

For three days Black Sheep was shut in his own bedroom—to prepare his heart. "That means two beatings. One at school and one here. *That* one will hurt
most." And it fell even as he thought. He was thrashed
at school before the Jews and the *hubshi,* for the hei-
nous crime of bringing home false reports of progress.

He was thrashed at home by Aunty Rosa on the same account, and then the placard was produced. Aunty Rosa stitched it between his shoulders and bade him go for a walk with it upon him.

"If you make me do that," said Black Sheep, very quietly, "I shall burn this house down, and perhaps I'll kill you. I don't know whether I *can* kill you— you're so bony—but I'll try."

No punishment followed this blasphemy, though Black Sheep held himself ready to work his way to Aunty Rosa's withered throat, and grip there till he was beaten off. Perhaps Aunty Rosa was afraid, for Black Sheep, having reached the Nadir of Sin, bore himself with a new recklessness.

In the midst of all the trouble, there came a visitor from over the seas to Downe Lodge, who knew papa and mamma, and was commissioned to see Punch and Judy. Black Sheep was sent to the drawing-room and charged into a solid tea-table laden with china.

"Gently, gently, little man," said the visitor, turning Black Sheep's face to the light, slowly. "What's that big bird on the palings?"

"What bird?" asked Black Sheep.

The visitor looked deep down into Black Sheep's eyes for half a minute, and then said, suddenly: "Good God, the little chap's nearly blind!"

It was a most business-like visitor. He gave orders, on his own responsibility, that Black Sheep was not to go to school or open a book until mamma came home. "She'll be here in three weeks, as you know, of course," said he; "and I'm Inverarity Sahib. I ushered you into this wicked world, young man, and a nice use you seem to have made of your time. You must do nothing whatever. Can you do that?"

"Yes," said Punch, in a dazed way. He had known that mamma was coming. There was a chance, then, of another beating. Thank Heaven, papa wasn't coming, too. Aunty Rosa had said of late that he ought to be beaten by a man.

For the next three weeks Black Sheep was strictly allowed to do nothing. He spent his time in the old nursery looking at the broken toys, for all of which account must be rendered to mamma. Aunty Rosa hit him over the hands if even a wooden boat were broken. But that sin was of small importance compared to the other revelations, so darkly hinted at by Aunty Rosa. "When your mother comes, and hears what I have to tell her, she may appreciate you properly," she said, grimly, and mounted guard over Judy lest that small maiden should attempt to comfort her brother, to the peril of her own soul.

And mamma came—in a four-wheeler and a flutter of tender excitement. Such a mamma! She was young, frivolously young, and beautiful, with delicately flushed cheeks, eyes that shone like stars, and a voice that needed no additional appeal of outstretched arms to draw little ones to her heart. Judy ran straight to her, but Black Sheep hesitated. Could this wonder be "showing off?" She would not put out her arms when she knew of his crimes. Meantime, was it possible that by fondling she wanted to get anything out of Black Sheep? Only all his love and all his confidence; but that Black Sheep

did not know. Aunty Rosa withdrew and left mamma
kneeling between her children, half laughing, half crying, in the very hall where Punch and Judy had wept
five years before.

"Well, chicks, do you remember me?"

"No," said Judy, frankly, "but I said 'God bless papa
and mamma' ev'vy night."

"A little," said Black Sheep. "Remember I wrote to
you every week, anyhow. That isn't to show off, but
'cause of what comes afterward."

"What comes after! What should come after, my
darling boy?" And she drew him to her again. He
came awkwardly, with many angles. "Not used to
petting," said the quick mother-soul. "The girl is."

"She's too little to hurt anyone," thought Black
Sheep, "and if I said I'd kill her, she'd be afraid. I
wonder what Aunty Rosa will tell."

There was a constrained late dinner, at the end of
which mamma picked up Judy and put her to bed with
endearments manifold. Faithless little Judy had shown
her defection from Aunty Rosa already; and that lady
resented it bitterly. Black Sheep rose to leave the room.

"Come and say good-night," said Aunty Rosa, offering a withered cheek.

"Huh!" said Black Sheep. "I never kiss you, and I'm
not going to show off. Tell that woman what I've
done, and see what she says."

Black Sheep climbed into bed feeling that he had lost
Heaven after a glimpse through the gates. In half an
hour "that woman" was bending over him. It wasn't

fair to come and hit him in the dark. Even Aunty
Rosa never tried that. But no blow followed.

"Are you showing off? I won't tell you anything
more than Aunty Rosa has, and *she* doesn't know
everything," said Black Sheep, as clearly as he could
for the arms round his neck.

"Oh, my son—my little, little son! It was my
fault—*my* fault, darling—and yet how could we help
it? Forgive me, Punch." The voice died out in a
broken whisper, and two hot tears fell on Black Sheep's
forehead.

"Has she been making you cry, too?" he asked.
"You should see Jane cry. But you're nice, and Jane
is a born liar—Aunty Rosa says so."

"Hush, Punch, hush! My boy, don't talk like that.
Try to love me a little bit—a little bit. You don't know
how I want it. Punch-*baba*, come back to me! I am
your mother—your own mother—and never mind the
rest. I know—yes, I know, dear. It doesn't matter
now. Punch, won't you care for me a little?"

It is astonishing how much petting a big boy of ten
can endure when he is quite sure that there is no one
to laugh at him. Black Sheep had never been made
much of before, and here was this beautiful woman
treating him—Black Sheep, the Child of the Devil and
the Inheritor of Undying Flame—as though he were
a small god.

"I care for you a great deal, mother dear," he whispered at last, "and I'm glad you've come back; but are
you sure Aunty Rosa told you everything?"

"Everything. What *does* it matter? But"—the

voice broke with a sob that was also laughter—"Punch, my poor, dear, half-blind darling, don't you think it was a little foolish of you?"

"*No*. It saved a lickin'."

Mamma shuddered and slipped away in the darkness to write a long letter to papa. Here is an extract:

" . . . Judy is a dear, plump little prig who adores the woman, and wears, with as much gravity as her religious opinions—only eight, Jack!—a venerable horse-hair atrocity which she calls her bustle! I have just burned it, and the child is asleep in my bed as I write. She will come to me at once. Punch I can not quite understand. He is well nourished, but seems to have been worried into a system of small deceptions which the woman magnifies into deadly sins. Don't you recollect our own up-bringing, dear, when the fear of the Lord was so often the beginning of falsehood? I shall win Punch to me before long. I am taking the children away into the country to get them to know me, and, on the whole, I am content, or shall be when you come home, dear boy; and then, thank God, we shall be all under one roof again at last!"

Three months later, Punch, no longer Black Sheep, has discovered that he is the veritable owner of a real live, lovely mamma, who is also a sister, comforter, and friend, and that he must protect her till the father comes home. Deception does not suit the part of a protector, and when one can do anything without question, where is the use of deception?

"Mother would be awfully cross if you walked

through that ditch," says Judy, continuing a conversation.

"Mother's never angry," says Punch. "She'd just say, 'You're a little *pagal';* and that's not nice, but I'll show."

Punch walks through the ditch and mires himself to the knees. "Mother dear," he shouts, "I'm as dirty as I can pos-*sib*-ly be!"

"Then change your clothes as quickly as you pos-*sib*-ly can!" rings out mother's clear voice from the house. "And don't be a little *pagal!*"

"There! Told you so," said Punch. "It's all different now, and we are just as much mother's as if she had never gone."

Not altogether, oh Punch, for when young lips have drunk deep of the bitter waters of Hate, Suspicion, and Despair, all the love in the world will not wholly take away that knowledge; though it may turn darkened eyes for awhile to the light, and teach Faith where no Faith was.

THE PHANTOM 'RICKSHAW

May no ill dreams disturb my rest,
Nor Powers of Darkness me molest.
—*Evening Hymn.*

ONE of the few advantages that India has over
England is a great Knowability. After five
years' service a man is directly or indirectly acquainted with the two or three hundred Civilians in his
Province, all the Messes of ten or twelve Regiments
and batteries, and some fifteen hundred other people of
the non-official caste. In ten years his knowledge
should be doubled, and at the end of twenty he knows,
or knows something about, every Englishman in the
Empire, and may travel anywhere and everywhere
without paying hotel-bills.

Globe-trotters who expect entertainment as a right,
have, even within my memory, blunted this open-
heartedness, but none the less to-day, if you belong to
the Inner Circle and are neither a Bear nor a Black
Sheep, all houses are open to you, and our small world
is very, very kind and helpful.

Rickett of Kamartha stayed with Polder of Kumaon
some fifteen years ago. He meant to stay two nights,
but was knocked down by rheumatic fever, and for six
weeks disorganized Polder's establishment, stopped

Polder's work, and nearly died in Polder's bedroom.
Polder behaved as though he had been placed under
eternal obligation by Rickett, and yearly sends the little
Ricketts a box of presents and toys. It is the same everywhere. The men who do not take the trouble to con-
ceal from you their opinion that you are an in-
competent ass, and the women who blacken your character and misunderstand your wife's amusements, will
work themselves to the bone in your behalf if you fall
sick or into serious trouble.

Heatherlegh, the Doctor, kept, in addition to his
regular practice, a hospital on his private account—an
arrangement of loose boxes for Incurables, his friend
called it—but it was really a sort of fitting-up shed for
craft that had been damaged by stress of weather. The
weather in India is often sultry, and since the tale of
bricks is always a fixed quantity, and the only liberty
allowed is permission to work overtime and get no
thanks, men occasionally break down and become as
mixed as the metaphors in this sentence.

Heatherlegh is the dearest doctor that ever was, and
his invariable prescription to all his patients is, "lie low,
go slow, and keep cool."

He says that more men are killed by overwork than
the importance of this world justifies. He maintains that
three years ago. He has, of course, the right to speak
authoritatively, and he laughs at my theory that there
was a crack in Pansay's head and a little bit of the Dark
World came through and pressed him to death. "Pansay went off the handle," says Heatherlegh, "after the
stimulus of long leave at Home. He may or he may

not have behaved like a blackguard to Mrs. Keith-
Wessington. My notion is that the work of the Kata-
bundi Settlement ran him off his legs, and that he took
to brooding and making much of an ordinary P. & O.
flirtation. He certainly was engaged to Miss Mannering, and she certainly broke off the engagement. Then
he took a feverish chill and all that nonsense about
ghosts developed. Overwork started his illness, kept it
alight, and killed him, poor devil. Write him off to
the System—one man to take the work of two and a
half men."

I do not believe this. I used to sit up with Pansay
sometimes when Heatherlegh was called out to patients, and I happened to be within claim. The man
would make me most unhappy by describing in a low,
even voice, the procession that was always passing at
the bottom of his bed. He had a sick man's command
of language. When he recovered I suggested that he
should write out the whole affair from beginning to
end, knowing that ink might assist him to ease his
mind. When little boys have learned a new bad word
they are never happy till they have chalked it up on a
door. And this also is Literature.

He was in a high fever while he was writing, and
the blood-and-thunder Magazine diction he adopted
did not calm him. Two months afterward he was reported fit for duty, but, in spite of the fact that he was
urgently needed to help an undermanned Commission
stagger through a deficit, he preferred to die; vowing
at last that he was hag-ridden. I got his manuscript

before he died, and this is his version of the affair, dated 1885:

My doctor tells me that I need rest and change of air. I is not improbable that I shall get both ere long —rest that neither the red-coated messenger nor the mid-day gun can break, and change of air far beyond that which any homeward-bound steamer can give me. In the meantime I am resolved to stay where I am; and, in flat defiance of my doctor's orders, to take all the world into my confidence. You shall learn for yourselves the precise nature of my malady; and shall, too, judge for yourselves whether any man born of woman on this weary earth was ever so tormented as I.

Speaking now as a condemned criminal might speak ere the drop-bolts are drawn, my story, wild and hideously improbable as it may appear, demands at least attention. That it will ever receive credence I utterly disbelieve. Two months ago I should have scouted as mad or drunk the man who had dared tell me the like. Two months ago I was the happiest man in India. To-day, from Peshawur to the sea, there is no one more wretched. My doctor and I are the only two who know this. His explanation is, that my brain, digestion, and eyesight are all slightly affected; giving rise to my frequent and persistent "delusions." Delusions, indeed! I call him a fool; but he attends me still with the same unwearied smile, the same bland professional manner, the same neatly trimmed red whiskers, till I begin to suspect that I am an ungrateful, evil-tempered invalid. But you shall judge for yourselves.

Three years ago it was my fortune—my great mis-
fortune—to sail from Gravesend to Bombay, on return
from long leave, with one Agnes Keith-Wessington,
wife of an officer on the Bombay side. It does not in
the least concern you to know what manner of woman
she was. Be content with the knowledge that, ere the
voyage had ended, both she and I were desperately and
unreasoningly in love with one another. Heaven
knows that I can make the admission now without one
particle of vanity. In matters of this sort there is always one who gives and another who accepts. From
the first day of our ill-omened attachment, I was con-
scious that Agnes's passion was a stronger, a more
dominant, and—if I may use the expression—a purer
sentiment than mine. Whether she recognized the fact
then, I do not know. Afterward it was bitterly plain
to both of us.

Arrived at Bombay in the spring of the year, we went
our respective ways, to meet no more for the next three
or four months, when my leave and her love took us
both to Simla. There we spent the season together;
and there my fire of straw burned itself out to a pitiful
end with the closing year. I attempt no excuse. I
make no apology. Mrs. Wessington had given up
much for my sake, and was prepared to give up all.
From my own lips, in August, 1882, she learned that
I was sick of her presence, tired of her company, and
weary of the sound of her voice. Ninety-nine women
out of a hundred would have wearied of me as I
wearied of them; seventy-five of that number would
have promptly avenged themselves by active and obtru-

sive flirtation with other men. Mrs. Wessington was the hundredth. On her neither my openly expressed aversion nor the cutting brutalities with which I garnished our interviews had the least effect.

"Jack, darling!" was her one eternal cuckoo cry: "I'm sure it's all a mistake—a hideous mistake; and we'll be good friends again some day. *Please* forgive me, Jack, dear."

I was the offender, and I knew it. That knowledge transformed my pity into passive endurance, and, eventually, into blind hate—the same instinct, I suppose, which prompts a man to savagely stamp on the spider he has but half killed. And with this hate in my bosom the season of 1882 came to an end.

Next year we met again at Simla—she with her monotonous face and timid attempts at reconciliation, and I with loathing of her in every fibre of my frame. Several times I could not avoid meeting her alone; and on each occasion her words were identically the same. Still the unreasoning wail that it was all a "mistake"; and still the hope of eventually "making friends." I might have seen had I cared to look, that that hope only was keeping her alive. She grew more wan and thin month by month. You will agree with me, at least, that such conduct would have driven any one to despair. It was uncalled for; childish; unwomanly. I maintain that she was much to blame. And again, sometimes, in the black, fever-stricken night-watches, I have begun to think that I might have been a little kinder to her. But that really *is* a "delusion." I could not have continued pretending to love her when I didn't; could I? It would have been unfair to us both.

Last year we met again—on the same terms as before. The same weary appeals, and the same curt answers from my lips. At least I would make her see how wholly wrong and hopeless were her attempts at resuming the old relationship. As the season wore on, we fell apart—that is to say, she found it difficult to meet me, for I had other and more absorbing interests to attend to. When I think it over quietly in my sickroom, the season of 1884 seems a confused nightmare wherein light and shade were fantastically intermingled —my courtship of little Kitty Mannering; my hopes, doubts, and fears; our long rides together; my trembling avowal of attachment; her reply; and now and again a vision of a white face flitting by in the 'rickshaw with the black and white liveries I once watched for so earnestly; the wave of Mrs. Wessington's gloved hand; and, when she met me alone, which was but seldom, the irksome monotony of her appeal. I loved Kitty Mannering; honestly, heartily loved her, and with my love for her grew my hatred for Agnes. In August Kitty and I were engaged. The next day I met those accursed "magpie" *jhampanies* at the back of Jakko, and, moved by some passing sentiment of pity, stopped to tell Mrs. Wessington everything. She knew it already.

"So I hear you're engaged, Jack dear." Then, without a moment's pause:—"I'm sure it's all a mistake— a hideous mistake. We shall be as good friends some day, Jack, as we ever were."

My answer might have made even a man wince. It

cut the dying woman before me like the blow of a whip. "Please forgive me, Jack; I didn't mean to make you angry; but it's true, it's true!"

And Mrs. Wessington broke down completely. I turned away and left her to finish her journey in peace, feeling, but only for a moment or two, that I had been an unutterably mean hound. I looked back, and saw that she had turned her 'rickshaw with the idea, I suppose, of overtaking me.

The scene and its surroundings were photographed on my memory. The rain-swept sky (we were at the end of the wet weather), the sodden, dingy pines, the muddy road, and the black powder-riven cliffs formed a gloomy background against which the black and white liveries of the *jhampanies,* the yellow-paneled 'rickshaw and Mrs. Wessington's down-bowed golden head stood out clearly. She was holding her handkerchief in her left hand and was leaning back exhausted against the 'rickshaw cushions. I turned my horse up a bypath near the Sanjowlie Reservoir and literally ran away. Once I fancied I heard a faint call of "Jack!" This may have been imagination. I never stopped to verify it. Ten minutes later I came across Kitty on horseback; and, in the delight of a long ride with her, forgot all about the interview.

A week later Mrs. Wessington died, and the inexpressible burden of her existence was removed from my life. I went Plainsward perfectly happy. Before three months were over I had forgotten all about her, except that at times the discovery of some of her old letters reminded me unpleasantly of our bygone relationship.

By January I had disinterred what was left of our correspondence from among my scattered belongings and had burned it. At the beginning of April of this year, 1885, I was at Simla—semideserted Simla—once more, and was deep in lover's talks and walks with Kitty. It was decided that we should be married at the end of June. You will understand, therefore, that, loving Kitty as I did, I am not saying too much when I pronounce myself to have been, at that time, the happiest man in India.

Fourteen delightful days passed almost before I noticed their flight. Then, aroused to the sense of what was proper among mortals circumstanced as we were, I pointed out to Kitty that an engagement ring was the outward and visible sign of her dignity as an engaged girl; and that she must forthwith come to Hamilton's to be measured for one. Up to that moment, I give you my word, we had completely forgotten so trivial a matter. To Hamilton's we accordingly went on the 15th of April, 1885. Remember that—whatever my doctor may say to the contrary—I was then in perfect health, enjoying a well-balanced mind and an *absolutely* tranquil spirit. Kitty and I entered Hamilton's shop together, and there, regardless of the order of affairs, I measured Kitty for the ring in the presence of the amused assistant. The ring was a sapphire with two diamonds. We then rode out down the slope that leads to the Combermere Bridge and Peliti's shop.

While my Waler was cautiously feeling his way over the loose shale, and Kitty was laughing and chattering at my side—while all Simla, that is to say as much of it as had then come from the Plains, was grouped round the Reading-room and Peliti's veranda,—I was aware that some one, apparently at a vast distance, was calling me by my Christian name. It struck me that I had heard the voice before, but when and where I could not at once determine. In the short space it took to cover the road between the path from Hamilton's shop and the first plank of the Combermere Bridge I had thought over half a dozen people who might have committed such a solecism, and had eventually decided that it must have been singing in my ears. Immediately opposite Peliti's shop my eye was arrested by the sight of four *jhampanies* in "magpie" livery, pulling a yellow-paneled, cheap, bazar 'rickshaw. In a moment my mind flew back to the previous season and Mrs. Wessington with a sense of irritation and disgust. Was it not enough that the woman was dead and done with, without her black and white servitors reappearing to spoil the day's happiness? Whoever employed them now I thought I would call upon, and ask as a personal favor to change her *jhampanies'* livery. I would hire the men myself, and, if necessary, buy their coats from off their backs. It is impossible to say here what a flood of undesirable memories their presence evoked.

"Kitty," I cried, "there are poor Mrs. Wessington's *jhampanies* turned up again! I wonder who has them now?"

Kitty had known Mrs. Wessington slightly last season, and had always been interested in the sickly woman.

"What? Where?" she asked. "I can't see them anywhere."

Even as she spoke, her horse, swerving from a laden mule, threw himself directly in front of the advancing 'rickshaw. I had scarcely time to utter a word of warning when, to my unutterable horror, horse and rider passed *through* men and carriage as if they had been thin air.

"What's the matter?" cried Kitty; "what made you call out so foolishly, Jack? If I *am* engaged I don't want all creation to know about it. There was lots of space between the mule and the veranda; and, if you think I can't ride— There!"

Whereupon wilful Kitty set off, her dainty little head in the air, at a hand-gallop in the direction of the Bandstand; fully expecting, as she herself afterward told me, that I should follow her. What was the matter? Nothing indeed. Either that I was mad or drunk, or that Simla was haunted with devils. I reined in my impatient cob, and turned round. The 'rickshaw had turned too, and now stood immediately facing me near the left railing of the Combermere Bridge.

"Jack! Jack, darling!" (There was no mistake about the words this time: they rang through my brain as if they had been shouted in my ear.) "It's some hideous mistake, I'm sure. *Please* forgive me, Jack, and let's be friends again."

The rickshaw-hood had fallen back, and inside, as I hope and pray daily for the death I dread by night, sat Mrs. Keith-Wessington, handkerchief in hand, and golden head bowed on her breast.

How long I stared motionless I do not know.
Finally, I was aroused by my syce taking the Waler's
bridle and asking whether I was ill. From the horrible to the commonplace is but a step. I tumbled off
my horse and dashed, half fainting, into Peliti's for a
glass of cherry-brandy. There two or three couples
were gathered round the coffee-tables discussing the
gossip of the day. Their trivialities were more com-
forting to me just then than the consolations of religion
could have been. I plunged into the midst of the
conversation at once; chatted, laughed, and jested with
a face (when I caught a glimpse of it in a mirror) as
white and drawn as that of a corpse. Three or four
men noticed my condition; and, evidently setting it
down to the results of over-many pegs, charitably en-
deavored to draw me apart from the rest of the
loungers. But I refused to be led away. I wanted the
company of my kind—as a child rushes into the midst
of the dinner-party after a fright in the dark. I must
have talked for about ten minutes or so, though it
seemed an eternity to me, when I heard Kitty's clear
voice outside inquiring for me. In another minute she
had entered the shop, prepared to roundly upbraid me
for failing so signally in my duties. Something in my
face stopped her.

"Why, Jack," she cried, "what *have* you been doing?
What *has* happened? Are you ill?" Thus driven into
a direct lie, I said that the sun had been a little too
much for me. It was close upon five o'clock of a cloudy
April afternoon, and the sun had been hidden all day.
I saw my mistake as soon as the words were out of my

mouth: attempted to recover it; blundered hopelessly
and followed Kitty in a regal rage, out of doors, amid
the smiles of my acquaintances. I made some excuse
(I have forgotten what) on the score of my feeling
faint; and cantered away to my hotel, leaving Kitty
to finish the ride by herself.

In my room I sat down and tried calmly to reason
out the matter. Here was I, Theobald Jack Pansay, a
well-educated Bengal Civilian in the year of grace 1885,
presumably sane, certainly healthy, driven in terror
from my sweetheart's side by the apparition of a
woman who had been dead and buried eight months
ago. These were facts that I could not blink. Nothing
was further from my thought than any memory of
Mrs. Wessington when Kitty and I left Hamilton's
shop. Nothing was more utterly commonplace than
the stretch of wall opposite Peliti's. It was broad daylight. The road was full of people; and yet here, look
you, in defiance of every law of probability, in direct
outrage of Nature's ordinance, there had appeared to
me a face from the grave.

Kitty's Arab had gone *through* the 'rickshaw: so that
my first hope that some woman marvelously like Mrs.
Wessington had hired the carriage and the coolies with
their old livery was lost. Again and again I went
round this treadmill of thought; and again and again
gave up baffled and in despair. The voice was as inex-
plicable as the apparition. I had originally some wild
notion of confiding it all to Kitty; of begging her to
marry me at once; and in her arms defying the ghostly
occupant of the 'rickshaw. "After all," I argued, "the

presence of the 'rickshaw is in itself enough to prove the existence of a spectral illusion. One may see ghosts of men and women, but surely never of coolies and carriages. The whole thing is absurd. Fancy the ghost of a hillman!"

Next morning I sent a penitent note to Kitty, imploring her to overlook my strange conduct of the previous afternoon. My Divinity was still very wroth, and a personal apology was necessary. I explained, with a fluency born of night-long pondering over a falsehood, that I had been attacked with a sudden palpitation of the heart—the result of indigestion. This eminently practical solution had its effect; and Kitty and I rode out that afternoon with the shadow of my first lie dividing us.

Nothing would please her save a canter round Jakko. With my nerves still unstrung from the previous night I feebly protested against the notion, suggesting Observatory Hill, Jutogh, the Boileaugunge road—anything rather than the Jakko round. Kitty was angry and a little hurt: so I yielded from fear of provoking further misunderstanding, and we set out together toward Chota Simla. We walked a greater part of the way, and, according to our custom, cantered from a mile or so below the Convent to the stretch of level road by the Sanjowlie Reservoir. The wretched horses appeared to fly, and my heart beat quicker and quicker as we neared the crest of the ascent. My mind had been full of Mrs. Wessington all the afternoon; and every inch of the Jakko road bore witness to our old-time walks and talks. The bowlders were full of it;

the pines sang it aloud overhead; the rain-fed torrents giggled and chuckled unseen over the shameful story; and the wind in my ears chanted the iniquity aloud.

As a fitting climax, in the middle of the level men call the Ladies' Mile the Horror was awaiting me. No other 'rickshaw was in sight—only the four black and white *jhampanies,* the yellow-paneled carriage, and the golden head of the woman within—all apparently just as I had left them eight months and one fortnight ago! For an instant I fancied that Kitty *must* see what I saw —we were so marvelously sympathetic in all things. Her next words undeceived me—"Not a soul in sight! Come along, Jack, and I'll race you to the Reservoir buildings!" Her wiry little Arab was off like a bird, my Waler following close behind, and in this order we dashed under the cliffs. Half a minute brought us within fifty yards of the 'rickshaw. I pulled my Waler and fell back a little. The 'rickshaw was directly in the middle of the road; and once more the Arab passed through it, my horse following. "Jack! Jack dear! *Please* forgive me," rang with a wail in my ears, and, after an interval:—"It's all a mistake, a hideous mistake!"

I spurred my horse like a man possessed. When I turned my head at the Reservoir works, the black and white liveries were still waiting—patiently waiting— under the grey hillside, and the wind brought me a mocking echo of the words I had just heard. Kitty bantered me a good deal on my silence throughout the remainder of the ride. I had been talking up till then wildly and at random. To save my life I could not speak afterward naturally, and from Sanjowlie to the Church wisely held my tongue.

I was to dine with the Mannerings that night, and had barely time to canter home to dress. On the road to Elysium Hill I overheard two men talking together in the dusk.—"It's a curious thing," said one, "how completely all trace of it disappeared. You know my wife was insanely fond of the woman ('never could see anything in her myself), and wanted me to pick up her old 'rickshaw and coolies if they were to be got for love or money. Morbid sort of fancy I call it; but I've got to do what the *Memsahib* tells me. Would you believe that the man she hired it from tells me that all four of the men—they were brothers—died of cholera on the way to Hardwar, poor devils; and the 'rickshaw has been broken up by the man himself. 'Told me he never used a dead *Memsahib's* 'rickshaw. 'Spoiled his luck. Queer notion, wasn't it? Fancy poor little Mrs. Wessington spoiling any one's luck except her own!" I laughed aloud at this point; and my laugh jarred on me as I uttered it. So there *were* ghosts of 'rickshaws after all, and ghostly employments in the other world! How much did Mrs. Wessington give her men? What were their hours? Where did they go?

And for visible answer to my last question I saw the infernal Thing blocking my path in the twilight. The dead travel fast, and by short cuts unknown to ordinary coolies. I laughed aloud a second time and checked my laughter suddenly, for I was afraid I was going mad. Mad to a certain extent I must have been, for I recollect that I reined in my horse at the head of the 'rickshaw, and politely wished Mrs. Wessington "Good-evening." Her answer was one I knew only too well. I listened to the end; and replied that I had heard it all before, but should be delighted if she had anything further to say. Some malignant devil stronger than I must have entered into me that evening, for I have a dim recollection of talking the commonplaces of the day for five minutes to the Thing in front of me.

"Mad as a hatter, poor devil—or drunk. Max, try and get him to come home."

Surely *that* was not Mrs. Wessington's voice! The two men had overheard me speaking to the empty air, and had returned to look after me. They were very kind and considerate, and from their words evidently gathered that I was extremely drunk. I thanked them confusedly and cantered away to my hotel, there changed, and arrived at the Mannerings' ten minutes late. I pleaded the darkness of the night as an excuse; was rebuked by Kitty for my unlover-like tardiness; and sat down.

The conversation had already become general; and under cover of it, I was addressing some tender small talk to my sweetheart when I was aware that at the further end of the table a short red-whiskered man was describing, with much broidery, his encounter with a mad unknown that evening.

A few sentences convinced me that he was repeating the incident of half an hour ago. In the middle of the story he looked round for applause, as professional story-tellers do, caught my eye, and straightway collapsed. There was a moment's awkward silence, and the red-whiskered man muttered something to the effect that he had "forgotten the rest," thereby sacrificing a reputation as a good story-teller which he had built up for six seasons past. I blessed him from the bottom of my heart, and—went on with my fish.

In the fulness of time that dinner came to an end; and with genuine regret I tore myself away from Kitty —as certain as I was of my own existence that It would be waiting for me outside the door. The red-whiskered man, who had been introduced to me as Doctor Heatherlegh of Simla, volunteered to bear me company as far as our roads lay together. I accepted his offer with gratitude.

My instinct had not deceived me. It lay in readiness in the Mall, and, in what seemed devilish mockery of our ways, with a lighted headlamp. The red-whiskered man went to the point at once, in a manner that showed he had been thinking over it all dinner time.

"I say, Pansay, what the deuce was the matter with you this evening on the Elysium road?" The suddenness of the question wrenched an answer from me before I was aware.

"That!" said I, pointing to It.

"*That* may be either D. T. or Eyes for aught I know. Now you don't liquor. I saw as much at dinner, so it can't be *D. T.* There's nothing whatever where you're pointing, though you're sweating and trembling with fright like a scared pony. Therefore, I conclude that it's Eyes. And I ought to understand all about them.

Come along home with me. I'm on the Blessington lower road."

To my intense delight the 'rickshaw instead of waiting for us kept about twenty yards ahead—and this, too, whether we walked, trotted, or cantered. In the course of that long night ride I had told my companion almost as much as I have told you here.

"Well, you've spoiled one of the best tales I've ever laid tongue to," said he, "but I'll forgive you for the sake of what you've gone through. Now come home and do what I tell you; and when I've cured you, young man, let this be a lesson to you to steer clear of women and indigestible food till the day of your death."

The 'rickshaw kept steady in front; and my red-whiskered friend seemed to derive great pleasure from my account of its exact whereabouts.

"Eyes, Pansay—all Eyes, Brain, and Stomach. And the greatest of these three is Stomach. You've too much conceited Brain, too little Stomach, and thoroughly unhealthy Eyes. Get your Stomach straight, and the rest follows. And all that's French for a liver pill. I'll take sole medical charge of you from this hour! for you're too interesting a phenomenon to be passed over."

By this time we were deep in the shadow of the Blessington lower road and the 'rickshaw came to a dead stop under a pine-clad, overhanging shale cliff. Instinctively I halted too, giving my reason. Heatherlegh rapped out an oath.

"Now, if you think I'm going to spend a cold night on the hillside for the sake of a Stomach-*cum*-Brain-

cum-Eye illusion . . . Lord, ha' mercy! What's that?"

There was a muffled report, a blinding smother of dust just in front of us, a crack, the noise of rent boughs, and about ten yards of the cliff-side—pines, undergrowth, and all—slid down into the road below, completely blocking it up. The uprooted trees swayed and tottered for a moment like drunken giants in the gloom, and then fell prone among their fellows with a thunderous crash. Our two horses stood motionless and sweating with fear. As soon as the rattle of falling earth and stone had subsided, my companion muttered:—"Man, if we'd gone forward we should have been ten feet deep in our graves by now. 'There are more things in heaven and earth.' . . . Come home, Pansay, and thank God. I want a peg badly."

We retraced our way over the Church Ridge, and I arrived at Dr. Heatherlegh's house shortly after midnight.

His attempts toward my cure commenced almost immediately, and for a week I never left his sight. Many a time in the course of that week did I bless the good-fortune which had thrown me in contact with Simla's best and kindest doctor. Day by day my spirits grew lighter and more equable. Day by day, too, I became more and more inclined to fall in with Heatherlegh's "spectral illusion" theory, implicating eyes, brain, and stomach. I wrote to Kitty, telling her that a slight sprain caused by a fall from my horse kept me indoors for a few days; and that I should be recovered before she had time to regret my absence.

Heatherlegh's treatment was simple to a degree. It

consisted of liver pills, cold-water baths, and strong exercise, taken in the dusk or at early dawn—for, as he sagely observed:—"A man with a sprained ankle doesn't walk a dozen miles a day, and your young woman might be wondering if she saw you."

At the end of the week, after much examination of pupil and pulse, and strict injunctions as to diet and pedestrianism, Heatherlegh dismissed me as brusquely as he had taken charge of me. Here is his parting benediction:—"Man, I certify to your mental cure, and that's as much as to say I've cured most of your bodily ailments. Now, get your traps out of this as soon as you can; and be off to make love to Miss Kitty."

I was endeavoring to express my thanks for his kindness. He cut me short.

"Don't think I did this because I like you. I gather that you've behaved like a blackguard all through. But, all the same, you're a phenomenon, and as queer a phenomenon as you are a blackguard. No!"—checking me a second time—"not a rupee please. Go out and see if you can find the eyes-brain-and-stomach business again. I'll give you a lakh for each time you see it."

Half an hour later I was in the Mannerings' drawing-room with Kitty—drunk with the intoxication of present happiness and the foreknowledge that I should never more be troubled with Its hideous presence. Strong in the sense of my new-found security, I proposed a ride at once; and, by preference, a canter round Jakko.

Never had I felt so well, so overladen with vitality and mere animal spirits, as I did on the afternoon of the 30th of April. Kitty was delighted at the change in my appearance, and complimented me on it in her delightfully frank and outspoken manner. We left the Mannerings' house together, laughing and talking, and cantered along the Chota Simla road as of old.

I was in haste to reach the Sanjowlie Reservoir and there make my assurance doubly sure. The horses did their best, but seemed all too slow to my impatient mind. Kitty was astonished at my boisterousness. "Why, Jack!" she cried at last, "you are behaving like a child. What are you doing?"

We were just below the Convent, and from sheer wantonness I was making my Waler plunge and curvet across the road as I tickled it with the loop of my riding-whip.

"Doing?" I answered; "nothing, dear. That's just it. If you'd been doing nothing for a week except lie up, you'd be as riotous as I.

" 'Singing and murmuring in your feastful mirth,
    Joying to feel yourself alive;
  Lord over Nature, Lord of the visible Earth,
    Lord of the senses five.' "

My quotation was hardly out of my lips before we had rounded the corner above the Convent; and a few yards further on could see across to Sanjowlie. In the centre of the level road stood the black and white liveries, the yellow-paneled 'rickshaw, and Mrs. Keith-Wessington. I pulled up, looked, rubbed my eyes, and, I believe, must have said something. The next thing I knew was that I was lying face downward on the road, with Kitty kneeling above me in tears.

"Has it gone, child!" I gasped. Kitty only wept more bitterly.

"Has what gone, Jack, dear? what does it all mean? There must be a mistake somewhere, Jack. A hideous mistake." Her last words brought me to my feet—mad —raving for the time being.

"Yes, there *is* a mistake somewhere," I repeated, "a hideous mistake. Come and look at It."

I have an indistinct idea that I dragged Kitty by the wrist along the road up to where It stood, and implored her for pity's sake to speak to It; to tell It that we were betrothed; that neither Death nor Hell could break the tie between us: and Kitty only knows how much more to the same effect. Now and again I appealed passionately to the Terror in the 'rickshaw to bear witness to all I had said, and to release me from a torture that was killing me. As I talked I suppose I must have told Kitty of my old relations with Mrs. Wessington, for I saw her listen intently with white face and blazing eyes.

"Thank you, Mr. Pansay," she said, "that's *quite* enough. *Syce ghora láo.*"

The syces, impassive as Orientals always are, had come up with the recaptured horses; and as Kitty sprang into her saddle I caught hold of the bridle, entreating her to hear me out and forgive. My answer was the cut of her riding-whip across my face from mouth to eye, and a word or two of farewell that even now I cannot write down. So I judged, and judged rightly, that Kitty knew all; and I staggered back to the side of the 'rickshaw. My face was cut and bleeding, and the blow of the riding-whip had raised a livid blue wheal on it. I had no self-respect. Just then, Heatherlegh, who must have been following Kitty and me at a distance, cantered up.

"Doctor," I said, pointing to my face, "here's Miss Mannering's signature to my order of dismissal and . . . I'll thank you for that lakh as soon as convenient."

Heatherlegh's face, even in my abject misery, moved me to laughter.

"I'll stake my professional reputation"—he began. "Don't be a fool," I whispered. "I've lost my life's happiness and you'd better take me home."

As I spoke the 'rickshaw was gone. Then I lost all knowledge of what was passing. The crest of Jakko seemed to heave and roll like the crest of a cloud and fall in upon me.

Seven days later (on the 7th of May, that is to say) I was aware that I was lying in Heatherlegh's room as weak as a little child. Heatherlegh was watching me intently from behind the papers on his writing-table. His first words were not encouraging; but I was too far spent to be much moved by them.

"Here's Miss Kitty has sent back your letters. You correspond a good deal, you young people. Here's a packet that looks like a ring, and a cheerful sort of a note from Mannering Papa, which I've taken the liberty of reading and burning. The old gentleman's not pleased with you."

"And Kitty?" I asked, dully.

"Rather more drawn than her father from what she says. By the same token you must have been letting

out any number of queer reminiscences just before I
met you. 'Says that a man who would have behaved
to a woman as you did to Mrs. Wessington ought to
kill himself out of sheer pity for his kind. She's a hot-
headed little virago, your mash. 'Will have it too that
you were suffering from *D. T.* when that row on the
Jakko road turned up. 'Says she'll die before she ever
speaks to you again."

I groaned and turned over on the other side.

"Now you've got your choice, my friend. This engagement has to be broken off; and the Mannerings
don't want to be too hard on you. Was it broken
through *D. T.* or epileptic fits? Sorry I can't offer you
a better exchange unless you'd prefer hereditary insanity. Say the word and I'll tell 'em it's fits. All
Simla knows about that scene on the Ladies' Mile.
Come! I'll give you five minutes to think over it."

During those five minutes I believe that I explored
thoroughly the lowest circles of the Inferno which it is
permitted man to tread on earth. And at the same
time I myself was watching myself faltering through
the dark labyrinths of doubt, misery, and utter despair.
I wondered, as Heatherlegh in his chair might have
wondered, which dreadful alternative I should adopt.
Presently I heard myself answering in a voice that I
hardly recognized,—

"They're confoundedly particular about morality in
these parts. Give 'em fits, Heatherlegh, and my love.
Now let me sleep a bit longer."

Then my two selves joined, and it was only I (half

crazed, devil-driven I) that tossed in my bed, tracing step by step the history of the past month.

"But I am in Simla," I kept repeating to myself. "I, Jack Pansay, am in Simla, and there are no ghosts here. It's unreasonable of that woman to pretend there are. Why couldn't Agnes have left me alone? I never did her any harm. It might just as well have been me as Agnes. Only I'd never have come back on purpose to kill *her*. Why can't I be left alone—left alone and happy?"

It was high noon when I first awoke: and the sun was low in the sky before I slept—slept as the tortured criminal sleeps on his rack, too worn to feel any further pain.

Next day I could not leave my bed. Heatherlegh told me in the morning that he had received an answer from Mr. Mannering, and that, thanks to his (Heatherlegh's) friendly offices, the story of my affliction had traveled through the length and breadth of Simla, where I was on all sides much pitied.

"And that's rather more than you deserve," he concluded, pleasantly, "though the Lord knows you've been going through a pretty severe mill. Never mind; we'll cure you yet, you perverse phenomenon."

I declined firmly to be cured. "You've been much too good to me already, old man," said I; "but I don't think I need trouble you further."

In my heart I knew that nothing Heatherlegh could do would lighten the burden that had been laid upon me.

With that knowledge came also a sense of hopeless,

impotent rebellion against the unreasonableness of it all. There were scores of men no better than I whose punishments had at least been reserved for another world; and I felt that it was bitterly, cruelly unfair that I alone should have been singled out for so hideous a fate. This mood would in time give place to another where it seemed that the 'rickshaw and I were the only realities in a world of shadows; that Kitty was a ghost; that Mannering, Heatherlegh, and all the other men and women I knew were all ghosts; and the great, grey hills themselves but vain shadows devised to torture me. From mood to mood I tossed backward and forward for seven weary days; my body growing daily stronger and stronger, until the bedroom looking-glass told me that I had returned to everyday life, and was as other men once more. Curiously enough my face showed no signs of the struggle I had gone through. It was pale indeed, but as expressionless and common-place as ever. I had expected some permanent altera-tion—visible evidence of the disease that was eating me away. I found nothing.

On the 15th of May I left Heatherlegh's house at eleven o'clock in the morning; and the instinct of the bachelor drove me to the Club. There I found that every man knew my story as told by Heatherlegh, and was, in clumsy fashion, abnormally kind and attentive. Nevertheless I recognized that for the rest of my natu-ral life I should be among but not of my fellows; and I envied very bitterly indeed the laughing coolies on the Mall below. I lunched at the Club, and at four o'clock wandered aimlessly down the Mall in the vague hope of meeting Kitty. Close to the Band-stand the black and white liveries joined me; and I heard Mrs. Wessington's old appeal at my side. I had been expecting this ever since I came out; and was only surprised at her delay. The phantom 'rickshaw and I went side by side along the Chola Simla road in silence. Close to the bazar, Kitty and a man on horseback overtook and passed us. For any sign she gave I might have been a dog in the road. She did not even pay me the compliment of quickening her pace; though the rainy afternoon had served for an excuse.

So Kitty and her companion, and I and my ghostly Light-o'-Love, crept round Jakko in couples. The road was streaming with water; the pines dripped like roof-pipes on the rocks below, and the air was full of fine, driving rain. Two or three times I found myself saying to myself almost aloud: "I'm Jack Pansay on leave at Simla—*at Simla!* Everyday, ordinary Simla. I mustn't forget that—I mustn't forget that." Then I would try to recollect some of the gossip I had heard at the Club: the price of So-and-So's horses—anything, in fact, that related to the workaday Anglo-Indian world I knew so well. I even repeated the multiplication-table rapidly to myself, to make quite sure that I was not taking leave of my senses. It gave me much comfort; and must have prevented my hearing Mrs. Wessington for a time.

Once more I wearily climbed the Convent slope and entered the level road. Here Kitty and the man started off at a canter, and I was left alone with Mrs. Wessington. "Agnes," said I, "will you put back your hood and

tell me what it all means?" The hood dropped noise-
lessly, and I was face to face with my dead and buried
mistress. She was wearing the dress in which I had
last seen her alive; carried the same tiny handkerchief
in her right hand; and the same cardcase in her left.
(A woman eight months dead with a cardcase!) I had
to pin myself down to the multiplication-table, and to
set both hands on the stone parapet of the road, to assure myself that that at least was real.

"Agnes," I repeated, "for pity's sake tell me what it
all means." Mrs. Wessington leaned forward, with
that odd, quick turn of the head I used to know so well,
and spoke.

If my story had not already so madly overleaped the
bounds of all human belief I should apologize to you
now. As I know that no one—no, not even Kitty, for
whom it is written as some sort of justification of my
conduct—will believe me, I will go on. Mrs. Wessington spoke and I walked with her from the Sanjowlie
road to the turning below the Commander-in-Chief's
house as I might walk by the side of any living woman's 'rickshaw, deep in conversation. The second and
most tormenting of my moods of sickness had suddenly
laid hold upon me, and like the Prince in Tennyson's
poem, "I seemed to move amid a world of ghosts."
There had been a garden-party at the Commander-in-
Chief's, and we two joined the crowd of homeward
bound folk. As I saw them then it seemed that *they*
were the shadows—impalpable, fantastic shadows—
that divided for Mrs. Wessington's 'rickshaw to pass
through. What we said during the course of that

weird interview I cannot—indeed, I dare not—tell. Heatherlegh's comment would have been a short laugh and a remark that I had been "mashing a brain-eye-and-stomach chimera." It was ghastly and yet in some indefinable way a marvelously dear experience. Could it be possible, I wondered, that I was in this life to woo a second time the woman I had killed by my own neglect and cruelty?

I met Kitty on the homeward road—a shadow among shadows.

If I were to describe all the incidents of the next fortnight in their order, my story would never come to an end; and your patience would be exhausted. Morning after morning and evening after evening the ghostly 'rickshaw and I used to wander through Simla together. Wherever I went there the four black and white liveries followed me and bore me company to and from my hotel. At the Theatre I found them amid the crowd of yelling *jhampanies;* outside the Club veranda, after a long evening of whist; at the Birthday Ball, waiting patiently for my reappearance; and in broad daylight when I went calling. Save that it cast no shadow, the 'rickshaw was in every respect as real to look upon as one of wood and iron. More than once, indeed, I have had to check myself from warning some hard-riding friend against cantering over it. More than once I have walked down the Mall deep in conversation with Mrs. Wessington to the unspeakable amazement of the passers-by.

Before I had been out and about a week I learned that the "fit" theory had been discarded in favor of insanity. However, I made no change in my mode of life. I called, rode, and dined out as freely as ever. I had a passion for the society of my kind which I had never felt before; I hungered to be among the realities of life; and at the same time I felt vaguely unhappy when I had been separated too long from my ghostly companion. It would be almost impossible to describe my varying moods from the 15th of May up to to-day.

The presence of the 'rickshaw filled me by turns with horror, blind fear, a dim sort of pleasure, and utter despair. I dared not leave Simla; and I knew that my stay there was killing me. I knew, moreover, that it was my destiny to die slowly and a little every day. My only anxiety was to get the penance over as quietly as might be. Alternately I hungered for a sight of Kitty and watched her outrageous flirtations with my successor—to speak more accurately, my successors—with amused interest. She was as much out of my life as I was out of hers. By day I wandered with Mrs. Wessington almost content. By night I implored Heaven to let me return to the world as I used to know it. Above all these varying moods lay the sensation of dull, numbing wonder that the Seen and the Unseen should mingle so strangely on this earth to hound one poor soul to its grave.

·   ·   ·   ·   ·   ·   ·

August 27.—Heatherlegh has been indefatigable in his attendance on me; and only yesterday told me that I ought to send in an application for sick leave. An application to escape the company of a phantom! A

request that the Government would graciously permit
me to get rid of five ghosts and an airy 'rickshaw by
going to England! Heatherlegh's proposition moved
me to almost hysterical laughter. I told him that I
should await the end quietly at Simla; and I am sure
that the end is not far off. Believe me that I dread its
advent more than any word can say; and I torture myself nightly with a thousand speculations as to the manner of my death.

Shall I die in my bed decently and as an English
gentleman should die; or, in one last walk on the Mall,
will my soul be wrenched from me to take its place forever and ever by the side of that ghastly phantasm?
Shall I return to my old lost allegiance in the next
world, or shall I meet Agnes loathing her and bound
to her side through all eternity? Shall we two hover
over the scene of our lives till the end of Time? As
the day of my death draws nearer, the intense horror
that all living flesh feels toward escaped spirits from
beyond the grave grows more and more powerful. It
is an awful thing to go down quick among the dead
with scarcely one-half of your life completed. It is a
thousand times more awful to wait as I do in your
midst, for I know not what unimaginable terror. Pity
me, at least on the score of my "delusion," for I know
you will never believe what I have written here. Yet
as surely as ever a man was done to death by the Powers
of Darkness I am that man.

In justice, too, pity her. For as surely as ever woman
was killed by man, I killed Mrs. Wessington. And the
last portion of my punishment is even now upon me.

BY WORD OF MOUTH

Not though you die to-night, O Sweet, and wail,
　　A spectre at my door,
Shall mortal Fear make Love immortal fail—
　　I shall but love you more,
Who, from Death's house returning, give me still
One moment's comfort in my matchless ill.
　　　　　　　　　　　—Shadow Houses.

THIS tale may be explained by those who know
how souls are made, and where the bounds of
the Possible are put down. I have lived long
enough in this India to know that it is best to know
nothing, and can only write the story as it happened.

Dumoise was our Civil Surgeon at Meridki, and we
called him "Dormouse," because he was a round little,
sleepy little man. He was a good Doctor and never
quarreled with any one, not even with our Deputy
Commissioner who had the manners of a bargee and
the tact of a horse. He married a girl as round and as
sleepy-looking as himself. She was a Miss Hillardyce,
daughter of "Squash" Hillardyce of the Bears, who
married his Chief's daughter by mistake. But that is
another story.

A honeymoon in India is seldom more than a week
long; but there is nothing to hinder a couple from ex-
tending it over two or three years. India is a delightful

country for married folk who are wrapped up in one
another. They can live absolutely alone and without
interruption—just as the Dormice did. Those two little
people retired from the world after their marriage, and
were very happy. They were forced, of course, to give
occasional dinners, but they made no friends thereby,
and the Station went its own way and forgot them;
only saying, occasionally, that Dormouse was the best
of good fellows though dull. A Civil Surgeon who
never quarrels is a rarity, appreciated as such.

Few people can afford to play Robinson Crusoe anywhere—least of all in India, where we are few in the
land and very much dependent on each other's kind
offices. Dumoise was wrong in shutting himself from
the world for a year, and he discovered his mistake
when an epidemic of typhoid broke out in the Station
in the heart of the cold weather, and his wife went
down. He was a shy little man, and five days were
wasted before he realized that Mrs. Dumoise was burning with something worse than simple fever, and three
days more passed before he ventured to call on Mrs.
Shute, the Engineer's wife, and timidly speak about his
trouble. Nearly every household in India knows that
Doctors are very helpless in typhoid. The battle must
be fought out between Death and the Nurses minute
by minute and degree by degree. Mrs. Shute almost
boxed Dumoise's ears for what she called his "criminal
delay," and went off at once to look after the poor girl
We had seven cases of typhoid in the Station that winter and, as the average of death is about one in every
five cases, we felt certain that we should have to lose

somebody. But all did their best. The women sat up
nursing the women, and the men turned to and tended
the bachelors who were down, and we wrestled with
those typhoid cases for fifty-six days, and brought them
through the Valley of the Shadow in triumph. But,
just when we thought all was over, and were going
to give a dance to celebrate the victory, little Mrs. Dumoise got a relapse and died in a week and the Station
went to the funeral. Dumoise broke down utterly at
the brink of the grave, and had to be taken away.

After the death, Dumoise crept into his own house
and refused to be comforted. He did his duties perfectly, but we all felt that he should go on leave, and
the other men of his own Service told him so. Dumoise
was very thankful for the suggestion—he was thankful
for anything in those days—and went to Chini on a
walking-tour. Chini is some twenty marches from
Simla, in the heart of the Hills, and the scenery is good
if you are in trouble. You pass through big, still
deodar-forests, and under big, still cliffs, and over big,
still grass-downs swelling like a woman's breasts; and
the wind across the grass, and the rain among the
deodars says—"Hush—hush—hush." So little Dumoise
was packed off to Chini, to wear down his grief with
a full-plate camera and a rifle. He took also a useless
bearer, because the man had been his wife's favorite
servant. He was idle and a thief, but Dumoise trusted
everything to him.

On his way back from Chini, Dumoise turned aside
to Bagi, through the Forest Reserve which is on the
spur of Mount Huttoo. Some men who have traveled

more than a little say that the march from Kotegarh to Bagi is one of the finest in creation. It runs through dark wet forest, and ends suddenly in bleak, nipped hillside and black rocks. Bagi dâk-bungalow is open to all the winds and is bitterly cold. Few people go to Bagi. Perhaps that was the reason why Dumoise went there. He halted at seven in the evening, and his bearer went down the hillside to the village to engage coolies for the next day's march. The sun had set, and the night-winds were beginning to croon among the rocks. Dumoise leaned on the railing of the veranda, waiting for his bearer to return. The man came back almost immediately after he had disappeared, and at such a rate that Dumoise fancied he must have crossed a bear. He was running as hard as he could up the face of the hill.

But there was no bear to account for his terror. He raced to the veranda and fell down, the blood spurting from his nose and his face iron-grey. Then he gurgled —"I have seen the *Memsahib!* I have seen the *Memsahib!*"

"Where?" asked Dumoise.

"Down there, walking on the road to the village. She was in a blue dress, and she lifted the veil of her bonnet and said—'Ram Dass, give my *salaams* to the *Sahib,* and tell him that I shall meet him next month at Nuddea.' Then I ran away, because I was afraid."

What Dumoise said or did I do not know. Ram Dass declares that he said nothing, but walked up and down the veranda all the cold night, waiting for the *Memsahib* to come up the hill and stretching out his arms into the dark like a madman. But no *Memsahib* came, and, next day, he went on to Simla cross-questioning the bearer every hour.

Ram Dass could only say that he had met Mrs. Dumoise and that she had lifted up her veil and given him the message which he had faithfully repeated to Dumoise. To this statement Ram Dass adhered. He did not know where Nuddea was, had no friends at Nuddea, and would most certainly never go to Nuddea; even though his pay were doubled.

Nuddea is in Bengal and has nothing whatever to do with a Doctor serving in the Punjab. It must be more than twelve hundred miles south of Meridki.

Dumoise went through Simla without halting, and returned to Meridki, there to take over charge from the man who had been officiating for him during his tour. There were some Dispensary accounts to be explained, and some recent orders of the Surgeon-General to be noted, and, altogether, the taking-over was a full day's work. In the evening, Dumoise told his *locum tenens,* who was an old friend of his bachelor days, what had happened at Bagi; and the man said that Ram Dass might as well have chosen Tuticorin while he was about it.

At that moment, a telegraph-peon came in with a telegram from Simla, ordering Dumoise not to take over charge at Meridki, but to go at once to Nuddea on special duty. There was a nasty outbreak of cholera at Nuddea, and the Bengal Government, being short-handed, as usual, had borrowed a Surgeon from the Punjab.

Dumoise threw the telegram across the table and said—"Well?"

The other Doctor said nothing. It was all that he could say.

Then he remembered that Dumoise had passed through Simla on his way from Bagi; and thus might, possibly, have heard first news of the impending transfer.

He tried to put the question, and the implied suspicion into words, but Dumoise stopped him with—"If I had desired *that,* I should never have come back from Chini. I was shooting there. I wish to live, for I have things to do . . . but I shall not be sorry."

The other man bowed his head, and helped, in the twilight, to pack up Dumoise's just opened trunks. Ram Dass entered with the lamps.

"Where is the *Sahib* going?" he asked.

"To Nuddea," said Dumoise, softly.

Ram Dass clawed Dumoise's knees and boots and begged him not to go. Ram Dass wept and howled till he was turned out of the room. Then he wrapped up all his belongings and came back to ask for a character. He was not going to Nuddea to see his *Sahib* die and, perhaps, to die himself.

So Dumoise gave the man his wages and went down to Nuddea alone; the other Doctor bidding him good-bye as one under sentence of death.

Eleven days later he had joined his *Memsahib;* and the Bengal Government had to borrow a fresh Doctor to cope with that epidemic at Nuddea. The first importation lay dead in Chooadanga Dâk-Bungalow.

BIMI

THE orang-outang in the big iron cage lashed to the sheep-pen began the discussion. The night was stiflingly hot, and as Hans Breitmann and I passed him, dragging our bedding to the forepeak of the steamer, he roused himself and chattered obscenely. He had been caught somewhere in the Malayan Archipelago, and was going to England to be exhibited at a shilling a head. For four days he had struggled, yelled and wrenched at the heavy iron bars of his prison without ceasing, and had nearly slain a Lascar incautious enough to come within reach of the great hairy paw.

"It would be well for, mine friend, if you was a liddle seasick," said Hans Breitmann, pausing by the cage. "You haf too much Ego in your Cosmos."

The orang-outang's arm slid out negligently from between the bars. No one would have believed that it would make a sudden snake-like rush at the German's breast. The thin silk of the sleep-suit tore out: Hans stepped back unconcernedly, to pluck a banana from a bunch hanging close to one of the boats.

"Too much Ego," said he, peeling the fruit and offering it to the caged devil, who was rending the silk to tatters.

Then we laid out our bedding in the bows, among the sleeping Lascars, to catch any breeze that the pace of the ship might give us. The sea was like smoky oil, except where it turned to fire under our forefoot and whirled back into the dark in smears of dull flame. There was a thunderstorm some miles away; we could see the glimmer of the lightning. The ship's cow, distressed by the heat and the smell of the ape-beast in the cage, lowed unhappily from time to time in exactly the same key as the lookout man at the bows answered the hourly call from the bridge. The trampling tune of the engines was very distinct, and the jarring of the ash-lift, as it was tipped into the sea, hurt the procession of hushed noise. Hans lay down by my side and lighted a good-night cigar. This was naturally the beginning of conversation. He owned a voice as soothing as the wash of the sea, and stores of experiences as vast as the sea itself; for his business in life was to wander up and down the world, collecting orchids and wild beasts and ethnological specimens for German and American dealers. I watched the glowing end of his cigar wax and wane in the gloom, as the sentences rose and fell, till I was nearly asleep. The orang-outang, troubled by some dream of the forests of his freedom, began to yell like a soul in purgatory, and to wrench madly at the bars of the cage.

"If he was out now dere would not be much of us left hereabouts," said Hans, lazily. "He screams good. See, now, how I shall tame him when he stops himself."

There was a pause in the outcry, and from Hans' mouth came an imitation of a snake's hiss, so perfect that I almost sprung to my feet. The sustained murderous sound rang along the deck, and the wrenching at the bars ceased. The orang-outang was quaking in an ecstasy of pure terror.

"Dot stop him," said Hans. "I learned dot trick in Mogoung Tanjong when I was collecting liddle monkeys for some peoples in Berlin. Efery one in der world is afraid of der monkeys—except der snake. So I blay snake against monkey, and he keep quite still. Dere was too much Ego in his Cosmos. Dot is der soul-custom of monkeys. Are you asleep, or will you listen, and I will tell a dale dot you shall not pelief?"

"There's no tale in the wide world that I can't believe," I said.

"If you have learned pelief you haf learned somedings. Now I shall try your pelief. Good! When I was collecting does liddle monkeys—it was in '79 or '80, und I was in der islands of der Archipelago—over dere in der dark"—he pointed southward to New Guinea generally—"Mein Gott! I would sooner collect life red devils than liddle monkeys. When dey do not bite off your thumbs dey are always dying from nostalgia— home-sick—for dey haf der imperfect soul, which is midway arrested in defelopment—und too much Ego. I was dere for nearly a year, und dere I found a man dot was called Bertran. He was a Frenchman, und he was a goot man—naturalist to the bone. Dey said he was an escaped convict, but he was a naturalist, und dot was enough for me. He would call all der life beasts from der forest, und dey would come. I said he was St. Francis of Assisi in a new dransmigration produced, und he laughed und said he haf never preach to der fishes. He sold dem for tripang—*beche-de-mer*.

"Und dot man, who was king of beasts-tamer men, he had in der house shush such anoder as dot devil-animal in der cage—a great orang-outang dot thought he was a man. He haf found him when he was a child —der orang-outang—und he was child and brother and opera comique all round to Bertran. He had his room in dot house—not a cage, but a room—mit a bed and sheets, and he would go to bed and get up in der morning and smoke his cigar und eat his dinner mit Bertran, und walk mit him hand-in-hand, which was most horrible. Herr Gott! I haf seen dot beast throw himself back in his chair und laugh when Bertran haf made fun of me. He was *not* a beast; he was a man, und he talked to Bertran, und Bertran comprehended, for I have seen dem. Und he was always politeful to me except when I talk too long to Bertran und say nodings at all to him. Den he would pull me away— dis great, dark devil, mit his enormous paws—shush as if I was a child. He was not a beast, he was a man.' Dis I saw pefore I know him three months, und Bertran he haf saw the same; and Bimi, der orang-outang, haf understood us both, mit his cigar between his big-dog teeth und der blue gum.

"I was dere a year, dere und at dere oder islands— somedimes for monkeys and somedimes for butterflies und orchits. One time Bertran says to me dot he will be married, pecause he haf found a girl dot was goot, and he inquire if this marrying idea was right. I would not say, pecause it was not me dot was going to be married. Den he go off courting der girl—she was a half-caste French girl—very pretty. Haf you got a new

light for my cigar? Oof! Very pretty. Only I say:
'Haf you thought of Bimi? If he pulls me away when
I talk to you, what will he do to your wife? He will
pull her in pieces. If I was you, Bertran, I would gif
my wife for wedding present der stuff figure of Bimi.'
By dot time I had learned somedings about der monkey peoples. 'Shoot him?' says Bertran. 'He is your
beast,' I said; 'if he was mine he would be shot now.'

"Den I felt at der back of my neck der fingers of
Bimi. Mein Gott! I tell you dot he talked through
dose fingers. It was der deaf-and-dumb alphabet all
gomplete. He slide his hairy arm round my neck, and
he tilt up my chin und look into my face, shust to see
if I understood his talk so well as he understood mine.

" 'See now dere!' says Bertran, 'und you would shoot
him while he is cuddling you? Dot is der Teuton in-
grate!'

"But I knew dot I had made Bimi a life's enemy,
pecause his fingers haf talk murder through the back
of my neck. Next dime I see Bimi dere was a pistol in
my belt, und he touch it once, and I open der breech
to show him it was loaded. He haf seen der liddle
monkeys killed in der woods and he understood.

"So Bertran he was married, und he forgot clean
about Bimi dot was skippin' alone on der beach mit der
half of a human soul in his belly. I was see him skip,
und he took a big bough und thrash der sand till he
half made a great hole like a grave. So I says to Bertran: 'For any sakes, kill Bimi. He is mad mit der
jealousy.'

"Bertran haf said: 'He is not mad at all. He haf

obey and love my wife, und if she speaks he will get her slippers,' und he looked at his wife across der room. She was a very pretty girl.

"Den I said to him: 'Dost thou pretend to know monkeys und dis beast dot is lashing himself mad upon der sands, pecause you do not talk to him? Shoot him when he comes to der house, for he haf der light in his eyes dot means killing—und killing.' Bimi come to der house, but dere was no light in his eyes. It was all put away, cunning—so cunning—und he fetch der girl her slippers, und Bertran turn to me und say: 'Dost thou know him in nine months more than I haf known him in twelve years? Shall a child stab his fader? I have fed him, und he was my child. Do not speak this nonsense to my wife or to me any more.'

"Dot next day Bertran came to my house to help me make some wood cases for der specimens, und he tell me dot he haf left his wife a liddle while mit Bimi in der garden. Den I finish my cases quick, und I say: 'Let us go to your house und get a trink.' He laugh und say: 'Come along, dry mans.'

"His wife was not in der garden, und Bimi did not come when Bertran called. Und his wife did not come when he called, und he knocked at her bedroom door und dot was shut tight—locked. Den he look at me, und his face was white. I broke down der door mit my shoulder, und der thatch of der roof was torn into a great hole, und der sun came in upon der floor. Haf you ever seen paper in der waste-basket, or cards at whist on der table scattered? Dere was no wife dot could be seen. I tell you dere was noddings in dot room dot might be a woman. Dere was stuff on der floor, und dot was all. I looked at dese things und I was very sick; but Bertran looked a liddle longer at what was upon the floor und der walls, und der hole in der thatch. Den he pegan to laugh, soft and low, und I knew und thank Got dot he was mad. He nefer cried, he nefer prayed. He stood still in der doorway und laugh to himself. Den he said: 'She haf locked herself in dis room, und he haf torn up der thatch. *Fi donc.* Dot is so. We will mend der thatch und wait for Bimi. He will surely come.'

"I tell you we waited ten days in dot house, after der room was made into a room again, and once or twice we saw Bimi comin' a liddle way from der woods. He was afraid pecause he haf done wrong. Bertran called him when he was come to look on the tenth day, und Bimi come skipping along der beach und making noises, mit a long piece of black hair in his hands. Den Bertran laugh and say, *'Fi donc!'* shust as if it was a glass broken upon der table; und Bimi come nearer, und Bertran was honey-sweet in his voice and laughed to himself. For three days he made love to Bimi, pecause Bimi would not let himself be touched. Den Bimi come to dinner at der same table mit us, und her hair on his hands was all black und thick mit—mit what had dried on his hands. Bertran gave him sangaree till Bimi was drunk and stupid, und den"—

Hans paused to puff at his cigar.

"And then?" said I.

"Und den Bertran kill him with his hands, und I go for a walk upon der beach. It was Bertran's own piziness. When I come back der ape he was dead, und Bertran he was dying abofe him; but still he laughed a liddle und low, and he was quite content. Now you know der formula of der strength of der orang-outang —it is more as seven to one in relation to man. But Bertran, he half killed Bimi mit sooch dings as Gott gif him. Dot was der miracle."

The infernal clamor in the cage recommenced. "Aha! Dot friend of ours haf still too much Ego in his Cosmos. Be quiet, thou!"

Hans hissed long and venomously. We could hear the great beast quaking in his cage.

"But why in the world didn't you help Bertran instead of letting him be killed?" I asked.

"My friend," said Hans, composedly stretching himself to slumber, "it was not nice even to mineself dot I should lif after I had seen dot room wit der hole in der thatch. Und Bertran, he was her husband. Gootnight, und sleep well."

THE MADNESS OF PRIVATE ORTHERIS

> Oh! Where would I be when my froat was dry?
> Oh! Where would I be when the bullets fly?
> Oh! Where would I be when I come to die?
> > Why,
> Somewheres anigh my chum.
> > If 'e's liquor 'e'll give me some,
> > If I'm dyin' 'e'll 'old my 'ead,
> > An' 'e'll write 'em 'Ome when I'm dead.—
> > Gawd send us a trusty chum!
> > > —*Barrack Room Ballad.*

MY friends Mulvaney and Ortheris had gone on a shooting-expedition for one day. Learoyd was still in hospital, recovering from fever picked up in Burma. They sent me an invitation to join them, and were genuinely pained when I brought beer—almost enough beer to satisfy two Privates of the Line . . . and Me.

" 'Twasn't for that we bid you welkim, sorr," said Mulvaney, sulkily. " 'Twas for the pleasure av your comp'ny."

Ortheris came to the rescue with—"Well, 'e won't be none the worse for bringin' liquor with 'im. We ain't a file o' Dooks. We're bloomin' Tommies, ye can-tankris Hirishman; an' 'eres your very good 'ealth!"

We shot all the forenoon, and killed two pariah-dogs,

four green parrots, sitting, one kite by the burning-
ghaut, one snake flying, one mud-turtle, and eight
crows. Game was plentiful. Then we sat down to
tiffin—"bull-mate an' bran-bread," Mulvaney called it—
by the side of the river, and took pot shots at the croco-
diles in the intervals of cutting up the food with our
only pocket-knife. Then we drank up all the beer, and
threw the bottles into the water and fired at them.
After that, we eased belts and stretched ourselves on the
warm sand and smoked. We were too lazy to continue
shooting.

Ortheris heaved a big sigh, as he lay on his stomach
with his head between his fists. Then he swore quietly
into the blue sky.

"Fwhat's that for?" said Mulvaney. "Have ye not
drunk enough?"

"Tott'nim Court Road, an' a gal I fancied there.
Wot's the good of sodgerin'?"

"Orth'ris, me son," said Mulvaney, hastily, " 'tis more
than likely you've got throuble in your inside wid the
beer. I feel that way mesilf whin my liver gets rusty."

Ortheris went on slowly, not heeding the interruption—

"I'm a Tommy—a bloomin', eight-anna, dog-stealin'
Tommy, with a number instead of a decent name.
Wot's the good o' me? If I 'ad a stayed at 'Ome, I
might a married that gal and a kep' a little shorp in the
'Ammersmith 'Igh.—'S. Orth'ris, Prac-ti-cal Taxi-der-
mist.' With a stuff fox, like they 'as in the Haylesbury
Dairies, in the winder, an' a little case of blue and yaller
glass-heyes, an' a little wife to call 'shorp!' 'shorp!'

when the door-bell rung. As it *his*, I'm on'y a Tommy
—a Bloomin', Gawd-forsaken, Beer-swillin' Tommy.
'Rest on your harms—*'versed*, Stan' at—*hease; 'Shun.*
'Verse—*harms*. Right an' lef'—*tarrn*. Slow—*march*.
'Alt—*front*. Rest on your harms—*'versed*. With blank-
cartridge—*load*.' An' that's the end o' me." He was
quoting fragments from Funeral Parties' Orders.

"Stop ut!" shouted Mulvaney. "Whin you've fired
into nothin' as often as me, over a better man than
yoursilf, you will not make a mock av thim orders.
'Tis worse than whistlin' the *Dead March* in barricks.
An' you full as a tick, an' the sun cool, an' all an' all!
I take shame for you. You're no better than a Pagin—
you an' your firin'-parties an' your glass-eyes. Won't
you stop ut, sorr?"

What could I do? Could I tell Ortheris anything
that he did not know of the pleasures of his life? I
was not a Chaplain nor a Subaltern, and Ortheris had
a right to speak as he thought fit.

"Let him run, Mulvaney," I said. "It's the beer."

"No! 'Tisn't the beer," said Mulvaney. "I know
fwhat's comin'. He's tuk this way now an' agin, an'
it's bad—it's bad—for I'm fond av the bhoy."

Indeed, Mulvaney seemed needlessly anxious; but I
knew that he looked after Ortheris in a fatherly way.

"Let me talk, let me talk," said Ortheris, dreamily.
"D'you stop your parrit screamin' of a 'ot day, when
the cage is a-cookin' is pore little pink toes orf, Mulvaney?"

"Pink toes! D'ye mane to say you've pink toes undher your bullswools, ye blandanderin',"—Mulvaney

gathered himself together for a terrific denunciation—
"school-misthress! Pink toes! How much Bass wid
the label did that ravin' child dhrink?"

" 'Tain't Bass," said Ortheris. "It's a bitterer beer
nor that. It's 'omesickness!"

"Hark to him! An' he goin' Home in the *Sherapis*
in the inside av four months!"

"I don't care. It's all one to me. 'Ow d'you know I
ain't 'fraid o' dyin' 'fore I gets my discharge paipers?"
He recommenced, in a sing-song voice, the Orders.

I had never seen this side of Ortheris' character before, but evidently Mulvaney had, and attached serious
importance to it. While Ortheris babbled, with his head
on his arms, Mulvaney whispered to me—

"He's always tuk this way whin he's been checked
overmuch by the childher they make Sarjints nowa-
days. That an' havin' nothin' to do. I can't make ut
out anyways."

"Well, what does it matter? Let him talk himself
through."

Ortheris began singing a parody of "The Ramrod
Corps," full of cheerful allusions to battle, murder, and
sudden death. He looked out across the river as he
sang; and his face was quite strange to me. Mulvaney
caught me by the elbow to ensure attention.

"Matther? It matthers everything! 'Tis some sort
av fit that's on him. I've seen ut. 'Twill hould him all
this night, an' in the middle av it he'll get out av his
cot an' go rakin' in the rack for his 'coutremints. Thin
he'll come over to me an' say, 'I'm goin' to Bombay.
Answer for me in the mornin'.' Thin me an' him will

fight as we've done before—him to go an' me to hould him—an' so we'll both come on the books for disturbin' in barracks. I've belted him, an' I've bruk his head, an' I've talked to him, but 'tis no manner av use whin the fit's on him. He's as good a bhoy as ever stepped whin his mind's clear. I know fwhat's comin', though, this night in barracks. Lord send he doesn't loose on me whin I rise to knock him down. 'Tis that that's in my mind day an' night."

This put the case in a much less pleasant light, and fully accounted for Mulvaney's anxiety. He seemed to be trying to coax Ortheris out of the fit; for he shouted down the bank where the boy was lying—

"Listen now, you wid the 'pore pink toes' an' the glass-eyes! Did you shwim the Irriwaddy at night, behin' me, as a bhoy shud; or were you hidin' under a bed, as you was at Ahmid Kheyl?"

This was at once a gross insult and a direct lie, and Mulvaney meant it to bring on a fight. But Ortheris seemed shut up in some sort of trance. He answered slowly, without a sign of irritation, in the same cadenced voice as he had used for his firing-party orders—

"*Hi* swum the Irriwaddy in the night, as you know, for to take the town of Lungtungpen, nakid an' without fear. *Hand* where I was at Ahmed Kheyl you know, and four bloomin' Pathans know too. But that was summat to do, an' I didn't think o' dyin'. Now I'm sick to go 'Ome—go 'Ome—go 'Ome! No, I ain't mammy-sick, because my uncle brung me up, but I'm sick for London again; sick for the sounds of 'er, an' the sights of 'er, and the stinks of 'er; orange peel and hasphalte an' gas comin' in over Vaux'all Bridge. Sick for the rail goin' down to Box'ill, with your gal on your knee an' a new clay pipe in your face. That, an' the Stran' lights where you knows ev'ry one, an' the Copper that takes you up is a old friend that tuk you up before, when you was a little, smitchy boy lying loose 'tween the Temple an' the Dark Harches. No bloomin' guard-mountin', no bloomin' rotten-stone, nor khaki, an' yourself your own master with a gal to take an' see the Humaners practicin' a-hookin' dead corpses out of the Serpentine o' Sundays. An' I lef' all that for to serve the Widder beyond the seas, where there ain't no women and there ain't no liquor worth 'avin', and there ain't nothin' to see, nor do, nor say, nor feel, nor think. Lord love you, Stanley Orth'ris, but you're a bigger bloomin' fool than the rest o' the reg'ment and Mulvaney wired together! There's the Widder sittin' at 'Ome with a gold crownd on 'er 'ead; and 'ere am Hi, Stanley Orth'ris, the Widder's property, a rottin' FOOL!"

His voice rose at the end of the sentence, and he wound up with a six-shot Anglo-Vernacular oath. Mulvaney said nothing, but looked at me as if he expected that I could bring peace to poor Ortheris' troubled brain.

I remembered once at Rawal Pindi having seen a man, nearly mad with drink, sobered by being made a fool of. Some regiments may know what I mean. I hoped that we might slake off Ortheris in the same way, though he was perfectly sober. So I said—

"What's the use of grousing there, and speaking against The Widow?"

"I didn't!" said Ortheris. "S'elp me, Gawd, I never said a word agin 'er, an' I wouldn't—not if I was to desert this minute!"

Here was my opening. "Well, you meant to, anyhow. What's the use of cracking-on for nothing? Would you slip it now if you got the chance?"

"On'y try me!" said Ortheris, jumping to his feet as if he had been stung.

Mulvaney jumped too. "Fwhat are you going to do?" said he.

"Help Ortheris down to Bombay or Karachi, whichever he likes. You can report that he separated from you before tiffin, and left his gun on the bank here!"

"I'm to report that—am I?" said Mulvaney, slowly. "Very well. If Orth'ris manes to desert now, and will desert now, an' you, sorr, who have been a frind to me an' to him, will help him to ut, I, Terence Mulvaney, on my oath which I've never bruk yet, will report as you say. But"—here he stepped up to Ortheris, and shook the stock of the fowling-piece in his face—"your fists help you, Stanley Orth'ris, if ever I come across you agin!"

"I don't care!" said Ortheris. "I'm sick o' this dorg's life. Give me a chanst. Don't play with me. Le' me go!"

"Strip," said I, "and change with me, and then I'll tell you what to do."

I hoped that the absurdity of this would check Ortheris; but he had kicked off his ammunition-boots and got rid of his tunic almost before I had loosed my shirt-collar. Mulvaney gripped me by the arm—

"The fit's on him: the fit's workin' on him still! By my Honor and Sowl, we shall be accessiry to a desartion yet. Only, twenty-eight days, as you say, sorr, or fifty-six, but think o' the shame—the black shame to him an' me!" I had never seen Mulvaney so excited.

But Ortheris was quite calm, and, as soon as he had exchanged clothes with me, and I stood up a Private of the Line, he said shortly, "Now! Come on. What nex'? D'ye mean fair. What must I do to get out o' this 'ere a-Hell?"

I told him that, if he would wait for two or three hours near the river, I would ride into the Station and come back with one hundred rupees. He would, with that money in his pocket, walk to the nearest side-station on the line, about five miles away, and would there take a first-class ticket for Karachi. Knowing that he had no money on him when he went out shooting, his regiment would not immediately wire to the seaports, but would hunt for him in the native villages near the river. Further, no one would think of seeking a deserter in a first-class carriage. At Karachi, he was to buy white clothes and ship, if he could, on a cargo-steamer.

Here he broke in. If I helped him to Karachi, he would arrange all the rest. Then I ordered him to wait where he was until it was dark enough for me to ride into the station without my dress being noticed. Now God in His wisdom has made the heart of the British Soldier, who is very often an unlicked ruffian, as soft as the heart of a little child, in order that he may believe in and follow his officers into tight and nasty places. He does not so readily come to believe in a "civilian," but, when he does, he believes implicitly and like a dog. I had had the honor of the friendship of Private Ortheris, at intervals, for more than three years, and we had dealt with each other as man by man. Consequently, he considered that all my words were true, and not spoken lightly.

Mulvaney and I left him in the high grass near the river-bank, and went away, still keeping to the high grass, toward my horse. The shirt scratched me horribly.

We waited nearly two hours for the dusk to fall and allow me to ride off. We spoke of Ortheris in whispers, and strained our ears to catch any sound from the spot where we had left him. But we heard nothing except the wind in the plume-grass.

"I've bruk his head," said Mulvaney, earnestly, "time an' agin. I've nearly kilt him wid the belt, an' *yet* I can't knock thim fits out av his soft head. No! An' he's not soft, for he's reasonable an' likely by natur'. Fwhat is ut? Is ut his breedin' which is nothin', or his edukashin which he niver got? You that think ye know things, answer me that."

But I found no answer. I was wondering how long Ortheris, in the bank of the river, would hold out, and whether I should be forced to help him to desert, as I had given my word.

Just as the dusk shut down and, with a very heavy

heart, I was beginning to saddle up my horse, we heard wild shouts from the river.

The devils had departed from Private Stanley Ortheris, No. 22639, B Company. The loneliness, the dusk, and the waiting had driven them out as I had hoped. We set off at the double and found him plunging about wildly through the grass, with his coat off—my coat off, I mean. He was calling for us like a madman.

When we reached him he was dripping with perspiration, and trembling like a startled horse. We had great difficulty in soothing him. He complained that he was in civilian kit, and wanted to tear my clothes off his body. I ordered him to strip, and we made a second exchange as quickly as possible.

The rasp of his own "greyback" shirt and the squeak of his boots seemed to bring him to himself. He put his hands before his eyes and said—

"Wot was it? I ain't mad, I ain't sunstrook, an' I've bin an' gone an' said, an' bin an' gone an' done. . . . *Wot* 'ave I bin an' done!"

"Fwhat have you done?" said Mulvaney. "You've dishgraced yourself—though that's no matter. You've dishgraced B Comp'ny, an' worst av all, you've dishgraced *Me!* Me that taught you how for to walk abroad like a man—whin you was a dhirty little, fish-backed little, whimperin' little recruity. As you are now, Stanley Orth'ris!"

Ortheris said nothing for a while. Then he unslung his belt, heavy with the badges of half a dozen regiments that his own had lain with, and handed it over to Mulvaney.

"I'm too little for to mill you, Mulvaney," said he, "an' you've strook me before; but you can take an' cut me in two with this 'ere if you like."

Mulvaney turned to me.

"Lave me to talk to him, sorr," said Mulvaney.

I left, and on my way home thought a good deal over Ortheris in particular, and my friend Private Thomas Atkins whom I love, in general.

But I could not come to any conclusion of any kind whatever.

IN THE HOUSE OF SUDDHOO

A stone's throw out on either hand
From that well-ordered road we tread,
    And all the world is wild and strange:
Churel and ghoul and *Djinn* and sprite
Shall bear us company to-night,
    For we have reached the Oldest Land
Wherein the Powers of Darkness range.
                —*From the Dusk to the Dawn.*

THE house of Suddhoo, near the Taksali Gate, is two-storied, with four carved windows of old brown wood, and a flat roof. You may recognize it by five red hand-prints arranged like the Five of Diamonds on the whitewash between the upper windows. Bhagwan Dass the grocer and a man who says he gets his living by seal-cutting live in the lower story with a troop of wives, servants, friends, and retainers. The two upper rooms used to be occupied by Janoo and Azizun and a little black-and-tan terrier that was stolen from an Englishman's house and given to Janoo by a soldier. To-day, only Janoo lives in the upper rooms. Suddhoo sleeps on the roof generally, except when he sleeps in the street. He used to go to Peshawar in the cold weather to visit his son who sells curiosities near the Edwardes' Gate, and then he slept under a real mud roof. Suddhoo is a great friend of mine, because his cousin had a son who secured, thanks to my recommendation, the post of head-messenger to a big firm in the Station. Suddhoo says that God will make me a Lieutenant-Governor one of these days. I dare say his prophecy will come true. He is very, very old, with white hair and no teeth worth showing, and he has outlived his wits—outlived nearly everything except his fondness for his son at Peshawar. Janoo and Azizun are Kashmiris, Ladies of the City, and theirs was an ancient and more or less honorable profession; but Azizun has since married a medical student from the Northwest and has settled down to a most respectable life somewhere near Bareilly. Bhagwan Dass is an extortionate and an adulterator. He is very rich. The man who is supposed to get his living by seal-cutting pretends to be very poor. This lets you know as much as is necessary of the four principal tenants in the house of Suddhoo. Then there is Me of course; but I am only the chorus that comes in at the end to explain things. So I do not count.

Suddhoo was not clever. The man who pretended to cut seals was the cleverest of them all—Bhagwan Dass only knew how to lie—except Janoo. She was also beautiful, but that was her own affair.

Suddhoo's son at Peshawar was attacked by pleurisy, and old Suddhoo was troubled. The seal-cutter man heard of Suddhoo's anxiety and made capital out of it. He was abreast of the times. He got a friend in Peshawar to telegraph daily accounts of the son's health. And here the story begins.

Suddhoo's cousin's son told me, one evening, that

Suddhoo wanted to see me; that he was too old and feeble to come personally, and that I should be conferring an everlasting honor on the House of Suddhoo if I went to him. I went; but I think, seeing how well off Suddhoo was then, that he might have sent something better than an *ekka*, which jolted fearfully, to haul out a future Lieutenant-Governor to the City on a muggy April evening. The *ekka* did not run quickly. It was full dark when we pulled up opposite the door of Ranjit Singh's Tomb near the main gate of the Fort. Here was Suddhoo, and he said that, by reason of my condescension, it was absolutely certain that I should become a Lieutenant-Governor while my hair was yet black. Then we talked about the weather and the state of my health, and the wheat crops, for fifteen minutes in the Huzuri Bagh, under the stars.

Suddhoo came to the point at last. He said that Janoo had told him that there was an order of the *Sirkar* against magic, because it was feared that magic might one day kill the Empress of India. I didn't know anything about the state of the law; but I fancied that something interesting was going to happen. I said that so far from magic being discouraged by the Government it was highly commended. The greatest officials of the State practiced it themselves. (If the Financial Statement isn't magic, I don't know what is.) Then, to encourage him further, I said that, if there was any *jadoo* afoot, I had not the least objection to giving it my countenance and sanction, and to seeing that it was clean *jadoo*—white magic, as distinguished from the unclean *jadoo* which kills folk. It took a long

time before Suddhoo admitted that this was just what
he had asked me to come for. Then he told me, in
jerks and quavers, that the man who said he cut seals
was a sorcerer of the cleanest kind; that every day he
gave Suddhoo news of the sick son in Peshawar more
quickly than the lightning could fly, and that this news
was always corroborated by the letters. Further, that
he had told Suddhoo how a great danger was threaten-
ing his son, which could be removed by clean *jadoo;*
and, of course, heavy payment. I began to see exactly
how the land lay, and told Suddhoo that I also understand a little *jadoo* in the Western line, and would go
to his house to see that everything was done decently
and in order. We set off together; and on the way
Suddhoo told me that he had paid the seal-cutter between one hundred and two hundred rupees already;
and the *jadoo* of that night would cost two hundred
more. What was cheap, he said, considering the great-
ness of his son's danger; but I do not think he meant it.

The lights were all cloaked in the front of the house
when we arrived. I could hear awful noises from behind the seal-cutter's shop-front, as if some one were
groaning his soul out. Suddhoo shook all over, and
while we groped our way upstairs told me that the
jadoo had begun, Janoo and Azizun met us at the stair-
head, and told that the *jadoo*-work was coming off in
their rooms, because there was more space there. Janoo
is a lady of a freethinking turn of mind. She whispered that the *jadoo* was an invention to get money out
of Suddhoo, and that the seal-cutter would go to a hot
place when he died. Suddhoo was nearly crying with

fear and old age. He kept walking up and down the
room in the half-light, repeating his son's name over
and over again, and asking Azizun if the seal-cutter
ought not to make a reduction in the case of his own
landlord. Janoo pulled me over to the shadow in the
recess of the carved bow-windows. The boards were
up, and the rooms were only lit by one tiny oil-limp.
There was no chance of my being seen if I stayed still.

Presently, the groans below ceased, and we heard
steps on the staircase. That was the seal-cutter. He
stopped outside the door as the terrier barked and
Azizun fumbled at the chain, and he told Suddhoo to
blow out the lamp. This left the place in jet darkness,
except for the red glow from the two *huqas* that belonged to Janoo and Azizun. The seal-cutter came in,
and I heard Suddhoo throw himself down on the floor
and groan. Azizun caught her breath, and Janoo
backed on to one of the beds with a shudder. There
was a clink of something metallic, and then shot up a
pale blue-green flame near the ground. The light was
just enough to show Azizun, pressed against one corner
of the room with the terrier between her knees; Janoo,
with her hands clasped, leaning forward as she sat on
the bed; Suddhoo, face down, quivering, and the seal-
cutter.

I hope I may never see another man like that seal-
cutter. He was stripped to the waist, with a wreath of
white jasmine as thick as my wrist round his forehead,
a salmon colored loin-cloth round his middle, and a
steel bangle on each ankle. This was not awe-inspir-
ing. It was the face of the man that turned me cold.

It was blue-grey in the first place. In the second, the eyes were rolled back till you could only see the whites of them; and, in the third, the face was the face of a demon—a ghoul—anything you please except of the sleek, oily old ruffian who sat in the daytime over his turning-lathe downstairs. He was lying on his stomach with his arms turned and crossed behind him, as if he had been thrown down pinioned. His head and neck were the only parts of him off the floor. They were neatly at right angles to the body, like the head of a cobra at spring. It was ghastly. In the centre of the room, on the bare earth floor, stood a big, deep, brass basin, with a pale blue-green light floating in the centre like a night-light. Round that basin the man on the floor wriggled himself three times. How he did it I do not know. I could see the muscles ripple along his spine and fall smooth again; but I could not see any other motion. The head seemed the only thing alive about him, except that slow curl and uncurl of the laboring back-muscles. Janoo from the bed was breathing seventy to the minute; Azizun held her hands before her eyes; and old Suddhoo, fingering at the dirt that had got into his white beard, was crying to himself. The horror of it was that the creeping, crawly thing made no sound—only crawled! And, remember, this lasted for ten minutes, while the terrier whined, and Azizun shuddered, and Janoo gasped, and Suddhoo cried.

I felt the hair lift at the back of my head, and my heart thump like a thermantidote paddle. Luckily, the seal-cutter betrayed himself by his most impressive trick and made me calm again. After he had finished that unspeakable triple crawl, he stretched his head away from the floor as high as he could, and sent out a jet of fire from his nostrils. Now I knew how fire-spouting is done—I can do it myself—so I felt at ease. The business was a fraud. If he had only kept to that crawl without trying to raise the effect, goodness knows what I might not have thought. Both the girls shrieked at the jet of fire and the head dropped, chin-down on the floor, with a thud; the whole body lying then like a corpse with its arms trussed. There was a pause of five full minutes after this, and the blue-green flame died down. Janoo stooped to settle one of her anklets, while Azizun turned her face to the wall and took the terrier in her arms. Suddhoo put out an arm mechanically to Janoo's *huqa,* and she slid it across the floor with her foot. Directly above the body and on the wall, were a couple of flaming portraits, in stamped-paper frames, of the Queen and the Prince of Wales. They looked down on the performance, and to my thinking, seemed to heighten the grotesqueness of it all.

Just when the silence was getting unendurable, the body turned over and rolled away from the basin to the side of the room, where it lay stomach-up. There was a faint "plop" from the basin—exactly like the noise a fish makes when it takes a fly—and the green light in the centre revived.

I looked at the basin, and saw, bobbing in the water, the dried, shrivelled, black head of a native baby—open eyes, open mouth, and shaved scalp. It was worse, being so very sudden, than the crawling exhibition.

We had no time to say anything before it began to speak.

Read Poe's account of the voice that came from the mesmerized dying man, and you will realize less than one half of the horror of that head's voice.

There was an interval of a second or two between each word, and a sort of "ring, ring, ring," in the note of the voice, like the timbre of a bell. It pealed slowly, as if talking to itself, for several minutes before I got rid of my cold sweat. Then the blessed solution struck me. I looked at the body lying near the doorway, and saw, just where the hollow of the throat joins on the shoulders, a muscle that had nothing to do with any man's regular breathing twitching away steadily. The whole thing was a careful reproduction of the Egyptian teraphin that one reads about sometimes; and the voice was as clever and as appalling a piece of ventriloquism as one could wish to hear. All this time the head was "lip-lip-lapping" against the side of the basin, and speaking. It told Suddhoo, on his face again whining, of his son's illness and of the state of the illness up to the evening of that very night. I always shall respect the seal-cutter for keeping so faithfully to the time of the Peshawar telegrams. It went on to say that skilled doctors were night and day watching over the man's life; and that he would eventually recover if the fee to the potent sorcerer, whose servant was the head in the basin, were doubled.

Here the mistake from the artistic point of view came in. To ask for twice your stipulated fee in a voice that Lazarus might have used when he rose from the dead, 's absurd. Janoo, who is really a woman of masculine intellect, saw this as quickly as I did. I heard her say "*Asli nahin! Fareib!*" scornfully under her breath; and just as she said so, the light in the basin died out, the head stopped talking, and we heard the room door creak on its hinges. Then Janoo struck a match, lit the lamp, and we saw that head, basin, and seal-cutter were gone. Suddhoo was wringing his hands and explaining to any one who cared to listen, that, if his chances of eternal salvation depended on it, he could not raise another two hundred rupees. Azizun was nearly in hysterics in the corner; while Janoo sat down composedly on one of the beds to discuss the probabilities of the whole thing being a *bunao,* or "make-up."

I explained as much as I knew of the seal-cutter's way of *jadoo;* but her argument was much more simple—"The magic that is always demanding gifts is no true magic," said she. "My mother told me that the only potent love-spells are those which are told you for love. This seal-cutter man is a liar and a devil. I dare not tell, do anything, or get anything done, because I am in debt to Bhagwan Dass the bunnia for two gold rings and a heavy anklet. I must get my food from his shop. The seal-cutter is the friend of Bhagwan Dass, and he would poison my food. A fool's *jadoo* has been going on for ten days, and has cost Suddhoo many rupees each night. The seal-cutter used black hens and lemons and *mantras* before. He never showed anything like this till to-night. Azizun is a fool, and will be a *purdahnashin* soon. Suddhoo has lost his strength and his wits. See now! I had hoped to get from Suddhoo many rupees while he lived, and many more after his death; and behold, he is spending everything on that offspring of a devil and a she-ass, the seal-cutter!"

Here I said, "But what induced Suddhoo to drag me into the business? Of course I can speak to the seal-cutter, and he shall refund. The whole thing is child's talk—shame—and senseless."

"Suddhoo *is* an old child," said Janoo. "He has lived on the roofs these seventy years and is as senseless as a milch-goat. He brought you here to assure himself that he was not breaking any law of the *Sirkar*, whose salt he ate many years ago. He worships the dust off the feet of the seal-cutter, and that cow-devourer has forbidden him to go and see his son. What does Suddhoo know of your laws or the lightning-post? I have to watch his money going day by day to that lying beast below."

Janoo stamped her foot on the floor and nearly cried with vexation; while Suddhoo was whimpering under a blanket in the corner, and Azizun was trying to guide the pipe-stem to his foolish old mouth.

·   ·   ·   ·   ·   ·   ·

Now, the case stands thus. Unthinkingly, I have laid myself open to the charge of aiding and abetting the seal-cutter in obtaining money under false pretences, which is forbidden by Section 420 of the Indian Penal Code. I am helpless in the matter for these reasons. I cannot inform the Police. What witnesses would support my statements? Janoo refuses flatly, and Azizun is a veiled woman somewhere near Bareilly—lost in this big India of ours. I dare not again take the law into my own hands, and speak to the seal-cutter; for certain am I that, not only would Suddhoo disbelieve me, but this step would end in the poisoning of Janoo, who is bound hand and foot by her debt to the *bunnia.* Suddhoo is an old dotard; and whenever we meet mumbles my idiotic joke that the *Sirkar* rather patronizes the Black Art than otherwise. His son is well now; but Suddhoo is completely under the influence of the seal-cutter, by whose advice he regulates the affairs of his life. Janoo watches daily the money that she hoped to wheedle out of Suddhoo taken by the seal-cutter, and becomes daily more furious and sullen.

She will never tell, because she dare not; but, unless something happens to prevent her, I am afraid that the seal-cutter would die of cholera—the white arsenic kind—about the middle of May. And thus I shall be privy to a murder in the House of Suddhoo.

THE STORY OF MUHAMMAD DIN

Who is the happy man? He that sees in his own house at home, little children crowned with dust, leaping and falling and crying.—*Munichandra,* translated by Professor Peterson.

THE polo-ball was an old one, scarred, chipped, and dinted. It stood on the mantelpiece among the pipe-stems which Imam Din, *khitmatgar,* was cleaning for me.

"Does the Heaven-born want this ball?" said Imam Din, deferentially.

The Heaven-born set no particular store by it; but of what use was a polo-ball to a *khitmatgar?*

"By your Honor's favor, I have a little son. He has seen this ball, and desires it to play with. I do not want it for myself."

No one would for an instant accuse portly old Imam Din of wanting to play with polo-balls. He carried out the battered thing into the veranda; and there followed a hurricane of joyful squeaks, a patter of small feet, and the *thud-thud-thud* of the ball rolling along the ground. Evidently the little son had been waiting outside the door to secure his treasure. But how had he managed to see that polo-ball?

Next day, coming back from office half an hour earlier than usual, I was aware of a small figure in the dining-room—a tiny, plump figure in a ridiculously in-adequate shirt which came, perhaps, half-way down the tubby stomach. It wandered round the room, thumb in mouth, crooning to itself as it took stock of the pic-tures. Undoubtedly this was the "little son."

He had no business in my room, of course; but was so deeply absorbed in his discoveries that he never noticed me in the doorway. I stepped into the room and startled him nearly into a fit. He sat down on the ground with a gasp. His eyes opened, and his mouth followed suit. I knew what was coming, and fled, followed by a long, dry howl which reached the serv-ants' quarters far more quickly than any command of mine had ever done. In ten seconds Imam Din was in the dining-room. Then despairing sobs arose, and I returned to find Imam Din admonishing the small sinner who was using most of his shirt as a hand-kerchief.

"This boy," said Imam Din, judicially, "is a *bud-mash*—a big *budmash*. He will, without doubt, go to the *jail-khana* for his behavior." Renewed yells from the penitent, and an elaborate apology to myself from Imam Din.

"Tell the baby," said I, "that the *Sahib* is not angry, and take him away." Imam Din conveyed my for-giveness to the offender, who had now gathered all his shirt round his neck, stringwise, and the yell subsided into a sob. The two set off for the door. "His name," said Imam Din, as though the name were part of the crime, "is Muhammad Din, and he is a *budmash*." Freed from present danger, Muhammad Din turned round in his father's arms, and said gravely, "It is true that my name is Muhammad Din, *Tahib,* but I am not a *budmash.* I am a *man!"*

From that day dated my acquaintance with Muhammad Din. Never again did he come into my dining-room, but on the neutral ground of the garden, we greeted each other with much state, though our conversation was confined to *"Talaam, Tahib"* from his side, and *"Salaam, Muhammad Din"* from mine. Daily on my return from office, the little white shirt, and the fat little body used to rise from the shade of the creeper-covered trellis where they had been hid; and daily I checked my horse here, that my salutation might not be slurred over or given unseemly.

Muhammad Din never had any companions. He used to trot about the compound, in and out of the castor-oil bushes, on mysterious errands of his own. One day I stumbled upon some of his handiwork far down the grounds. He had half buried the polo-ball in dust, and stuck six shriveled old marigold flowers in a circle round it. Outside that circle again was a rude square, traced out in bits of red brick alternating with fragments of broken china; the whole bounded by a little bank of dust. The water-man from the well-curb put in a plea for the small architect, saying that it was only the play of a baby and did not much disfigure my garden.

Heaven knows that I had no intention of touching the child's work then or later; but, that evening, a stroll through the garden brought me unawares full on it; so that I trampled, before I knew, marigold-heads, dust-bank, and fragments of broken soap-dish into confusion past all hope of mending. Next morning, I came upon Muhammad Din crying softly to himself over the ruin I had wrought. Some one had cruelly told him that the *Sahib* was very angry with him for spoiling the garden, and had scattered his rubbish, using bad language the while. Muhammad Din labored for an hour at effacing every trace of the dust-bank and pottery fragments, and it was with a tearful and apologetic face that he said *"Talaam, Tahib,"* when I came home from office. A hasty inquiry resulted in Imam Din informing Muhammad Din that, by my singular favor, he was permitted to disport himself as he pleased. Whereat the child took heart and fell to tracing the ground-plan of an edifice which was to eclipse the marigold-polo-ball creation.

For some months, the chubby little eccentricity revolved in his humble orbit among the castor-oil bushes and in the dust; always fashioning magnificent palaces from stale flowers thrown away by the bearer, smooth water-worn pebbles, bits of broken glass, and feathers pulled, I fancy, from my fowls—always alone, and always crooning to himself.

A gaily-spotted sea-shell was dropped one day close to the last of his little buildings; and I looked that Muhammad Din should build something more than ordinarily splendid on the strength of it. Nor was I disappointed. He meditated for the better part of an hour, and his crooning rose to a jubilant song. Then he began tracing in the dust. It would certainly be a wondrous palace, this one, for it was two yards long

and a yard broad in ground-plan. But the palace was
never completed.

Next day there was no Muhammad Din at the head
of the carriage-drive, and no *"Talaam, Tahib"* to welcome my return. I had grown accustomed to the greeting, and its omission troubled me. Next day Imam
Din told me that the child was suffering slightly from
fever and needed quinine. He got the medicine, and
an English Doctor.

"They have no stamina, these brats," said the Doctor,
as he left Imam Din's quarters.

A week later, though I would have given much to
have avoided it, I met on the road to the Mussulman
burying-ground Imam Din, accompanied by one other
friend, carrying in his arms, wrapped in a white cloth
all that was left of little Muhammad Din.

THE BIG DRUNK DRAF'

We're goin' 'ome, we're goin' 'ome—
Our ship is *at* the shore,
An' you mus' pack your 'aversack,
For we won't come back no more.
Ho, don't you grieve for me,
My lovely Mary Ann,
For I'll marry you yet on a fourp'ny bit,
As a time-expired ma-a-an!
—*Barrack Room Ballad.*

AN awful thing has happened! My friend, Private
Mulvaney, who went home in the *Serapis,* time-
expired, not very long ago, has come back to India as a civilian! It was all Dinah Shadd's fault. She
could not stand the poky little lodgings, and she missed
her servant Abdullah more than words could tell. The
fact was that the Mulvaneys had been out here too long,
and had lost touch of England.

Mulvaney knew a contractor on one of the new Central India lines, and wrote to him for some sort of work.
The contractor said that if Mulvaney could pay the
passage he would give him command of a gang of
coolies for old sake's sake. The pay was eighty-five
rupees a month, and Dinah Shadd said that if Terence
did not accept she would make his life a "basted purgathory." Therefore the Mulvaneys came out as "civil-

ians," which was a great and terrible fall; though Mulvaney tried to disguise it, by saying that he was 'Ker'nel on the railway line, an' a consequinshal man."

He wrote me an invitation, on a tool-indent form, to visit him; and I came down to the funny little "construction" bungalow at the side of the line. Dinah Shadd had planted peas about and about, and nature had spread all manner of green stuff around the place. There was no change in Mulvaney except the change of clothing, which was deplorable, but could not be helped. He was standing upon his trolly, haranguing a gang-man, and his shoulders were as well drilled, and his big, thick chin was as clean-shaven as ever.

"I'm a civilian now," said Mulvaney. "Cud you tell that I was iver a martial man? Don't answer, sorr, av you're strainin' betune a complimint an' a lie. There's no houldin' Dinah Shadd now she's got a house av her own. Go inside, an' dhrink tay out av chiny in the drrrrawin'-room, an' thin we'll dhrink like Christians undher the tree here. Scutt, ye naygur-folk! There's a Sahib come to call on me, an' that's more than he'll iver do for you onless you run! Get out, an' go on pilin' up the earth, quick, till sundown."

When we three were comfortably settled under the big *sisham* in front of the bungalow, and the first rush of questions and answers about Privates Ortheris and Learoyd and old times and places had died away, Mulvaney said, reflectively—"Glory be there's no p'rade tomorrow, an' no bun-headed Corp'ril-bhoy to give you his lip. An' yit I don't know. 'Tis harrd to be something ye niver were an' niver meant to be, an' all the

ould days shut up along wid your papers. Eyah! I'm
growin' rusty, an' 'tis the will av God that a man
mustn't serve his Quane for time an' all."

He helped himself to a fresh peg, and sighed furiously.

"Let your beard grow, Mulvaney," said I, "and then
you won't be troubled with those notions. You'll be a
real civilian."

Dinah Shadd had told me in the drawing-room of
her desire to coax Mulvaney into letting his beard grow.
" 'Twas so civilian-like," said poor Dinah, who hated
her husband's hankering for his old life.

"Dinah Shadd, you're a dishgrace to an honust, clane-
scraped man!" said Mulvaney, without replying to me.
"Grow a beard on your own chin, darlint, and lave my
razors alone. They're all that stand betune me and dis-
ris-pect-ability. Av I didn't shave, I wud be torminted
wid an outrajis thurrst; for there's nothin' so dhryin' to
the throat as a big billy-goat beard waggin' undher the
chin. Ye wudn't have me dhrink *always,* Dinah
Shadd? By the same token, you're kapin' me crool
dhry now. Let me look at that whiskey."

The whiskey was lent and returned, but Dinah
Shadd, who had been just as eager as her husband in
asking after old friends, rent me with—

"I take shame for you, sorr, coming down here—
though the Saints know you're as welkim as the daylight whin you *do* come—an' upsettin' Terence's head
wid your nonsense about—about fwhat's much better
forgotten. He bein' a civilian now, an' you niver was

aught else. Can you not let the Arrmy rest? 'Tis not good for Terence."

I took refuge by Mulvaney, for Dinah Shadd has a temper of her own.

"Let be—let be," said Mulvaney. " 'Tis only wanst in a way I can talk about the ould days." Then to me:—"Ye say Dhrumshticks is well, an' his lady tu? I niver knew how I liked the grey garron till I was shut av him an' Asia."—"Dhrumshticks" was the nickname of the Colonel commanding Mulvaney's old regiment.—"Will you be seein' him again? You will. Thin tell him"—Mulvaney's eyes began to twinkle—"tell him wid Privit"—

"*Mister,* Terence," interrupted Dinah Shadd.

"Now the Divil an' all his angils an' the Firmament av Hiven fly away wid the 'Mister,' an' the sin av making me swear be on your confession, Dinah Shadd! *Privit,* I tell ye. Wid *Privit* Mulvaney's best obedience, that but for me the last time-expired wud be still pullin' hair on their way to the sea."

He threw himself back in the chair, chuckled, and was silent.

"Mrs. Mulvaney," I said, "please take up the whiskey, and don't let him have it until he has told the story."

Dinah Shadd dexterously whipped the bottle away, saying at the same time, " 'Tis nothing to be proud av," and thus captured by the enemy, Mulvaney spake:—

" 'Twas on Chuseday week. I was behaderin' round wid the gangs on the 'bankmint—I've taught the hoppers how to kape step an' stop screechin'—whin a head gangman comes up to me, wid about two inches av shirt-tail hanging round his neck an' a disthressful light in his oi. 'Sahib,' sez he, 'there's a reg'mint an' a half av soldiers up at the junction, knockin' red cinders out av ivrything an' ivrybody! They thried to hang me in my cloth,' he sez, 'an' there will be murder an' ruin an' rape in the place before nightfall! They say they're comin' down here to wake us up. What will we do wid our women-folk?'

" 'Fetch my throlly!' sez I; 'my heart's sick in my ribs for a wink at anything wid the Quane's uniform on ut. Fetch my throlly, an' six av the jildiest men, and run me up in shtyle.' "

"He tuk his best coat," said Dinah Shadd, reproach-fully.

" 'Twas to do honor to the Widdy. I cud ha' done no less, Dinah Shadd. You and your digresshins in-terfere wid the coorse av the narrative. Have you iver considhered fwhat I wud look like wid me *head* shaved as well as my chin? You bear that in your mind, Dinah darlin'.

"I was throllied up six miles, all to get a shquint at that draf'. I *knew* 'twas a spring draf' goin' home, for there's no rig'mint hereabouts, more's the pity."

"Praise the Virgin!" murmured Dinah Shadd. But Mulvaney did not hear.

"Whin I was about three-quarters av a mile off the rest-camp, powtherin' along fit to burrst, I heard the noise av the men an', on my sowl, sorr, I cud catch the voice av Peg Barney bellowin' like a bison wid the belly-ache. You remimber Peg Barney that was in D Comp'ny—a red, hairy scraun, wid a scar on his jaw?

Peg Barney that cleared out the Blue Lights' Jubilee meeting wid the cook-room mop last year?

"Thin I knew ut was a draf' of the ould rig'mint, an' I was conshumed wid sorrow for the bhoy that was in charge. We was harrd scrapin's at any time. Did I iver tell you how Horker Kelley went into clink nakid as Phœbus Apollonius, wid the shirts av the Corp'ril an' file undher his arrum? An' *he* was a moild man! But I'm digreshin'. 'Tis a shame both to the rig'mints and the Arrmy sendin' down little orf'cer bhoys wid a draf' av strong men mad wid liquor an' the chanst av gettin' shut av India, an' *niver a punishment that's fit to be given right down an' away from cantonmints to the dock!* 'Tis this nonsince. Whin I am servin' my time, I'm undher the Articles av War, an' can be whipped on the peg for *thim*. But whin I've *served* my time, I'm a Reserve man, an' the Articles av War haven't any hould on me. An orf'cer *can't* do anthin' to a time-expired savin' confinin' him to barricks. 'Tis a wise rig'lation bekaze a time-expired does *not* have any barricks; bein' on the move all the time. 'Tis a Solomon av a rig'lation, is that. I wud like to be in-throduced to the man that made ut. 'Tis easier to get colts from a Kibbereen horse-fair into Galway than to take a bad draf' over ten miles av country. Consiquintly that rig'lation—for fear that the men wud be hurt by the little orf'cer bhoy. No matther. The nearer my throlly came to the rest-camp, the woilder was the shine, an' the louder was the voice av Peg Barney. ' 'Tis good I am here,' thinks I to myself, 'for Peg alone is employmint for two or three.' He bein', I well knew, as copped as a dhrover.

"Faith, that rest-camp was a sight! The tent-ropes was all skew-nosed, an' the pegs looked as dhrunk as the men—fifty av thim—the scourin's, an' rinsin's, an' Divil's lavin's av the Ould Rig'mint. I tell you, sorr, they were dhrunker than any men you've ever seen in your moitial life. *How* does a draf' get dhrunk? How does a frog get fat? They suk ut in through their shkins.

"There was Peg Barney sittin' on the groun' in his shirt—wan shoe off an' wan shoe on—whackin' a tent-peg over the head wid his boot, an' singin' fit to wake the dead. 'Twas no clane song that he sung, though. 'Twas the Divil's Mass."

"What's that?" I asked.

"Whin a bad egg is shut av the Army, he sings the Divil's Mass for a good riddance; an' that manes swearin' at ivrything from the Commandher-in-Chief down to the Room Corp'ril, such as you niver in your days heard. Some men can swear so as to make green turf crack! Have you iver heard the Curse in an Orange Lodge? The Divil's Mass is ten times worse, an' Peg Barney was singin' ut, whackin' the tent-peg on the head wid his boot for each man that he cursed. A powerful big voice had Peg Barney, an' a hard swearer he was whin sober. I stood forninst him, an' 'twas not me oi alone that cud tell Peg was dhrunk as a coot.

"'Good mornin', Peg,' I sez, whin he dhrew breath afther cursin' the Adj'tint Gen'ral; 'I've put on my best coat to see you, Peg Barney,' sez I.

" 'Thin take ut off again,' sez Peg Barney, latherin' away wid the boot; 'take ut off an' dance, ye lousy civilian!'

"Wid that he begins cursin' ould Dhrumshticks, be-ing so full he clean disremimbers the Brigade-Major an' the Judge Advokit Gen'ral.

" 'Do you not know me, Peg?' sez I, though me blood was hot in me wid being called a civilian."

"An' him a decent married man!" wailed Dinah Shadd.

" 'I do not,' sez Peg, 'but dhrunk or sober I'll tear the hide off your back wid a shovel whin I've stopped singin'.'

" ' 'Say you so, Peg Barney?' sez I. ' 'Tis clear as mud you've forgotten me. I'll assist your autobiography.' Wid that I stretched Peg Barney, boot an' all, an' wint into the camp. An awful sight ut was!

" 'Where's the orf'cer in charge av the detachment?' sez I to Scrub Greene—the manest little worm that ever walked.

" 'There's no orf'cer, ye ould cook,' sez Scrub; 'we're a bloomin' Republic.'

" ' 'Are you that?' sez I; 'thin I'm O'Connell the Dic-tator, an' by this you will larn to keep a civil tongue in your rag-box.'

"Wid that I stretched Scrub Greene an' wint to the orf'cer's tent. 'Twas a new little bhoy—not wan I'd iver seen before. He was sittin' in his tent, purtendin' not to 'ave ear av the racket.

"I saluted—but for the life av me I mint to shake

hands whin I went in. 'Twas the sword hangin' on the tent-pole changed my will.

" 'Can't I help, sorr?' sez I; ' 'tis a strong man's job they've given you, an' you'll be wantin' help by sundown.' He was a bhoy wid bowils, that child, an' a rale gintleman.

" 'Sit down,' sez he.

" 'Not before my orf'cer,' sez I; an' I tould him fwhat my service was.

" 'I've heard uv you,' sez he. 'You tuk the town av Lungtungpen nakid.'

" 'Faith,' thinks I, 'that's Honor an' Glory;' for 'twas Lift'nint Brazenose did that job. 'I'm wid ye, sorr,' sez I, 'if I'm av use. They shud niver ha' sent you down wid the draf'. Savin' your presince, sorr,' I sez, ' 'tis only Lift'nint Hackerston in the Ould Reg'mint can manage a Home draf'.'

" 'I've niver had charge of men like this before,' sez he, playin' wid the pens on the table; 'an' I see by the Rig'lations'—

" 'Shut your oi to the Rig'lations, sorr,' I sez, 'till the throoper's into blue wather. By the Rig'lations you've got to tuck thim up for the night, or they'll be runnin' foul av my coolies an' makin' a shiverarium half through the country. Can you trust your noncoms, sorr?'

" 'Yes,' sez he.

" 'Good,' sez I; 'there'll be throuble before the night. Are you marchin', sorr?'

" 'To the next station,' sez he.

" 'Better still,' sez I; 'there'll be big throuble.'

"'Can't be too hard on a Home draf',' sez he; 'the great thing is to get thim in-ship.'

"'Faith you've larnt the half av your lesson, sorr,' sez I, 'but av you shtick to the Rig'lations you'll niver get thim in-ship at all, at all. Or there won't be a rag av kit betune thim whin you do.'

"'Twas a dear little orf'cer bhoy, an' by way av kapin' his heart up, I tould him fwhat I saw wanst in a draf' in Egypt."

"What was that, Mulvaney?" said I.

"Sivin an' fifty men sittin' on the bank av a canal, laughin' at a poor little squidgereen av an orf'cer that they'd made wade into the slush an' pitch the things out av the boats for their Lord High Mightinesses. That made me orf'cer bhoy woild wid indignation.

"'Soft an' aisy, sorr,' sez I; 'you've niver had your draf' in hand since you left cantonmints. Wait till the night, an' your work will be ready to you. Wid your permission, sorr, I will investigate the camp, an' talk to my ould friends. 'Tis no manner av use thryin' to shtop the divilmint now.'

"Wid that I wint out into the camp an' inthrojuced mysilf to ivry man sober enough to remimber me. I was some wan in the ould days, an' the bhoys was glad to see me—all excipt Peg Barney wid a oi like a tomata five days in the bazar, an' a nose to match. They come round me an' shuk me, an' I tould thim I was in privit employ wid an income av me own, an' a drrrawin'-room fit to bate the Quane's; an' wid me lies an' me shtories an' nonsinse gin'rally, I kept 'em quiet in wan way an' another, knockin' roun' the camp.

'Twas *bad* even thin whin I was the Angil av Peace.

"I talked to me ould non-coms—*they* was sober— an' betune me an' thim we wore the draf' over into their tents at the proper time. The little orf'cer bhoy he comes round, decint an' civil-spoken as might be.

" 'Rough quarters, men,' sez he, 'but you can't look to be as comfortable as in barricks. We must make the best av things. I've shut my eyes to a dale av dog's tricks to-day, an' now there must be no more av ut.'

" 'No more we will. Come an' have a dhrink, me son,' sez Peg Barney, staggerin' where he stud. Me little orf'cer bhoy kep' his timper.

" 'You're a sulky swine, you are,' sez Peg Barney, an' at that the men in the tent began to laugh.

"I tould you me orf'cer bhoy had bowils. He cut Peg Barney as near as might be on the oi that I'd squshed whin we first met. Peg wint spinnin' acrost the tent.

" 'Peg him out, sorr,' sez I, in a whisper.

" 'Peg him out!' sez me orf'cer bhoy, up loud, just as if 'twas battalion-p'rade an' he pickin' his wurds from the Sargint.

"The non-coms tuk Peg Barney—a howlin' handful he was—an' in three minuts he was pegged out—chin down, tight-dhrawn—on his stummick, a tent-peg to each arm an' leg, swearin' fit to turn a naygur white.

"I tuk a peg an' jammed ut into his ugly jaw.—'Bite on that, Peg Barney,' I sez; 'the night is settin' frosty, an' you'll be wantin' divarsion before the mornin'. But for the Rig'lations you'd be bitin' on a bullet now at the thriangles, Peg Barney,' sez I.

"All the draf' was out av their tents watchin' Barney bein' pegged.

" ' 'Tis agin the Rig'lations! He strook him!' screeches out Scrub Greene, who was always a lawyer; an' some of the men tuk up the shoutin'.

" 'Peg out that man!' sez my orf'cer bhoy, niver losin' his timper; an' the non-coms wint in and pegged out Scrub Greene by the side av Peg Barney.

" 'I cud see that the draf' was comin' roun'. The men stud not knowin' fwhat to do.

" 'Get to your tents!' sez me orf'cer bhoy. 'Sargint, put a sintry over these two men.'

"The men wint back into the tents like jackals, an' the rest av the night there was no noise at all excipt the stip av the sintry over the two, an' Scrub Greene blubberin' like a child. 'Twas a chilly night, an' faith, ut sobered Peg Barney.

"Just before Revelly, my orf'cer bhoy comes out an' sez: 'Loose those men an' send thim to their tents!' Scrub Greene wint away widout a word, but Peg Barney, stiff wid the cowld, stud like a sheep, thryin' to make his orf'cer undershtand he was sorry for playin' the goat.

"There was no tucker in the draf' whin ut fell in for the march, an' divil a wurrd about 'illegality' cud I hear.

"I wint to the ould Color Sargint and I sez:—'Let me die in glory,' sez I. 'I've seen a man this day!'

" ' 'A man he is,' sez ould Hother; 'the draf's as sick as a herrin'. They'll all go down to the sea like lambs. That bhoy has the bowils av a cantonmint av Gin'rals.'

" 'Amin,' sez I, 'an' good luck go wid him, wheriver he be, by land or by sea. Let me know how the draf' gets clear.'

"An do you know how they *did?* That bhoy, so I was tould by letter from Bombay, bullydamned 'em down to the dock, till they cudn't call their sowls their own. From the time they left me oi till they was 'tween decks, not wan av thim was more than dacintly dhrunk. An', by the Holy Articles av War, whin they wint abroad they cheered him till they cudn't spake, an' *that,* mark you, has not come about wid a draf' in the mim'ry av livin' man! You look to that little orf'cer bhoy. He has bowils. 'Tis not ivry child that wud chuck the Rig'lations to Flanders an' stretch Peg Barney on a wink from a brokin' an' dilapidated ould carkiss like mesilf. I'd be proud to serve"—

"Terence, you're a civilian," said Dinah Shadd, warningly.

"So I am—so I am. Is ut likely I wud forget ut? But he was a gran' bhoy all the same, an' I'm only a mudtipper wid a hod on my shoulthers. The whiskey's in the heel av your hand, sorr. Wid your good lave we'll dhrink to the Ould Rig'mint—three fingers—standin' up!"

And we drank.

HIS MAJESTY THE KING

"Where the word of a King is, there is power: And who
may say unto him—What doest thou?"

"YETH! And Chimo to sleep at ve foot of ve bed,
and ve pink pikky-book, and ve bwead—'cause
I will be hungwy in ve night—and vat's all,
Miss Biddums. And now give me one kiss and I'll go
to sleep.—So! Kite quiet. Ow! Ve pink pikky-book
has slidded under ve pillow and ve bwead is cwum-
bling! Miss Biddums! Miss *Bid*dums! I'm *so* un-
comfy! Come and tuck me up, Miss Biddums."

His Majesty the King was going to bed; and poor,
patient Miss Biddums, who had advertised herself hum-
bly as a "young person, European, accustomed to the
care of little children," was forced to wait upon his
royal caprices. The going to bed was always a lengthy
process, because His Majesty had a convenient knack
of forgetting which of his many friends, from the
mehter's son to the Commissioner's daughter, he had
prayed for, and, lest the Deity should take offence, was
used to toil through his little prayers, in all reverence,
five times in one evening. His Majesty the King believed in the efficacy of prayer as devoutly as he believed
in Chimo the patient spaniel, or Miss Biddums, who
could reach him down his gun—"with cursuffun caps

259

—*reel* ones"—from the upper shelves of the big nursery cupboard.

At the door of the nursery his authority stopped. Beyond lay the empire of his father and mother—two very terrible people who had no time to waste upon His Majesty the King. His voice was lowered when he passed the frontier of his own dominions, his actions were fettered, and his soul was filled with awe because of the grim man who lived among a wilderness of pigeon-holes and the most fascinating pieces of red tape, and the wonderful woman who was always getting into or stepping out of the big carriage.

To the one belonged the mysteries of the "*duftar-room*"; to the other the great, reflected wilderness of the "Memsahib's room" where the shiny, scented dresses hung on pegs, miles and miles up in the air, and the just-seen plateau of the toilet-table revealed an acreage of speckly combs, broidered "hanafitch bags," and "white-headed" brushes.

There was no room for His Majesty the King either in official reserve or mundane gorgeousness. He had discovered that, ages and ages ago—before even Chimo came to the house, or Miss Biddums had ceased grizzling over a packet of greasy letters which appeared to be her chief treasure on earth. His Majesty the King, therefore, wisely confined himself to his own territories, where only Miss Biddums, and she feebly, disputed his sway.

From Miss Biddums he had picked up his simple theology and welded it to the legends of gods and devils that he had learned in the servants' quarters.

To Miss Biddums he confided with equal trust his tattered garments and his more serious griefs. She would make everything whole. She knew exactly how the Earth had been born, and had reassured the trembling soul of His Majesty the King that terrible time in July when it rained continuously for seven days and seven nights, and—there was no Ark ready and all the ravens had flown away! She was the most powerful person with whom he was brought into contact—always excepting the two remote and silent people beyond the nursery door.

How was His Majesty the King to know that, six years ago, in the summer of his birth, Mrs. Austell, turning over her husband's papers, had come upon the intemperate letter of a foolish woman who had been carried away by the silent man's strength and personal beauty? How could he tell what evil the overlooked slip of note-paper had wrought in the mind of a desperately jealous wife? How could he, despite his wisdom, guess that his mother had chosen to make of it excuse for a bar and a division between herself and her husband, that strengthened and grew harder to break with each year; that she, having unearthed this skeleton in the cupboard, had trained it into a household God which should be about their path and about their bed, and poison all their ways?

These things were beyond the province of His Majesty the King. He only knew that his father was daily absorbed in some mysterious work for a thing called the *Sirkar* and that his mother was the victim alternately of the *Nautch* and the *Burrak'hana*. To these entertainments she was escorted by a Captain-Man for whom His Majesty the King had no regard.

"He *doesn't* laugh," he argued with Miss Biddums, who would fain have taught him charity. "He only makes faces wiv his mouf, and when he wants to o-muse me I am *not* o-mused." And His Majesty the King shook his head as one who knew the deceitfulness of this world.

Morning and evening it was his duty to salute his father and mother—the former with a grave shake of the hand, and the latter with an equally grave kiss. Once, indeed, he had put his arms round his mother's neck, in the fashion he used toward Miss Biddums. The openwork of his sleeve-edge caught in an earring, and the last stage of His Majesty's little overture was a suppressed scream and summary dismissal to the nursery.

"It's w'ong," thought His Majesty the King, "to hug Memsahibs wiv fings in veir ears. I will amember." He never repeated the experiment.

Miss Biddums, it must be confessed, spoiled him as much as his nature admitted, in some sort of recompense for what she called "the hard ways of his Papa and Mamma." She, like her charge, knew nothing of the trouble between man and wife—the savage contempt for a woman's stupidity on the one side, or the dull, rankling anger on the other. Miss Biddums had looked after many little children in her time, and served in many establishments. Being a discreet woman, she observed little and said less, and, when her pupils went over the sea to the Great Unknown which she, with

touching confidence in her hearers, called "Home,"
packed up her slender belongings and sought for employment afresh, lavishing all her love on each successive batch of ingrates. Only His Majesty the King
had repaid her affection with interest; and in his uncomprehending ears she had told the tale of nearly all
her hopes, her aspirations, the hopes that were dead, and
the dazzling glories of her ancestral home in "*Cal*cutta,
close to Wellington Square."

Everything above the average was in the eyes of His
Majesty the King "Calcutta good." When Miss Biddums had crossed his royal will, he reversed the epithet
to vex that estimable lady, and all things evil were, until
the tears of repentance swept away spite, "Calcutta
bad."

Now and again Miss Biddums begged for him the
rare pleasure of a day in the society of the Commissioner's child—the wilful four-year-old Patsie, who, to
the intense amazement of His Majesty the King, was
idolized by her parents. On thinking the question out
at length, by roads unknown to those who have left
childhood behind, he came to the conclusion that Patsie
was petted because she wore a big blue sash and yellow
hair.

This precious discovery he kept to himself. The
yellow hair was absolutely beyond his power, his own
tousled wig being potato-brown; but something might
be done toward the blue sash. He tied a large knot in
his mosquito-curtains in order to remember to consult
Patsie on their next meeting. She was the only child
he had ever spoken to, and almost the only one that he

had ever seen. The little memory and the very large and ragged knot held good.

"Patsie, lend me your blue wiband," said His Majesty the King.

"You'll bewy it," said Patsie, doubtfully, mindful of certain fearful atrocities committed on her doll.

"No, I won't—twoofanhonor. It's for me to wear."

"Pooh!" said Patsie. "Boys don't wear sa-ashes. Zey's only for dirls."

"I didn't know." The face of His Majesty the King fell.

"Who wants ribands? Are you playing horses, chickabiddies?" said the Commissioner's wife, stepping into the veranda.

"Toby wanted my sash," explained Patsie.

"I don't now," said His Majesty the King, hastily, feeling that with one of these terrible "grown-ups" his poor little secret would be shamelessly wrenched from him, and perhaps—most burning desecration of all— laughed at.

"I'll give you a cracker-cap," said the Commissioner's wife. "Come along with me, Toby, and we'll choose it."

The cracker-cap was a stiff, three-pointed vermilion-and-tinsel splendor. His Majesty the King fitted it on his royal brow. The Commissioner's wife had a face that children instinctively trusted, and her action, as she adjusted the toppling middle spike, was tender.

"Will it do as well?" stammered His Majesty the King.

"As what, little one?"

"As ve wiban?"

"Oh, quite. Go and look at yourself in the glass."

The words were spoken in all sincerity and to help forward any absurd "dressing-up" amusement that the children might take into their minds. But the young savage has a keen sense of the ludicrous. His Majesty the King swung the great cheval-glass down, and saw his head crowned with the staring horror of a fool's cap—a thing which his father would rend to pieces if it ever came into his office. He plucked it off, and burst into tears.

"Toby," said the Commissioner's wife, gravely, "you shouldn't give way to temper. I am very sorry to see it. It's wrong."

His Majesty the King sobbed inconsolably, and the heart of Patsie's mother was touched. She drew the child on to her knee. Clearly it was not temper alone.

"What is it, Toby? Won't you tell me? Aren't you well?"

The torrent of sobs and speech met, and fought for a time, with chokings and gulpings and gasps. Then, in a sudden rush, His Majesty the King was delivered of a few inarticulate sounds, followed by the words:— "Go a—way you—dirty—little debbil!"

"Toby! What do you mean?"

"It's what he'd say. I *know* it is. He said vat when vere was only a little, little eggy mess, on my t-t-unic; and he'd say it again, and laugh, if I went in wif vat on my head."

"Who would say that?"

"M-m-my Papa! And I fought if I had ve blue

wiban, he'd let me play in ve waste-paper basket under ve table."

"*What* blue riband, childie?"

"Ve same vat Patsie had—ve big blue wiban w-w-wound my t-ttummy!"

"What is it, Toby? There's something on your mind. Tell me all about it, and perhaps I can help."

"Isn't anyfing," sniffed His Majesty, mindful of his manhood, and raising his head from the motherly bosom upon which it was resting. "I only fought vat you—you petted Patsie 'cause she had ve blue wiban, and—and if I'd had ve blue wiban too, m-my Papa w-would pet me."

The secret was out, and His Majesty the King sobbed bitterly in spite of the arms round him, and the murmur of comfort on his heated little forehead.

Enter Patsie tumultuously, embarrassed by several lengths of the Commissioner's pet *mahseer-rod*. "Tum along, Toby! Zere's a *chu-chu* lizard in ze *chick*, and I've told Chimo to watch him till we tum. If we poke him wiz zis his tail will go *wiggle-wiggle* and fall off. Tum along! I can't weach."

"I'm coming," said His Majesty the King, climbing down from the Commissioner's wife's knee after a hasty kiss.

Two minutes later, the *chu-chu* lizard's tail was wriggling on the matting of the veranda, and the children were gravely poking it with splinters from the *chick*, to urge its exhausted vitality into "just one wiggle more, 'cause it doesn't hurt *chu-chu*."

The Commissioner's wife stood in the doorway and

watched:—"Poor little mite! A blue sash . . . and my own precious Patsie! I wonder if the best of us, or we who love them best, ever understand what goes on in their topsy-turvy little heads."

A big tear splashed on the Commissioner's wife's wedding ring, and she went indoors to devise a tea for the benefit of His Majesty the King.

"Their souls aren't in their tummies at that age in this climate," said the Commissioner's wife, "but they are not far off. I wonder if I could make Mrs. Austell understand. Poor little fellow!"

With simple craft, the Commissioner's wife called on Mrs. Austell and spoke long and lovingly about children; inquiring specially for His Majesty the King.

"He's with his governess," said Mrs. Austell, and the tone intimated that she was not interested.

The Commissioner's wife, unskilled in the art of war, continued her questionings. "I don't know," said Mrs. Austell. "These things are left to Miss Biddums, and, of course, she does not ill-treat the child."

The Commissioner's wife left hastily. The last sentence jarred upon her nerves. "Doesn't *ill-treat* the child! As if that were all! I wonder what Tom would say if I only 'didn't ill-treat' Patsie!"

Thenceforward, His Majesty the King was an honored guest at the Commissioner's house, and the chosen friend of Patsie, with whom he blundered into as many scrapes as the compound and the servants' quarters afforded. Patsie's Mamma was always ready to give counsel, help, and sympathy, and, if need were and callers few, to enter into their games with an *abandon* that would have shocked the sleek-haired subalterns who squirmed painfully in their chairs when they came to call on her whom they profanely nick-named "Mother Bunch."

Yet, in spite of Patsie and Patsie's Mamma, and the love that these two lavished upon him, His Majesty the King fell grievously from grace, and committed no less a sin than that of theft—unknown, it is true, but burdensome.

There came a man to the door one day, when His Majesty was playing in the hall and the bearer had gone to dinner, with a packet for His Majesty's Mamma. And he put it upon the hall-table, said that there was no answer, and departed.

Presently, the pattern of the dado ceased to interest His Majesty, while the packet, a white, neatly wrapped one of fascinating shape, interested him very much indeed. His Mamma was out, so was Miss Biddums, and there was pink string round the packet. He greatly desired pink string. It would help him in many of his little businesses—the haulage across the floor of his small cane-chair, the torturing of Chimo, who could never understand harness—and so forth. If he took the string it would be his own, and nobody would be any the wiser. He certainly could not pluck up sufficient courage to ask Mamma for it. Wherefore, mounting upon a chair, he carefully untied the string and, behold, the stiff white paper spread out in four directions, and revealed a beautiful little leather box with gold lines upon it! He tried to replace the string, but that was a failure. So he opened the box to get full

satisfaction for his iniquity, and saw a most beautiful
Star that shone and winked, and was altogether lovely
and desirable.

"Vat," said His Majesty, meditatively, "is a 'parkle
cwown, like what I will wear when I go to heaven. I
will wear it on my head—Miss Biddums says so. I
would like to wear it *now*. I would like to play wiv
it. I will take it away and play wiv it, very careful,
until Mamma asks for it. I fink it was bought for me
to play wiv—same as my cart."

His Majesty the King was arguing against his conscience, and he knew it, for he thought immediately
after: "Never mind. I will keep it to play wiv until
Mamma says where is it, and then I will say:—'I tookt
it and I am sorry.' I will not hurt it because it is a
'parkle cwown. But Miss Biddums will tell me to put
it back. I will not show it to Miss Biddums."

If Mamma had come in at that moment all would
have gone well. She did not, and His Majesty the
King stuffed paper, case, and jewel into the breast of
his blouse and marched to the nursery.

"When Mamma asks I will tell," was the salve that
he laid upon his conscience. But Mamma never asked,
and for three whole days His Majesty the King gloated
over his treasure. It was of no earthly use to him, but
it was splendid, and, for aught he knew, something
dropped from the heavens themselves. Still Mamma
made no inquiries, and it seemed to him, in his furtive
peeps, as though the shiny stones grew dim. What was
the use of a 'parkle cwown if it made a little boy feel
all bad in his inside? He had the pink string as well

as the other treasure, but greatly he wished that he had not gone beyond the string. It was his first experience of iniquity, and it pained him after the flush of possession and secret delight in the "'parkle cwown" had died away.

Each day that he delayed rendered confession to the people beyond the nursery doors more impossible. Now and again he determined to put himself in the path of the beautifully attired lady as she was going out, and explain that he and no one else was the possessor of a "'parkle cwown," most beautiful and quite uninquired for. But she passed hurriedly to her carriage, and the opportunity was gone before His Majesty the King could draw the deep breath which clinches noble resolve. The dread secret cut him off from Miss Biddums, Patsie, and the Commissioner's wife, and—doubly hard fate—when he brooded over it Patsie said, and told her mother, that he was cross.

The days were very long to His Majesty the King, and the nights longer still. Miss Biddums had informed him, more than once, what was the ultimate destiny of "fieves," and when he passed the interminable mud flanks of the Central Jail, he shook in his little strapped shoes.

But release came after an afternoon spent in playing boats by the edge of the tank at the bottom of the garden. His Majesty the King went to tea, and, for the first time in his memory, the meal revolted him. His nose was very cold, and his cheeks were burning hot. There was a weight about his feet, and he pressed his

head several times to make sure that it was not swelling as he sat.

"I feel vevy funny," said His Majesty the King, rubbing his nose. "Vere's a buzz-buzz in my head."

He went to bed quietly. Miss Biddums was out and
the bearer undressed him.

The sin of the " 'parkle cwown" was forgotten in
the acuteness of the discomfort to which he roused after
a leaden sleep of some hours. He was thirsty, and the
bearer had forgotten to leave the drinking-water. "Miss
Biddums! Miss Biddums! I'm so kirsty!"

No answer. Miss Biddums had leave to attend the
wedding of a Calcutta schoolmate. His Majesty the
King had forgotten that.

"I want a dwink of water!" he cried, but his voice
was dried up in his throat. "I want a dwink! Vere
is ve glass?"

He sat up in bed and looked round. There was a
murmur of voices from the other side of the nursery
door. It was better to face the terrible unknown than
to choke in the dark. He slipped out of bed, but his
feet were strangely wilful, and he reeled once or twice.
Then he pushed the door open and staggered—a puffed
and purple-faced little figure—into the brilliant light of
the dining-room full of pretty ladies.

"I'm vevy hot! I'm vevy uncomfitivle," moaned His
Majesty the King, clinging to the portière, "and vere's
no water in ve glass, and I'm *so* kirsty. Give me a
dwink of water."

An apparition in black and white—His Majesty the
King could hardly see distinctly—lifted him up to the

level of the table, and felt his wrists and forehead. The water came, and he drank deeply, his teeth chattering against the edge of the tumbler. Then every one seemed to go away—every one except the huge man in black and white, who carried him back to his bed; the mother and father following. And the sin of the " 'parkle cwown" rushed back and took possession of the terrified soul.

"I'm a fief!" he gasped. "I want to tell Miss Biddums vat I'm a fief. Vere is Miss Biddums?"

Miss Biddums had come and was bending over him. "I'm a fief," he whispered. "A fief—like ve men in the pwison. But I'll tell now. I tookt . . . I tookt ve 'parkle cwown when the man that came left it in ve hall. I bwoke ve paper and ve little bwown box, and it looked shiny, and I tookt it to play wif, and I was afwaid. It's in ve dooly-box at ve bottom. No one *never* asked for it, but I was afwaid. Oh, go an' get ve dooly-box!"

Miss Biddums obediently stooped to the lowest shelf of the *almirah* and unearthed the big paper box in which His Majesty the King kept his dearest possessions. Under the tin soldiers, and a layer of mud pellets for a pellet-bow, winked and blazed a diamond star, wrapped roughly in a half-sheet of note-paper whereon were a few words.

Somebody was crying at the head of the bed, and a man's hand touched the forehead of His Majesty the King, who grasped the packet and spread it on the bed.

"Vat is ve 'parkle cwown," he said, and wept bitterly;

for now that he had made restitution he would fain
have kept the shining splendor with him.

"It concerns you too," said a voice at the head of the
bed. "Read the note. This is not the time to keep back
anything."

The note was curt, very much to the point, and
signed by a single initial. *"If you wear this to-morrow
night I shall know what to expect."* The date was three
weeks old.

A whisper followed, and the deeper voice returned:
"And you drifted as far apart as *that!* I think it makes
us quits now, doesn't it? Oh, can't we drop this folly
once and for all? Is it worth it, darling?"

"Kiss me too," said His Majesty the King, dreamily.
"You isn't *vevy* angwy, is you?"

The fever burned itself out, and His Majesty the
King slept.

When he waked, it was in a new world—peopled by
his father and mother as well as Miss Biddums: and
there was much love in that world and no morsel of
fear, and more petting than was good for several little
boys. His Majesty the King was too young to moralize
on the uncertainty of things human, or he would have
been impressed with the singular advantages of crime
—ay, black sin. Behold, he had stolen the " 'parkle
cwown," and his reward was Love, and the right to
play in the waste-paper basket under the table "for always."

.   .   .   .

He trotted over to spend an afternoon with Patsie,
and the Commissioner's wife would have kissed him.

"No, not vere," said His Majesty the King, with superb insolence, fencing one corner of his mouth with his hand. "Vat's my Mamma's place—vere *she* kisses me." "Oh!" said the Commissioner's wife, briefly. Then to herself: "Well, I suppose I ought to be glad for his sake. Children are selfish little grubs and—I've got my Patsie."

BLACK JACK

To the wake av Tim O'Hara
Came company,
All St. Patrick's Alley
Was there to see.
—*Robert Buchanan.*

AS the Three Musketeers share their silver, tobacco,
and liquor together, as they protect each other
in barracks or camp, and as they rejoice together
over the joy of one, so do they divide their sorrows.
When Ortheris's irrepressible tongue has brought him
into cells for a season, or Learoyd has run amok through
his kit and accoutrements, or Mulvaney has indulged
in strong waters, and under their influence reproved his
Commanding Officer, you can see the trouble in the
faces of the untouched two. And the rest of the regiment know that comment or jest is unsafe. Generally
the three avoid Orderly Room and the Corner Shop
that follows, leaving both to the young bloods who
have not sown their wild oats; but there are occasions—

For instance, Ortheris was sitting on the drawbridge
of the main gate of Fort Amara, with his hands in his
pockets and his pipe, bowl down, in his mouth. Learoyd was lying at full length on the turf of the glacis,
kicking his heels in the air, and I came round the
corner and asked for Mulvaney.

275

Ortheris spat into the ditch and shook his head. "No good seein' 'im now," said Ortheris; "'e's a bloomin' camel. Listen."

I heard on the flags of the veranda opposite to the cells, which are close to the Guard-Room, a measured step that I could have identified in the tramp of an army. There were twenty paces *crescendo,* a pause, and then twenty *diminuendo.*

"That's 'im," said Ortheris; "my Gawd, that's 'im! All for a bloomin' button you could see your face in an' a bit o' lip that a bloomin' Hark-angel would 'a' guv back."

Mulvaney was doing pack-drill—was compelled, that is to say, to walk up and down for certain hours in full marching order, with rifle, bayonet, ammunition, knapsack, and overcoat. And his offence was being dirty on parade! I nearly fell into the Fort Ditch with astonishment and wrath, for Mulvaney is the smartest man that ever mounted guard, and would as soon think of turning out uncleanly as of dispensing with his trousers.

"Who was the Sergeant that checked him?" I asked.

"Mullins, o' course," said Ortheris. "There ain't no other man would whip 'im on the peg so. But Mullins ain't a man. 'E's a dirty little pigscraper, that's wot 'e is."

"What did Mulvaney say? He's not the make of man to take that quietly."

"Said! Bin better for 'im if 'e'd shut 'is mouth. Lord, 'ow we laughed! 'Sargint,' 'e sez, 'ye say I'm dirty. Well,' sez 'e, 'when your wife lets you blow your own nose for yourself, perhaps you'll know wot dirt is. You're himperfectly eddicated, Sargint,' sez 'e, an' then we fell in. But after p'rade, 'e was up an' Mullins was swearin' 'imself black in the face at Ord'ly Room that Mulvaney 'ad called 'im a swine an' Lord knows wot all. You know Mullins. 'E'll 'ave 'is 'ead broke in one o' these days. 'E's too big a bloomin' liar for ord'nary consumption. 'Three hours' can an' kit,' sez the Colonel; 'not for bein' dirty on p'rade, but for 'avin said somethin' to Mullins, tho' I do not believe,' sez 'e, 'you said wot 'e said you said.' An' Mulvaney fell away sayin' nothin'.' You know 'e never speaks to the Colonel for fear o' gettin' 'imself fresh copped."

Mullins, a very young and very much married Sergeant, whose manners were partly the result of innate depravity and partly of imperfectly digested Board School, came over the bridge, and most rudely asked Ortheris what he was doing.

"Me?" said Ortheris. "Ow! I'm waiting for my C'mission. 'Seed it comin' along yit?"

Mullins turned purple and passed on. There was the sound of a gentle chuckle from the glacis where Learoyd lay.

" 'E expects to get 'is C'mission some day," explained Orth'ris; "Gawd 'elp the Mess that 'ave to put their 'ands into the same kiddy as 'im! Wot time d'you make it, sir? Fower! Mulvaney'll be out in 'arf an hour. You don't want to buy a dorg, sir, do you? A pup you can trust—'arf Rampore by the Colonel's grey-'ound."

"Ortheris," I answered, sternly, for I knew what was in his mind, "do you mean to say that" —

"I didn't mean to arx money o' you, any'ow," said Ortheris; "I'd 'a' sold you the dorg good an' cheap, but —but—I know Mulvaney'll want somethin' after we've walked 'im orf, an' I ain't got nothin', nor 'e 'asn't neither. I'd sooner sell you the dorg, sir. 'S trewth I would!"

A shadow fell on the drawbridge, and Ortheris began to rise into the air, lifted by a huge hand upon his collar.

"Onything but t' braass," said Learoyd, quietly, as he held the Londoner over the ditch. "Onything but t' braass, Orth'ris, ma son! Ah've got one rupee eight annas of ma own." He showed two coins, and re-placed Ortheris on the drawbridge rail.

"Very good," I said; "where are you going to?"

"Goin to walk 'im orf wen 'e comes out—two miles or three or fower," said Ortheris.

The footsteps within ceased. I heard the dull thud of a knapsack falling on a bedstead, followed by the rat-tle of arms. Ten minutes later, Mulvaney, faultlessly dressed, his lips tight and his face as black as a thunder-storm, stalked into the sunshine on the drawbridge. Learoyd and Ortheris sprang from my side and closed in upon him, both leaning toward as horses lean upon the pole. In an instant they had disappeared down the sunken road to the cantonments, and I was left alone. Mulvaney had not seen fit to recognize me; so I knew that his trouble must be heavy upon him.

I climbed one of the bastions and watched the figures

of the Three Musketeers grow smaller and smaller across the plain. They were walking as fast as they could put foot to the ground, and their heads were bowed. They fetched a great compass round the parade-ground, skirted the Cavalry lines, and vanished in the belt of trees that fringes the low land by the river.

I followed slowly, and sighted them—dusty, sweating, but still keeping up their long, swinging tramp—on the river bank. They crashed through the Forest Reserve, headed toward the Bridge of Boats, and presently established themselves on the bow of one of the pontoons. I rode cautiously till I saw three puffs of white smoke rise and die out in the clear evening air, and knew that peace had come again. At the bridge-head they waved me forward with gestures of welcome.

"Tie up your 'orse," shouted Ortheris, "an' come on, sir. We're all goin' 'ome in this 'ere bloomin' boat."

From the bridge-head to the Forest Officer's bungalow is but a step. The mess-man was there, and would see that a man held my horse. Did the Sahib require aught else—a peg, or beer? Ritchie Sahib had left half a dozen bottles of the latter, but since the Sahib was a friend of Ritchie Sahib, and he, the mess-man, was a poor man—

I gave my order quietly, and returned to the bridge. Mulvaney had taken off his boots, and was dabbling his toes in the water; Learoyd was lying on his back on the pontoon; and Ortheris was pretending to row with a big bamboo.

"I'm an ould fool," said Mulvaney, reflectively,

"dhraggin' you two out here bekaze I was undher the Black Dog—sulkin' like a child. Me that was soldierin' when Mullins, an' be damned to him, was shquealin' on a counterpin for five shillin' a week—an' that not paid! Bhoys, I've took you five miles out av natural pervarsity. Phew!"

"Wot's the odds so long as you're 'appy?" said Ortheris, applying himself afresh to the bamboo. "As well 'ere as anywhere else."

Learoyd held up a rupee and an eight-anna bit, and shook his head sorrowfully. "Five mile from t' Canteen, all along o' Mulvaney's blaasted pride."

"I know ut," said Mulvaney, penitently. "Why will ye come wid me? An' yet I wud be mortial sorry if ye did not—any time—though I am ould enough to know betther. But I will do penance. I will take a dhrink av wather."

Ortheris squeaked shrilly. The butler of the Forest bungalow was standing near the railings with a basket, uncertain how to clamber down to the pontoon. "Might 'a' know'd you'd 'a' got liquor out o' bloomin' desert, sir," said Ortheris, gracefully, to me. Then to the mess-man: "Easy with them there bottles. They're worth their weight in gold. Jock, ye long-armed beggar, get out o' that an' hike 'em down."

Learoyd had the basket on the pontoon in an instant, and the Three Musketeers gathered round it with dry lips. They drank my health in due and ancient form, and thereafter tobacco tasted sweeter than ever. They absorbed all the beer, and disposed themselves in picturesque attitudes to admire the setting sun—no man speaking for a while.

Mulvaney's head dropped upon his chest, and we thought that he was asleep.

"What on earth did you come so far for?" I whispered to Ortheris.

"To walk 'im orf, o' course. When 'e's been checked we allus walks 'im orf. 'E ain't fit to be spoke to those times—nor 'e ain't fit to leave alone neither. So we takes 'im till 'e is."

Mulvaney raised his head, and stared straight into the sunset. "I had my rifle," said he, dreamily, "an' I had my bay'nit, an' Mullins came round the corner, an' he looked in my face an' grinned dishpiteful. '*You* can't blow your own nose,' sez he. Now, I cannot tell fwhat Mullins's expayrience may ha' been, but, Mother av God, he was nearer to his death that minut' than I have iver been to mine—and that's less than the thicknuss av a hair!"

"Yes," said Ortheris, calmly, "you'd look fine with all your buttons took orf, an' the Band in front o' you, walkin' roun' slow time. We're both front-rank men, me an' Jock, when the reg'ment's in 'ollow square. Bloomin' fine you'd look. 'The Lord giveth an' the Lord taketh awai,—Heasy with that there drop!— Blessed be the naime o' the Lord,'" he gulped in a quaint and suggestive fashion.

"Mullins! Wot's Mullins?" said Learoyd, slowly. "Ah'd take a coomp'ny o' Mullinses—ma hand behind me. Sitha, Mulvaney, don't be a fool."

"*You* were not checked for fwhat you did not do, an'

made a mock av afther. 'Twas for less than that the Tyrone wud ha' sent O'Hara to hell, instid av lettin' him go by his own choosin', whin Rafferty shot him," retorted Mulvaney.

"And who stopped the Tyrone from doing it?" I asked.

"That ould fool who's sorry he didn't stick the pig Mullins." His head dropped again. When he raised it he shivered and put his hands on the shoulders of his two companions.

"Ye've walked the Divil out av me, bhoys," said he. Ortheris shot out the red-hot dottel of his pipe on the back of the hairy fist. "They say 'Ell's 'otter than that," said he, as Mulvaney swore aloud. "You be warned so. Look yonder!"—he pointed across the river to a ruined temple—"Me an' you an' *'im*"—he indicated me by a jerk of his head—"was there one day when Hi made a bloomin' show o' myself. You an' 'im stopped me doin' such—an' Hi was on'y wishful for to desert. You are makin' a bigger bloomin' show o' yourself now."

"Don't mind him, Mulvaney," I said; "Dinah Shadd won't let you hang yourself yet awhile, and you don't intend to try it either. Let's hear about the Tyrone and O'Hara. Rafferty shot him for fooling with his wife. What happened before that?"

"There's no fool like an ould fool. You know you can do anythin' wid me whin I'm talkin'. Did I say I wud like to cut Mullins's liver out? I deny the imputashin, for fear that Orth'ris here wud report me— Ah! You wud tip me into the river, wud you? Sit quiet, little man. Anyways, Mullins is not worth the trouble av an extry p'rade, an' I will trate him wid outrajis contimpt. The Tyrone an' O'Hara! O'Hara an' the Tyrone, begad! Ould days are hard to bring back into the mouth, but they're always inside the head."

Followed a long pause.

"O'Hara was a Divil. Though I saved him, for the honor av the rig'mint, from his death that time, I say it now. He was a Divil—a long, bould, black-haired Divil."

"Which way?" asked Ortheris.

"Women."

"Then I know another."

"Not more than in reason, if you mane me, ye warped walkin'-shtick. I have been young, an' for why should I not have tuk what I cud? Did I iver, whin I was Corp'ril, use the rise av my rank—wan step an' that taken away, more's the sorrow an' the fault av me!— to prosecute a nefarious inthrigue, as O'Hara did? Did I, whin I was Corp'ril, lay my spite upon a man an' make his life a dog's life from day to day? Did I lie, as O'Hara lied, till the young wans in the Tyrone turned white wid the fear av the Judgment av God killin' thim all in a lump, as ut killed the woman at Devizes? I did not! I have sinned my sins an' I have made my confesshin, an' Father Victor knows the worst av me. O'Hara was tuk, before he cud spake, on Rafferty's doorstep, an' no man knows the worst av him. But this much I know!

"The Tyrone was recruited any fashion in the ould days. A draf' from Connemara—a draf' from Ports-

mouth—a draf' from Kerry, an' that was a blazin' bad
draf'—here, there and iverywhere—but the large av
thim was Oirish—Black Oirish. Now there are Oirish
an' Oirish. The good are good as the best, but the bad
are wurrst than the wurrst. 'Tis this way. They clog
together in pieces as fast as thieves, an' no wan knows
fwhat they will do till wan turns informer an' the gang
is bruk. But ut begins again, a day later, meetin' in
holes an' corners an' swearin' bloody oaths an' shtickin'
a man in the back an' runnin' away, an' thin waitin'
for the blood-money on the reward papers—to see if
ut's worth enough. Those are the Black Oirish, an' 'tis
they that bring dishgrace upon the name av Oireland,
an' thim I wud kill—as I nearly killed wan wanst.

"But to reshume. My room—'twas before I was married—was wid twelve av the scum av the earth—the
pickin's av the gutter—mane men that wud neither
laugh nor talk nor yet get dhrunk as a man shud. They
thried some av their dog's thricks on me, but I dhrew
a line round my cot, an' the man that thransgressed ut
wint into hospital for three days good.

"O'Hara had put his spite on the room—he was my
Color Sargint—an' nothin' cud we do to plaze him. I
was younger than I am now, an' I tuk what I got in
the way av dressing down and punishmint-dhrill wid
my tongue in my cheek. But it was diff'rint wid the
others, an' why I cannot say, excipt that some men are
borrun mane an' go to dhirty murdher where a fist is
more than enough. Afther a whoile, they changed
their chune to me an' was desp'rit frien'ly—all twelve
av thim cursin' O'Hara in chorus.

" 'Eyah,' sez I, 'O'Hara's a divil an' I'm not for deny-
in' ut, but is he the only man in the wurruld? Let him
go. He'll get tired av findin' our kit foul an' our 'coutrements onproperly kep.' '

" 'We will *not* let him go,' sez they.

" 'Thin take him,' sez I, 'an' a dashed poor yield you
will get for your throuble.'

" 'Is he not misconductin' himself wid Slimmy's
wife?' sez another.

" 'She's common to the rig'mint,' sez I. 'Fwhat has
made ye this partic'lar on a suddint?'

" 'Has he not put his spite on the roomful av us?
Can we do anythin' that he will not check us for?' sez
another.

" 'That's thrue,' sez I.

" 'Will ye not help us to do aught,' sez another—'a
big bould man like you?'

" 'I will break his head upon his shoulthers av he
puts hand on me,' sez I. 'I will give him the lie av he
says that I'm dhirty, an' I wud not mind duckin' him
in the Artillery troughs if ut was not that I'm thryin'
for my shtripes.'

" 'Is that all ye will do?' sez another. 'Have ye no
more spunk than that, ye blood-dhrawn calf?'

" 'Blood-dhrawn I may be,' sez I, gettin' back to my
cot an' makin' my line round ut; 'but ye know that the
man who comes acrost this mark will be more blood-
dhrawn than me. No man gives me the name in my
mouth,' I sez. 'Ondersthand, I will have no part wid
you in anythin' ye do, nor will I raise my fist to my
shuperior. Is any wan comin' on?' sez I.

"They made no move, tho' I gave them full time, but stud growlin' an' snarlin' together at wan ind av the room. I tuk up my cap and wint out to Canteen, thinkin' no little av mesilf, and there I grew most ondacintly dhrunk in my legs. My head was all reasonable.

" 'Houligan,' I sez to a man in E Comp'ny that was by way av bein' a frind av mine; 'I'm overtuk from the belt down. Do you give me the touch av your shoulther to presarve my formation an' march me acrost the ground into the high grass. I'll sleep ut off there,' sez I; an' Houligan—he's dead now, but good he was while he lasted—walked wid me, givin' me the touch whin I wint wide, ontil we came to the high grass, an', my faith, the sky an' the earth was fair rowlin' undher me. I made for where the grass was thickust, an' there I slep' off my liquor wid an easy conscience. I did not desire to come on books too frequent; my characther havin' been shpotless for the good half av a year.

"Whin I roused, the dhrink was dyin' out in me, an' I felt as though a she-cat had littered in my mouth. I had not learned to hould my liquor wid comfort in thim days. 'Tis little betther I am now. 'I will get Houligan to pour a bucket over my head,' thinks I, an' I wud ha' risen, but I heard some wan say: 'Mulvaney can take the blame av ut for the backslidin' hound he is.'

" 'Oho!' sez I, an' my head rang like a guard-room gong: 'fwhat is the blame that this young man must

take to oblige Tim Vulmea?' For 'twas Tim Vulmea
that shpoke.

"I turned on my belly an' crawled through the grass,
a bit at a time, to where the spache came from. There
was the twelve av my room sittin' down in a little
patch, the dhry grass wavin' above their heads an' the
sin av black murdher in their hearts. I put the stuff
aside to get a clear view.

" 'Fwhat's that?' sez wan man, jumpin' up.

" 'A dog,' says Vulmea. 'You're a nice hand to this
job! As I said, Mulvaney will take the blame—av ut
comes to a pinch.'

" ' 'Tis harrd to swear a man's life away,' sez a young
wan.

" 'Thank ye for that,' thinks I. 'Now, fwhat the divil
are you paragins conthrivin' against me?'

" ' 'Tis as easy as dhrinkin' your quart,' sez Vulmea.
'At seven or thereon. O'Hara will come acrost to the
Married Quarters, goin' to call on Slimmy's wife, the
swine! Wan av us'll pass the wurrd to the room an'
we shtart the divil an' all av a shine—laughin' an'
crackin' on an' t'rowin' our boots about. Thin O'Hara
will come to give us the ordher to be quiet, the more
by token bekaze the room-lamp will be knocked over
in the larkin'. He will take the straight road to the ind
door where there's the lamp in the veranda, an' that'll
bring him clear against the light as he shtands. He
will not be able to look into the dhark. Wan av us will
loose off, an' a close shot ut will be, an' shame to the
man that misses. 'Twill be Mulvaney's rifle, she that

that is at the head av the rack—there's no mistakin' long-shtocked, cross-eyed bitch even in the dhark.'

"The thief misnamed my ould firin'-piece out av jealousy—I was pershuaded av that—an' ut made me more angry than all.

"But Vulmea goes on: 'O'Hara will dhrop, an' by the time the light's lit again, there'll be some six av us on the chest av Mulvaney, cryin' murdher an' rape. Mulvaney's cot is near the ind door, an' the shmokin' rifle will be lyin' undher him whin we've knocked him over. We know, an' all the rig'mint knows, that Mulvaney has given O'Hara more lip than any man av us. Will there be any doubt at the Coort-martial? Wud twelve honust sodger-bhoys swear away the life av a dear, quiet, swate-timpered man such as is Mulvaney— wid his line av pipe-clay roun' his cot, threatenin' us wid murdher av we overshtepped ut, as we can truthful testify?'

" 'Mary, Mother av Mercy!' thinks I to mesilf; 'it is this to have an unruly mimber an' fistes fit to use! Oh the sneakin' hounds!'

"The big dhrops ran down my face, for I was wake wid the liquor an' had not the full av my wits about me. I laid shtill an' heard thim workin' themselves up to swear my life by tellin' tales av ivry time I had put my mark on wan or another; an' my faith, they was few that was not so dishtinguished. 'Twas all in the way av fair fight, though, for niver did I raise my hand excipt whin they had provoked me to ut.

" ' 'Tis all well,' sez wan av thim, 'but who's to do this shootin'?'

" 'Fwhat matther?' sez Vulmea. ' 'Tis Mulvaney will do that—at the Coort-martial.'

" 'He will so,' sez the man, 'but whose hand is put to the trigger—*in the room?*'

" 'Who'll do ut?' sez Vulmea, lookin' round, but divil a man answeared. They began to dishpute till Kiss, that was always playin' Shpoil Five, sez: 'Thry the kyards!' Wid that he opined his tunic an' tuk out the greasy palammers, an' they all fell in wid the notion.

" 'Deal on!' sez Vulmea, wid a big rattlin' oath, 'an' the Black Curse av Shielygh' come to the man that will not do his duty as the kyards say. Amin!'

" 'Black Jack is the masther,' sez Kiss, dealin'. Black Jack, sorr, I shud expaytiate to you, is the Ace av Shpades which from time immimorial has been intimately connect wid battle, murdher an' suddin death.

"*Wanst* Kiss dealt an' there was no sign, but the men was whoite wid the workin's av their sowls. *Twice* Kiss dealt, an' there was a grey shine on their cheeks like the mess av an egg. *Three* times Kiss dealt an' they was blue. 'Have ye not lost him?' sez Vulmea, wipin' the sweat on him; 'Let's ha' done quick!' 'Quick ut is,' sez Kiss t'rowin' him the kyard; an' ut fell face up on his knee—Black Jack!

"Thin they all cackled wid laughin'. 'Duty thrippence,' sez wan av thim, 'an' damned cheap at that price!' But I cud see they all dhrew a little away from Vulmea an' lef' him sittin' playin' wid the kyard. Vulmea sez no word for a whoile but licked his lips— cat-wavs. Thin he threw up his head an' made the men swear by ivry oath known to stand by him not alone in the room but at the Coort-martial that was to set on *me!* He tould off five av the biggest to stretch me on my cot whin the shot was fired, an' another man he tould off to put out the light, an' yet another to load my rifle. He wud not do that himself; an' that was quare, for 'twas but a little thing considerin'.

"Thin they swore over again that they wud not bethray wan another, an' crep' out av the grass in diff'rint ways, two by two. A mercy ut was that they did not come on me. I was sick wid fear in the pit av my stummick—sick, sick, sick! Afther they was all gone, I wint back to Canteen an' called for a quart to put a thought in me. Vulmea was there, dhrinkin' heavy, an' politeful to me beyond reason. 'Fwhat will I do— fwhat will I do?' thinks I to mesilf whin Vulmea wint away.

"Presintly the Arm'rer Sargint comes in stiffin' an' crackin' on, not pleased wid any wan, bekaze the Martini Henri bein' new to the rig'mint in those days we used to play the mischief wid her arrangements. 'Twas a long time before I cud get out av the way av thryin' to pull back the back-sight an' turnin' her over afther firin'—as if she was a Snider.

"'Fwhat tailor-men do they give me to work wid?' sez the Arm'rer Sargint. 'Here's Hogan, his nose flat as a table, laid by for a week, an' ivry Comp'ny sendin' their arrums in knocked to small shivreens.'

"'Fwhat's wrong wid Hogan, Sargint?' sez I.

"'Wrong!' sez the Arm'rer Sargint; 'I showed him, as though I had been his mother, the way av shtrippin' a 'Tini, an' he shtrup her clane an' easy. I tould him to put her to again an' fire a blank into the blow-pit to show how the dirt hung on the groovin'. He did that, but he did not put in the pin av the fallin'-block, an' av coorse whin he fired he was strook by the block jumpin' clear. Well for him 'twas but a blank—a full charge wud ha' cut his oi out.'

"I looked a thrifle wiser than a boiled sheep's head. 'How's that, Sargint?' sez I.

" 'This way, ye blundherin' man, an' don't you be doin' ut,' sez he. Wid that he shows me a Waster action—the breech av her all cut away to show the inside—an' so plazed he was to grumble that he dimonstrated fwhat Hogan had done twice over. 'An' that comes av not knowin' the wepping you're purvided wid,' sez he.

" 'Thank ye, Sargint,' sez I; 'I will come to you again for further information.'

" 'Ye will not,' sez he. 'Kape your clanin'-rod away from the breech-pin or you will get into throuble.'

"I wint outside an' I could ha' danced wid delight for the grandeur av ut. 'They will load my rifle, good luck to thim, whoile I'm away,' thinks I, and back I wint to the Canteen to give them their clear chanst.

"The Canteen was fillin' wid men at the ind av the day. I made feign to be far gone in dhrink, an', wan by wan, all my roomful came in wid Vulmea. I wint away, walkin' thick an' heavy, but not so thick an' heavy that any wan cud ha' tuk me. Sure and thrue, there was a kyartridge gone from my pouch an' lyin' snug in my rifle. I was hot wid rage against thim all,

an' I worried the bullet out wid my teeth as fast as I
cud, the room bein' empty. Then I tuk my boot an'
the clanin'-rod and knocked out the pin av the fallin'-
block. Oh, 'twas music when that pin rowled on the
flure! I put ut into my pouch an' stuck a dab av dirt
on the holes in the plate, puttin' the fallin'-block back.
'That'll do your business, Vulmea,' sez I, lyin' easy on
the cot. 'Come an' sit on my chest the whole room av
you, an' I will take you to my bosom for the biggest
divils that iver cheated halter.' I would have no mercy
on Vulmea. His oi or his life—little I cared!

"At dusk they came back, the twelve av thim, an'
they had all ben dhrinkin.' I was shammin' sleep on
the cot. Wan man wint outside in the veranda. Whin
he whishtled they began to rage roun' the room an'
carry on tremenjus. But I niver want to hear men
laugh as they did—skylarkin' too! 'Twas like mad
jackals.

"'Shtop that blasted noise!' sez O'Hara in the dark,
an' pop goes the room lamp. I cud hear O'Hara runnin' up an' the rattlin' av my rifle in the rack an' the
men breathin' heavy as they stud roun' my cot. I cud
see O'Hara in the light av the veranda lamp, an' thin
I heard the crack av my rifle. She cried loud, poor
darlint, bein' mishandled. Next minut' five men were
houldin' me down. 'Go easy,' I sez; 'fwhat's ut all
about?'

"Thin Vulmea, on the flure, raised a howl you cud
hear from wan ind av cantonmints to the other. 'I'm
dead, I'm butchered, I'm blind!' sez he. 'Saints have
mercy on my sinful sowl! Sind for Father Constant!

Oh sind for Father Constant an' let me go clean!' By that I knew he was not so dead as I cud ha' wished.

"O'Hara picks up the lamp in the veranda wid a hand as stiddy as a rest. 'Fwhat damned dog's thrick is this av yours?' sez he, and turns the light on Tim Vulmea that was shwimmin' in blood from top to toe. The fallin'-block had sprung free behin' a full charge av powther—good care I tuk to bite down the brass afther takin' out the bullet that there might be somethin' to give ut full worth—an' had cut Tim from the lip to the corner av the right eye, lavin' the eyelid in tatthers, an' so up an' along by the forehead to the hair. 'Twas more av a rakin' plough, if you will ondherstand, than a clean cut; an' niver did I see a man bleed as Vulmea did. The dhrink an' the stew that he was in pumped the blood strong. The minut' the men sittin' on my chest heard O'Hara spakin' they scatthered each wan to his cot, an' cried out very politeful: 'Fwhat is ut, Sargint?'

" 'Fwhat is ut!' sez O'Hara, shakin' Tim. 'Well an' good do you know fwhat ut is, ye skulkin' ditch-lurkin' dogs! Get a *doolie,* an' take this whimperin' scutt away. There will be more heard av ut than any av you will care for.'

"Vulmea sat up rockin' his head in his hand an' moanin' for Father Constant.

" 'Be done!' sez O'Hara, dhraggin' him up by the hair. 'You're none so dead that you cannot go fifteen years for thryin' to shoot me.'

" 'I did not,' sez Vulmea; 'I was shootin' mesilf.'

" 'That's quare,' sez O'Hara, 'for the front av my

jackut is black wid your powther.' He tuk up the rifle that was still warm an' began to laugh. 'I'll make your life Hell to you,' sez he, 'for attempted murdher an' kapin' your rifle onproperly. You'll be hanged first an' thin put undher stoppages for four fifteen. The rifle's done for,' sez he.

"'Why, 'tis my rifle!' sez I, comin' up to look; 'Vulmea, ye divil, fwhat were you doin' wid her—answer me that?'

"'Lave me alone,' sez Vulmea; 'I'm dyin'!'

"'I'll wait till you're betther,' sez I, 'an' thin we two will talk ut out umbrageous.'

"O'Hara pitched Tim into the *doolie,* none too tinder, but all the bhoys kep' by their cots, which was not the sign av innocint men. I was huntin' ivrywhere for my fallin'-block, but not findin' ut at all. I niver found ut.

"'*Now* fwhat will I do?' sez O'Hara, swinging the veranda light in his hand an' lookin' down the room. I had hate and contimpt av O'Hara an' I have now, dead tho' he is, but, for all that, will I say he was a brave man. He is baskin' in Purgathory this tide, but I wish he cud hear that, whin he stud lookin' down the room an' the bhoys shivered before the oi av him, I knew him for a brave man an' I liked him *so*.

"'Fwhat will I do?' sez O'Hara agin, an' we heard the voice av a woman low an' sof' in the veranda. 'Twas Slimmy's wife, come over at the shot, sittin' on wan av the benches an' scarce able to walk.

"'O Denny!—Denny, dear,' sez she, 'have they kilt you?'

"O'Hara looked down the room again an' showed his teeth to the gum. Then he spat on the flure.

" 'You're not worth ut,' sez he. 'Light that lamp, ye dogs,' an' wid that he turned away, an' I saw him walkin' off wid Slimmy's wife; she thryin' to wipe off the powther-black on the front av his jackut wid her handkerchief. 'A brave man you are,' thinks I—'a brave man an' a bad woman.'

"No wan said a word for a time. They was all ashamed, past spache.

" 'Fwhat d' you think he will do?' sez wan av thim at last. 'He knows we're all in ut.'

" 'Are we so?' sez I from my cot. 'The man that sez that to me will be hurt. I do not know,' sez I, 'fwhat onderhand divilmint you have conthrived, but by what I've seen I know that you cannot commit murdher wid another man's rifle—such shakin' cowards you are. I'm goin' to slape,' I sez, 'an' you can blow my head off whoile I lay.' I did not slape, though, for a long time. Can ye wonder?

"Next morn the news was through all the rig'mint, an' there was nothin' that the men did not tell. O'Hara reports, fair an' easy, that Vulmea was come to grief through tamperin' wid his rifle in barricks, all for to show the mechanism. An' by my sowl' he had the impart'nince to say that he was on the sphot at the time an' cud certify that ut was an accidint! You might ha' knocked my roomful down wid a straw whin they heard that. 'Twas lucky for thim that the bhoys were always thryin' to find out how the new rifle was made, an' a lot av thim had come up for easin' the pull by shtickin' bits av grass an' such in the part av the lock that showed near the thrigger. The first issues of the 'Tinis was not covered in, an' I mesilf have eased the pull av mine time an' agin. A light pull is ten points on the range to me.

" 'I will not have this foolishness!' sez the Colonel. 'I will twist the tail off Vulmea!' sez he; but whin he saw him, all tied up an' groanin' in hospital, he changed his will. 'Make him an early convalescint,' sez he to the Doctor, an' Vulmea was made so for a warnin'. His big bloody bandages an' face puckered up to wan side did more to kape the bhoys from messin' wid the insides av their rifles than any punishmint.

"O'Hara gave no reason for fwhat he'd said, an' all my roomful were too glad to inquire, tho' he put his spite upon thim more wearin' than before. Wan day, howiver, he tuk me apart very polite, for he cud be that at the choosin'.

" 'You're a good sodger, tho' you're a damned in-solint man,' sez he.

" 'Fair words, Sargint,' sez I, 'or I may be insolint again.'

" ' 'Tis not like you,' sez he, 'to lave your rifle in the rack widout the breech-pin, for widout the breech-pin she was whin Vulmea fired. I should ha' found the break av ut in the eyes av the holes, else,' he sez.

" 'Sargint,' sez I, 'fwhat wud your life ha' been worth av the breech-pin had been in place, for, on my sowl, my life wud be worth just as much to me av I tould you whether ut was or was not. Be thankful the bullet was not there,' I sez.

" 'That's thrue,' sez he, pulling his moustache; 'but I do not believe that you, for all your lip, was in that business.'

" 'Sargint,' sez I, 'I cud hammer the life out av a man in ten minuts wid my fistes if that man dishpleased me; for I am a good sodger, an' I will be threated as such, an' whoile my fistes are my own they're strong enough for all work I have to do. They do not fly back toward me!' sez I, lookin' him betune the eyes.

" 'You're a good man,' sez he, lookin' me betune the eyes—an' oh he was a gran'-built man to see!—'you're a good man,' he sez, 'an' I cud wish, for the pure frolic av ut, that I was not a Sargint, or that you were not a privit; an' you will think me no coward whin I say this thing.'

" 'I do not,' sez I. 'I saw you whin Vulmea mishandled the rifle. But, Sargint,' I sez, 'take the wurrd from me now, spakin' as man to man wid the shtripes off, tho' 'tis little right I have to talk, me being fwhat I am by natur'. This time ye tuk no harm, an' next time ye may not, but, in the ind, so sure as Slimmy's wife came into the veranda, so sure will ye take harm —an' bad harm. Have thought, Sargint,' sez I. 'Is ut worth ut?'

" 'Ye're a bould man,' sez he, breathin' harrd. 'A very bould man. But I am a bould man tu. Do you go your way, Privit Mulvaney, an' I will go mine.'

"We had no further spache thin or afther, but, wan by another, he drafted the twelve av my room out into other rooms an' got thim spread among the Comp'nies, for they was not a good breed to live together, an' the

Comp'ny orf'cers saw ut. They wud ha' shot me in the night av they had known fwhat I knew; but that they did not.

"An', in the ind, as I said, O'Hara met his death from Rafferty for foolin' wid his wife. He wint his own way too well—Eyah, too well! Shtraight to that affair, widout turnin' to the right or to the lef', he wint, an' may the Lord have mercy on his sowl. Amin!"

"'Ear! 'Ear!" said Ortheris, pointing the moral with a wave of his pipe. "An' this is 'im 'oo would be a bloomin' Vulmea all for the sake of Mullins an' a bloomin' button! Mullins never went after a woman in his life. Mrs. Mullins, she saw 'im one day"—

"Ortheris," I said, hastily, for the romances of Private Ortheris are all too daring for publication, "look at the sun. It's quarter past six!"

"O Lord! Three quarters of an hour for five an' a 'arf miles! We'll 'ave to run like Jimmy O."

The Three Musketeers clambered on to the bridge, and departed hastily in the direction of the cantonment road. When I overtook them I offered them two stirrups and a tail, which they accepted enthusiastically. Ortheris held the tail, and in this manner we trotted steadily through the shadows by an unfrequented road.

At the turn into the cantonments we heard carriage wheels. It was the Colonel's barouche, and in it sat the Colonel's wife and daughter. I caught a suppressed chuckle, and my beast sprang forward with a lighter step.

The Three Musketeers had vanished into the night.

THE TAKING OF LUNGTUNGPEN

So we loosed a bloomin' volley,
  An' we made the beggars cut,
An' when our pouch was emptied out,
  We used the bloomin' butt,
    Ho! My!
  Don't yer come anigh,
When Tommy is a playin' with the baynit an' the butt.
    —*Barrack Room Ballad.*

MY friend Private Mulvaney told me this, sitting on the parapet of the road to Dagshai, when we were hunting butterflies together. He had theories about the Army, and colored clay pipes perfectly. He said that the young soldier is the best to work with, "on account av the surpassing innocinse av the child."

"Now, listen!" said Mulvaney, throwing himself full length on the wall in the sun. "I'm a born scutt av the barrick-room! The Army's mate an' dhrink to me, bekaze I'm wan av the few that can't quit ut. I've put in sivinteen years, an' the pipe-clay's in the marrow av me. Av I cud have kept out av wan big dhrink a month, I wud have been a Hon'ry Lift'nint by this time —a nuisance to my betthers, a laughin'-shtock to my equils, an' a curse to meself. Bein' fwhat I am, I'm Privit Mulvaney, wid no good conduc' pay an' a devourin' thirst. Always barrin' me little frind Bobs Bahadur, I know as much about the Army as most men."

I said something here.

"Wolseley be shot! Betune you an' me an' that butterfly net, he's a ramblin', incoherint sort av a divil, wid wan oi on the Quane an' the Coort, an' the other on his blessed silf—everlastin'ly playing Saysar an' Alexandrier rowled into a lump. Now Bobs is a sinsible little man. Wid Bobs an' a few three-year-olds, I'd swape any army av the earth into a towel, an' throw it away aftherward. Faith, I'm not jokin'! 'Tis the bhoys—the raw bhoys—that don't know fwhat a bullut manes, an' wudn't care av they did—that dhu the work. They're crammed wid bullmate till they fairly *ramps* wid good livin'; and thin, av they don't fight, they blow each other's hids off. 'Tis the trut' I'm tellin' you. They shud be kept on water an' rice in the hot weather; but there'd be a mut'ny av 'twas done.

"Did ye iver hear how Privit Mulvaney tuk the town av Lungtungpen? I thought not! 'Twas the Lift'nint got the credit; but 'twas me planned the schame. A little before I war inviladed from Burma, me an' four-an'-twenty young wans undher a Lift'nint Brazenose, was ruinin' our dijeshins thryin' to catch dacoits. An' such double-ended divils I niver knew! 'Tis only a *dah* an' a Snider that makes a dacoit. Widout thim, he's a paceful cultivator, an' felony for to shoot. We hunted, an' we hunted, an' tuk fever an' elephints now an' again; but no dacoits. Evenshually, we *puckarowed* wan man. 'Tra'e him tinderly,' sez the Lift'nint. So

I tuk him away into the jungle, wid the Burmese Interprut'r an' my clanin'-rod. Sez I to the man, 'My
paceful squireen,' sez I, 'you shquot on your hunkers
an' dimonstrate to *my* frind here, where *your* frinds
are whin they're at home?' Wid that I introjuced him
to the clanin'-rod, an' he comminst to jabber; the Interprut'r interprutin' in betweens, an' me helpin' the
Intilligince Departmint wid my clanin'-rod whin the
man misremimbered.

"Prisintly, I learned that, acrost the river, about nine
miles away, was a town just dhrippin' wid dahs, an'
bohs an' arrows, an' dacoits, and elephints, an' *jingles*.
'Good!' sez I; 'this office will now close!'

"That night, I went to the Lift'nint an' communi-
cates my information. I never thought much of Lift'-
nint Brazenose till that night. He was shtiff wid
books an' the-ouries, an' all manner av thrimmin's no
manner av use. 'Town did ye say?' sez he. 'Accordin'
to the the-ouries av War, we shud wait for reinforce-
mints.'—'Faith!' thinks I, 'we'd betther dig our graves
thin'; for the nearest throops was up to their shtocks in
the marshes out Mimbu way. 'But,' says the Lift'nint,
'since 'tis a speshil case, I'll make an excepshin. We'll
visit this Lungtungpen to-night.'

"The bhoys was fairly woild wid deloight whin I
tould 'em; an', by this an' that, they wint through the
jungle like buck-rabbits. About midnight we come to
the shtrame which I had clane forgot to minshin to my
orficer. I was on, ahead, wid four bhoys, an' I thought
that the Lift'nint might want to the-ourise. 'Shtrip
boys!' sez I. 'Shtrip to the buff, an' shwim in where

glory waits!'—'But I *can't* shwim!' sez two av thim.
'To think I should live to hear that from a bhoy wid
a board-school edukashin!' sez I. 'Take a lump av
timber, an' me an' Conolly here will ferry ye over, ye
young ladies!'

"We got an ould tree-trunk, an' pushed off wid the
kits an' the rifles on it. The night was chokin' dhark,
an' just as we was fairly embarked, I heard the Lift'-
nint behind av me callin' out. 'There's a bit av a *nullah* here, sorr,' sez I, 'but I can feel the bottom already.'
So I cud, for I was not a yard from the bank.

" 'Bit av a *nullah!* Bit av an eshtuary!' sez the Lift'-
nint. 'Go on, ye made Irishman! Shtrip bhoys!' I
heard him laugh; an' the bhoys begun shtrippin' an'
rollin' a log into the wather to put their kits on. So me
an' Conolly shtruck out through the warm wather wid
our log, an' the rest come on behind.

"That shtrame was miles woide! Orth'ris, on the
rear-rank log, whispers we had got into the Thames
below Sheerness by mistake. 'Kape on shwimmin', ye
little blayguard,' sez I, 'an' don't go pokin' your dirty
jokes at the Irriwaddy.'—'Silince, men!' sings out the
Lift'nint. So we shwum on into the black dhark, wid
our chests on the logs, trustin' in the Saints an' the luck
av the British Army.

"Evenshually, we hit ground—a bit av sand—an' a
man. I put my heel on the back av him. He skreeched
an' ran.

" '*Now* we've done it!' sez Lift'nint Brazenose.
'Where the Divil *is* Lungtungpen?' There was about
a minute and a half to wait. The bhoys laid a hould

av their rifles an' some thried to put their belts on; we was marchin' wid fixed baynits av coorse. Thin we knew where Lungtungpen was; for we had hid the river-wall av it in the dhark, an' the whole town blazed wid thim messin' *jingles* an' Sniders like a cat's back on a frosty night. They was firin' all ways at wanst; but over our hids into the shtrame.

" 'Have you got your rifles?' sez Brazenose. 'Got 'em!' sez Orth'ris. 'I've got that thief Mulvaney's for all my back-pay, an' she'll kick my heart sick wid that blunderin' long shtock av hers.'—'Go on!' yells Brazenose, whippin' his sword out. 'Go on an' take the town! An' the Lord have mercy on our sowls!'

"Thin the bhoys gave wan divastatin' howl, an' pranced into the dhark, feelin' for the town, an' blindin' an' stiffin' like Cavalry Ridin' Masters whin the grass pricked their bare legs. I hammered wid the butt at some bamboo-thing that felt wake, an' the rest come an' hammered contagious, while the *jingles* was jingling, an' feroshus yells from inside was shplittin' our ears. We was too close under the wall for thim to hurt us.

"Evenshually, the thing, whatever ut was, bruk; an' the six-and-twenty av us tumbled, wan after the other, naked as we was borrun, into the town of Lungtungpen. There was a *melly* av a sumpshus kind for a whoile; but whether they tuk us, all white an' wet, for a new breed av divil, or a new kind av dacoit, I don't know. They ran as though we was both, an' we wint into thim, baynit an' butt, shriekin' wid laughin'. There was torches in the shtreets, an' I saw little Orth'-

ris rubbin' his showlther ivry time he loosed my long-
-shtock Martini; an' Brazenose walkin' into the gang
wid his sword, like Diarmid av the Gowlden Collar—
barring he hadn't a stitch av clothin' on him. We dis-
kivered elephints wid dacoits under their bellies, an',
what wid wan thing an' another, we was busy till
mornin' takin' possession av the town of Lungtungpen.

"Thin we halted an' formed up, the wimmen
howlin' in the houses an' Lift'nint Brazenose blushin'
pink in the light av the mornin' sun. 'Twas the most
ondasint p'rade I iver tuk a hand in. Foive-and-twenty
privits an' a orficer av the Line in review ordher, an'
not as much as wud dust a fife betune 'em all in the way
of clothin'! Eight av us had their belts an' pouches on;
but the rest had gone in wid a handful av cartridges an'
the skin God gave thim. *They* was as nakid as Vanus.

"'Number off from the right!' sez the Lift'nint.
'Odd numbers fall out to dress; even numbers pathrol
the town till relieved by the dressing party.' Let me tell
you, pathrollin' a town wid nothing on is an ex*payri*-
ence. I pathrolled for tin minutes, an' begad, before
'twas over, I blushed. The women laughed so. I niver
blushed before or since; but I blushed all over my carkiss thin. Orth'ris didn't pathrol. He sez only, 'Port-
smith Barricks an' the 'Ard av a Sunday!' Thin he lay
down an' rowled any ways wid laughin'.

"Whin we was all dhressed, we counted the dead—
sivinty-foive dacoits besides wounded. We tuk five elephints, a hunder' an' sivinty Sniders, two hunder' dahs,
and a lot av other burglarious thruck. Not a man av

us was hurt—excep' maybe the Lift'nint, an' he from
the shock to his dasincy.

"The Headman av Lungtungpen, who surrinder'd
himself, asked the Interprut'r—"Av the English fight
like that wid their clo'es off, what in the wurruld do
they do wid their clo'es on?' Orth'ris began rowlin' his
eyes an' crackin' his fingers an' dancin' a step-dance for
to impress the Headman. He ran to his house; an' we
spint the rest av the day carryin' the Lift'nint on our
showlthers round the town, an' playin' wid the Burmese babies—fat, little, brown little divils, as pretty as
picturs.

"When I was inviladed for the dysent'ry to India, I
sez to the Lift'nint, 'Sorr,' sezs I, 'you've the makin's in
you av a great man; but, av you'll let an ould sodger
spake, you're too fond of the-ourisn'.' He shuk hands
wid me and sez, 'Hit high, hit low, there's no plasin'
you, Mulvaney. You've seen me waltzin' through Lungtungpen like a red Injin widout the warpaint, an' you
say I'm too fond av the-ourisin'?'—'Sorr,' sez I, for I
loved the bhoy; 'I wud waltz wid you in that condishin
through *Hell*, an' so wud the rest av the men!' Thin I
wint downshtrame in the flat an' left him my blessin'.
May the Saints carry ut where ut shud go, for he was
a fine upstandin' young orficer.

"To reshume. Fwhat I've said jist shows the use av
three-year-olds. Wud fifty seasoned sodgers have taken
Lungtungpen in the dhark that way? No! They'd
know the risk av fever and chill. Let alone the
shootin'. Two hundher' might have done ut. But the
three-year-olds know little an' care less; an' where

there's no fear, there's no danger. Catch thim young, feed thim high, an' by the honor av that great, little man Bobs, behind a good orficer 'tisn't only dacoits they'd smash wid their clo'es off—'tis Con-ti-nental Ar-r-r-mies! They tuk Lungtungpen nakid; an' they'd take St. Pethersburg in their dhrawers! Begad, they would that!

"Here's your pipe, sorr. Shmoke her tinderly wid honey-dew, afther letting the reek av the Canteen plug die away. But 'tis no good, thanks to you all the same, fillin' my pouch wid your chopped hay. Canteen baccy's like the Army. It shpoils a man's taste for moilder things."

So saying, Mulvaney took up his butterfly-net, and returned to barracks.

THE MAN WHO WOULD BE KING

"Brother to a Prince and fellow to a beggar if he be found worthy."

THE Law, as quoted, lays down a fair conduct of life, and one not easy to follow. I have been fellow to a beggar again and again under circumstances which prevented either of us finding out whether the other was worthy. I have still to be brother to a Prince, though I once came near to kinship with what might have been a veritable King and was promised the reversion of a Kingdom—army, lawcourts, revenue and policy all complete. But, to-day, I greatly fear that my King is dead, and if I want a crown I must go and hunt it for myself.

The beginning of everything was in a railway train upon the road to Mhow from Ajmir. There had been a Deficit in the Budget, which necessitated traveling, not Second-class, which is only half as dear as First-class, but by Intermediate, which is very awful indeed. There are no cushions in the Intermediate class, and the population are either Intermediate, which is Eurasian, or native, which for a long night journey is nasty, or Loafer, which is amusing though intoxicated. Intermediates do not patronize refreshment-rooms. They carry their food in bundles and pots, and buy

307

sweets from the native sweetmeat-sellers, and drink the roadside water. That is why in the hot weather Intermediates are taken out of the carriages dead, and in all weathers are most properly looked down upon.

My particular Intermediate happened to be empty till I reached Nasirabad, when a huge gentleman in shirt-sleeves entered, and, following the custom of Intermediates, passed the time of day. He was a wanderer and a vagabond like myself, but with an educated taste for whiskey. He told tales of things he had seen and done, of out-of-the-way corners of the Empire into which he had penetrated, and of adventures in which he risked his life for a few days' food. "If India was filled with men like you and me, not knowing more than the crows where they'd get their next day's rations, it isn't seventy millions of revenue the land would be paying—it's seven hundred millions," said he; and as I looked at his mouth and chin I was disposed to agree with him. We talked politics—the politics of Loaferdom that sees things from the underside where the lath and plaster is not smoothed off—and we talked postal arrangements because my friend wanted to send a telegram back from the next station to Ajmir, which is the turning-off place from the Bombay to the Mhow line as you travel westward. My friend had no money beyond eight annas which he wanted for dinner, and I had no money at all, owing to the hitch in the Budget before mentioned. Further, I was going into a wilderness where, though I should resume touch with the Treasury, there were no telegraph offices. I was, therefore, unable to help him in any way.

"We might threaten a Station-master, and make him send a wire on tick," said my friend, "but that'd mean inquiries for you and for me, and I've got my hands full these days. Did you say you are traveling back along this line within any days?"

"Within ten," I said.

"Can't you make it eight?" said he. "Mine is rather urgent business."

"I can send your telegram within ten days if that will serve you," I said.

"I couldn't trust the wire to fetch him now I think of it. It's this way. He leaves Delhi on the 23d for Bombay. That means he'll be running through Ajmir about the night of the 23d."

"But I'm going into the Indian Desert," I explained.

"Well *and* good," said he. "You'll be changing at Marwar Junction to get into Jodhpore territory—you must do that—and he'll be coming through Marwar Junction in the early morning of the 24th by the Bombay Mail. Can you be at Marwar Junction on that time? 'Twon't be inconveniencing you because I know that there's precious few pickings to be got out of these Central India States—even though you pretend to be correspondent of the *Backwoodsman*."

"Have you ever tried that trick?" I asked.

"Again and again, but the Residents finds you out, and then you get escorted to the Border before you've time to get your knife into them. But about my friend here. I *must* give him a word o' mouth to tell him what's come to me or else he won't know where to go. I would take it more than kind of you if you was to

come out of Central India in time to catch him at
Marwar Junction, and say to him:—'He has gone
South for the week.' He'll know what that means.
He's a big man with a red beard, and a great swell he
is. You'll find him sleeping like a gentleman with all
his luggage round him in a Second-class compartment.
But don't you be afraid. Slip down the window, and
say:—'He has gone South for the week,' and he'll
tumble. It's only cutting your time of stay in those
parts by two days. I ask you as a stranger—going to
the West," he said, with emphasis.

"Where have *you* come from?" said I.

"From the East," said he, "and I am hoping that you
will give him the message on the Square—for the sake
of my Mother as well as your own."

Englishmen are not usually softened by appeals to the
memory of their mothers, but for certain reasons, which
will be fully apparent, I saw fit to agree.

"It's more than a little matter," said he, "and that's
why I ask you to do it—and now I know that I can
depend on you doing it. A Second-class carriage at
Marwar Junction, and a redhaired man asleep in it.
You'll be sure to remember. I get out at the next station, and I must hold on there till he comes or sends me
what I want."

"I'll give the message if I catch him," I said, "and
for the sake of your Mother as well as mine I'll give
you a word of advice. Don't try to run the Central
India States just now as the correspondent of the *Backwoodsman*. There's a real one knocking about here,
and it might lead to trouble."

"Thank you," said he, simply, "and when will the swine be gone? I can't starve because he's ruining my work. I wanted to get hold of the Degumber Rajah down here about his father's widow, and give him a jump."

"What did he do to his father's widow, then?"

"Filled her up with red pepper and slippered her to death as she hung from a beam. I found that out myself and I'm the only man that would dare going into the State to get hush-money for it. They'll try to poison me, same as they did in Chortumna when I went on the loot there. But you'll give the man at Marwar Junction my message?"

He got out at a little roadside station, and I reflected. I had heard, more than once, of men personating correspondents of newspapers and bleeding small Native States with threats of exposure, but I had never met any of the caste before. They lead a hard life, and generally die with great suddenness. The Native States have a wholesome horror of English newspapers, which may throw light on their peculiar methods of government, and do their best to choke correspondents with champagne, or drive them out of their mind with four-in-hand barouches. They do not understand that nobody cares a straw for the internal administration of Native States so long as oppression and crime are kept within decent limits, and the ruler is not drugged, drunk, or diseased from one end of the year to the other. Native States were created by Providence in order to supply picturesque scenery, tigers, and tall-writing. They are the dark places of the earth, full of unimaginable cruelty, touching the Railway and the Telegraph on one side, and, on the other, the days of Harun-al-Raschid. When I left the train I did business with divers Kings, and in eight days passed through many changes of life. Sometimes I wore dress-clothes and consorted with Princes and Politicals, drinking from crystal and eating from silver. Sometimes I lay out upon the ground and devoured what I could get, from a plate made of a flapjack, and drank the running water, and slept under the same rug as my servant. It was all in the day's work.

Then I headed for the Great Indian Desert upon the proper date, as I had promised, and the night Mail set me down at Marwar Junction, where a funny little, happy-go-lucky, native-managed railway runs to Jodhpore. The Bombay Mail from Delhi makes a short halt at Marwar. She arrived as I got in, and I had just time to hurry to her platform and go down the carriages. There was only one Second-class on the train. I slipped the window and looked down upon a flaming red beard, half covered by a railway rug. That was my man, fast asleep, and I dug him gently in the ribs. He woke with a grunt and I saw his face in the light of the lamps. It was a great and shining face.

"Tickets again?" said he.

"No," said I. "I am to tell you that he is gone South for the week. He is gone South for the week!"

The train had begun to move out. The red man rubbed his eyes. "He has gone South for the week," he repeated. "Now that's just like his impidence. Did he say that I was to give you anything?—'Cause I won't."

"He didn't," I said, and dropped away, and watched the red lights die out in the dark. It was horribly cold because the wind was blowing off the sands. I climbed into my own train—not an Intermediate Carriage this time—and went to sleep.

If the man with the beard had given me a rupee I should have kept it as a memento of a rather curious affair. But the consciousness of having done my duty was my only reward.

Later on I reflected that two gentlemen like my friends could not do any good if they foregathered and personated correspondents of newspapers, and might, if they "stuck up" one of the little rat-trap states of Central India or Southern Rajputana, get themselves into serious difficulties. I therefore took some trouble to describe them as accurately as I could remember to people who would be interested in deporting them: and succeeded, so I was later informed, in having them headed back from the Degumber borders.

Then I became respectable, and returned to an Office where there were no Kings and no incidents except the daily manufacture of a newspaper. A newspaper office seems to attract every conceivable sort of person, to the prejudice of discipline. Zenana-mission ladies arrive, and beg that the Editor will instantly abandon all his duties to describe a Christian prize-giving in a back-slum of a perfectly inaccessible village; Colonels who have been overpassed for commands sit down and sketch the outline of a series of ten, twelve, or twenty-four leading articles on Seniority *versus* Selection; missionaries wish to know why they have not been permitted to escape from their regular vehicles of abuse and swear at a brother-missionary under special patronage of the editorial We; stranded theatrical companies troop up to explain that they cannot pay for their advertisements, but on their return from New Zealand or Tahiti will do so with interest; inventors of patent punkah-pulling machines, carriages couplings and unbreakable swords and axle-trees call with specifications in their pockets and hours at their disposal; tea-companies enter and elaborate their prospectuses with the office pens; secretaries of ball-committees clamor to have the glories of their last dance more fully expounded; strange ladies rustle in and say:—"I want a hundred lady's cards printed *at once,* please," which is manifestly part of an Editor's duty; and every dissolute ruffian that ever tramped the Grand Trunk Road makes it his business to ask for employment as a proofreader. And, all the time, the telephone-bell is ringing madly, and Kings are being killed on the Continent, and Empires are saying—"You're another," and Mister Gladstone is calling down brimstone upon the British Dominions, and the little black copy-boys are whining, *"kaa-pi chay-ha-yeh"* (copy wanted) like tired bees, and most of the paper is as blank as Modred's shield.

But that is the amusing part of the year. There are other six months wherein none ever come to call, and the thermometer walks inch by inch up to the top of the glass, and the office is darkened to just above reading

light, and the press machines are red-hot of touch, and
nobody writes anything but accounts of amusements in
the Hill-stations or obituary notices. Then the telephone becomes a tinkling terror, because it tells you of
the sudden deaths of men and women that you knew
intimately, and the prickly-heat covers you as with a
garment, and you sit down and write:—"A slight increase of sickness is reported from the Khuda Janta
Khan District. The outbreak is purely sporadic in its
nature, and, thanks to the energetic efforts of the District authorities, is now almost at an end. It is, however, with deep regret we record the death, etc."

Then the sickness really breaks out, and the less recording and reporting the better for the peace of the
subscribers. But the Empires and the Kings continue
to divert themselves as selfishly as before, and the Foreman thinks that a daily paper really ought to come out
once in twenty-four hours, and all the people at the
Hill-stations in the middle of their amusements say:—
"Good gracious! Why can't the paper be sparkling?
I'm sure there's plenty going on up here."

That is the dark half of the moon, and, as the advertisements say, "must be experienced to be appreciated."

It was in that season, and a remarkably evil season,
that the paper began running the last issue of the week
on Saturday night, which is to say Sunday morning,
after the custom of a London paper. This was a great
convenience, for immediately after the paper was put
to bed, the dawn would lower the thermometer from
96° to almost 84° for half an hour, and in that chill—

you have no idea how cold is 84° on the grass until you begin to pray for it—a very tired man could set off to sleep ere the heat roused him.

One Saturday night it was my pleasant duty to put the paper to bed alone. A King or courtier or a courtesan or a community was going to die or get a new Constitution, or do something that was important on the other side of the world, and the paper was to be held open till the latest possible minute in order to catch the telegram. It was a pitchy black night, as stifling as a June night can be, and the *loo,* the red-hot wind from the westward, was booming among the tinder-dry trees and pretending that the rain was on its heels. Now and again a spot of almost boiling water would fall on the dust with the flop of a frog, but all our weary world knew that was only pretence. It was a shade cooler in the press-room than the office, so I sat there, while the type ticked and clicked, and the night-jars hooted at the windows, and the all but naked compositors wiped the sweat from their foreheads and called for water. The thing that was keeping us back, whatever it was, would not come off, though the *loo* dropped and the last type was set, and the whole round earth stood still in the choking heat, with its fingers on its lip, to wait the event. I drowsed, and wondered whether the telegraph was a blessing, and whether this dying man, or struggling people, was aware of the inconvenience the delay was causing. There was no special reason beyond the heat and worry to make tension, but, as the clock hands crept up to three o'clock and the machines spun their fly-wheels two and three

times to see that all was in order, before I said the word
that would set them off, I could have shrieked aloud.

Then the roar and rattle of the wheels shivered the
quiet into little bits. I rose to go away, but two men
in white clothes stood in front of me. The first one
said:—"It's him!" The second said:—"So it is!" And
they both laughed almost as loudly as the machinery
roared, and mopped their foreheads. "We see there
was a light burning across the road and we were sleeping in that ditch there for coolness, and I said to my
friend here, The office is open. Let's come along and
speak to him as turned us back from the Degumber
State," said the smaller of the two. He was the man
I had met in the Mhow train, and his fellow was the
red-bearded man of Marwar Junction. There was no
mistaking the eyebrows of the one or the beard of the
other.

I was not pleased, because I wished to go to sleep, not
to squabble with loafers. "What do you want?" I
asked.

"Half an hour's talk with you cool and comfortable,
in the office," said the red-bearded man. "We'd *like*
some drink—the Contrack doesn't begin yet, Peachey,
so you needn't look—but what we really want is advice.
We don't want money. We ask you as a favor, because
you did us a bad turn about Degumber."

I led from the press-room to the stifling office with
the maps on the walls, and the red-haired man rubbed
his hands. "That's something like," said he. "This
was the proper shop to come to. Now, Sir, let me introduce to you Brother Peachey Carnehan, that's him,

and Brother Daniel Dravot, that is *me,* and the less said about our professions the better, for we have been most things in our time. Soldier, sailor, compositor, photographer, proof-reader, street-preacher, and correspondents of the *Backwoodsman* when we thought the paper wanted one. Carnehan is sober, and so am I. Look at us first and see that's sure. It will save you cutting into my talk. We'll take one of your cigars apiece, and you shall see us light."

I watched the test. The men were absolutely sober, so I gave them each a tepid peg.

"Well *and* good," said Carnehan of the eyebrows, wiping the froth from his moustache. "Let me talk now, Dan. We have been all over India, mostly on foot. We have been boiler-fitters, engine-drivers, petty contractors, and all that, and we have decided that India isn't big enough for such as us."

They certainly were too big for the office. Dravot's beard seemed to fill half the room and Carnehan's shoulders the other half, as they sat on the big table. Carnehan continued:—"The country isn't half worked out because they that governs it won't let you touch it. They spend all their blessed time in governing it, and you can't lift a spade, nor chip a rock, nor look for oil, nor anything like that without all the Government saying—'Leave it alone and let us govern.' Therefore, such as it is, we will let it alone, and go away to some other place where a man isn't crowded and can come to his own. We are not little men, and there is nothing that we are afraid of except Drink, and we have signed

a Contrack on that. *Therefore,* we are going away to
be Kings."

"Kings in our own right," muttered Dravot.

"Yes, of course," I said. "You've been tramping in
the sun, and it's a very warm night, and hadn't you better sleep over the notion? Come to-morrow."

"Neither drunk nor sunstruck," said Dravot. "We
have slept over the notion half a year, and require to
see Books and Atlases, and we have decided that there
is only one place now in the world that two strong
men can Sar-a-*whack*. They call it Kafiristan. But my
reckoning it's the top right-hand corner of Afghanistan,
not more than three hundred miles from Peshawur.
They have two and thirty heathen idols there, and we'll
be the thirty-third. It's a mountainous country, and
the women of those parts are very beautiful."

"But that is provided against in the Contrack," said
Carnehan. "Neither Women nor Liqu-or, Daniel."

"And that's all we know, except that no one has
gone there, and they fight, and in any place where they
fight a man who knows how to drill men can always
be a King. We shall go to those parts and say to any
King we find—'D' you want to vanquish your foes?'
and we will show him how to drill men; for that we
know better than anything else. Then we will subvert
that King and seize his Throne and establish a Dy-
nasty."

"You'll be cut to pieces before you're fifty miles
across the Border," I said. "You have to travel through
Afghanistan to get to that country. It's one mass of
mountains and peaks and glaciers, and no Englishman

has been through it. The people are utter brutes, and even if you reached them you couldn't do anything."

"That's more like," said Carnehan. "If you could think us a little more mad we would be more pleased. We have come to you to know about this country, to read a book about it, and to be shown maps. We want you to tell us that we are fools and to show us your books." He turned to the bookcases.

"Are you at all in earnest?" I said.

"A little," said Dravot, sweetly. "As big a map as you have got, even if it's all blank where Kafiristan is, and any books you've got. We can read, though we aren't very educated."

I uncased the big thirty-two-miles-to-the-inch map of India, and two smaller Frontier maps, hauled down volume INF-KAN of the *Encyclopædia Britannica,* and the men consulted them.

"See here!" said Dravot, his thumb on the map. "Up to Jagdallak, Peachey and me know the road. We was there with Roberts's Army. We'll have to turn off to the right at Jagdallak through Laghmann territory. Then we get among the hills—fourteen thousand feet —fifteen thousand—it will be cold work there, but it don't look very far on the map."

I handed him Wood on the *Sources of the Oxus.* Carnehan was deep in the *Encyclopædia.*

"They're a mixed lot," said Dravot, reflectively; "and it won't help us to know the names of their tribes. The more tribes the more they'll fight, and the better for us. From Jagdallak to Ashang. H'mm!"

' But all the information about the country is as

sketchy and inaccurate as can be," I protested. "No
one knows anything about it really. Here's the file of
the *United Services' Institute*. Read what Bellew says."

"Blow Bellew!" said Carnehan. "Dan, they're an all-
fired lot of heathens, but this book here says they think
they're related to us English."

I smoked while the men pored over *Raverty, Wood,*
the maps and the *Encyclopædia*.

"There is no use your waiting," said Dravot, politely.
"It's about four o'clock now. We'll go before six
o'clock if you want to sleep, and we won't steal any of
the papers. Don't you sit up. We're two harmless
lunatics, and if you come, to-morrow evening, down to
the Serai we'll say good-bye to you."

"You *are* two fools," I answered. "You'll be turned
back at the Frontier or cut up the minute you set
foot in Afghanistan. Do you want any money or a
recommendation down-country? I can help you to
the chance of work next week."

"Next week we shall be hard at work ourselves,
thank you," said Dravot. "It isn't so easy being a King
as it looks. When we've got our Kingdom in going
order we'll let you know, and you can come up and
help us to govern it."

"Would two lunatics make a Contrack like that?"
said Carnehan, with subdued pride, showing me a
greasy half-sheet of note-paper on which was written
the following. I copied it then and there, as a curiosity:

*This Contract between me and you persuing wit-
nesseth in the name of God—Amen and so forth.*

(One) That me and you will settle this matter to-
gether: i.e., to be Kings of Kafiristan.
(Two) That you and me will not, while this matter
is being settled, look at any Liquor, nor
any woman, black, white or brown, so as
to get mixed up with one or the other
harmful.
(Three) *That we conduct ourselves with dignity and*
discretion, and if one of us gets into trouble
the other will stay by him.
Signed by you and me this day.
Peachey Taliaferro Carnehan.
Daniel Dravot.
Both Gentlemen at Large.

"There was no need for the last article," said Carnehan, blushing modestly; "but it looks regular. Now
you know the sort of men that loafers are—we *are*
loafers, Dan, until we get out of India—and *do* you
think that we would sign a Contrack like that unless
we was in earnest? We have kept away from the two
things that make life worth having."

"You won't enjoy your lives much longer if you are
going to try this idiotic adventure. Don't set the office
on fire," I said, "and go away before nine o'clock."

I left them still poring over the maps and making
notes on the back of the "Contrack." "Be sure to
come down to the Serai to-morrow," were their parting words.

The Kumharsen Serai is the great four-square sink
of humanity where the strings of camels and horses

from the North load and unload. All the nationalities of Central Asia may be found there, and most of the folk of India proper. Balkh and Bokhara there meet Bengal and Bombay, and try to draw eye-teeth. You can buy ponies, turquoises, Persian pussy-cats, saddle-bags, fat-tailed sheep and musk in the Kumharsen Serai, and get many strange things for nothing. In the afternoon I went down there to see whether my friends intended to keep their word or were lying about drunk.

A priest attired in fragments of ribbons and rags stalked up to me, gravely twisting a child's paper whirligig. Behind him was his servant bending under the load of a crate of mud toys. The two were load-ing up two camels, and the inhabitants of the Serai watched them with shrieks of laughter.

"The priest is mad," said a horse-dealer to me. "He is going up to Kabul to sell toys to the Amir. He will either be raised to honor or have his head cut off. He came in here this morning and has been behaving madly ever since."

"The witless are under the protection of God," stammered a flat-cheeked Usbeg in broken Hindi. "They foretell future events."

"Would they could have foretold that my caravan would have been cut up by the Shinwaris almost within shadow of the Pass!" grunted the Eusufzai agent of a Rajputana trading-house whose goods had been feloni-ously diverted into the hands of other robbers just across the Border, and whose misfortunes were the laughing-stock of the bazaar. "Ohé, priest, whence come you and whither do you go?"

"From Roum have I come," shouted the priest, waving his whirligig; "from Roum, blown by the breath of a hundred devils across the sea! O thieves, robbers, liars, the blessing of Pir Khan on pigs, dogs, and perjurers! Who will take the Protected of God to the North to sell charms that are never still to the Amir? The camels shall not gall, the sons shall not fall sick, and the wives shall remain faithful while they are away, of the men who give me place in their caravan. Who will assist me to slipper the King of the Ross with a golden slipper with a silver heel? The protection of Pir Khan be upon his labors!" He spread out the skirts of his gaberdine and pirouetted between the lines of tethered horses.

"There starts a caravan from Peshawur to Kabul in twenty days, *Huzrut,*" said the Eusufzai trader. "My camels go therewith. Do thou also go and bring us good-luck."

"I will go even now!" shouted the priest. "I will depart upon my winged camels, and be at Pashawur in a day! Ho! Hazar Mir Khan," he yelled to his servant, "drive out the camels, but let me first mount my own."

He leaped on the back of his beast as it knelt, and, turning round to me, cried:—"Come thou also, Sahib, a little along the road, and I will sell thee a charm—an amulet that shall make thee King of Kafiristan."

Then the light broke upon me, and I followed the two camels out of the Serai till we reached open road and the priest halted.

"What d' you think o' that?" said he in English.

"Carnehan can't talk their patter, so I've made him my servant. He makes a handsome servant. 'Tisn't for nothing that I've been knocking about the country for fourteen years. Didn't I do that talk neat? We'll hitch on to a caravan at Peshawur till we get to Jagdallak, and then we'll see if we can get donkeys for our camels, and strike into Kafiristan. Whirligigs for the Amir, O Lor! Put your hand under the camel-bags and tell me what you feel."

I felt the butt of a Martini, and another and another.

"Twenty of 'em," said Dravot, placidly. "Twenty of 'em, and ammunition to correspond, under the whirligigs and the mud dolls."

"Heaven help you if you are caught with those things!" I said. "A Martini is worth her weight in silver among the Pathans."

"Fifteen hundred rupees of capital—every rupee we could beg, borrow, or steal—are invested on these two camels," said Dravot. "We won't get caught. We're going through the Khaiber with a regular caravan. Who'd touch a poor mad priest?"

"Have you got everything you want?" I asked, overcome with astonishment.

"Not yet, but we shall soon. Give us a memento of your kindness, *Brother*. You did me a service yesterday, and that time in Marwar. Half my Kingdom shall you have, as the saying is." I slipped a small charm compass from my watch-chain and handed it up to the priest.

"Good-bye," said Dravot, giving me hand cautiously. "It's the last time we'll shake hands with an English-

man these many days. Shake hands with him, Carnehan," he cried, as the second camel passed me.

Carnehan leaned down and shook hands. Then the
camels passed away along the dusty road, and I was
left alone to wonder. My eye could detect no failure
in the disguises. The scene in Serai attested that they
were complete to the native mind. There was just the
chance, therefore, that Carnehan and Dravot would be
able to wander through Afghanistan without detection.
But, beyond, they would find death, certain and awful
death.

Ten days later a native friend of mine, giving me the
news of the day from Peshawur, wound up his letter
with:—"There has been much laughter here on account
of a certain mad priest who is going in his estimation
to sell petty gauds and insignificant trinkets which he
ascribes as great charms to H. H. the Amir of Bokhara.
He passed through Peshawur and associated himself to
the Second Summer caravan that goes to Kabul. The
merchants are pleased because through superstition they
imagine that such mad fellows bring good-fortune."

The two, then, were beyond the Border. I would
have prayed for them, but, that night, a real King died
in Europe, and demanded an obituary notice.

.   .   .   .   .   .

The wheel of the world swings through the same
phases again and again. Summer passed and winter
thereafter, and came and passed again. The daily paper
continued and I with it, and upon the third summer
there fell a hot night, a night-issue, and a strained wait-

ing for something to be telegraphed from the other side of the world, exactly as had happened before. A few great men had died in the past two years, the machines worked with more clatter, and some of the trees in the Office garden were a few feet taller. But that was all the difference.

I passed over to the press-room, and went through just a scene as I have already described. The nervous tension was stronger than it had been two years before, and I felt the heat more acutely. At three o'clock I cried, "Print off," and turned to go, when there crept to my chair what was left of a man. He was bent into a circle, his head was sunk between his shoulders, and he moved his feet one over the other like a bear. I could hardly see whether he walked or crawled—this rag-wrapped, whining cripple who addressed me by name, crying that he was come back. "Can you give me a drink?" he whimpered. "For the Lord's sake, give me a drink!"

I went back to the office, the man following with groans of pain, and I turned up the lamp.

"Don't you know me?" he gasped, dropping into a chair, and he turned his drawn face, surmounted by a shock of grey hair, to the light.

I looked at him intently. Once before had I seen eyebrows that met over the nose in an inch-broad black band, but for the life of me I could not tell where.

"I don't know you," I said, handing him the whiskey. "What can I do for you?"

He took a gulp of the spirit raw, and shivered in spite of the suffocating heat.

"I've come back," he repeated; "and I was the King of Kafiristan—me and Dravot—crowned Kings we was! In this office we settled it—you setting there and giving us the books. I am Peachey—Peachey Taliaferro Carnehan, and you've been setting here ever since —O Lord!"

I was more than a little astonished, and expressed my feelings accordingly.

"It's true," said Carnehan, with a dry cackle, nursing his feet, which were wrapped in rags. "True as gospel. Kings we were, with crowns upon our heads —me and Dravot—poor Dan—oh, poor, poor Dan, that would never take advice, not though I begged of him!"

"Take the whiskey," I said, "and take your own time. Tell me all you can recollect of everything from beginning to end. You got across the border on your camels, Dravot dressed as a mad priest and you his servant. Do you remember that?"

"I ain't mad—yet, but I shall be that way soon. Of course I remember. Keep looking at me, or maybe my words will go all to pieces. Keep looking at me in my eyes and don't say anything."

I leaned forward and looked into his face as steadily as I could. He dropped one hand upon the table and I grasped it by the wrist. It was twisted like a bird's claw, and upon the back was a ragged, red, diamond-shaped scar.

"No, don't look there. Look at *me*," said Carnehan.

"That comes afterward, but for the Lord's sake don't distrack me. We left with that caravan, me and Dravot playing all sorts of antics to amuse the people we were with. Dravot used to make us laugh in the evenings when all the people was cooking their dinners—cooking their dinners, and . . . what did they do then? They lit little fires with sparks that went into Dravot's beard, and we all laughed—fit to die. Little red fires they was, going into Dravot's big red beard—so funny." His eyes left mine and he smiled foolishly.

"You went as far as Jagdallak with that caravan," I said, at a venture "after you had lit those fires. To Jagdallak, where you turned off to try to get into Kafiristan."

"No, we didn't neither. What are you talking about? We turned off before Jagdallak, because we heard the roads was good. But they wasn't good enough for our two camels—mine and Dravot's. When we left the caravan, Dravot took off all his clothes and mine too, and said we would be heathen, because the Kafirs didn't allow Mohammedans to talk to them. So we dressed betwixt and between, and such a sight as Daniel Dravot I never saw yet nor expect to see again. He burned half his beard, and slung a sheep-skin over his shoulder, and shaved his head into patterns. He shaved mine, too, and made me wear outrageous things to look like a heathen. That was in a most mountainous country, and our camels couldn't go along any more because of the mountains. They were tall and black, and coming home I saw them fight like wild goats—there are lots of goats in Kafiristan. And these mountains, they never keep still, no more than the goats. Always fighting they are, and don't let you sleep at night."

"Take some more whiskey," I said, very slowly. "What did you and Daniel Dravot do when the camels could go no further because of the rough roads that led into Kafiristan?"

"What did which do? There was a party called Peachey Taliaferro Carnehan that was with Dravot. Shall I tell you about him? He died out there in the cold. Slap from the bridge fell old Peachey, turning and twisting in the air like a penny whirligig that you can sell to the Amir.—No; they was two for three ha' pence, those whirligigs, or I am much mistaken and woful sore. And then these camels were no use, and Peachey said to Dravot—'For the Lord's sake, let's get out of this before our heads are chopped off,' and with that they killed the camels all among the mountains, not having anything in particular to eat, but first they took off the boxes with the guns and the ammunition, till two men came along driving four mules. Dravot up and dances in front of them, singing,—'Sell me four mules.' Says the first man,—'If you are rich enough to buy, you are rich enough to rob;' but before ever he could put his hand to his knife, Dravot breaks his neck over his knee, and the other party runs away. So Carnehan loaded the mules with the rifles that was taken off the camels, and together we starts forward into those bitter cold mountaineous parts, and never a road broader than the back of your hand."

He paused for a moment, while I asked him if he could remember the nature of the country through which he had journeyed.

"I am telling you as straight as I can, but my head

isn't as good as it might be. They drove nails through
it to make me hear better how Dravot died. The country was mountaineous and the mules were most contrary, and the inhabitants was dispersed and solitary.
They went up and up, and down and down, and that
other party, Carnehan, was imploring of Dravot not to
sing and whistle so loud, for fear of bringing down
the tremenjus avalanches. But Dravot says that if a
King couldn't sing it wasn't worth being King, and
whacked the mules over the rump, and never took no
heed for ten cold days. We came to a big level valley all among the mountains, and the mules were near
dead, so we killed them, not having anything in special
for them or us to eat. We sat upon the boxes, and
played odd and even with the cartridges that was jolted
out.

"Then ten men with bows and arrows ran down
that valley, chasing twenty men with bows and arrows,
and the row was tremenjus. They was fair men—fairer
than you or me—with yellow hair and remarkable well
built. Says Dravot, unpacking the guns—'This is the
beginning of the business. We'll fight for the ten men,'
and with that he fires two rifles at the twenty men, and
drops one of them at two hundred yards from the rock
where we was sitting. The other men began to run,
but Carnehan and Dravot sits on the boxes picking
them off at all ranges, up and down the valley. Then
we goes up to the ten men that had run across the snow
too, and they fires a footy little arrow at us. Dravot he
shoots above their heads and they all falls down flat.
Then he walks over them and kicks them, and then he

lifts them up and shakes hands all round to make them friendly like. He calls them and gives them the boxes to carry, and waves his hand for all the world as though he was King already. They takes the boxes and him across the valley and up the hill into pine wood on the top, where there was half a dozen big stone idols. Dravot he goes to the biggest—a fellow they call Imbra —and lays a rifle and a cartridge at his feet, rubbing his nose respectful with his own nose, patting him on the head, and saluting in front of it. He turns round to the men and nods his head, and says,—'That's all right. I'm in the know too, and all these old jim-jams are my friends.' Then he opens his mouth and points down it, and when the first man brings him food, he says—'No'; and when the second man brings him food, he says—'No'; but when one of the old priests and the boss of the village brings him food, he says—'Yes'; very haughty, and eats it slow. That was how we came to our first village, without any trouble, just as though we had tumbled from the skies. But we tumbled from one of those damned rope-bridges, you see, and you couldn't expect a man to laugh much after that."

"Take some more whiskey and go on," I said. "That was the first village you came into. How did you get to be King?"

"I wasn't King," said Carnehan. "Dravot he was the King, and a handsome man he looked with the gold crown on his head and all. Him and the other party stayed in that village, and every morning Dravot sat by the side of old Imbra, and the people came and worshipped. That was Dravot's order. Then a lot of

men came into the valley, and Carnehan and Dravot
picks them off with the rifles before they knew where
they was, and runs down into the valley and up again
the other side, and finds another village, same as the
first one, and the people all falls down flat on their
faces, and Dravot says,—'Now what is the trouble between you two villages?' and the people points to a
woman, as fair as you or me, that was carried off, and
Dravot takes her back to the first village and counts
up the dead—eight there was. For each dead man
Dravot pours a little milk on the ground and waves his
arms like a whirligig and 'That's all right,' says he.
Then he and Carnehan takes the big boss of each village by the arm and walks them down the valley, and
shows them how to scratch a line with a spear right
down the valley, and gives each a sod of turf from both
sides o' the line. Then all the people comes down and
shouts like the devil and all, and Dravot says,—'Go
and dig the land, and be fruitful and multiply,' which
they did, though they didn't understand. Then we
asks the names of things in their lingo—bread and
water and fire and idols and such, and Dravot leads
the priest of each village up to the idol, and says he
must sit there and judge the people, and if anything
goes wrong he is to be shot.

"Next week they was all turning up the land in the
valley as quiet as bees and much prettier, and the priests
heard all the complaints and told Dravot in dumb show
what it was about. 'That's just the beginning,' says
Dravot. 'They think we're Gods.' He and Carnehan
picks out twenty good men and shows them how to

click off a rifle, and form fours, and advance in line, and they was very pleased to do so, and clever to see the hang of it. Then he takes out his pipe and his baccy-pouch and leaves one at one village and one at the other, and off we two goes to see what was to be done in the next valley. That was all rock, and there was a little village there, and Carnehan says,—'Send 'em to the old valley to plant,' and takes 'em there and gives 'em some land that wasn't took before. They were a poor lot, and we blooded 'em with a kid before letting 'em into the new Kingdom. That was to impress the people, and then they settled down quiet, and Carnehan went back to Dravot who had got into another valley, all snow and ice and most mountaineous. There was no people there and the Army got afraid, so Dravot shoots one of them, and goes on till he finds some people in a village, and the Army explains that unless the people wants to be killed they had better not shoot their little matchlock; for they had matchlocks. We makes friends with the priest and I stays there alone with two of the Army, teaching the men how to drill, and a thundering big Chief comes across the snow with kettle-drums and horns twanging, because he heard there was a new God kicking about. Carnehan sights for the brown of the men half a mile across the snow and wings one of them. Then he sends a message to the Chief that, unless he wished to be killed, he must come and shake hands with me and leave his arms behind. The Chief comes alone first, and Carnehan shakes hands with him and whirls his arms about, same as Dravot used, and very much surprised that

Chief was, and strokes my eyebrows. Then Carnehan goes alone to the Chief, and asks him in dumb show if he had an enemy he hated. 'I have,' says the Chief. So Carnehan weeds out the pick of his men, and sets the two of the Army to show them drill and at the end of two weeks the men can manœuvre about as well as Volunteers. So he marches with the Chief to a great big plain on the top of a mountain, and the Chief's men rushes into a village and takes it; we three Martinis firing into the brown of the enemy. So we took that village too, and I gives the Chief a rag from my coat and says, 'Occupy till I come:' which was scriptural. By way of a reminder, when me and the Army was eighteen hundred yards away, I drops a bullet near him standing on the snow, and all the people falls flat on their faces. Then I sends a letter to Dravot, wherever he be by land or by sea."

At the risk of throwing the creature out of train I interrupted,—"How could you write a letter up yonder?"

"The letter?—Oh!—The Letter! Keep looking at me between the eyes, please. It was a string-talk letter, that we'd learned the way of it from a blind beggar in the Punjab."

I remember that there had once come to the office a blind man with a knotted twig and a piece of string which he wound round the twig according to some cypher of his own. He could, after the lapse of days or hours, repeat the sentence which he had reeled up. He had reduced the alphabet to eleven primitive sounds; and tried to teach me his method, but failed.

"I sent that letter to Dravot," said Carnehan; "and told him to come back because this Kingdom was growing too big for me to handle, and then I struck for the first valley, to see how the priests were working. They called the village we took along with the Chief, Bashkai, and the first village we took, Er-Heb. The priests at Er-Heb was doing all right, but they had a lot of pending cases about land to show me, and some men from another village had been firing arrows at night. I went out and looked for that village and fired four rounds at it from a thousand yards. That used all the cartridges I cared to spend, and I waited for Dravot, who had been away two or three months, and I kept my people quiet.

"One morning I heard the devil's own noise of drums and horns, and Dan Dravot marches down the hill with his Army and a tail of hundreds of men, and, which was the most amazing—a great gold crown on his head. 'My Gord, Carnehan,' says Daniel, 'this is a tremenjus business, and we've got the whole country as far as it's worth having. I am the son of Alexander by Queen Semiramis, and you're my younger brother and a God too! It's the biggest thing we've ever seen. I've been marching and fighting for six weeks with the Army, and every footy little village for fifty miles has come in rejoiceful; and more than that, I've got the key of the whole show, as you'll see, and I've got a crown for you! I told 'em to make two of 'em at a place called Shu, where the gold lies in the rock like suet in mutton. Gold I've seen, and turquoise I've kicked out of the cliffs, and there's garnets in the sands of the river, and here's a chunk of amber that a man brought me. Call up all the priests and, here, take your crown.'

"One of the men opens a black hair bag and I slips the crown on. It was too small and too heavy, but I wore it for the glory. Hammered gold it was—five pound weight, like a hoop of a barrel.

" 'Peachey,' says Dravot, 'we don't want to fight no more. The Craft's the trick so help me!' and he brings forward that same Chief that I left at Bashkai—Billy Fish we called him afterward, because he was so like Billy Fish that drove the big tank-engine at Mach on the Bolan in the old days. 'Shake hands with him,' says Dravot, and I shook hands and nearly dropped, for Billy Fish gave me the Grip. I said nothing, but tried him with the Fellow Craft Grip. He answers, all right, and I tried the Master's Grip, but that was a slip. 'A Fellow Craft he is!' I says to Dan. 'Does he know the word?' 'He does,' says Dan, 'and all the priests know. It's a miracle! The Chiefs and the priests can work a Fellow Craft Lodge in a way that's very like ours, and they've cut the marks on the rocks, but they don't know the Third Degree, and they've come to find out. It's Gord's Truth. I've known these long years that the Afghans knew up to the Fellow Craft Degree, but this is a miracle. A God and a Grand-Master of the Craft am I, and a Lodge in the Third Degree I will open, and we'll raise the head priests and the Chiefs of the villages.'

" 'It's against all the law,' I says, 'holding a Lodge without warrant from any one; and we never held office in any Lodge.'

" 'It's a master-stroke of policy,' says Dravot. 'It means running the country as easy as a four-wheeled bogy on a down grade. We can't stop to inquire now, or they'll turn against us. I've forty Chiefs at my heel, and passed and raised according to their merit they shall be. Billet these men on the villages and see that we run up a Lodge of some kind. The temple of Imbra will do for the Lodge-room. The women must make aprons as you show them. I'll hold a levee of Chiefs to-night and Lodge to-morrow.'

"I was fair run off my legs, but I wasn't such a fool as not to see what a pull this Craft business gave us. I showed the priests' families how to make aprons of the degrees, but for Dravot's apron the blue border and marks was made of turquoise lumps on white hide, not cloth. We took a great square stone in the temple for the Master's chair, and little stones for the officers' chairs, and painted the black pavement with white squares, and did what we could to make things regular.

"At the levee which was held that night on the hillside with big bonfires, Dravot gives out that him and me were Gods and sons of Alexander, and Past Grand-Masters in the Craft, and was come to make Kafiristan a country where every man should eat in peace and drink in quiet, and specially obey us. Then the Chiefs come round to shake hands, and they was so hairy and white and fair it was just shaking hands with old friends. We gave them names according as they was like men we had known in India—Billy Fish, Holly Dilworth, Pikky Kergan that was Bazar-master when I was at Mhow, and so on and so on.

"*The* most amazing miracle was at Lodge next night. One of the old priests was watching us continuous, and I felt uneasy, for I knew we'd have to fudge the Ritual, and I didn't know what the men knew. The old priest was a stranger come in from beyond the village of Bashkai. The minute Dravot puts on the Master's apron that the girls had made for him, the priest fetches a whoop and a howl, and tries to overturn the stone that Dravot was sitting on. 'It's all up now,' I says. 'That comes of meddling with the Craft without warrant!' Dravot never winked an eye, not when ten priests took and tilted over the Grand-Master's chair—which was to say the stone of Imbra. The priest begins rubbing the bottom end of it to clear away the black dirt, and presently he shows all the other priests the Master's Mark, same as was on Dravot's apron, cut into the stone. Not even the priests of the temple of Imbra knew it was there. The old chap falls flat on his face at Dravot's feet and kisses 'em. 'Luck again,' says Dravot, across the Lodge to me, 'they say it's the missing Mark that no one could understand the why of. We're more than safe now.' Then he bangs the butt of his gun for a gavel and says:—'By virtue of the authority vested in me by my own right hand and the help of Peachey, I declare myself Grand-Master of all Freemasonry in Kafiristan in this the Mother Lodge o' the country, and King of Kafiristan equally with Peachey!' At that he puts on his crown and I puts on mine—I was doing Senior Warden—and we opens the Lodge in most ample form. It was a amazing miracle! The priests moved in Lodge through the first two de-

grees almost without telling, as if the memory was coming back to them. After that, Peachey and Dravot
raised such as was worthy—high priests and Chiefs of
far-off villages. Billy Fish was the first, and I can tell
you we scared the soul out of him. It was not in any
way according to Ritual, but it served our turn. We
didn't raise more than ten of the biggest men because
we didn't want to make the Degree common. And
they was clamoring to be raised.

" 'In another six months,' says Dravot, 'we'll hold
another Communication and see how you are working.'
Then he asks them about their villages, and learns that
they was fighting one against the other and were fair
sick and tired of it. And when they wasn't doing that
they was fighting with the Mohammedans. 'You can
fight those when they come into our country,' says
Dravot. 'Tell off every tenth man of your tribes for a
Frontier guard, and send two hundred at a time to this
valley to be drilled. Nobody is going to be shot or
speared any more so long as he does well, and I know
that you won't cheat me because you're white people—
sons of Alexander—and not like common, black Mohammedans. You are *my* people and by God,' says he,
running off into English at the end—'I'll make a
damned fine Nation of you, or I'll die in the making!'

"I can't tell all we did for the next six months because Dravot did a lot I couldn't see the hang of, and he
learned their lingo in a way I never could. My work
was to help the people plough, and now and again go
out with some of the Army and see what the other villages were doing, and make 'em throw rope-bridges

across the ravines which cut up the country horrid. Dravot was very kind to me, but when he walked up and down in the pine wood pulling that bloody red beard of his with both fists I knew he was thinking plans I could not advise him about, and I just waited for orders.

"But Dravot never showed me disrespect before the people. They were afraid of me and the Army, but they loved Dan. He was the best of friends with the priests and the Chiefs; but any one could come across the hills with a complaint and Dravot would hear him out fair, and call four priests together and say what was to be done. He used to call in Billy Fish from Bashkai, and Pikky Kergan from Shu, and an old Chief we called Kafuzelum—it was like enough to his real name—and hold councils with 'em when there was any fighting to be done in small villages. That was his Council of War, and the four priests of Bashkai, Shu, Khawak, and Madora was his Privy Council. Between the lot of 'em they sent me, with forty men and twenty rifles, and sixty men carrying turquoises, into the Ghorband country to buy those hand-made Martini rifles, that come out of the Amir's workshops at Kabul, from one of the Amir's Herati regiments that would have sold the very teeth out of their mouths for turquoises.

"I stayed in Ghorband a month, and gave the Governor there the pick of my baskets for hush-money, and bribed the Colonel of the regiment some more, and, between the two and the tribes-people, we got more than a hundred hand-made Martinis, a hundred good Kohat Jezails that'll throw to six hundred yards, and forty man-loads of very bad ammunition for the rifles. I came back with what I had, and distributed 'em among the men that the Chiefs sent to me to drill. Dravot was too busy to attend to those things, but the old Army that we first made helped me, and we turned out five hundred men that could drill, and two hundred that knew how to hold arms pretty straight. Even those cork-screwed, hand-made guns was a miracle to them. Dravot talked big about powder-shops and factories, walking up and down in the pine wood when the winter was coming on.

"'I won't make a Nation,' says he. 'I'll make an Empire! These men aren't niggers; they're English! Look at their eyes—look at their mouths. Look at the way they stand up. They sit on chairs in their own houses. They're the Lost Tribes, or something like it, and they've grown to be English. I'll take a census in the spring if the priests don't get frightened. There must be a fair two million of 'em in these hills. The villages are full o' little children. Two million people —two hundred and fifty thousand fighting men—and all English! They only want the rifles and a little drilling. Two hundred and fifty thousand men, ready to cut in on Russia's right flank when she tries for India! Peachey, man,' he says, chewing his beard in great hunks, 'we shall be Emperors—Emperors of the Earth! Rajah Brooke will be a suckling to us. I'll treat with the Viceroy on equal terms. I'll ask him to send me twelve picked English—twelve that I know of—to help us govern a bit. There's Mackray, Sergeant-pensioner at Segowli—many's the good dinner he's given me, and his wife a pair of trousers. There's Donkin, the Warder of Tounghoo Jail; there's hundreds that I could lay my hand on if I was in India. The Viceroy shall do it for me. I'll send a man through in the spring for those men, and I'll write for a dispensation from the Grand Lodge for what I've done as Grand-Master. That—and all the Sniders that'll be thrown out when the native troops in India take up the Martini. They'll be worn smooth, but they'll do for fighting in these hills. Twelve English, a hundred thousand Sniders run through the Amir's country in driblets—I'd be content with twenty thousand in one year—and we'd be an Empire. When everything was shipshape, I'd hand over the crown—this crown I'm wearing now—to Queen Victoria on my knees, and she'd say: "Rise up, Sir Daniel Dravot." Oh, it's big! It's big, I tell you! But there's so much to be done in every place—Bashkai, Khawak, Shu, and everywhere else.'

" 'What is it?' I says. 'There are no more men coming in to be drilled this autumn. Look at those fat, black clouds. They're bringing the snow.'

" 'It isn't that,' says Daniel, putting his hand very hard on my shoulder; 'and I don't wish to say anything that's against you, for no other living man would have followed me and made me what I am as you have done. You're a first-class Commander-in-Chief, and the people know you; but—it's a big country, and somehow you can't help me, Peachey, in the way I want to be helped.'

" 'Go to your blasted priests, then!' I said, and I was sorry when I made that remark, but it did hurt me sore to find Daniel talking so superior when I'd drilled all the men, and done all he told me.

" 'Don't let's quarrel, Peachey,' says Daniel, without cursing. 'You're a King too, and the half of this Kingdom is yours; but can't you see, Peachey, we want cleverer men than us now—three or four of 'em, that we can scatter about for our Deputies. It's a hugeous great State, and I can't always tell the right thing to do, and I haven't time for all I want to do, and here's the winter coming on and all.' He put half his beard into his mouth, and it was as red as the gold of his crown.

" 'I'm sorry, Daniel,' says I. 'I've done all I could. I've drilled the men and shown the people how to stack their oats better; and I've brought in those tinware rifles from Ghorband—but I know what you're driving at. I take it Kings always feel oppressed that way.'

" 'There's another thing, too,' says Dravot, walking up and down. 'The winter's coming and these people won't be giving much trouble, and if they do we can't move about. I want a wife.'

" 'For Gord's sake leave the women alone!' I says. 'We've both got all the work we can, though I *am* a fool. Remember the Contrack, and keep clear o' women.'

" 'The Contrack only lasted till such time as we was Kings; and Kings we have been these months past,' says Dravot, weighing his crown in his hand. 'You go get a wife too, Peachey—a nice, strappin', plump girl that'll keep you warm in the winter. They're prettier than English girls, and we can take the pick of 'em.

Boil 'em once or twice in hot water, and they'll come as fair as chicken and ham.'

" 'Don't tempt me!' I says. 'I will not have any dealings with a woman not till we are a dam' side more settled than we are now. I've been doing the work o' two men, and you've been doing the work o' three. Let's lie off a bit, and see if we can get some better tobacco from Afghan country and run in some good liquor; but no women.'

" 'Who's talking o' *women?*' says Dravot. 'I said *wife*—a Queen to breed a King's son for the King. A Queen out of the strongest tribe, that'll make them your blood-brothers, and that'll lie by your side and tell you all the people thinks about you and their own affairs. That's what I want.'

" 'Do you remember that Bengali woman I kept at Mogul Serai when I was a plate-layer?' says I. 'A fat lot o' good she was to me. She taught me the lingo and one or two other things; but what happened? She ran away with the Station Master's servant and half my month's pay. Then she turned up at Dadur Junction in tow of a half-caste, and had the impidence to say I was her husband—all among the drivers in the running-shed!'

" 'We've done with that,' says Dravot. 'These women are whiter than you or me, and a Queen I will have for the winter months.'

" 'For the last time o' asking, Dan, do *not*,' I says. 'It'll only bring us harm. The Bible says that Kings ain't to waste their strength on women, 'specially when they've got a new raw Kingdom to work over.'

" 'For the last time of answering I will,' said Dravot, and he went away through the pine-trees looking like a big red devil. The low sun hit his crown and beard on one side and the two blazed like hot coals.

"But getting a wife was not as easy as Dan thought. He put it before the Council, and there was no answer till Billy Fish said that he'd better ask the girls. Dravot damned them all round. 'What's wrong with me?' he shouts, standing by the idol Imbra. 'Am I a dog or am I not enough of a man for your wenches? Haven't I put the shadow of my hand over this country? Who stopped the last Afghan raid?' It was me really, but Dravot was too angry to remember. 'Who brought your guns? Who repaired the bridges? Who's the Grand-Master of the sign cut in the stone?' and he thumped his hand on the block that he used to sit on in Lodge, and at Council, which opened like Lodge always. Billy Fish said nothing and no more did the others. 'Keep your hair on, Dan,' said I; 'and ask the girls. That's how it's done at Home, and these people are quite English.'

" 'The marriage of the King is a matter of State,' says Dan, in a white-hot rage, for he could feel, I hope, that he was going against his better mind. He walked out of the Council-room, and the others sat still, looking at the ground.

" 'Billy Fish,' says I to the Chief of Bashkai, 'what's the difficulty here? A straight answer to a true friend.' 'You know,' says Billy Fish. 'How should a man tell you who know everything? How can daughters of men marry Gods or Devils? It's not proper.'

"I remembered something like that in the Bible; but if, after seeing us as long as they had, they still believed we were Gods, it wasn't for me to undeceive them.

" 'A God can do anything,' says I. 'If the King is fond of a girl he'll not let her die.' 'She'll have to,' said Billy Fish. 'There are all sorts of Gods and Devils in these mountains, and now and again a girl marries one of them and isn't seen any more. Besides, you two know the Mark cut in the stone. Only the Gods know that. We thought you were men till you showed the sign of the Master.'

"I wished then that we had explained about the loss of the genuine secrets of a Master-Mason at the first go-off; but I said nothing. All that night there was a blowing of horns in a little dark temple half-way down the hill, and I heard a girl crying fit to die. One of the priests told us that she was being prepared to marry the King.

" 'I'll have no nonsense of that kind,' says Dan. 'I don't want to interfere with your customs, but I'll take my own wife.' 'The girl's a little bit afraid,' says the priest. 'She thinks she's going to die, and they are a-heartening of her up down in the temple.'

" 'Hearten her very tender, then,' says Dravot, 'or I'll hearten you with the butt of a gun so that you'll never want to be heartened again.' He licked his lips, did Dan, and stayed up walking about more than half the night, thinking of the wife that he was going to get in the morning. I wasn't any means comfortable, for I knew that dealings with a woman in foreign parts, though you was a crowned King twenty times over, could not but be risky. I got up very early in the morning while Dravot was asleep, and I saw the priests talking together in whispers, and the Chiefs talking together too, and they looked at me out of the corners of their eyes.

" 'What is up, Fish?' I says to the Bashkai man, who was wrapped up in his furs and looking splendid to behold.

" 'I can't rightly say,' says he; 'but if you can induce the King to drop all this nonsense about marriage, you'll be doing him and me and yourself a great service.'

" 'That I do believe,' says I. 'But sure, you know, Billy, as well as me, having fought against and for us, that the King and me are nothing more than two of the finest men that God Almighty ever made. Nothing more, I do assure you.'

" 'That may be,' says Billy Fish, 'and yet I should be sorry if it was.' He sinks his head upon his great fur cloak for a minute and thinks. 'King,' says he, 'be you man or God or Devil, I'll stick by you to-day. I have twenty of my men with me, and they will follow me. We'll go to Bashkai until the storm blows over.'

"A little snow had fallen in the night, and everything was white except the greasy fat clouds that blew down and down from the north. Dravot came out with his crown on his head, swinging his arms and stamping his feet, and looking more pleased than Punch.

" 'For the last time, drop it, Dan,' says I, in a whisper. 'Billy Fish here says that there will be a row.'

" 'A row among my people!' says Dravot. 'Not much. Peachey, you're a fool not to get a wife too.

Where's the girl?' says he, with a voice as loud as the braying of a jackass. 'Call up all the Chiefs and priests, and let the Emperor see if his wife suits him.'

"There was no need to call any one. They were all there leaning on their guns and spears round the clearing in the centre of the pine wood. A deputation of priests went down to the little temple to bring up the girl, and the horns blew up fit to wake the dead. Billy Fish saunters round and gets as close to Daniel as he could, and behind him stood his twenty men with matchlocks. Not a man of them under six feet. I was next to Dravot, and behind me was twenty men of the regular Army. Up comes the girl, and a strapping wench she was, covered with silver and turquoises but white as death, and looking back every minute at the priests.

" 'She'll do,' said Dan, looking her over. 'What's to be afraid of, lass? Come and kiss me.' He puts his arm round her. She shuts her eyes, gives a bit of a squeak, and down goes her face in the side of Dan's flaming red beard.

" 'The slut's bitten me!' says he, clapping his hand to his neck, and, sure enough, his hand was red with blood. Billy Fish and two of his matchlock-men catches hold of Dan by the shoulders and drags him into the Bashkai lot, while the priests howl in their lingo,—'Neither God nor Devil but a man!' I was all taken aback, for a priest cut at me in front, and the Army behind began firing into the Bashkai men.

" 'God A-mighty!' says Dan. 'What is the meaning o' this?'

" 'Come back! Come away!' says Billy Fish. 'Ruin and Mutiny is the matter. We'll break for Bashkai if we can.'

"I tried to give some sort of orders to my men—the men o' the regular Army—but it was no use, so I fired into the brown of 'em with an English Martini and drilled three beggars in a line. The valley was full of shouting, howling creatures, and every soul was shrieking, 'Not a God nor a Devil but only a man!' The Bashkai troops stuck to Billy Fish all they were worth, but their matchlocks wasn't half as good as the Kabul breech-loaders, and four of them dropped. Dan was bellowing like a bull, for he was very wrathy; and Billy Fish had a hard job to prevent him running out at the crowd.

" 'We can't stand,' says Billy Fish. 'Make a run for it down the valley! The whole place is against us.' The matchlock-men ran, and we went down the valley in spite of Dravot's protestations. He was swearing horribly and crying out that he was a King. The priests rolled great stones on us, and the regular Army fired hard, and there wasn't more than six men, not counting Dan, Billy Fish, and Me, that came down to the bottom of the valley alive.

"Then they stopped firing and the horns in the temple blew again. 'Come away—for Gord's sake come away!' says Billy Fish. 'They'll send runners out to all the villages before ever we get to Bashkai. I can protect you there, but I can't do anything now.'

"My own notion is that Dan began to go mad in his head from that hour. He stared up and down like a

stuck pig. Then he was all for walking back alone
and killing the priests with his bare hands; which he
could have done. 'An Emperor am I,' says Daniel,
'and next year I shall be a Knight of the Queen.'

"'All right, Dan,' says I; 'but come along now while
there's time.'

"'It's your fault,' says he, 'for not looking after your
Army better. There was mutiny in the midst, and you
didn't know—you damned engine-driving, plate-laying,
missionary's-pass-hunting hound!' He sat upon a rock
and called me every foul name he could lay tongue to.
I was too heart-sick to care, though it was all his foolishness that brought the smash.

"'I'm sorry, Dan,' says I, 'but there's no accounting
for natives. This business is our Fifty-Seven. Maybe
we'll make something out of it yet, when we've got to
Bashkai.'

"'Let's get to Bashkai,' says Dan, 'and, by God,
when I come back here again I'll sweep the valley so
there isn't a bug in a blanket left!'

"We walked all that day, and all that night Dan was
stumping up and down on the snow, chewing his beard
and muttering to himself.

"'There's no hope o' getting clear,' said Billy Fish.
'The priests will have sent runners to the villages to say
that you are only men. Why didn't you stick on as
Gods till things was more settled? I'm a dead man,'
says Billy Fish, and he throws himself down on the
snow and begins to pray to his Gods.

"Next morning we was in a cruel bad country—all
up and down, no level ground at all, and no food either.

The six Bashkai men looked at Billy Fish hungry-wise
as if they wanted to ask something, but they said never
a word. At noon we came to the top of a flat mountain all covered with snow, and when we climbed up
into it, behold, there was an Army in position waiting
in the middle!

" 'The runners have been very quick,' says Billy Fish,
with a little bit of a laugh. 'They are waiting for us.'

"Three or four men began to fire from the enemy's
side, and a chance shot took Daniel in the calf of the
leg. That brought him to his senses. He looks across
the snow at the Army, and sees the rifles that we had
brought into the country.

" 'We're done for,' says he. 'They are Englishmen,
these people,—and it's my blasted nonsense that has
brought you to this. Get back, Billy Fish, and take
your men away; you've done what you could, and now
cut for it. Carnehan,' says he, 'shake hands with me
and go along with Billy. Maybe they won't kill you.
I'll go and meet 'em alone. It's me that did it. Me,
the King!'

" 'Go!' says I. 'Go to Hell, Dan. I'm with you here.
Billy Fish, you clear out, and we two will meet those
folk.'

" 'I'm a Chief,' says Billy Fish, quite quiet. 'I stay
with you. My men can go.'

"The Bashkai fellows didn't wait for a second word
but ran off, and Dan and Me and Billy Fish walked
across to where the drums were drumming and the
horns were horning. It was cold—awful cold. I've got

that cold in the back of my head now. There's a lump
of it there."

The punkah-coolies had gone to sleep. Two kero-
sene lamps were blazing in the office, and the perspiration poured down my face and splashed on the blotter
as I leaned forward. Carnehan was shivering, and I
feared that his mind might go. I wiped my face, took
a fresh grip of the piteously mangled hands, and said:
—"What happened after that?"

The momentary shift of my eyes had broken the
clear current.

"What was you pleased to say?" whined Carnehan.
"They took them without any sound. Not a little whisper all along the snow, not though the King knocked
down the first man that set hand on him—not though
old Peachey fired his last cartridge into the brown of
'em. Not a single solitary sound did those swines
make. They just closed up tight, and I tell you their
furs stunk. There was a man called Billy Fish, a good
friend of us all, and they cut his throat, Sir, then and
there, like a pig; and the King kicks up the bloody
snow and says:—'We've had a dashed fine run for our
money. What's coming next?' But Peachey, Peachey
Taliaferro, I tell you, Sir, in confidence as betwixt two
friends, he lost his head, Sir. No, he didn't neither.
The King lost his head, so he did, all along o' one of
those cunning rope-bridges. Kindly let me have the
paper-cutter, Sir. It tilted this way. They marched
him a mile across that snow to a rope-bridge over a ravine with a river at the bottom. You may have seen
such. They prodded him behind like an ox. 'Damn

your eyes!' says the King. 'D'you suppose I can't die like a gentleman?' He turns to Peachey—Peachey that was crying like a child. 'I've brought you to this, Peachey,' says he. 'Brought you out of your happy life to be killed in Kafiristan, where you was late Commander-in-Chief of the Emperor's forces. Say you forgive me, Peachey.' 'I do,' says Peachey. 'Fully and freely do I forgive you, Dan.' 'Shake hands, Peachey,' says he. 'I'm going now.' Out he goes, looking neither right nor left, and when he was plumb in the middle of those dizzy dancing ropes, 'Cut, you beggars,' he shouts; and they cut, and old Dan fell, turning round and round and round twenty thousand miles, for he took half an hour to fall till he struck the water, and I could see his body caught on a rock with the gold crown close beside.

"But do you know what they did to Peachey between two pine trees? They crucified him, Sir, as Peachey's hand will show. They used wooden pegs for his hands and his feet; and he didn't die. He hung there and screamed, and they took him down next day, and said it was a miracle that he wasn't dead. They took him down—poor old Peachey that hadn't done them any harm—that hadn't done them any . . ."

He rocked to and fro and wept bitterly, wiping his eyes with the back of his scarred hands and moaning like a child for some ten minutes.

"They was cruel enough to feed him up in the temple, because they said he was more of a God than old Daniel that was a man. Then they turned him out on the snow, and told him to go home, and Peachey came home in about a year, begging along the roads quite safe; for Daniel Dravot he walked before and said:— 'Come along, Peachey. It's a big thing we're doing.' The mountains they danced at night, and the mountains they tried to fall on Peachey's head, but Dan he held up his hand, and Peachey came along bent double. He never let go of Dan's hand, and he never let go of Dan's head. They gave it to him as a present in the temple, to remind him not to come again, and though the crown was pure gold, and Peachey was starving, never would Peachey sell the same. You knew Dravot, Sir! You knew Right Worshipful Brother Dravot! Look at him now!"

He fumbled in the mass of rags round his bent waist; brought out a black horsehair bag embroidered with silver thread; and shook therefrom on to my table— the dried, withered head of Daniel Dravot! The morning sun that had long been paling the lamps struck the red beard and blind sunken eyes; struck, too, a heavy circlet of gold studded with raw turquoises, that Carnehan placed tenderly on the battered temples.

"You behold now," said Carnehan, "the Emperor in his habit as he lived—the King of Kafiristan with his crown upon his head. Poor old Daniel that was a monarch once!"

I shuddered, for, in spite of defacements manifold, I recognized the head of the man of Marwar Junction. Carnehan rose to go. I attempted to stop him. He was not fit to walk abroad. "Let me take away the whiskey, and give me a little money," he gasped. "I was a King once. I'll go to the Deputy Commissioner and ask to set in the Poorhouse till I get my health. No, thank you, I can't wait till you get a carriage for me. I've urgent private affairs—in the south—at Marwar."

He shambled out of the office and departed in the direction of the Deputy Commissioner's house. That day at noon I had occasion to go down the blinding hot Mall, and I saw a crooked man crawling along the white dust of the roadside, his hat in his hand, quavering dolorously after the fashion of street-singers at Home. There was not a soul in sight, and he was out of all possible earshot of the houses. And he sang through his nose, turning his head from right to left:

"The Son of Man goes forth to war,
    A golden crown to gain;
His blood-red banner streams afar—
    Who follows in his train?"

I waited to hear no more, but put the poor wretch into my carriage and drove him off to the nearest missionary for eventual transfer to the Asylum. He repeated the hymn twice while he was with me whom he did not in the least recognize, and I left him singing it to the missionary.

Two days later I inquired after his welfare of the Superintendent of the Asylum.

"He was admitted suffering from sunstroke. He died early yesterday morning," said the Superintendent. "It it true that he was half an hour bareheaded in the sun at midday?"

"Yes," said I, "but do you happen to know if he had anything upon him by any chance when he died?"

"Not to my knowledge," said the Superintendent. And there the matter rests.

PRIVATE LEAROYD'S STORY

And he told a tale.—Chronicles of Gautama Buddha.

FAR from the haunts of Company Officers who
insist upon kit-inspections, far from keen-nosed
Sergeants who sniff the pipe stuffed into the bed-
ding-roll, two miles from the tumult of the barracks,
lies the Trap. It is an old dry well, shadowed by a
twisted *pipal* tree and fenced with high grass. Here,
in the years gone by, did Private Ortheris establish his
depôt and menagerie for such possessions, dead and
living, as could not safely be introduced to the barrack-
room. Here were gathered Houdin pullets, and fox-
terriers of undoubted pedigree and more than doubtful
ownership, for Ortheris was an inveterate poacher and
preëminent among a regiment of neat-handed dog-
stealers.

Never again will the long lazy evenings return
wherein Ortheris, whistling softly, moved surgeon-wise
among the captives of his craft at the bottom of the
well; when Learoyd sat in the niche, giving sage counsel on the management of "tykes," and Mulvaney, from
the crook of the overhanging *pipal,* waved his enormous boots in benediction above our heads, delighting
us with tales of Love and War, and strange experiences
of cities and men.

Ortheris—landed at last in the "little stuff bird-shop" for which your soul longed; Learoyd—back again in the smoky, stone-ribbed North, amid the clang of the Bradford looms; Mulvaney—grizzled, tender, and very wise Ulysses, sweltering on the earthwork of a Central India line—judge if I have forgotten old days in the Trap!

Orth'ris, as allus thinks he knaws more than other foaks, said she wasn't a real laady, but nobbut a Hew-rasian. I don't gainsay as her culler was a bit doosky like. But she *was* a laady. Why, she rode iv a carriage, an' good 'osses, too, an' her 'air was that oiled as you could see your faice in it, an' she wore dimond rings an' a goold chain, an' silk an' satin dresses as mun 'a' cost a deal, for it isn't a cheap shop as keeps enough o' one pattern to fit a figure like hers. Her name was Mrs. DeSussa, an' t' waay I coom to be acquainted wi' her was along of our Colonel's Laady's dog Rip.

I've seen a vast o' dogs, but Rip was t' prettiest picter of a cliver fox-tarrier 'at iver I set eyes on. He could do owt you like to speeak, an' t' Colonel's Laady set more store by him than if he hed been a Christian. She hed bairns of her awn, but they was i' England, and Rip seemed to get all t' coodlin' and pettin' as be-longed to a bairn by good right.

But Rip were a bit on a rover, an' hed a habit o' breakin' out o' barricks like, and trottin' round t' plaice as if he were t' Cantonment Magistrate coom round in-spectin'. The Colonel leathers him once or twice, but Rip didn't care an' kept on gooin' his rounds, wi' his

taail a-waggin' as if he were flag-signallin' to t' world
at large 'at he was "gettin' on nicely, thank yo', and
how's yo'sen?" An' then t' Colonel, as was noa sort of
a hand wi' a dog, tees him oop. A real clipper of a dog,
an' it's noa wonder yon laady, Mrs. DeSussa, should tek
a fancy tiv him. Theer's one o' t' Ten Commandments
says yo maun't cuvvet your neebor's ox nor his jackass,
but it doesn't say nowt about his tarrier dogs, an' happen thot's t' reason why Mrs. DeSussa cuvveted Rip,
tho' she went to church reg'lar along wi' her husband
who was so mich darker 'at if he hedn't such a good
coaat tiv his back yo' might ha' called him a black man
and nut tell a lee nawther. They said he addled his
brass i' jute, an' he'd a rare lot on it.

Well, you seen, when they teed Rip up, t' poor awd
lad didn't enjoy very good 'elth. So t' Colonel's Laady
sends for me as 'ad a naame for bein' knowledgeable
about a dog, an' axes what's ailin' wi' him.

"Why," says I, "he's getten t' mopes, an' what he
wants is his libbaty an' coompany like t' rest on us; wal
happen a rat or two 'ud liven him oop. It's low, mum,"
says I, "is rats, but it's t' nature of a dog; an' soa's cuttin' round an' meetin' another dog or two an' passin'
t' time o' day, an' hevvin' a bit of a turn-up wi' him like
a Christian."

So she says *her* dog maunt niver fight an' noa Christians iver fought.

"Then what's a soldier for?" says I; an' I explains to
her t' contrairy qualities of a dog, 'at, when yo' coom
to think on't, is one o' t' curusest things as is. For they
larn to behave theirsens like gentlemen born, fit for t'

fost o' coompany—they tell me t' Widdy herself is fond
of a good dog and knaws one when she sees it as well
as onny body: then on t' other hand a-tewin' round
after cats an' gettin' mixed oop i' all manners o' black-
guardly street-rows, an' killin' rats, an' fightin' like
divils.

T' Colonel's Laady says:—"Well, Learoyd, I doan't
agree wi' you, but you're right in a way o' speeakin',
an' I should like yo' to tek Rip out a-walkin' wi' you
sometimes; but yo' maun't let him fight, nor chase cats,
nor do nowt 'orrid"; an' them was her very wods.

Soa Rip an' me gooes out a-walkin' o' evenin's, he
bein' a dog as did credit tiv a man, an' I catches a lot
o' rats an' we hed a bit of a match on in an awd dry
swimmin'-bath at back o' t' cantonments, an' it was
none so long afore he was as bright as a button again.
He hed a way o' flyin' at them big yaller pariah dogs
as if he was a harrow offan a bow, an' though his
weight were nowt, he tuk 'em so suddint-like they
rolled over like skittles in a halley, an' when they coot
he stretched after 'em as if he were rabbit-runnin'.
Saame with cats when he cud get t' cat agaate o'
runnin'.

One evenin', him an' me was trespassin' ovver a compound wall after one of them mongooses 'at he'd
started, an' we was busy grubbin' round a prickle-bush,
an' when we looks up there was Mrs. DeSussa wi' a
parasel ovver her shoulder, a-watchin' us. "Oh my!"
she sings out; "there's that lovelee dog! Would he let
me stroke him, Mister Soldier?"

"Ay, he would, mum," sez I, "for he's fond o' laady's

coompany. Coom here, Rip, an' speeak to this kind
laady." An' Rip, seein' 'at t' mongoose hed getten clean
awaay, cooms up like t' gentleman he was, nivver a
hauporth shy or okkord.

"Oh, you beautiful—you prettee dog!" she says, clip-
pin' an' chantin' her speech in a way them sooart has o'
their awn; "I would like a dog like you. You are so
verree lovelee—so awfullee prettee," an' all thot sort o'
talk, 'at a dog o' sense mebbe thinks nowt on, tho' he
bides it by reason o' his breedin'.

An' then I meks him joomp ovver my swagger-cane,
an' shek hands, an' beg, an' lie dead, an' a lot o' them
tricks as laadies teeaches dogs, though I doan't haud
with it mysen, for it's makin' a fool o' a good dog to
do such like.

An' at lung length it cooms out 'at she'd been
thrawin' sheep's eyes, as t' sayin' is, at Rip for many a
day. Yo' see, her childer was grown up, an' she'd
nowt mich to do, an' were allus fond of a dog. Soa
she axes me if I'd tek somethin' to dhrink. An' we
goes into t' drawn-room wheer her 'usband was a-set-
tin'. They meks a gurt fuss ovver t' dog an' I has a
bottle o' aale, an' he gave me a handful o' cigars.

Soa I coomed away, but t' awd lass sings out—"Oh,
Mister Soldier, please coom again and bring that prettee
dog."

I didn't let on to t' Colonel's Laady about Mrs. De-
Sussa, and Rip, he says nowt nawther; an' I gooes
again, an' ivry time there was a good dhrink an' a
handful o' good smooaks. An' I telled t' awd lass a
heeap more about Rip than I'd ever heeared; how he

tuk t' fost prize at Lunnon dog-show and cost thotty-
three pounds fower shillin' from t' man as bred him;
'at his own brother was t' propputty o' t' Prince o'
Wailes, an' 'at he had a pedigree as long as a Dook's.
An' she lapped it all oop an' were niver tired o' ad-
mirin' him. But when t' awd lass took to givin' me
money an' I seed 'at she were gettin' fair fond about t'
dog, I began to suspicion summat. Onny body may
give a soldier t' price of a pint in a friendly way an'
theer's no 'arm done, but when it cooms to five rupees
slipt into your hand, sly like, why, it's what t' 'lection-
eerin' fellows calls bribery an' corruption. Specially
when Mrs. DeSussa threwed hints how t' cold weather
would soon be ovver an' she was goin' to Munsooree
Pahar an' we was goin' to Rawalpindi, an' she would
niver see Rip any more onless somebody she knowed
on would be kind tiv her.

Soa I tells Mulvaney an' Ortheris all t' taale thro',
beginnin' to end.

" 'Tis larceny that wicked ould laady manes," says t'
Irishman, " 'tis felony she is sejuicin' ye into, my frind
Learoyd, but I'll purtect your innocince. I'll save ye
from the wicked wiles av that wealthy ould woman,
an' I'll go wid ye this evenin' and spake to her the
wurrds av truth an' honesty. But, Jock," says he, waggin' his heead, " 'twas not like ye to kape all that good
dhrink an' thim fine cigars to yerself, while Orth'ris
here an' me have been prowlin' round wid throats as
dry as lime-kilns, and nothin' to smoke but Canteen
plug. 'Twas a dhirty thrick to play on a comrade, for
why should you, Learoyd, he balancin' yourself on the

butt av a satin chair, as if Terence Mulvaney was not the aquil av anybody who thrades in jute!"

"Let alone me," sticks in Orth'ris, "but that's like life. Them wot's really fitted to decorate society get no show while a blunderin' Yorkshireman like you"—

"Nay," says I, "it's none o' t' blunderin' Yorkshireman she wants; it's Rip. He's t' gentleman this journey."

Soa t' next day, Mulvaney an' Rip an' me goes to Mrs. DeSussa's, an' t' Irishman bein' a strainger she wor a bit shy at fost. But yo've heeard Mulvaney talk, an' yo' may believe as he fairly bewitched t' awd lass wal she let out 'at she wanted to tek Rip away wi' her to Munsooree Pahar. Then Mulvaney changes his tune an' axes her solemn-like if she'd thought o' t' consequences o' gettin' two poor but honest soldiers sent t' Andamning Islands. Mrs. DeSussa began to cry, so Mulvaney turns round oppen t' other tack and smooths her down, allowin' 'at Rip ud be a vast better off in t' Hills than down i' Bengal, and 'twas a pity he shouldn't go wheer he was so well beliked. And soa he went on, backin' an' fillin' an' workin' up t' awd lass wal she felt as if her life warn't worth nowt if she didn't hev t' dog.

Then all of a suddint he says:—"But ye *shall* have him, marm, for I've a feelin' heart, not like this couldblooded Yorkshireman; but 'twill cost ye not a penny less than three hundher rupees."

"Don't yo' believe him, mum," says I; "t' Colonel's Laaoy wouldn't tek five hundred for him."

"Who said she would?" says Mulvaney; "it's not buyin' him mane, but for the sake o' this kind, good laady, I'll do what I never dreamt to do in my life. I'll stale him!"

"Don't say steal," says Mrs. DeSussa; "he shall have the happiest home. Dogs often get lost, you know, and then they stray, an' he likes me and I like him as I niver liked a dog yet, an' I *must* hev him. If I got him at t' last minute I could carry him off to Munsooree Pahar and nobody would niver knaw."

Now an' again Mulvaney looked acrost at me, an' though I could mak nowt o' what he was after, I concluded to take his leead.

"Well, mum," I says, "I never thowt to coom down to dog-steealin', but if my comrade sees how it could be done to oblige a laady like yo'sen, I'm nut t' man to hod back, tho' it's a bad business I'm thirkin', an' three hundred rupees is a poor set-off again t' chance of them Damning Islands as Mulvaney talks on."

"I'll mek it three fifty," says Mrs. DeSussa; "only let me hev t' dog!"

So we let her persuade us, an' she teks Rip's measure theer an' then, an' sent to Hamilton's to order a silver collar again t' time when he was to be her awn, which was to be t' day she set off for Munsooree Pahar.

"Sitha, Mulvaney," says I, when we was outside, "you're niver goin' to let her hev Rip!"

"An' would ye disappoint a poor old woman?" says he; "she shall have *a* Rip."

"An' wheer's he to come through?" says I.

"Learoyd, my man," he sings out, "you're a pretty man av your inches an' a good comrade, but your head is made av duff. Isn't our friend Orth'ris a Taxider-

mist, an' a rale artist wid his nimble white fingers?
An' what's a Taxidermist but a man who can thrate
shkins? Do ye mind the white dog that belongs to the
Canteen Sargint, bad cess to him—he that's lost half
his time an' snarlin' the rest? He shall be lost for *good*
now; an' do ye mind that he's the very spit in shape
an' size av the Colonel's, barrin' that his tail is an inch
too long, an' he has none av the color that divarsifies
the rale Rip, an' his timper is that av his masther an'
worse. But fwhat is an inch on a dog's tail? An'
fwhat to a professional like Orth'ris is a few ring-
straked shpots av black, brown, an' white? Nothin' at
all, at all."

Then we meets Orth'ris, an' that little man, bein'
sharp as a needle, seed his way through t' business in a
minute. An' he went to work a-practicin' 'air-dyes the
very next day, beginnin' on some white rabbits he had,
an' then he drored all Rip's markin's on t' back of a
white Commissariat bullock, so as to get his 'and in an'
be sure of his colors; shadin' off brown into black as
nateral as life. If Rip *hed* a fault it was too mich
markin', but it was straingely reg'lar an' Orth'ris settled
himself to make a fost-rate job on it when ·· got haud
o' t' Canteen Sargint's dog. Theer niver ··· sich a dog
as thot for bad temper, an' it did nut get no better when
his tail hed to be fettled an inch an' a half shorter.
But they may talk o' theer Royal Academies as they
like. *I* niver seed a bit o' animal paintin' to beat t' copy
as Orth'ris made of Rip's marks, wal t' picter itself was
snarlin' all t' time an' tryin' to get at Rip standin' theer
to be copied as good as goold.

Orth'ris allus hed as mich conceit on himsen as would lift a balloon, an' he wor so pleeased wi' his sham Rip he wor for tekking him to Mrs. DeSussa before she went away. But Mulvaney an' me stopped thot, knowin' Orth'ris's work, though niver so cliver, was nobbut skin-deep.

An' at last Mrs. DeSussa fixed t' day for startin' to Munsooree Pahar. We was to tek Rip to t' stayshun i' a basket an' hand him ovver just when they was ready to start, an' then she'd give us t' brass—as was agreed upon.

An' my wod! It were high time she were off, for them 'air-dyes upon t' cur's back took a vast of paintin' to keep t' reet culler, tho' Orth'ris spent a matter o' seven rupees six annas i' t' best drooggist shops i' Calcutta.

An' t' Canteen Sargint was lookin' for 'is dog every-wheer; an', wi' bein' tied up, t' beast's timper got waur nor ever.

It wor i' t' evenin' when t' train started thro' Howrah, an' we 'elped Mrs. DeSussa wi' about sixty boxes, an' then we gave her t' basket. Orth'ris, for pride av his work, axed us to let him coom along wi' us, an' he couldn't help liftin' t' lid an' showin' t' cur as he lay coiled oop.

"Oh!" says t' awd lass; "the beautee! How sweet he looks!" An' just then t' beauty snarled an' showed his teeth, so Mulvaney shuts down t' lid and says: "Ye'll be careful, marm, whin ye tek him out. He's disaccus-tomed to traveling by t' railway, an' he'll be sure to want his rale mistress an' his friend Learoyd, so ye'll make allowance for his feelings at fost."

She would do all thot an' more for the dear, good Rip, an' she would nut oppen t' basket till they were miles away, for fear anybody should recognize him, an' we were real good and kind soldier-men, we were, an' she honds me a bundle o' notes, an' then cooms up a few of her relations an' friends to say good-bye—not more than seventy-five there wasn't—an' we cuts away.

What coom to t' three hundred and fifty rupees? Thot's what I can scarcelins tell yo', but we melted it— we melted it. It was share an' share alike, for Mulvaney said: "If Learoyd got hold of Mrs. DeSussa first, sure, 'twas I that remimbered the Sargint's dog just in the nick av time, an' Orth'ris was the artist av janius that made a work av art out av that ugly piece av ill-nature. Yet, by way av a thank-offerin' that I was not led into felony by that wicked ould woman, I'll send a thrifle to Father Victor for the poor people he's always beggin' for."

But me an' Orth'ris, he bein' Cockney, an' I bein' pretty far north, did nut see it i' t' saame way. We'd getten t' brass, an' we meaned to keep it. An' soa we did—for a short time.

Noa, noa, we niver heeard a wod more o' t' awd lass. Our rig'mint went to Pindi, an' t' Canteen Sargint he got himself another tyke insteead o' t' one 'at got lost so reg'lar, an' was lost for good at last.

THE SENDING OF DANA DA

When the Devil rides on your chest remember the *chamar.*—
Native Proverb.

ONCE upon a time, some people in India made
a new Heaven and a new Earth out of broken
tea-cups, a missing brooch or two, and a hair-
brush. These were hidden under brushes, or stuffed
into holes in the hillside, and an entire Civil Service of
subordinate Gods used to find or mend them again;
and every one said: "There are more things in Heaven
and Earth than are dreamed of in our philosophy."
Several other things happened also, but the Religion
never seemed to get much beyond its first manifestations; though it added an air-line postal service, and
orchestral effects in order to keep abreast of the times,
and choke off competition.

This Religion was too elastic for ordinary use. It
stretched itself and embraced pieces of everything that
the medicine-men of all ages have manufactured. It
approved of and stole from Freemasonry; looted the
Latter-day Rosicrucians of half their pet words; took
any fragments of Egyptian philosophy that it found in
the *Encyclopædia Britannica;* annexed as many of the
Vedas as had been translated into French or English,
and talked of all the rest; built in the German versions

369

of what is left of the Zend Avesta; encouraged White, Grey and Black Magic, including spiritualism, palmistry, fortune-telling by cards, hot chestnuts, double-kerneled nuts and tallow droppings; would have adopted Voodoo and Oboe had it known anything about them, and showed itself, in every way, one of the most accommodating arrangements that had ever been invented since the birth of the Sea.

When it was in thorough working order, with all the machinery, down to the subscriptions, complete, Dana Da came from nowhere, with nothing in his hands, and wrote a chapter in its history which has hitherto been unpublished. He said that his first name was Dana, and his second was Da. Now, setting aside Dana of the New York *Sun,* Dana is a Bhil name, and Da fits no native of India unless you except the Bengali Dé as the original spelling. Da is Lap or Finnish; and Dana Da was neither Finn, Chin, Bhil, Bengali, Lap, Nair, Gond, Romaney, Magh, Bokhariot, Kurd, Armenian, Levantine, Jew, Persian, Punjabi, Madrasi, Parsee, nor anything else known to ethnologists. He was simply Dana Da, and declined to give further information. For the sake of brevity and as roughly indicating his origin, he was called "The Native." He might have been the original Old Man of the Mountains, who is said to be the only authorized head of the Tea-cup Creed. Some people said that he was; but Dana Da used to smile and deny any connection with the cult; explaining that he was an "Independent Experimenter."

As I have said, he came from nowhere, with his

hands behind his back, and studied the Creed for three weeks; sitting at the feet of those best competent to explain its mysteries. Then he laughed aloud and went away, but the laugh might have been either of devotion or derision.

When he returned he was without money, but his pride was unabated. He declared that he knew more about the Things in Heaven and Earth than those who taught him, and for this contumacy was abandoned altogether.

His next appearance in public life was at a big cantonment in Upper India, and he was then telling fortunes with the help of three leaden dice, a very dirty old cloth, and a little tin box of opium pills. He told better fortunes when he was allowed half a bottle of whiskey; but the things which he invented on the opium were quite worth the money. He was in reduced circumstances. Among other people's he told the fortune of an Englishman who had once been interested in the Simla Creed, but who, later on, had married and forgotten all his old knowledge in the study of babies and things. The Englishman allowed Dana Da to tell a fortune for charity's sake, and gave him five rupees, a dinner, and some old clothes. When he had eaten, Dana Da professed gratitude, and asked if there were anything he could do for his host—in the esoteric line.

"Is there any one that you love?" said Dana Da. The Englishman loved his wife, but had no desire to drag her name into the conversation. He therefore shook his head.

"Is there any one that you hate?" said Dana Da. The Englishman said that there were several men whom he hated deeply.

"Very good," said Dana Da, upon whom the whiskey and the opium were beginning to tell. "Only give me their names, and I will despatch a Sending to them and kill them."

Now a Sending is a horrible arrangement, first invented, they say, in Iceland. It is a Thing sent by a wizard, and may take any form, but, most generally, wanders about the land in the shape of a little purple cloud till it finds the Sendee, and him it kills by changing into the form of a horse, or a cat, or a man without a face. It is not strictly a native patent, though *chamars* of the skin and hide castes can, if irritated, despatch a Sending which sits on the breast of their enemy by night and nearly kills him. Very few natives care to irritate *chamars* for this reason.

"Let me despatch a Sending," said Dana Da; "I am nearly dead now with want, and drink, and opium; but I should like to kill a man before I die. I can send a Sending anywhere you choose, and in any form except in the shape of a man."

The Englishman had no friends that he wished to kill, but partly to soothe Dana Da, whose eyes were rolling, and partly to see what would be done, he asked whether a modified Sending could not be arranged for —such a Sending as should make a man's life a burden to him, and yet do him no harm. If this were possible, he notified his willingness to give Dana Da ten rupees for the job.

"I am not what I was once," said Dana Da, "and I must take the money because I am poor. To what Englishman shall I send it?"

"Send a Sending to Lone Sahib," said the Englishman, naming a man who had been most bitter in rebuking him for his apostasy from the Tea-cup Creed. Dana Da laughed and nodded.

"I could have chosen no better man myself," said he. "I will see that he finds the Sending about his path and about his bed."

He lay down on the hearth-rug, turned up the whites of his eyes, shivered all over and began to snort. This was Magic, or Opium, or the Sending, or all three. When he opened his eyes he vowed that the Sending had started upon the war-path, and was at that moment flying up to the town where Lone Sahib lives.

"Give me my ten rupees," said Dana Da, wearily, "and write a letter to Lone Sahib, telling him, and all who believe with him, that you and a friend are using a power greater than theirs. They will see that you are speaking the truth."

He departed unsteadily, with the promise of some more rupees if anything came of the Sending.

The Englishman sent a letter to Lone Sahib, couched in what he remembered of the terminology of the Creed. He wrote: "I also, in the days of what you held to be my backsliding, have obtained Enlightenment, and with Enlightenment has come Power." Then he grew so deeply mysterious that the recipient of the letter could make neither head nor tail of it, and was proportionately impressed; but he fancied that his friend had become a "fifth-rounder." When a man is a "fifth-rounder" he can do more than Slade and Houdin combined.

Lone Sahib read the letter in five different fashions, and was beginning a sixth interpretation when his bearer dashed in with the news that there was a cat on the bed. Now if there was one thing that Lone Sahib hated more than another, it was a cat. He scolded the bearer for not turning it out of the house. The bearer said that he was afraid. All the doors of the bedroom had been shut throughout the morning, and no *real* cat could possibly have entered the room. He would prefer not to meddle with the creature.

Lone Sahib entered the room gingerly, and there, on the pillow of his bed, sprawled and whimpered a wee white kitten; not a jumpsome, frisky little beast, but a slug-like crawler with its eyes barely opened and its paws lacking strength or direction—a kitten that ought to have been in a basket with its mamma. Lone Sahib caught it by the scurff of its neck, handed it over to the sweeper to be drowned, and fined the bearer four annas.

That evening, as he was reading in his room, he fancied that he saw something moving about on the hearth-rug, outside the circle of light from his reading-lamp. When the thing began to myowl, he realized that it was a kitten—a wee white kitten, nearly blind and very miserable. He was seriously angry, and spoke bitterly to his bearer, who said that there was no kitten in the room when he brought in the lamp, and *real* kittens of tender age generally had mother-cats in attendance.

"If the Presence will go out into the veranda and listen," said the bearer, "he will hear no cats. How, therefore, can the kitten on the bed and the kitten on the hearth-rug be real kittens?"

Lone Sahib went out to listen, and the bearer followed him, but there was no sound of any one mewing for her children. He returned to his room, having hurled the kitten down the hillside, and wrote out the incidents of the day for the benefit of his co-religionists. Those people were so absolutely free from superstition that they ascribed anything a little out of the common to Agencies. As it was their business to know all about the Agencies, they were on terms of almost indecent familiarity with Manifestations of every kind. Their letters dropped from the ceiling—unstamped—and Spirits used to squatter up and down their staircases all night; but they had never come into contact with kittens. Lone Sahib wrote out the facts, noting the hour and the minute, as every Psychical Observer is bound to do, and appending the Englishman's letter because it was the most mysterious document and might have had a bearing upon anything in this world or the next. An outsider would have translated all the tangle thus: "Look out! You laughed at me once, and now I am going to make you sit up."

Lone Sahib's co-religionists found that meaning in it; but their translation was refined and full of four-syllable words. They held a sederunt, and were filled with tremulous joy, for, in spite of their familiarity with all the other worlds and cycles, they had a very human awe of things sent from Ghost-land. They met in Lone Sahib's room in shrouded and sepulchral gloom, and their conclave was broken up by clinking among the photo-frames on the mantelpiece. A wee white kitten, nearly blind, was looping and writhing itself between the clock and the candlesticks. That stopped all investigations or doubtings. Here was the Manifestation in the flesh. It was, so far as could be seen, devoid of purpose, but it was a Manifestation of undoubted authenticity.

They drafted a Round Robin to the Englishman, the backslider of old days, adjuring him in the interests of the Creed to explain whether there was any connection between the embodiment of some Egyptian God or other (I have forgotten the name) and his communication. They called the kitten Ra, or Toth, or Tum, or some thing; and when Lone Sahib confessed that the first one had, at his most misguided instance, been drowned by the sweeper, they said consolingly that in his next life he would be a "bounder," and not even a "rounder" of the lowest grade. These words may not be quite correct, but they accurately express the sense of the house.

When the Englishman received the Round Robin— it came by post—he was startled and bewildered. He sent into the bazar for Dana Da, who read the letter and laughed. "That is my Sending," said he. "I told you I would work well. Now give me another ten rupees."

"But what in the world is this gibberish about Egyptian Gods?" asked the Englishman.

"Cats," said Dana Da, with a hiccough, for he had

discovered the Englishman's whiskey bottle. "Cats, and cats, and cats! Never was such a Sending. A hundred of cats. Now give me ten more rupees and write as I dictate."

Dana Da's letter was a curiosity. It bore the Englishman's signature, and hinted at cats—at a Sending of Cats. The mere words on paper were creepy and uncanny to behold.

"What have you done, though?" said the Englishman; "I am as much in the dark as ever. Do you mean to say that you can actually send this absurd Sending you talk about?"

"Judge for yourself," said Dana Da. "What does that letter mean? In a little time they will all be at my feet and yours, and I—O Glory!—will be drugged or drunk all day long."

Dana Da knew his people.

When a man who hates cats wakes up in the morning and finds a little squirming kitten on his breast, or puts his hands into his ulster-pocket and finds a little half-dead kitten where his gloves should be, or opens his trunk and finds a vile kitten among his dress-shirts, or goes for a long ride with his mackintosh strapped on his saddle-bow and shakes a little squawling kitten from its folds when he opens it, or goes out to dinner and finds a little blind kitten under his chair, or stays at home and finds a writhing kitten under the quilt, or wriggling among his boots, or hanging, head downward, in his tobacco-jar, or being mangled by his terrier in the veranda,—when such a man finds one kitten, neither more nor less, once a day in a place where no

kitten rightly could or should be, he is naturally upset.
When he dare not murder his daily trove because he
believes it to be a Manifestation, an Emissary, an Embodiment, and half a dozen other things all out of the
regular course of nature, he is more than upset. He is
actually distressed. Some of Lone Sahib's co-religionists thought that he was a highly favored individual;
but many said that if he had treated the first kitten
with proper respect—as suited a Toth-Ra-Tum-Sen-
nacherib Embodiment—all this trouble would have
been averted. They compared him to the Ancient
Mariner, but none the less they were proud of him and
proud of the Englishman who had sent the Manifestation. They did not call it a Sending because Icelandic
magic was not in their programme.

After sixteen kittens, that is to say after one fortnight,
for there were three kittens on the first day to impress
the fact of the Sending, the whole camp was uplifted
by a letter—it came flying through a window—from
the Old Man of the Mountains—the Head of all the
Creed—explaining the Manifestation in the most beautiful language and soaking up all the credit of it for
himself. The Englishman, said the letter, was not there
at all. He was a backslider without Power or Asceti-
cism, who couldn't even raise a table by force of voli-
tion, much less project an army of kittens through
space. The entire arrangement, said the letter, was
strictly orthodox, worked and sanctioned by the highest Authorities within the pale of the Creed. There
was great joy at this, for some of the weaker brethren
seeing that an outsider who had been working on in-

dependent lines could create kittens, whereas their own
rulers had never gone beyond crockery—and broken at
best—were showing a desire to break line on their own
trail. In fact, there was the promise of a schism. A
second Round Robin was drafted to the Englishman,
beginning: "O Scoffer," and ending with a selection
of curses from the Rites of Mizraim and Memphis and
the Commination of Jugana, who was a "fifth-rounder,"
upon whose name an unstart "third-rounder" once
traded. A papal excommunication is a *billet-doux*
compared to the Commination of Jugana. The Englishman had been proved, under the hand and seal of
the Old Man of the Mountains, to have appropriated
Virtue and pretended to have Power which, in reality,
belonged only to the Supreme Head. Naturally the
Round Robin did not spare him.

He handed the letter to Dana Da to translate into
decent English. The effect on Dana Da was curious.
At first he was furiously angry, and then he laughed
for five minutes.

"I had thought," he said, "that they would have come
to me. In another week I would have shown that I
sent the Sending, and they would have discrowned the
Old Man of the Mountains who has sent this Sending
of mine. Do you do nothing. The time has come for
me to act. Write as I dictate, and I will put them to
shame. But give me ten more rupees."

At Dana Da's dictation the Englishman wrote nothing less than a formal challenge to the Old Man of the
Mountains. It wound up: "And if this Manifestation
be from your hand, then let it go forward; but if it be

from my hand, I will that the Sending shall cease in two days' time. On that day there shall be twelve kittens and thenceforward none at all. The people shall judge between us." This was signed by Dana Da, who added pentacles and pentagrams, and a *crux ansata,* and half a dozen *swastikas,* and a Triple Tau to his name, just to show that he was all he laid claim to be.

The challenge was read out to the gentlemen and ladies, and they remembered then that Dana Da had laughed at them some years ago. It was officially announced that the Old Man of the Mountains would treat the matter with contempt; Dana Da being an Independent Investigator without a single "round" at the back of him. But this did not soothe his people. They wanted to see a fight. They were very human for all their spirituality. Lone Sahib, who was really being worn out with kittens, submitted meekly to his fate. He felt that he was being "kittened to prove the power of Dana Da," as the poet says.

When the stated day dawned, the shower of kittens began. Some were white and some were tabby, and all were about the same loathsome age. Three were on his hearth-rug, three in his bath-room, and the other six turned up at intervals among the visitors who came to see the prophecy break down. Never was a more satisfactory Sending. On the next day there were no kittens, and the next and all the other days were kittenless and quiet. The people murmured and looked to the Old Man of the Mountains for an explanation. A letter, written on a palm-leaf, dropped from the ceiling, but every one except Lone Sahib felt that letters were

not what the occasion demanded. There should have
been cats, there should have been cats,—full-grown
ones. The letter proved conclusively that there had
been a hitch in the Psychic Current which, colliding
with a Dual Identity, had interfered with the Percipi-
ent Activity all along the main line. The kittens were
still going on, but owing to some failure in the De-
veloping Fluid, they were not materialized. The air
was thick with letters for a few days afterward. Unseen hands played Glück and Beethoven on finger-
bowls and clock-shades; but all men felt that Psychic
Life was a mockery without materialized Kittens.
Even Lone Sahib shouted with the majority on this
head. Dana Da's letters were very insulting, and if he
had then offered to lead a new departure, there is no
knowing what might not have happened.

But Dana Da was dying of whiskey and opium in
the Englishman's godown, and had small heart for
honors.

"They have been put to shame," said he. "Never
was such a Sending. It has killed me."

"Nonsense," said the Englishman, "you are going to
die, Dana Da, and that sort of stuff must be left behind.
I'll admit that you have made some queer things come
about. Tell me honestly, now, how was it done?"

"Give me ten more rupees," said Dana Da, faintly,
"and if I die before I spend them, bury them with me."
The silver was counted out while Dana Da was fighting with Death. His hand closed upon the money and
he smiled a grim smile.

"Bend low," he whispered. The Englishman bent.

"Bunnia — Mission-school — expelled — *box-wallah* (peddler)—Ceylon pearl-merchant—all mine English education—out-casted, and made up name Dana Da— England with American thought-reading man and— and—you gave me ten rupees several times—I gave the Sahib's bearer two-eight a month for cats—little, little cats. I wrote, and he put them about—very clever man. Very few kittens now in the *bazar.* Ask Lone Sahib's sweeper's wife."

So saying, Dana Da gasped and passed away into a land where, if all be true, there are no materializations and the making of new creeds is discouraged.

But consider the gorgeous simplicity of it all!

TO BE FILED FOR REFERENCE

By the hoof of the Wild Goat up-tossed
From the Cliff where She lay in the Sun,
Fell the Stone
To the Tarn where the daylight is lost;
So She fell from the light of the Sun,
And alone.

Now the fall was ordained from the first,
With the Goat and the Cliff and the Tarn,
But the Stone
Knows only Her life is accursed,
As She sinks in the depths of the Tarn,
And alone.

Oh, Thou who hast builded the world!
Oh, Thou who hast lighted the Sun!
Oh, Thou who hast darkened the Tarn!
Judge Thou
The sin of the Stone that was hurled
By the Goat from the light of the Sun,
As She sinks in the mire of the Tarn,
Even now—even now—even now!
—*From the Unpublished Papers of McIntosh Jellaludin.*

"SAY is it dawn, is it dusk in thy Bower,
Thou whom I long for, who longest for me?
Oh, be it night—be it"—

Here he fell over a little camel-colt that was sleeping in the Serai where the horse-traders and the best of the blackguards from Central Asia live; and, because he was very drunk indeed and the night was dark, he could not rise again till I helped him. That was the beginning of my acquaintance with McIntosh Jellaludin. When a loafer, and drunk, sings "The Song of the Bower," he must be worth cultivating. He got off the camel's back and said, rather thickly, "I—I— I'm a bit screwed, but a dip in Loggerhead will put me right again; and, I say, have you spoken to Symonds about the mare's knees?"

Now Loggerhead was six thousand weary miles away from us, close to Mesopotamia, where you mustn't fish and poaching is impossible, and Charley Symond's stable a half mile farther across the paddocks. It was strange to hear all the old names, on a May night, among the horses and camels of the Sultan Caravanserai. Then the man seemed to remember himself and sober down at the same time. We leaned against the camel and pointed to a corner of the Serai where a lamp was burning.

"I live there," said he, "and I should be extremely obliged if you would be good enough to help my mutinous feet thither; for I am more than usually drunk —most—most phenomenally tight. But not in respect to my head. 'My brain cries out against'—how does it go? But my head rides on the—rolls on the dunghill I should have said, and controls the qualm."

I helped him through the gangs of tethered horses and he collapsed on the edge of the veranda in front of the line of native quarters.

"Thanks—a thousand thanks! O Moon and little, little Stars! To think that a man should so shamelessly

. . . Infamous liquor too. Ovid in exile drank no worse. Better. It was frozen. Alas! I had no ice. Good-night. I would introduce you to my wife were I sober—or she civilized."

A native woman came out of the darkness of the room, and began calling the man names; so I went away. He was the most interesting loafer that I had had the pleasure of knowing for a long time; and later on, he became a friend of mine. He was a tall, well-built, fair man, fearfully shaken with drink, and he looked nearer fifty than the thirty-five which, he said, was his real age. When a man begins to sink in India, and is not sent Home by his friends as soon as may be, he falls very low from a respectable point of view. By the time that he changes his creed, as did McIntosh, he is past redemption.

In most big cities, natives will tell you of two or three *Sahibs,* generally low-caste, who have turned Hindu or Mussulman, and who live more or less as such. But it is not often that you can get to know them. As McIntosh himself used to say, "If I change my religion for my stomach's sake, I do not seek to become a martyr to missionaries, nor am I anxious for notoriety."

At the outset of acquaintance McIntosh warned me. "Remember this. I am not an object for charity. I require neither your money, your food, nor your cast-off raiment. I am that rare animal, a self-supporting drunkard. If you choose. I will smoke with you, for the tobacco of the bazars does not, I admit, suit my palate; and I will borrow any books which you may not specially value. It is more than likely that I shall sell them for bottles of excessively filthy country liquors. In return, you shall share such hospitality as my house affords. Here is a charpoy on which two can sit, and it is possible that there may, from time to time, be food in that platter. Drink, unfortunately, you will find on the premises at any hour: and thus I make you welcome to all my poor establishment."

I was admitted to the McIntosh household—I and my good tobacco. But nothing else. Unluckily, one cannot visit a loafer in the Serai by day. Friends buying horses would not understand it. Consequently, I was obliged to see McIntosh after dark. He laughed at this, and said simply, "You are perfectly right. When I enjoyed a position in society, rather higher than yours, I should have done exactly the same thing. Good heavens! I was once"—he spoke as though he had fallen from the Command of a Regiment—"an Oxford Man!" This accounted for the reference to Charley Symond's stable.

"You," said McIntosh, slowly, "have not had that advantage; but, to outward appearance, you do not seem possessed of a craving for strong drinks. On the whole, I fancy that you are the luckier of the two. Yet I am not certain. You are—forgive my saying so even while I am smoking your excellent tobacco—painfully ignorant of many things."

We were sitting together on the edge of his bedstead, for he owned no chairs, watching the horses being watered for the night, while the native woman was preparing dinner. I did not like being patronized by a loafer, but I was his guest for the time being, though

he owned only one very torn alpaca-coat and a pair of
trousers made out of gunny-bags. He took the pipe out
of his mouth, and went on judicially, "All things considered, I doubt whether you are the luckier. I do not
refer to your extremely limited classical attainments,
or your excruciating quantities, but to your gross
ignorance of matters more immediately under your notice. That, for instance," he pointed to a woman cleaning a samovar near the well in the centre of the Serai.
She was flicking the water out of the spout in regular
cadenced jerks.

"There are ways and ways of cleaning samovars. If
you knew why she was doing her work in that particular fashion, you would know what the Spanish
Monk meant when he said—

> I the Trinity illustrate,
> Drinking watered orange-pulp—
> In three sips the Arian frustrate,
> While he drains his at one gulp—

and many other things which now are hidden from
your eyes. However, Mrs. McIntosh has prepared dinner. Let us come and eat after the fashion of the people
of the country—of whom, by the way, you know
nothing."

The native woman dipped her hand in the dish with
us. This was wrong. The wife should always wait
until the husband has eaten. McIntosh Jellaludin
apologized, saying—

"It is an English prejudice which I have not been
able to overcome; and she loves me. Why, I have
never been able to understand. I foregathered with

her at Jullundur, three years ago, and she has remained with me ever since. I believe her to be moral, and know her to be skilled in cookery."

He patted the woman's head as he spoke, and she cooed softly. She was not pretty to look at.

McIntosh never told me what position he had held before his fall. He was, when sober, a scholar and a gentleman. When drunk, he was rather more of the first than the second. He used to get drunk about once a week for two days. On those occasions the native woman tended him while he raved in all tongues except his own. One day, indeed, he began reciting *Atalanta in Calydon*, and went through it to the end, beating time to the swing of the verse with a bedstead-leg. But he did most of his ravings in Greek or German. The man's mind was a perfect rag-bag of useless things. Once, when he was beginning to get sober, he told me that I was the only rational being in the Inferno into which he had descended—a Virgil in the Shades, he said—and that, in return for my tobacco, he would, before he died, give me the materials of a new Inferno that should make me greater than Dante. Then he fell asleep on a horse-blanket and woke up quite calm.

"Man," said he, "when you have reached the uttermost depths of degradation, little incidents which would vex a higher life, are to you of no consequence. Last night, my soul was among the Gods; but I make no doubt that my bestial body was writhing down here in the garbage."

"You were abominably drunk if that's what you mean," I said.

"I *was* drunk—filthily drunk. I who am the son of a man with whom you have no concern—I who was once Fellow of a College whose buttery-hatch you have not seen. I was loathsomely drunk. But consider how lightly I am touched. It is nothing to me. Less than nothing; for I do not even feel the headache which should be my portion. Now, in a higher life, how ghastly would have been my punishment, how bitter my repentance! Believe me my friend with the neglected education, the highest is as the lowest—always supposing each degree extreme."

He turned round on the blanket, put his head between his fists and continued—

"On the Soul which I have lost and on the Conscience which I have killed, I tell you that I cannot feel! I am as the Gods, knowing good and evil, but untouched by either. Is this enviable cr is it not?"

When a man has lost the warning of "next morning's head," he must be in a bad state. I answered, looking at McIntosh on the blanket, with his hair over his eyes and his lips blue-white, that I did not think the insensibility good enough.

"For pity's sake, don't say that! I tell you, it *is* good and most enviable. Think of my consolations!"

"Have you so many, then, McIntosh?"

"Certainly; your attempts at sarcasm which is essentially the weapon of a cultured man, are crude. First, my attainments, my classical and literary knowledge, blurred, perhaps, by immoderate drinking—which reminds me that before my soul went to the Gods last night, I sold the Pickering Horace you so kindly loaned me. Ditta Mull the clothesman has it. It fetched ten annas, and may be redeemed for a rupee—but still infinitely superior to yours. Secondly, the abiding affection of Mrs. McIntosh, best of wives. Thirdly, a monument, more enduring than brass, which I have built up in the seven years of my degradation."

He stopped here; and crawled across the room for a drink of water. He was very shaky and sick.

He referred several times to his "treasure"—some great possession that he owned—but I held this to be the raving of drink. He was as poor and as proud as he could be. His manner was not pleasant, but he knew enough about the natives, among whom seven years of his life had been spent, to make his acquaintance worth having. He used actually to laugh at Strickland as an ignorant man—"ignorant West and East"—he said. His boast was, first, that he was an Oxford Man of rare and shining parts, which may or may not have been true—I did not know enough to check his statements—and, secondly, that he "had his hand on the pulse of native life"—which was a fact. As an Oxford Man, he struck me as a prig: he was always throwing his education about. As a Mohammedan *faquir*—as McIntosh Jellaludin—he was all that I wanted for my own ends. He smoked several pounds of my tobacco, and taught me several ounces of things worth knowing; but he would never accept any gifts, not even when the cold weather came, and gripped the poor thin chest under the poor thin alpaca-coat. He grew very angry, and said that I had insulted him, and that he was not going into hospital. He had lived like a beast and he would die rationally, like a man.

As a matter of fact, he died of pneumonia; and on the night of his death sent over a grubby note asking me to come and help him to die.

The native woman was weeping by the side of the bed. McIntosh, wrapped in a cotton cloth, was too weak to resent a fur coat being thrown over him. He was very active as far as his mind was concerned, and his eyes were blazing. When he had abused the Doctor who came with me, so foully that the indignant old fellow left, he cursed me for a few minutes and calmed down.

Then he told his wife to fetch out "The Book" from a hole in the wall. She brought out a big bundle, wrapped in the tail of a petticoat, of old sheets of miscellaneous note-paper, all numbered and covered with fine cramped writing. McIntosh ploughed his hand through the rubbish and stirred it up lovingly.

"This," he said, "is my work—the Book of McIntosh Jellaludin, showing what he saw and how he lived, and what befell him and others; being also an account of the life and sins and death of Mother Maturin. What Mirza Murad Ali Beg's book is to all other books on native life, will my work be to Mirza Murad Ali Beg's!"

This, as will be conceded by any one who knows Mirza Murad Ali Beg's book, was a sweeping statement. The papers did not look specially valuable; but

McIntosh handled them as if they were currency-notes. Then said he slowly—

"In despite the many weaknesses of your education, you have been good to me. I will speak of your tobacco when I reach the Gods. I owe you much thanks for many kindnesses. But I abominate indebtedness. For this reason, I bequeath to you now the monument more enduring than brass—my one book—rude and imperfect in parts, but oh how rare in others! I wonder if you will understand it. It is a gift more honorable than . . . Bah! where is my brain rambling to? You will mutilate it horribly. You will knock out the gems you call Latin quotations, you Philistine, and you will butcher the style to carve into your own jerky jargon; but you cannot destroy the whole of it. I bequeath it to you. Ethel . . . My brain again! . . . Mrs. McIntosh, bear witness that I give the *Sahib* all these papers. They would be of no use to you, Heart of my Heart; and I lay it upon you," he turned to me here, "that you do not let my book die in its present form. It is yours unconditionally—the story of McIntosh Jellaludin, which is *not* the story of McIntosh Jellaludin, but of a greater man than he, and of a far greater woman. Listen now; I am neither mad nor drunk! That book will make you famous."

I said, "Thank you," as the native woman put the bundle into my arms.

"My only baby!" said McIntosh, with a smile. He was sinking fast, but he continued to talk as long as breath remained. I waited for the end; knowing that, in six cases out of ten a dying man calls for his mother. He turned on his side and said—

"Say how it came into your possession. No one will believe you, but my name, at least, will live. You will treat it brutally, I know you will. Some of it must go; the public are fools and prudish fools. I was their servant once. But do your mangling gently—very gently. It is a great work, and I have paid for it in seven years' damnation."

His voice stopped for ten or twelve breaths, and then he began mumbling a prayer of some kind in Greek. The native woman cried very bitterly. Lastly, he rose in bed and said, as loudly as slowly—"Not guilty, my Lord!"

Then he fell back, and the stupor held him till he died. The native woman ran into the Serai among the horses, and screamed and beat her breasts; for she had loved him.

Perhaps his last sentence in life told what McIntosh had once gone through; but, saving the big bundle of old sheets in the cloth, there was nothing in his room to say who or what he had been.

The papers were in a hopeless muddle.

Strickland helped me to sort them, and he said that the writer was either an extreme liar or a most wonderful person. He thought the former. One of these days, you may be able to judge for yourselves. The bundle needed much expurgation and was full of Greek nonsense, at the head of the chapters, which has all been cut out.

If the thing is ever published, some one may perhaps

remember this story, now printed as a safeguard to prove that McIntosh Jellaludin and not I myself wrote the Book of Mother Maturin.

I don't want the *Giant's Robe* to come true in my case.

NAMGAY DOOLA

ONCE upon a time there was a king who lived on the road to Thibet, very many miles in the Himalaya Mountains. His kingdom was 11,000 feet above the sea, and exactly four miles square, but most of the miles stood on end, owing to the nature of the country. His revenues were rather less than £400 yearly, and they were expended on the maintenance of one elephant and a standing army of five men. He was tributary to the Indian government, who allowed him certain sums for keeping a section of the Himalaya-Thibet road in repair. He further increased his revenues by selling timber to the railway companies, for he would cut the great deodar trees in his own forest and they fell thundering into the Sutlej River and were swept down to the Plains, 300 miles away, and became railway ties. Now and again this king, whose name does not matter, would mount a ring-streaked horse and ride scores of miles to Simlatown to confer with the lieutenant-governor on matters of state, or assure the viceroy that his sword was at the service of the queen-empress. Then the viceroy would cause a ruffle of drums to be sounded and the ring-streaked horse and the cavalry of the state—two men in tatters—and the herald who bore the Silver Stick before the king would trot back to their own place,

which was between the tail of a heaven-climbing glacier
and a dark birch forest.

Now, from such a king, always remembering that he
possessed one veritable elephant and could count his
descent for 1,200 years, I expected, when it was my fate
to wander through his dominions, no more than mere
license to live.

The night had closed in rain, and rolling clouds
blotted out the lights of the villages in the valley.
Forty miles away, untouched by cloud or storm, the
white shoulder of Dongo Pa—the Mountain of the
Council of the Gods—upheld the evening star. The
monkeys sung sorrowfully to each other as they hunted
for dry roots in the fern-draped trees, and the last puff
of the day-wind brought from the unseen villages the
scent of damp wood smoke, hot cakes, dripping undergrowth, and rotting pine-cones. That smell is the true
smell of the Himalayas, and if it once gets into the
blood of a man he will, at the last, forgetting everything else, return to the Hills to die. The clouds closed
and the smell went away, and there remained nothing
in all the world except chilling white mists and the
boom of the Sutlej River.

A fat-tailed sheep, who did not want to die, bleated
lamentably at my tent-door. He was scuffling with the
prime minister and the director-general of public education, and he was a royal gift to me and my camp
servants. I expressed my thanks suitably and inquired
if I might have audience of the king. The prime
minister readjusted his turban—it had fallen off in the
struggle—and assured me that the king would be very

pleased to see me. Therefore I dispatched two bottles
as a foretaste, and when the sheep had entered upon
another incarnation, climbed up to the king's palace
through the wet. He had sent his army to escort me,
but it stayed to talk with my cook. Soldiers are very
much alike all the world over.

The palace was a four-roomed, whitewashed mud-
and-timber house, the finest in all the Hills for a day's
journey. The king was dressed in a purple velvet
jacket, white muslin trousers, and a saffron-yellow turban of price. He gave me audience in a little car-
peted room opening off the palace court-yard, which
was occupied by the elephant of state. The great beast
was sheeted and anchored from trunk to tail, and the
curve of his back stood out against the sky line.

The prime minister and the director-general of public
instruction were present to introduce me; but all the
court had been dismissed lest the two bottles aforesaid
should corrupt their morals. The king cast a wreath
of heavy, scented flowers round my neck as I bowed,
and inquired how my honored presence had the felicity
to be. I said that through seeing his auspicious countenance the mists of the night had turned into sunshine,
and that by reason of his beneficent sheep his good
deeds would be remembered by the gods. He said that
since I had set my magnificent foot in his kingdom the
crops would probably yield seventy per cent more than
the average. I said that the fame of the king had
reached to the four corners of the earth, and that the
nations gnashed their teeth when they heard daily of
the glory of his realm and the wisdom of his moon.

like prime minister and lotus-eyed director-general of public education.

Then we sat down on clean white cushions, and I was at the king's right hand. Three minutes later he was telling me that the condition of the maize crop was something disgraceful, and that the railway companies would not pay him enough for his timber. The talk shifted to and fro with the bottles. We discussed very many quaint things, and the king became confidential on the subject of government generally. Most of all he dwelt on the shortcomings of one of his subjects, who, from what I could gather, had been paralyzing the executive.

"In the old days," said the king, "I could have ordered the elephant yonder to trample him to death. Now I must e'en send him seventy miles across the hills to be tried, and his keep for that time would be upon the state. And the elephant eats everything."

"What be the man's crimes, Rajah Sahib?" said I.

"Firstly, he is an 'outlander,' and no man of mine own people. Secondly, since of my favor I gave him land upon his coming, he refuses to pay revenue. Am I not the lord of the earth, above and below—entitled by right and custom to one-eighth of the crop? Yet this devil, establishing himself, refuses to pay a single tax . . . and he brings a poisonous spawn of babes."

"Cast him into jail," I said.

"Sahib," the king answered, shifting a little on the cushions, "once and only once in these forty years sickness came upon me so that I was not able to go abroad. In that hour I made a vow to my God that I would

never again cut man or woman from the light of the
sun and the air of God, for I perceived the nature of
the punishment. How can I break my vow? Were it
only the lopping off of a hand or a foot, I should not
delay. But even that is impossible now that the English have rule. One or another of my people"—he
looked obliquely at the director-general of public education—"would at once write a letter to the viceroy, and
perhaps I should be deprived of that ruffle of drums."

He unscrewed the mouthpiece of his silver water-
pipe, fitted a plain amber one, and passed the pipe to
me. "Not content with refusing revenue," he continued, "this outlander refuses also to beegar" (this is
the corvee or forced labor on the roads), "and stirs my
people up to the like treason. Yet he is, if so he wills,
an expert log-snatcher. There is none better or bolder
among my people to clear a block of the river when
the logs stick fast."

"But he worships strange gods," said the prime minister, deferentially.

"For that I have no concern," said the king, who was
as tolerant as Akbar in matters of belief. "To each
man his own god, and the fire or Mother Earth for us
at the last. It is the rebellion that offends me."

"The king has an army," I suggested. "Has not the
king burned the man's house, and left him naked to
the night dews?"

"Nay. A hut is a hut, and it holds the life of a man.
But once I sent my army against him when his excuses
became wearisome. Of their heads he brake three

across the top with a stick. The other two men ran away. Also the guns would not shoot."

I had seen the equipment of the infantry. One-third of it was an old muzzle-loading fowling-piece with ragged rust holes where the nipples should have been; one-third a wire-bound match-lock, with a worm-eaten stock, and one-third a four-bore flint duck-gun, without a flint.

"But it is to be remembered," said the king, reaching out for the bottle, "that he is a very expert log-snatcher and a man of a merry face. What shall I do to him, Sahib?"

This was interesting. The timid hill-folk would as soon have refused taxes to their king as offerings to their gods. The rebel must be a man of character.

"If it be the king's permission," I said, "I will not strike my tents till the third day, and I will see this man. The mercy of the king is godlike, and rebellion is like unto the sin of witchcraft. Moreover, both the bottles, and another, be empty."

"You have my leave to go," said the king.

Next morning the crier went through the state proclaiming that there was a log-jam on the river and that it behooved all loyal subjects to clear it. The people poured down from their villages to the moist, warm valley of poppy fields, and the king and I went with them.

Hundreds of dressed deodar logs had caught on a snag of rock, and the river was bringing down more logs every minute to complete the blockade. The water snarled and wrenched and worried at the timber, while

the population of the state prodded at the nearest logs
with poles, in the hope of easing the pressure. Then
there went up a shout of "Namgay Doola! Namgay
Doola!" and a large, red-haired villager hurried up,
stripping off his clothes as he ran.

"That is he. That is the rebel!" said the king. "Now
will the dam be cleared."

"But why has he red hair?" I asked, since red hair
among hill-folk is as uncommon as blue or green.

"He is an outlander," said the king. "Well done!
Oh, well done!"

Namgay Doola had scrambled on the jam and was
clawing out the butt of a log with a rude sort of a boat-
hook. It slid forward slowly, as an alligator moves,
and three or four others followed it. The green water
spouted through the gaps. Then the villagers howled
and shouted and leaped among the logs, pulling and
pushing the obstinate timber, and the red head of Namgay Doola was chief among them all. The logs swayed
and chafed and groaned as fresh consignments from
up-stream battered the now weakening dam. It gave
way at last in a smother of foam, racing butts, bobbing
black heads, and a confusion indescribable, as the river
tossed everything before it. I saw the red head go
down with the last remnants of the jam and disappear
between the great grinding tree trunks. It rose close
to the bank, and blowing like a grampus, Namgay
Doola wiped the water out of his eyes and made obeisance to the king.

I had time to observe the man closely. The virulent
redness of his shock head and beard was most startling,

and in the thicket of hair twinkled above high cheek-
bones two very merry blue eyes. He was indeed an
outlander, but yet a Thibetan in language, habit and
attire. He spoke the Lepcha dialect with an indescribable softening of the gutturals. It was not so much a
lisp as an accent.

"Whence comest thou?" I asked, wondering.

"From Thibet." He pointed across the hills and
grinned. That grin went straight to my heart. Mechanically I held out my hand, and Namgay Doola
took it. No pure Thibetan would have understood the
meaning of the gesture. He went away to look for his
clothes, and as he climbed back to his village, I heard
a joyous yell that seemed unaccountably familiar. It
was the whooping of Namgay Doola.

"You see now," said the king, "why I would not kill
him. He is a bold man among my logs, but," and he
shook his head like a schoolmaster, "I know that before long there will be complaints of him in the court.
Let us return to the palace and do justice."

It was that king's custom to judge his subjects every
day between eleven and three o'clock. I heard him do
justice equitably on weighty matters of trespass,
slander, and a little wife-stealing. Then his brow
clouded and he summoned me.

"Again it is Namgay Doola," he said, despairingly.
"Not content with refusing revenue on his own part,
he has bound half his village by an oath to the like
treason. Never before has such a thing befallen me!
Nor are my taxes heavy."

A rabbit-faced villager, with a blush-rose stuck behind his ear, advanced trembling. He had been in Namgay Doola's conspiracy, but had told everything and hoped for the king's favor.

"Oh, king!" said I, "if it be the king's will, let this matter stand over till the morning. Only the gods can do right in a hurry, and it may be that yonder villager has lied."

"Nay, for I know the nature of Namgay Doola; but since a guest asks, let the matter remain. Wilt thou, for my sake, speak harshly to this redheaded outlander? He may listen to thee."

I made an attempt that very evening, but for the life of me I could not keep my countenance. Namgay Doola grinned so persuasively and began to tell me about a big brown bear in a poppy field by the river. Would I care to shoot that bear? I spoke austerely on the sin of detected conspiracy and the certainty of punishment. Namgay Doola's face clouded for a moment. Shortly afterward he withdrew from my tent, and I heard him singing softly among the pines. The words were unintelligible to me, but the tune, like his liquid, insinuating speech, seemed the ghost of something strangely familiar.

"Dir hane mard-i-yemen dir
To weeree ala gee,"

crooned Namgay Doola again and again, and I racked my brain for that lost tune. It was not till after dinner that I discovered some one had cut a square foot of velvet from the center of my best camera-cloth. This made me so angry that I wandered down the valley in the hope of meeting the big brown bear. I could hear him grunting like a discontented pig in the poppy field as I waited shoulder deep in the dewdripping Indian corn to catch him after his meal. The moon was at full and drew out the scent of the tasseled crop. Then I heard the anguished bellow of a Himalayan cow—one of the little black crummies no bigger than Newfoundland dogs. Two shadows that looked like a bear and her cub hurried past me. I was in the act of firing when I saw that each bore a brilliant red head. The lesser animal was trailing something rope-like that left a dark track on the path. They were within six feet of me, and the shadow of the moonlight lay velvet-black on their faces. Velvet-black was exactly the word, for by all the powers of moonlight they were masked in the velvet of my camera-cloth. I marveled, and went to bed.

Next morning the kingdom was in an uproar. Namgay Doola, men said, had gone forth in the night and with a sharp knife had cut off the tail of a cow belonging to the rabbit-faced villager who had betrayed him. It was sacrilege unspeakable against the holy cow! The state desired his blood, but he had retreated to his hut, barricaded the doors and windows with big stones, and defied the world.

The king and I and the populace approached the hut cautiously. There was no hope of capturing our man without loss of life, for from a hole in the wall projected the muzzle of an extremely well-cared-for gun—the only gun in the state that could shoot. Namgay Doola had narrowly missed a villager just before we came up.

The standing army stood.

It could do no more, for when it advanced pieces of sharp shale flew from the windows. To these were added from time to time showers of scalding water. We saw red heads bobbing up and down within. The family of Namgay Doola were aiding their sire. Blood-curding yells of defiance were the only answer to our prayers.

"Never," said the king, puffing, "has such a thing befallen my state. Next year I will certainly buy a little cannon." He looked at me imploringly.

"Is there any priest in the kingdom to whom he will listen?" said I, for a light was beginning to break upon me.

"He worships his own god," said the prime minister. "We can but starve him out."

"Let the white man approach," said Namgay Doola from within. "All others I will kill. Send me the white man."

The door was thrown open and I entered the smoky interior of a Thibetan hut crammed with children. And every child had flaming red hair. A fresh-gathered cow's tail lay on the floor, and by its side two pieces of black velvet—my black velvet—rudely hacked into the semblance of masks.

"And what is this shame, Namgay Doola?" I asked.

He grinned more charmingly than ever. "There is no shame," said he. "I did but cut off the tail of that man's cow. He betrayed me. I was minded to shoot him, Sahib, but not to death. Indeed, not to death; only in the legs."

"And why at all, since it is the custom to pay revenue to the king? Why at all?"

"By the god of my father, I can not tell," said Namgay Doola.

"And who was thy father?"

"The same that had this gun." He showed me his weapon, a Tower musket, bearing date 1832 and the stamp of the Honorable East India Company.

"And thy father's name?" said I.

"Timlay Doola," said he. "At the first, I being then a little child, it is in my mind that he wore a red coat."

"Of that I have no doubt; but repeat the name of thy father twice or thrice."

He obeyed, and I understood whence the puzzling accent in his speech came. "Thimla Dhula!" said he, excitedly. "To this hour I worship his god."

"May I see that god?"

"In a little while—at twilight time."

"Rememberest thou aught of thy father's speech?"

"It is long ago. But there was one word which he said often. Thus, ''Shun!' Then I and my brethren stood upon our feet, our hands to our sides, thus."

"Even so. And what was thy mother?"

"A woman of the Hills. We be Lepchas of Darjiling, but me they call an outlander because my hair is as thou seest."

The Thibetan woman, his wife, touched him on the arm gently. The long parley outside the fort had lasted far into the day. It was now close upon twilight—the hour of the Angelus. Very solemnly the red-headed brats rose from the floor and formed a semicircle.

Namgay Doola laid his gun aside, lighted a little oil-lamp, and set it before a recess in the wall. Pulling back a wisp of dirty cloth, he revealed a worn brass crucifix leaning against the helmet badge of a long-forgotten East India Company's regiment. "Thus did my father," he said, crossing himself clumsily. The wife and children followed suit. Then, all together, they struck up the wailing chant that I heard on the hill-side:

> "Dir hane mard-i-yemen dir
> To weeree ala gee."

I was puzzled no longer. Again and again they sung, as if their hearts would break, their version of the chorus of "The Wearing of the Green":

> "They're hanging men and women, too,
> For the wearing of the green."

A diabolical inspiration came to me. One of the brats, a boy about eight years old—could he have been in the fields last night?—was watching me as he sung. I pulled out a rupee, held the coin between finger and thumb, and looked—only looked—at the gun leaning against the wall. A grin of brilliant and perfect comprehension overspread his porringer-like face. Never for an instant stopping the song, he held out his hand for the money, and then slid the gun to my hand. I might have shot Namgay Doola dead as he chanted, but I was satisfied. The inevitable blood-instinct held true. Namgay Doola drew the curtain across the recess. Angelus was over.

"Thus my father sung. There was much more, but

I have forgotten, and I do not know the purport of even these words, but it may be that the god will understand. I am not of this people, and I will not pay revenue."

"And why?"

Again that soul-compelling grin. "What occupation would be to me between crop and crop? It is better than scaring bears. But these people do not understand."

He picked the masks off the floor and looked in my face as simply as a child.

"By what road didst thou attain knowledge to make those deviltries?" I said, pointing.

"I can not tell. I am but a Lepcha of Darjiling, and yet the stuff—"

"Which thou hast stolen," said I.

"Nay, surely. Did I steal? I desired it so. The stuff—the stuff. What else should I have done with the stuff." He twisted the velvet between his fingers.

"But the sin of maiming the cow—consider that."

"Oh, Sahib, the man betrayed me; the heifer's tail waved in the moonlight, and I had my knife. What else should I have done? The tail came off ere I was aware. Sahib, thou knowest more than I."

"That is true," said I. "Stay within the door. I go to speak to the king." The population of the state were ranged on the hill-side. I went forth and spoke.

"Oh, king," said I, "touching this man, there be two courses open to thy wisdom. Thou canst either hang him from a tree—he and his brood—till there remains no hair that is red within thy land."

"Nay," said the king. "Why should I hurt the little children?"

They had poured out of the hut and were making plump obeisances to everybody. Namgay Doola waited at the door with his gun across his arm.

"Or thou canst, discarding their impiety of the cow-maiming, raise him to honor in thy army. He comes of a race that will not pay revenue. A red flame is in his blood which comes out at the top of his head in that glowing hair. Make him chief of thy army. Give him honor as may befall and full allowance of work, but look to it, oh, king, that neither he nor his hold a foot of earth from thee henceforward. Feed him with words and favor, and also liquor from certain bottles that thou knowest of, and he will be a bulwark of defense. But deny him even a tuftlet of grass for his own. This is the nature that God has given him. Moreover, he has brethren—"

The state groaned unanimously.

"But if his brethren come they will surely fight with each other till they die; or else the one will always give information concerning the other. Shall he be of thy army, oh, king? Choose."

The king bowed his head, and I said: "Come forth, Namgay Doola, and command the king's army. Thy name shall no more be Namgay in the mouths of men, but Patsay Doola, for, thou hast truly said, I know."

Then Namgay Doola, new-christened Patsay Doola, son of Timlay Doola—which is Tim Doolan—clasped the king's feet, cuffed the standing army, and hurried in an agony of contrition from temple to temple making offerings for the sin of the cattle-maiming.

And the king was so pleased with my perspicacity that he offered to sell me a village for £20 sterling. But I buy no village in the Himalayas so long as one red head flares between the tail of the heaven-climbing glacier and the dark birch forest.

I know that breed.

THE ARREST OF LIEUTENANT GOLIGHTLY

"'I've forgotten the countersign,' sez 'e.
'Oh! You 'ave, 'ave you?' sez I.
'But I'm the Colonel,' sez 'e.
'Oh! You are, are you?' sez I. 'Colonel nor no Colonel,
you waits 'ere till I'm relieved, an' the Sarjint reports on your
ugly old mug. Coop!' sez I.

. . . .

An' s'elp me soul, 'twas the Colonel after all! But I was a
recruity then."
                    —*The Unedited Autobiography of Private Ortheris.*

IF there was one thing on which Golightly prided
    himself more than another, it was looking like "an
    Officer and a Gentleman." He said it was for the
honor of the Service that he attired himself so elabo-
rately; but those who knew him best said it was just
personal vanity. There was no harm about Golightly
—not an ounce. He recognized a horse when he saw
one, and could do more than fill a cantle. He played a
very fair game at billiards, and was a sound man at the
whist-table. Everyone liked him; and nobody ever
dreamed of seeing him handcuffed on a station platform as a deserter. But this sad thing happened.

He was going down from Dalhousie, at the end of
his leave—riding down. He had cut his leave as fine as
he dared, and wanted to come down in a hurry.

411

It was fairly warm at Dalhousie, and, knowing what to expect below, he descended in a new khaki suit—tight fitting—of a delicate olive-green; a peacock-blue tie, white collar, and a snowy white solah helmet. He prided himself on looking neat even when he was riding post. He did look neat, and he was so deeply concerned about his appearance before he started that he quite forgot to take anything but small change with him. He left all his notes at the hotel. His servants had gone down the road before him, to be ready in waiting at Pathankote with a change of gear. That was what he called traveling in "light marching-order." He was proud of his faculty of organization—what we call bundobust.

Twenty-two miles out of Dalhousie it began to rain—not a mere hill-shower but a good, tepid monsoonish downpour. Golightly bustled on, wishing that he had brought an umbrella. The dust on the roads turned into mud, and the pony mired a good deal. So did Golightly's khaki gaiters. But he kept on steadily and tried to think how pleasant the coolth was.

His next pony was rather a brute at starting and Golightly's hands being slippery with the rain, contrived to get rid of Golightly at a corner. He chased the animal, caught it, and went ahead briskly. The spill had not improved his clothes or his temper, and he had lost one spur. He kept the other one employed. By the time that stage was ended, the pony had had as much exercise as he wanted and, in spite of the rain, Golightly was sweating freely. At the end of another miserable half-hour, Golightly found the world disappear before his eyes in clammy pulp. The rain had turned the pith of his huge and snowy solah-topee into an evil-smelling dough, and it had closed on his head like a half-opened mushroom. Also the green lining was beginning to run.

Golightly did not say anything worth recording here. He tore off and squeezed up as much of the brim as was in his eyes and ploughed on. The back of the helmet was flapping on his neck and the sides stuck to his ears, but the leather band and green lining kept things roughly together, so that the hat did not actually melt away where it flapped.

Presently the pulp and the green stuff made a sort of slimy mildew which ran over Golightly in several directions—down his back and bosom for choice. The khaki color ran too—it was really shockingly bad dye—and sections of Golightly were brown, and patches were violet, and contours were ochre, and streaks were ruddy red, and blotches were nearly white, according to the nature and peculiarities of the dye. When he took out his handkerchief to wipe his face and the green of the hat-lining and the purple stuff that had soaked through on to his neck from the tie became thoroughly mixed, the effect was amazing.

Near Dhar the rain stopped and the evening sun came out and dried him up slightly. It fixed the colors, too. Three miles from Pathankote the last pony fell dead lame, and Golightly was forced to walk. He pushed on into Pathankote to find his servants. He did not know then that his khitmatgar had stopped by the roadside to get drunk, and would come on the next day saying that he had sprained his ankle. When he got into Pathankote, he couldn't find his servants, his boots were stiff and ropy with mud, and there were large quantities of dirt about his body. The blue tie had run as much as the khaki. So he took it off with the collar and threw it away. Then he said something about servants generally and tried to get a peg. He paid eight annas for the drink, and this revealed to him that he had only six annas more in his pocket—or in the world as he stood at that hour.

He went to the Station-Master to negotiate for a first-class ticket to Khasa, where he was stationed. The booking-clerk said something to the Station-Master, the Station-Master said something to the Telegraph Clerk, and the three looked at him with curiosity. They asked him to wait for half-an-hour, while they telegraphed to Umritsar for authority. So he waited and four constables came and grouped themselves picturesquely round him. Just as he was preparing to ask them to go away, the Station-Master said that he would give the Sahib a ticket to Umritsar, if the Sahib would kindly come inside the booking-office. Golightly stepped inside, and the next thing he knew was that a constable was attached to each of his legs and arms, while the Station-Master was trying to cram a mail-bag over his head.

There was a very fair scuffle all round the booking-office, and Golightly received a nasty cut over his eye through falling against a table. But the constables were too much for him, and they and the Station-Master handcuffed him securely. As soon as the mail-bag was slipped, he began expressing his opinions, and the head-constable said:"Without doubt this is the soldier-Englishman we required. Listen to the abuse!" Then Golightly asked the Station-Master what the this and the that the proceedings meant. The Station-Master told him he was "Private John Binkle of the ——— Regiment, 5 ft. 9 in., fair hair, gray eyes, and a dissipated appearance, no marks on the body," who had deserted a fortnight ago. Golightly began explaining at great length: and the more he explained the less the Station-Master believed him. He said that no Lieutenant could look such a ruffian as did Golightly, and that his instructions were to send his capture under proper escort to Umritsar. Golightly was feeling very damp and uncomfortable, and the language he used was not fit for publication, even in an expurgated form. The four constables saw him safe to Umritsar in an "intermediate" compartment, and he spent the four-hour journey in abusing them as fluently as his knowledge of the vernaculars allowed.

At Umritsar he was bundled out on the platform into the arms of a Corporal and two men of the ———Regiment. Golightly drew himself up and tried to carry off matters jauntily. He did not feel too jaunty in handcuffs, with four constables behind him, and the blood from the cut on his forehead stiffening on his left cheek. The Corporal was not jocular either. Golightly got as far as:—"This is a very absurd mistake, my men," when the Corporal told him to "stow his lip" and come along. Golightly did not want to come along. He desired to stop and explain. He explained

very well indeed, until the Corporal cut in with:—
"You a orficer! It's the like o' you as brings disgrace
on the likes of us. Bloomin' fine orficer you are. I
know your regiment. The Rogue's March is the quickstep where you come from. You're a black shame to
the Service."

Golightly kept his temper, and began explaining all
over again from the beginning. Then he was marched
out of the rain into the refreshment-room and told not
to make a qualified fool of himself. The men were
going to run him up to Fort Govindghar. And "running up" is a performance almost as undignified as the
Frog March.

Golightly was nearly hysterical with rage and the
chill and the mistake and the handcuffs' and the
headache that the cut on his forehead had given him.
He really laid himself out to express what was in his
mind. When he had quite finished and his throat was
feeling dry, one of the men said:—"I've 'eard a few
beggars in the click blind, stiff and crack on a bit; but
I've never 'eard any one to touch this 'ere 'orficer.'"
They were not angry with him. They rather admired
him. They had some beer at the refreshment-room,
and offered Golightly some too, because he had "swore
won'erful." They asked him to tell them all about the
adventures of Private John Binkle while he was loose
on the country-side; and that made Golightly wilder
than ever. If he had kept his wits about him he would
have kept quiet until an officer came; but he attempted
to run.

Now the butt of a Martini in the small of your back

hurts a great deal, and rotten, rain-soaked khaki tears easily when two men are jerking at your collar.

Golightly rose from the floor feeling very sick and giddy, with his shirt ripped open all down his breast and nearly all down his back. He yielded to his luck, and at that point the downtrain from Lahore came in, carrying one of Golightly's Majors.

This is the Major's evidence in full:—

"There was the sound of a scuffle in the second-class refreshment-room, so I went in and saw the most villainous loafer that I ever set eyes on. His boots and breeches were plastered with mud and beer-stains. He wore a muddy-white dunghill sort of thing on his head, and it hung down in slips on his shoulders which were a good deal scratched. He was half in and half out of a shirt as nearly in two pieces as it could be, and he was begging the guard to look at the name on the tail of it. As he had rucked the shirt all over his head, I couldn't at first see who he was, but I fancied that he was a man in the first stage of D. T. from the way he swore while he wrestled with his rags. When he turned round, and I had made allowances for a lump as big as a pork-pie over one eye, and some green war-paint on the face, and some violet stripes round the neck, I saw that it was Golightly. He was very glad to see me," said the Major, "and he hoped I would not tell the Mess about it. I didn't, but you can, if you like, now that Golightly has gone Home."

Golightly spent the greater part of that summer in trying to get the Corporal and the two soldiers tried by

Court-Martial for arresting an "officer and a gentle-man." They were, of course, very sorry for their error. But the tale leaked into the regimental canteen, and thence ran about the Province.

MOTI GUJ—MUTINEER

ONCE upon a time there was a coffee-planter in
India who wished to clear some forest land for
coffee-planting. When he had cut down all
the trees and burned the underwood, the stumps still
remained. Dynamite is expensive and slow fire slow.
The happy medium for stump-clearing is the lord of
all beasts, who is the elephant. He will either push
the stump out of the ground with his tusks, if he has
any, or drag it out with ropes. The planter, therefore,
hired elephants by ones and twos and threes, and fell to
work. The very best of all the elephants belonged to
the very worst of all the drivers or mahouts; and this
superior beast's name was Moti Guj. He was the absolute property of his mahout, which would never have
been the case under native rule; for Moti Guj was a
creature to be desired by kings and his name, being
translated, meant the Pearl Elephant. Because the
British government was in the land, Deesa, the mahout,
enjoyed his property undisturbed. He was dissipated.
When he had made much money through the strength
of his elephant, he would get extremely drunk and give
Moti Guj a beating with a tent-peg over the tender
nails of the forefoot. Moti Guj never trampled the life
out of Deesa on these occasions, for he knew that after
the beating was over Deesa would embrace his trunk

and weep and call him his love and his life and the liver of his soul, and give him some liquor. Moti Guj was very fond of liquor—arrack for choice, though he would drink palm-tree toddy if nothing better offered. Then Deesa would go to sleep between Moti Guj's forefeet, and as Deesa generally chose the middle of the public road, and as Moti Guj mounted guard over him, and would not permit horse, foot, or cart to pass by, traffic was congested till Deesa saw fit to wake up.

There was no sleeping in the day-time on the planter's clearing: the wages were too high to risk. Deesa sat on Moti Guj's neck and gave him orders, while Moti Guj rooted up the stumps—for he owned a magnificent pair of tusks; or pulled at the end of a rope—for he had a magnificent pair of shoulders—while Deesa kicked him behind the ears and said he was the king of elephants. At evening time Moti Guj would wash down his three hundred pounds' weight of green food with a quart of arrack, and Deesa would take a share, and sing songs between Moti Guj's legs till it was time to go to bed. Once a week Deesa led Moti Guj down to the river, and Moti Guj lay on his side luxuriously in the shallows, while Deesa went over him with a coir swab and a brick. Moti Guj never mistook the pounding blow of the latter for the smack of the former that warned him to get up and turn over on the other side. Then Deesa would look at his feet and examine his eyes, and turn up the fringes of his mighty ears in case of sores or budding ophthalmia. After inspection the two would "come up with a song from the sea," Moti Guj, all black and shining, waving a torn tree branch twelve feet long in his trunk, and Deesa knotting up his own long wet hair.

It was a peaceful, well-paid life till Deesa felt the return of the desire to drink deep. He wished for an orgy. The little draughts that led nowhere were taking the manhood out of him.

He went to the planter, and "My mother's dead," said he, weeping.

"She died on the last plantation two months ago, and she died once before when you were working for me last year," said the planter, who knew something of the ways of nativedom.

"Then it's my aunt, and she was just the same as a mother to me," said Deesa, weeping more than ever. "She has left eighteen small children entirely without bread, and it is I who must fill their little stomachs," said Deesa, beating his head on the floor.

"Who brought you the news?" said the planter.

"The post," said Deesa.

"There hasn't been a post here for the past week. Get back to your lines!"

"A devastating sickness has fallen on my village, and all my wives are dying," yelled Deesa, really in tears this time.

"Call Chihun, who comes from Deesa's village," said the planter. "Chihun, has this man got a wife?"

"He?" said Chihun. "No. Not a woman of our village would look at him. They'd sooner marry the elephant."

Chihun snorted. Deesa wept and bellowed.

"You will get into a difficulty in a minute," said the planter. "Go back to your work!"

"Now I will speak Heaven's truth," gulped Deesa, with an inspiration. "I haven't been drunk for two months. I desire to depart in order to get properly drunk afar off and distant from this heavenly plantation. Thus I shall cause no trouble."

A flickering smile crossed the planter's face. "Deesa," said he, "you've spoken the truth, and I'd give you leave on the spot if anything could be done with Moti Guj while you're away. You know that he will only obey your orders."

"May the light of the heavens live forty thousand years. I shall be absent but ten little days. After that, upon my faith and honor and soul, I return. As to the inconsiderable interval, have I the gracious permission of the heaven-born to call up Moti Guj?"

Permission was granted, and in answer to Deesa's shrill yell, the mighty tusker swung out of the shade of a clump of trees where he had been squirting dust over himself till his master should return.

"Light of my heart, protector of the drunken, mountain of might, give ear!" said Deesa, standing in front of him.

Moti Guj gave ear, and saluted with his trunk. "I am going away," said Deesa.

Moti Guj's eyes twinkled. He liked jaunts as well as his master. One could snatch all manner of nice things from the road-side then.

"But you, you fussy old pig, must stay behind and work.'"

The twinkle died out as Moti Guj tried to look delighted. He hated stump-hauling on the plantation.
It hurt his teeth.

"I shall be gone for ten days, oh, delectable one!
Hold up your near forefoot and I'll impress the fact
upon it, warty toad of a dried mud-puddle." Deesa
took a tent-peg and banged Moti Guj ten times on the
nails. Moti Guj grunted and shuffled from foot to foot.

"Ten days," said Deesa, "you will work and haul
and root the trees as Chihun here shall order you. Take
up Chihun and set him on your neck!" Moti Guj
curled the tip of his trunk, Chihun put his foot there,
and was swung on to the neck. Deesa handed Chihun
the heavy *ankus*—the iron elephant goad.

Chihun thumped Moti Guj's bald head as a paver
thumps a curbstone.

Moti Guj trumpeted.

"Be still, hog of the backwoods! Chihun's your
mahout for ten days. And now bid me good-bye, beast
after my own heart. Oh, my lord, my king! Jewel of
all created elephants, lily of the herd, preserve your
honored health; be virtuous. Adieu!"

Moti Guj lapped his trunk round Deesa and swung
him into the air twice. This was his way of bidding
him good-bye.

"He'll work now," said Deesa to the planter. "Have
I leave to go?"

The planter nodded, and Deesa dived into the woods.
Moti Guj went back to haul stumps.

Chihun was very kind to him, but he felt unhappy
and forlorn for all that. Chihun gave him a ball of

spices, and tickled him under the chin, and Chihun's little baby cooed to him after work was over, and Chihun's wife called him a darling; but Moti Guj was a bachelor by instinct, as Deesa was. He did not understand the domestic emotions. He wanted the light of his universe back again—the drink and the drunken slumber, the savage beatings and the savage caresses.

None the less he worked well, and the planter wondered. Deesa had wandered along the roads till he met a marriage procession of his own caste, and, drinking, dancing, and tippling, had drifted with it past all knowledge of the lapse of time.

The morning of the eleventh day dawned, and there returned no Deesa. Moti Guj was loosed from his ropes for the daily stint. He swung clear, looked round, shrugged his shoulders, and began to walk away, as one having business elsewhere.

"Hi! ho! Come back you!" shouted Chihun. "Come back and put me on your neck, misborn mountain! Return, splendor of the hill-sides! Adornment of all India, heave to, or I'll bang every toe off your fat forefoot!"

Moti Guj gurgled gently, but did not obey. Chihun ran after him with a rope and caught him up. Moti Guj put his ears forward, and Chihun knew what that meant, though he tried to carry it off with high words.

"None of your nonsense with me," said he. "To your pickets, devil-son!"

"Hrrump!" said Moti Guj, and that was all—that and the forebent ears.

Moti Guj put his hands in his pockets, chewed a

branch for a toothpick, and strolled about the clearing, making fun of the other elephants who had just set to work.

Chihun reported the state of affairs to the planter, who came out with a dog-whip and cracked it furiously. Moti Guj paid the white man the compliment of charging him nearly a quarter of a mile across the clearing and "Hrrumphing" him into his veranda. Then he stood outside the house, chuckling to himself and shaking all over with the fun of it, as an elephant will.

"We'll thrash him," said the planter. "He shall have the finest thrashing ever elephant received. Give Kala Nag and Nazim twelve foot of chain apiece, and tell them to lay on twenty."

Kala Nag—which means Black Snake—and Nazim were two of the biggest elephants in the lines, and one of their duties was to administer the graver punishment, since no man can beat an elephant properly.

They took the whipping-chains and rattled them in their trunks as they sidled up to Moti Guj, meaning to hustle him between them. Moti Guj had never, in all his life of thirty-nine years, been whipped, and he did not intend to begin a new experience. So he waited, waving his head from right to left, and measuring the precise spot in Kala Nag's fat side where a blunt tusk could sink deepest. Kala Nag had no tusks; the chain was the badge of his authority; but for all that, he swung wide of Moti Guj at the last minute, and tried to appear as if he had brought the chain out for amusement. Nazim turned round and went home early.

He did not feel fit that morning, and so Moti Guj was
left standing alone with his ears cocked.

That decided the planter to argue no more, and Moti
Guj rolled back to his amateur inspection of the clearing. An elephant who will not work and is not tied
up is about as manageable as an eighty-one-ton gun
loose in a heavy seaway. He slapped old friends on the
back and asked them if the stumps were coming away
easily; he talked nonsense concerning labor and the
inalienable rights of elephants to a long "nooning;"
and, wandering to and fro, he thoroughly demoralized
the garden till sundown, when he returned to his picket
for food.

"If you won't work, you sha'n't eat," said Chihun,
angrily. "You're a wild elephant, and no educated
animal at all. Go back to your jungle."

Chihun's little brown baby was rolling on the floor
of the hut, and stretching out its fat arms to the huge
shadow in the doorway. Moti Guj knew well that it
was the dearest thing on earth to Chihun. He swung
out his trunk with a fascinating crook at the end, and
the brown baby threw itself, shouting, upon it. Moti
Guj made fast and pulled up till the brown baby was
crowing in the air twelve feet above his father's head.

"Great Lord!" said Chihun. "Flour cakes of the best,
twelve in number, two feet across and soaked in rum,
shall be yours on the instant, and two hundred pounds
weight of fresh-cut young sugar cane therewith. Deign
only to put down safely that insignificant brat who is
my heart and my life to me!"

Moti Guj tucked the brown baby comfortably be-

tween his forefeet, that could have knocked into tooth-
picks all Chihun's hut, and waited for his food. He
ate it, and the brown baby crawled away. Moti Guj
dozed and thought of Deesa. One of many mysteries
connected with the elephant is that his huge body needs
less sleep than anything else that lives. Four or five
hours in the night suffice—two just before midnight,
lying down on one side; two just after one o'clock, lying down on the other. The rest of the silent hours
are filled with eating and fidgeting, and long grumbling soliloquies.

At midnight, therefore, Moti Guj strode out of his
pickets, for a thought had come to him that Deesa
might be lying drunk somewhere in the dark forest
with none to look after him. So all that night he
chased through the undergrowth, blowing and trumpeting and shaking his ears. He went down to the
river and blared across the shallows where Deesa used
to wash him, but there was no answer. He could not
find Deesa, but he disturbed all the other elephants in
the line, and nearly frightened to death some gypsies
in the woods.

At dawn Deesa returned to the plantation. He had
been very drunk indeed, and he expected to get into
trouble for outstaying his leave. He drew a long breath
when he saw that the bungalow and the plantation
were still uninjured for he knew something of Moti
Guj's temper, and reported himself with many lies and
salaams. Moti Guj had gone to his pickets for breakfast. The night exercise had made him hungry.

"Call up your beast," said the planter; and Deesa

shouted in the mysterious elephant language that some mahouts believe came from China at the birth of the world, when elephants and not men were masters. Moti Guj heard and came. Elephants do not gallop. They move from places at varying rates of speed. If an elephant wished to catch an express train he could not gallop, but he could catch the train. So Moti Guj was at the planter's door almost before Chihun noticed that he had left his pickets. He fell into Deesa's arms trumpeting with joy, and the man and beast wept and slobbered over each other, and handled each other from head to heel to see that no harm had befallen.

"Now we will get to work," said Deesa. "Lift me up, my son and my joy!"

Moti Guj swung him up, and the two went to the coffee-clearing to look for difficult stumps.

The planter was too astonished to be very angry.

THE ROUT OF THE WHITE HUSSARS

It was not in the open fight
  We threw away the sword,
But in the lonely watching
  In the darkness by the ford.
The waters lapped, the night-wind blew
Full-armed the Fear was born and grew
And we were flying ere we knew,
  From panic in the night.

—Beoni Bar.

SOME people hold that an English Cavalry regiment cannot run. This is a mistake. I have seen four hundred and thirty-seven sabers flying over the face of the country in abject terror—have seen the best Regiment that ever drew bridle wiped off the Army List for the space of two hours. If you repeat this tale to the White Hussars they will, in all probability, treat you severely. They are not proud of the incident.

You may know the White Hussars by their "side," which is greater than that of all the Cavalry Regiments on the roster. If this is not a sufficient mark, you may know them by their old brandy. It has been sixty years in the Mess and is worth going far to taste. Ask for the "McGaire" old brandy, and see that you get it. If the Mess Sergeant thinks that you are uneducated, and that the genuine article will be lost on you, he will treat you accordingly. He is a good man. But, when you are at Mess, you must never talk to your hosts about forced marches or long-distance rides. The Mess are very sensitive; and, if they think that you are laughing at them, will tell you so.

As the White Hussars say, it was all the Colonel's fault. He was a new man, and he ought never to have taken the Command. He said that the Regiment was not smart enough. This to the White Hussars, who knew that they could walk round any Horse and through any Guns, and over any Foot on the face of the earth! That insult was the first cause of offense.

Then the Colonel cast the Drum-Horse—the Drum-Horse of the White Hussars! Perhaps you do not see what an unspeakable crime he had committed. I will try to make it clear. The soul of the Regiment lives in the Drum-Horse who carries the silver kettle-drums. He is nearly always a big piebald Waler. That is a point of honor; and a Regiment will spend anything you please on a piebald. He is beyond the ordinary laws of casting. His work is very light, and he only manœuvres at a foot-pace. Wherefore so long as he can step out and look handsome, his wellbeing is assured. He knows more about the Regiment than the Adjutant, and could not make a mistake if he tried.

The Drum-Horse of the White Hussars was only eighteen years old, and perfectly equal to his duties. He had at least six years' more work in him, and carried himself with all the pomp and dignity of a Drum-

Major of the Guards. The Regiment had paid Rs.1200 for him.

But the Colonel said that he must go, and he was cast in due form and replaced by a washy, bay beast, as ugly as a mule, with a ewe-neck, rat-tail, and cow-hocks. The Drummer detested that animal, and the best of the Band-horses put back their ears and showed the whites of their eyes at the very sight of him. They knew him for an upstart and no gentleman. I fancy that the Colonel's ideas of smartness extended to the Band, and that he wanted to make it take part in the regular parade movements. A Cavalry Band is a sacred thing. It only turns out for Commanding officers' pa-rades, and the Band Master is one degree more impor-tant than the Colonel. He is a High Priest and the "Keel Row" is his holy song. The "Keel Row" is the Cavalry Trot; and the man who has never heard that tune rising, high and shrill, above the rattle of the Regiment going past the saluting-base, has something yet to hear and understand.

When the Colonel cast the Drum-Horse of the White Hussars, there was nearly a mutiny.

The officers were angry, the Regiment were furious, and the Bandsmen swore—like troopers. The Drum-Horse was going to be put up to auction—public auc-tion—to be bought, perhaps, by a Parsee and put into a cart! It was worse than exposing the inner life of the Regiment to the whole world, or selling the Mess Plate to a Jew—a black Jew.

The Colonel was a mean man and a bully. He knew what the Regiment thought about his action; and, when the troopers offered to buy the Drum-Horse, he said that their offer was mutinous and forbidden by the Regulations.

But one of the Subalterns—Hogan-Yale, an Irishman —bought the Drum-Horse for Rs.160 at the sale, and the Colonel was wroth. Yale professed repentance— he was unnaturally submissive—and said that, as he had only made the purchase to save the horse from possible ill-treatment and starvation, he would now shoot him and end the business. This appeared to soothe the Colonel, for he wanted the Drum-Horse disposed of. He felt that he had made a mistake, and could not of course acknowledge it. Meantime, the presence of the Drum-Horse was an annoyance to him.

Yale took to himself a glass of the old brandy, three cheroots, and his friend Martyn; and they all left the Mess together. Yale and Martyn conferred for two hours in Yale's quarters; but only the bull terrier who keeps watch over Yale's boot-trees knows what they said. A horse, hooded and sheeted to his ears, left Yale's stables and was taken, very unwillingly, into the Civil Lines. Yale's groom went with him. Two men broke into the Regimental Theater and took several paint-pots and some large scenery-brushes. Then night fell over the Cantonments, and there was a noise as of a horse kicking his loose box to pieces in Yale's stables. Yale had a big, old, white Waler trap-horse.

The next day was a Thursday, and the men, hearing that Yale was going to shoot the Drum-Horse in the evening, determined to give the beast a regular regi-mental funeral—a finer one than they would have given the Colonel had he died just then. They got a bullock-cart and some sacking, and mounds and mounds of roses, and the body, under sacking, was carried out to the place where the anthrax cases were cremated; two-thirds of the Regiment following. There was no Band, but they all sang "The Place where the old Horse died" as something respectful and appropriate to the occasion. When the corpse was dumped into the grave and the men began throwing down armfuls of roses to cover it, the Farrier-Sergeant ripped out an oath and said aloud "Why, it ain't the Drum-Horse any more than it's me!" The Troop Sergeant-Majors asked him whether he had left his head in the Canteen. The Farrier-Sergeant said that he knew the Drum-Horse's feet as well as he knew his own; but he was silenced when he saw the regimental number burnt in on the poor stiff, upturned near-fore.

Thus was the Drum-Horse of the White Hussars buried; the Farrier-Sergeant grumbling. The sacking that covered the corpse was smeared in places with black paint; and the Farrier-Sergeant drew attention to this fact. But the Troop-Sergeant-Major of E Troop kicked him severely on the shin, and told him that he was undoubtedly drunk.

On the Monday following the burial, the Colonel sought revenge on the White Hussars. Unfortunately, being at that time temporarily in Command of the Station, he ordered a Brigade field-day. He said that he wished to make the Regiment "sweat for their insolence," and he carried out his notion thoroughly. That Monday was one of the hardest days in the memory of

the White Hussars. They were thrown against a skele-
ton-enemy, and pushed forward, and withdrawn, and
dismounted, and "scientifically handled" in every possible fashion over dusty country, till they sweated profusely. Their only amusement came late in the day
when they fell upon the battery of Horse Artillery and
chased it for two miles. This was a personal question,
and most of the troopers had money on the event; the
Gunners saying openly that they had the legs of the
White Hussars. They were wrong. A march-past concluded the campaign, and when the Regiment got back
to their Lines, the men were coated with dirt from
spur to chin-strap.

The White Hussars have one great and peculiar
privilege. They won it at Fontenoy, I think.

Many Regiments possess special rights such as wearing collars with undress uniforms, or a bow or riband
between the shoulders, or red and white roses in their
helmets on certain days of the year. Some rights are
connected with regimental saints, and some with regimental successes. All are valued highly; but none so
highly as the right of the White Hussars to have the
Band playing when their horses are being watered in
the Lines. Only one tune is played, and that tune
never varies. I don't know its real name, but the White
Hussars call it, "Take me to London again." It sounds
very pretty. The Regiment would sooner be struck off
the roster than forego their distinction.

After the "dismiss" was sounded, the officers rode off
home to prepare for stables; and the men filed into
the lines riding easy. That is to say, they opened their

tight buttons, shifted their helmets, and began to joke or to swear as the humor took them; the more careful slipping off and easing girths and curbs. A good trooper values his mount exactly as much as he values himself, and believes, or should believe, that the two together are irresistible where women or men, girls or guns, are concerned.

Then the Orderly-Officer gave the order, "Water horses," and the Regiment loafed off to the squadron troughs which were in rear of the stables and between these and the barracks. There were four huge troughs, one for each squadron, arranged *en echelon,* so that the whole Regiment could water in ten minutes if it liked. But it lingered for seventeen, as a rule, while the Band played.

The Band struck up as the squadrons filed off to the troughs, and the men slipped their feet out of the stirrups and chaffed each other. The sun was just setting in a big, hot bed of red cloud, and the road to the Civil Lines seemed to run straight into the sun's eye. There was a little dot on the road. It grew and grew till it showed as a horse, with a sort of gridiron-thing on his back. The red cloud glared through the bars of the gridiron. Some of the troopers shaded their eyes with their hands and said—"What the mischief 'as that there 'orse got on 'im?"

In another minute they heard a neigh that every soul —horse and man—in the Regiment knew, and saw, heading straight towards the Band, the dead Drum-Horse of the White Hussars!

On his withers banged and bumped the kettledrums

draped in crape, and on his back, very stiff and soldierly, sat a bareheaded skeleton.

The Band stopped playing, and, for a moment, there was a hush.

Then some one in E Troop—men said it was the Troop-Sergeant-Major—swung his horse round and yelled. No one can account exactly for what happened afterwards; but it seems that, at least, one man in each troop set an example of panic, and the rest followed like sheep. The horses that had barely put their muzzles into the troughs reared and capered; but as soon as the Band broke, which it did when the ghost of the Drum-Horse was about a furlong distant, all hooves followed suit, and the clatter of the stampede—quite different from the orderly throb and roar of a movement on parade, or the rough horse-play of watering in camp—made them only more terrified. They felt that the men on their backs were afraid of something. When horses once know that, all is over except the butchery.

Troop after troop turned from the troughs and ran —anywhere and everywhere—like spilt quicksilver. It was a most extraordinary spectacle, for men and horses were in all stages of easiness, and the carbine-buckets flopping against their sides urged the horses on. Men were shouting and cursing, and trying to pull clear of the Band which was being chased by the Drum-Horse whose rider had fallen forward and seemed to be spurring for a wager.

The Colonel had gone over to the Mess for a drink. Most of the officers were with him, and the Subaltern of the Day was preparing to go down to the lines, and receive the watering reports from the Troop-Sergeant-Majors. When "Take me to London again" stopped after twenty bars, every one in the Mess said, "What on earth has happened?" A minute later, they heard unmilitary noises, and saw, far across the plain, the White Hussars, scattered and broken, and flying.

The Colonel was speechless with rage, for he thought that the Regiment had risen against him or was unanimously drunk. The Band, a disorganized mob, tore past, and at its heels labored the Drum-Horse—the dead and buried Drum-Horse—with the jolting, clattering skeleton. Hogan-Yale whispered softly to Martyn— "No wire will stand that treatment," and the Band, which had doubled like a hare, came back again. But the rest of the Regiment was gone, was rioting all over the Province, for the dusk had shut in and each man was howling to his neighbor that the Drum-Horse was on his flank. Troop-horses are far too tenderly treated as a rule. They can, on emergencies, do a great deal, even with seventeen stone on their backs. As the troopers found out.

How long this panic lasted I cannot say. I believe that when the moon rose the men saw they had nothing to fear, and, by twos and threes and half troops, crept back into Cantonments very much ashamed of themselves. Meantime, the Drum-Horse, disgusted at his treatment by old friends, pulled up, wheeled round, and trotted up to the Mess verandah-steps for bread. No one liked to run; but no one cared to go forward till the Colonel made a movement and laid hold of the skeleton's foot. The Band had halted some distance away, and now came back slowly. The Colonel called it, individually and collectively, every evil name that occurred to him at the time; for he had set his hand on the bosom of the Drum-Horse and found flesh and blood. Then he beat the kettle-drums with his clenched fist, and discovered that they were but made of silver paper and bamboo. Next, still swearing, he tried to drag the skeleton out of the saddle, but found that it had been wired into the cantle. The sight of the Colonel, with his arms round the skeleton's pelvis and his knee in the old Drum-Horse's stomach, was striking. Not to say amusing. He worried the thing off in a minute or two, and threw it down on the ground, saying to the Band—"Here, you curs, that's what you're afraid of." The skeleton did not look pretty in the twilight. The Band-Sergeant seemed to recognize it for he began to chuckle and choke. "Shall I take it away, sir?" said the Band-Sergeant. "Yes," said the Colonel, "take it and yourselves!"

The Band-Sergeant saluted, hoisted the skeleton across his saddle-bow, and led off to the stables. Then the Colonel began to make inquiries for the rest of the Regiment, and the language he used was wonderful. He would disband the Regiment—he would court-martial every soul in it—he would not command such a set of rabble, and so on, and so on. As the men dropped in, his language grew wilder, until at last it exceeded the utmost limits of free speech allowed even to a Colonel of Horse.

Martyn took Hogan-Yale aside and suggested compulsory retirement from the Service as a necessity when all was discovered. Martyn was the weaker man of the two. Hogan-Yale put up his eyebrows and remarked, firstly, that he was the son of a Lord, and, secondly, that he was as innocent as the babe unborn of the theatrical resurrection of the Drum-Horse.

"My instructions," said Yale, with a singularly sweet smile, "were that the Drum-Horse should be sent back as impressively as possible. I ask you, am I responsible if a mule-headed friend sends him back in such a manner as to disturb the peace of mind of a regiment of Her Majesty's Cavalry?"

Martyn said, "You are a great man, and will in time become a General; but I'd give my chance of a troop to be safe out of this affair."

Providence saved Martyn and Hogan-Yale. The Second-in-Command led the Colonel away to the little curtained alcove wherein the Subalterns of the White Hussars were accustomed to play poker of nights; and there, after many oaths on the Colonel's part, they talked together in low tones. I fancy that the Second-in-Command must have represented the scare as the work of some trooper whom it would be hopeless to detect; and I know that he dwelt upon the sin and the shame of making a public laughing-stock of the scare.

"They will call us," said the Second-in-Command, who had really a fine imagination—"they will call us the 'Fly-by-Nights;' they will call us the 'Ghost Hunters;' they will nickname us from one end of the Army List to the other. All the explanation in the world won't make outsiders understand that the officers were away when the panic began. For the honor of the Regiment and for your own sake keep this thing quiet."

The Colonel was so exhausted with anger that soothing him down was not so difficult as might be imagined. He was made to see, gently and by degrees, that it was obviously impossible to court-martial the whole Regiment and equally impossible to proceed against any subaltern who, in his belief, had any concern in the hoax.

"But the beast's alive! He's never been shot at all!" shouted the Colonel. "It's flat flagrant disobedience! I've known a man broke for less. They're mocking me, I tell you, Mutman! They're mocking me!"

Once more, the Second-in-Command set himself to soothe the Colonel, and wrestled with him for half an hour. At the end of that time the Regimental Sergeant-Major reported himself. The situation was rather novel to him; but he was not a man to be put out by circumstances. He saluted and said, "Regiment all come back, Sir." Then, to propitiate the Colonel— "An' none of the 'orses any worse, Sir."

The Colonel only snorted and answered—"You'd better tuck the men into their cots, then, and see that they don't wake up and cry in the night." The Sergeant withdrew.

His little stroke of humor pleased the Colonel, and, further, he felt slightly ashamed of the language he had been using. The Second-in-Command worried him again, and the two sat talking far into the night.

Next day but one, there was a Commanding Officer's parade, and the Colonel harangued the White Hussars vigorously. The pith of his speech was that, since the Drum-Horse in his old age had proved himself capable of cutting up the whole Regiment, he should return to his post of pride at the head of the Band, but the Regiment were a set of ruffians with bad consciences.

The White Hussars shouted, and threw everything movable about them into the air, and when the parade was over, they cheered the Colonel till they couldn't speak. No cheers were put up for Lieutenant Hogan-Yale, who smiled very sweetly in the background.

Said the Second-in-Command to the Colonel, unofficially—

"These little things ensure popularity, and do not the least affect discipline."

"But I went back on my word," said the Colonel.

"Never mind," said the Second-in-Command. "The White Hussars will follow you anywhere from to-day. Regiments are just like women. They will do anything for trinketry."

A week later Hogan-Yale received an extraordinary letter from some one who signed himself "Secretary, Charity and Zeal, 3709, E. C.," and asked for "the return of our skeleton which we have reason to believe is in your possession."

"Who the deuce is this lunatic who trades in bones?" said Hogan-Yale.

"Beg your pardon, Sir," said the Band-Sergeant, "but the skeleton is with me, an' I'll return it if you'll pay the carriage into the Civil Lines. There's a coffin with it, Sir."

Hogan-Yale smiled and handed two rupees to the

Band-Sergeant, saying, "Write the date on the skull, will you?"

If you doubt this story, and know where to go, you can see the date on the skeleton. But don't mention the matter to the White Hussars.

I happen to know something about it, because I prepared the Drum-Horse for his resurrection. He did not take kindly to the skeleton at all.

TODS' AMENDMENT

The World hath set its heavy yoke
Upon the old white-bearded folk
  Who strive to please the King.
God's mercy is upon the young,
God's wisdom in the baby tongue
  That fears not anything.
    —*The Parable of Chajju Bhagat.*

NOW, Tods' Mamma was a singularly charming
woman, and every one in Simla knew Tods.
Most men had saved him from death on occasions. He was beyond his ayah's control altogether,
and periled his life daily to find out what would happen if you pulled a Mountain Battery mule's tail. He
was an utterly fearless young Pagan, about six years
old, and the only baby who ever broke the holy calm
of the Supreme Legislative Council.

It happened this way: Tods' pet kid got loose, and
fled up the hill, off the Boileaugunge Road, Tods after
it, until it burst in to the Viceregal Lodge lawn, then
attached to "Peterhoff." The Council were sitting at
the time, and the windows were open because it was
warm. The Red Lancer in the porch told Tods to go
away; but Tods knew the Red Lancer and most of the
Members of the Council personally. Moreover, he had
firm hold of the kid's collar, and was being dragged

all across the flower-beds. "Give my salaam to the long Councillor Sahib, and ask him to help me take Moti back!" gasped Tods. The Council heard the noise through the open windows; and, after an interval, was seen the shocking spectacle of a Legal Member and a Lieutenant-Governor helping, under the direct patronage of a Commander-in-Chief and a Viceroy, one small and very dirty boy in a sailor's suit and a tangle of brown hair, to coerce a lively and rebellious kid. They headed it off down the path to the Mall, and Tods went home in triumph and told his Mamma that all the Councillor Sahibs had been helping him to catch Moti. Whereat his Mamma smacked Tods for interfering with the administration of the Empire; but Tods met the Legal Member the next day, and told him in confidence that if the Legal Member ever wanted to catch a goat, he, Tods, would give him all the help in his power. "Thank you, Tods," said the Legal Member.

Tods was the idol of some eighty jhampanis, and half as many saises. He saluted them all as "O Brother." It never entered his head that any living human being could disobey his orders; and he was the buffer between the servants and his Mamma's wrath. The working of that household turned on Tods, who was adored by every one from the dhoby to the dog-boy. Even Futteh Khan, the villainous loafer khit from Mussoorie, shirked risking Tods' displeasure for fear his co-mates should look down on him.

So Tods had honor in the land from Boileaugunge to Chota Simla, and ruled justly according to his lights.

Of course, he spoke Urdu, but he had also mastered many queer side-speeches like the chotee bolee of the women, and held grave converse with shopkeepers and Hill-coolies alike. He was precocious for his age, and his mixing with natives had taught him some of the more bitter truths of life: the meanness and the sordidness of it. He used, over his bread and milk, to deliver solemn and serious aphorisms, translated from the vernacular into the English, that made his Mamma jump and vow that Tods must go Home next hot weather.

Just when Tods was in the bloom of his power, the Supreme Legislature were hacking out a Bill for the Sub-Montane Tracts, a revision of the then Act, smaller than the Punjab Land Bill, but affecting a few hundred thousand people none the less. The Legal Member had built, and bolstered, and embroidered, and amended that Bill, till it looked beautiful on paper. Then the Council began to settle what they called the "minor details." As if any Englishman legislating for natives knows enough to know which are the minor and which are the major points, from the native point of view, of any measure! That Bill was a triumph of "safeguarding the interests of the tenant." One clause provided that land should not be leased on longer terms than five years at a stretch; because, if the landlord had a tenant bound down for, say, twenty years, he would squeeze the very life out of him. The notion was to keep up a stream of independent cultivators in the Sub-Montane Tracts; and ethnologically and politically the notion was correct. The only drawback was that it was altogether wrong. A native's life in India implies the life of his son. Wherefore, you cannot legislate for one generation at a time. You must consider the next from the native point of view. Curiously enough, the native now and then, and in Northern India more particularly, hates being over-protected against himself. There was a Naga village once, where they lived on dead and buried Commissariat mules. . . . But that is another story.

For many reasons, to be explained later, the people concerned objected to the Bill. The Native Member in Council knew as much about Punjabis as he knew about Charing Cross. He had said in Calcutta that "the Bill was entirely in accord with the desires of that large and important class, the cultivators;" and so on, and so on. The Legal Member's knowledge of natives was limited to English-speaking Durbaris and his own red chaprassis, the Sub-Montane Tracts concerned no one in particular, the Deputy Commissioners were a good deal too driven to make representations, and the measure was one which dealt with small land-holders only. Nevertheless, the Legal Member prayed that it might be correct, for he was a nervously conscientious man. He did not know that no man can tell what natives think unless he mixes with them with the varnish off. And not always then. But he did the best he knew. And the measure came up to the Supreme Council for the final touches, while Tods patrolled the Burra Simla Bazaar in his morning rides, and played with the monkey belonging to Ditta Mull, the bunnia, and listened, as a child listens, to all the stray talk about this new freak of the Lord Sahib's.

One day there was a dinner-party at the house of Tods' Mamma, and the Legal Member came. Tods was in bed, but he kept awake till he heard the bursts of laughter from the men over the coffee. Then he paddled out in his little red flannel dressing-gown and his night-shirt and took refuge by the side of his father, knowing that he would not be sent back. "See the miseries of having a family!" said Tods' father, giving Tods three prunes, some water in a glass that had been used for claret, and telling him to sit still. Tods sucked the prunes slowly, knowing that he would have to go when they were finished, and sipped the pink water like a man of the world, as he listened to the conversation. Presently, the Legal Member, talking "shop" to the Head of a Department, mentioned his Bill by its full name—"The Sub-Montane Tracts Ryotwary Revised Enactment." Tods caught the one native word and lifting up his small voice said—

"Oh, I know all about that! Has it been murramutted yet, Councillor Sahib?"

"How much?" said the Legal Member.

"Murramutted—mended.—Put theek, you know—made nice to please Ditta Mull!"

The Legal Member left his place and moved up next to Tods.

"What do you know about ryotwari, little man?" he said.

"I'm not a little man, I'm Tods, and I know all about it. Ditta Mull, and Choga Lall, and Amir Nath, and

—oh, lakhs of my friends tell me about it in the bazars when I talk to them."

"Oh, they do—do they? What do they say, Tods?"

Tods tucked his feet under his red flannel dressing-gown and said—"I must fink."

The Legal Member waited patiently. Then Tods with infinite compassion—

"You don't speak my talk, do you, Councillor Sahib?"

"No; I am sorry to say I do not," said the Legal Member.

"Very well," said Tods, "I must fink in English."

He spent a minute putting his ideas in order, and began very slowly, translating in his mind from the vernacular to English, as many Anglo-Indian children do. You must remember that the Legal Member helped him on by questions when he halted, for Tods was not equal to the sustained flight of oratory that follows:

"Ditta Mull says, 'This thing is the talk of a child, and was made up by fools.' But I don't think you are a fool, Councillor Sahib," said Tods hastily. "You caught my goat. This is what Ditta Mull says—'I am not a fool, and why should the Sirkar say I am a child? I can see if the land is good and if the landlord is good. If I am a fool, the sin is upon my own head. For five years I take my ground for which I have saved money, and a wife I take too, and a little son is born.' Ditta Mull has one daughter now, but he says he will have a son soon. And he says, 'At the end of five years, by this new bundobust, I must go. If I do not go, I must get fresh seals and takkus-stamps on the papers, per-

haps in the middle of the harvest, and to go to the
law-courts once is wisdom, but to go twice is Jehannum.' That is quite true," explained Tods gravely.
"All my friends say so. And Ditta Mull says, 'Always
fresh takkus and paying money to vakils and chaprassis and law-courts every five years, or else the landlord makes me go. Why do I want to go? Am I a
fool? If I am a fool and do not know, after forty
years, good land when I see it, let me die! But if the
new bundobust says for fifteen years, this is good and
wise. My little son is a man, and I am burnt, and he
takes the ground or another ground, paying only once
for the takkus-stamps on the papers, and his little son
is born, and at the end of fifteen years is a man too.
But what profit is there in five years and fresh papers?
Nothing but dikh, trouble, dikh. We are not young
men who take these lands, but old ones—not farmers,
but tradesmen with a little money—and for fifteen
years we shall have peace. Nor are we children that
the Sirkar should treat us so.'"

Here Tods stopped short, for the whole table were
listening. The Legal Member said to Tods, "Is that
all?"

"All I can remember," said Tods. "But you should
see Ditta Mull's big monkey. It's just like a Councillor
Sahib."

"Tods! Go to bed," said his father.

Tods gathered up his dressing-gown tail and departed.

The Legal Member brought his hand down on the
table with a crash—"By Jove!" said the Legal Member,

"I believe the boy is right. The short tenure is the weak point."

He left early, thinking over what Tods had said. Now, it was obviously impossible for the Legal Member to play with a bunnia's monkey, by way of getting understanding; but he did better. He made inquiries, always bearing in mind the fact that the real native—not the hybrid, University-trained mule—is as timid as a colt, and, little by little, he coaxed some of the men whom the measure concerned most intimately to give in their views, which squared very closely with Tods' evidence.

So the bill was amended in that clause; and the Legal Member was filled with an uneasy suspicion that Native Members represent very little except the Orders they carry on their bosoms. But he put the thought from him as illiberal. He was a most Liberal man.

After a time, the news spread through the bazars that Tods had got the Bill recast in the tenure-clause, and if Tods' Mamma had not interfered, Tods would have made himself sick on the baskets of fruit and pistachio nuts and Cabuli grapes and almonds that crowded the verandah. Till he went Home, Tods ranked some few degrees before the Viceroy in popular estimation. But for the little life of him Tods could not understand why.

In the Legal Member's private-paper-box still lies the rough draft of the Sub-Montane Tracts Ryotwary Revised Enactment; and, opposite the twenty-second clause, penciled in blue chalk, and signed by the Legal Member, are the words, "Tods' Amendment."

THE INCARNATION OF KRISHNA
MULVANEY

Wohl auf, my bully cavaliers,
  We ride to church to-day,
The man that hasn't got a horse
  Must steal one straight away.

.   .   .   .   .

Be reverent, men, remember
  This is a Gottes haus.
Du, Conrad, cut along der aisle
  And schenck der whiskey aus.
  —*Hans Breitmann's Ride to Church.*

ONCE upon a time, very far from England, there lived three men who loved each other so greatly that neither man nor woman could come between them. They were in no sense refined, nor to be admitted to the outer-door mats of decent folk, because they happened to be private soldiers in Her Majesty's Army; and private soldiers of our service have small time for self-culture. Their duty is to keep themselves and their accoutrements specklessly clean, to refrain from getting drunk more often than is necessary, to obey their superiors, and to pray for a war. All these things my friends accomplished; and of their own motion threw in some fighting-work for which the Army Regulations did not call. Their fate sent them

to serve in India, which is not a golden country, though
poets have sung otherwise. There men die with great
swiftness, and those who live suffer many and curious
things. I do not think that my friends concerned
themselves much with the social or political aspects of
the East. They attended a not unimportant war on
the northern frontier, another one on our western
boundary, and a third in Upper Burma. Then their
regiment sat still to recruit, and the boundless monotony of cantonment life was their portion. They were
drilled morning and evening on the same dusty parade-
ground. They wandered up and down the same stretch
of dusty white road, attended the same church and the
same grog-shop, and slept in the same lime-washed
barn of a barrack for two long years. There was Mulvaney, the father in the craft, who had served with
various regiments from Bermuda to Halifax, old in
war, scarred, reckless, resourceful, and in his pious
hours an unequalled soldier. To him turned for help
and comfort six and a half feet of slow-moving, heavy-
footed Yorkshiremen, born on the wolds, bred in the
dales, and educated chiefly among the carriers' carts at
the back of York railway-station. His name was
Learoyd, and his chief virtue an unmitigated patience
which helped him to win fights. How Ortheris, a fox-
terrier of a Cockney, ever came to be one of the trio, is
a mystery which even to-day I cannot explain. "There
was always three av us," Mulvaney used to say. "An'
by the grace av God, so long as our service lasts, three
av us they'll always be. 'Tis betther so."
They desired no companionship beyond their own,

and it was evil for any man of the regiment who attempted dispute with them. Physical argument was out of the question as regarded Mulvaney and the Yorkshireman; and assault on Ortheris meant a combined attack from these twain—a business which no five men were anxious to have on their hands. Therefore they flourished, sharing their drinks, their tobacco, and their money; good luck and evil; battle and the chances of death; life and the chances of happiness from Calicut in southern, to Peshawur in northern India.

Through no merit of my own it was my good fortune to be in a measure admitted to their friendship—frankly by Mulvaney from the beginning, sullenly and with reluctance by Learoyd, and suspiciously by Ortheris, who held to it that no man not in the Army could fraternize with a red-coat. "Like to like," said he, "I'm a bloomin' sodger—he's a bloomin' civilian. 'Tain't natural—that's all."

But that was not all. They thawed progressively, and in the thawing told me more of their lives and adventures than I am ever likely to write.

Omitting all else, this tale begins with the Lamentable Thirst that was at the beginning of First Causes. Never was such a thirst—Mulvaney told me so. They kicked against their compulsory virtue, but the attempt was only successful in the case of Ortheris. He, whose talents were many, went forth into the highways and stole a dog from a "civilian"—*videlicet,* some one, he knew not who, not in the Army. Now that civilian was but newly connected by marriage with the colonel of the regiment, and outcry was made from quarters least anticipated by Ortheris, and, in the end, he was forced, lest a worse thing should happen, to dispose at ridiculously unremunerative rates of as promising a small terrier as ever graced one end of a leading string. The purchase-money was barely sufficient for one small outbreak which led him to the guard-room. He escaped, however, with nothing worse than a severe reprimand, and a few hours of punishment drill. Not for nothing had he acquired the reputation of being "the best soldier of his inches" in the regiment. Mulvaney had taught personal cleanliness and efficiency as the first articles of his companions' creed. "A dhirty man," he was used to say, in the speech of his kind, "goes to Clink for a weakness in the knees, an' is coortmartialled for a pair av socks missin'; but a clane man, such as is an ornament to his service—a man whose buttons are gold, whose coat is wax upon him, an' whose 'coutrements are widout a speck—*that* man may, spakin' in reason, do fwhat he likes an' dhrink from day to divil. That's the pride av bein' dacint."

We sat together, upon a day, in the shade of a ravine far from the barracks, where a water-course used to run in rainy weather. Behind us was the scrub jungle, in which jackals, peacocks, the grey wolves of the Northwestern Provinces, and occasionally a tiger estrayed from Central India, were supposed to dwell. In front lay the cantonment, glaring white under a glaring sun; and on either side ran the broad road that led to Delhi.

It was the scrub that suggested to my mind the wisdom of Mulvaney taking a day's leave and going upon a shooting-tour. The peacock is a holy bird throughout India, and he who slays one is in danger of being mobbed by the nearest villagers; but on the last occasion that Mulvaney had gone forth, he had contrived, without in the least offending local religious susceptibilities, to return with six beautiful peacock skins which he sold to profit. It seemed just possible then—

"But fwhat manner av use is ut to me goin' out widout a dhrink? The ground's powdher-dhry underfoot, an' ut gets unto the throat fit to kill," wailed Mulvaney, looking at me reproachfully. "An' a peacock is not a bird you can catch the tail av onless ye run. Can a man run on wather—an' jungle-wather too?"

Ortheris had considered the question in all its bearings. He spoke, chewing his pipe-stem meditatively the while:

"Go forth, return in glory,
    To Clusium's royal 'ome:
An' round these bloomin' temples 'ang
    The bloomin' shields o' Rome.

You better go. You ain't like to shoot yourself—not while there's a chanst of liquor. Me an' Learoyd'll stay at 'ome an' keep shop—'case o' anythin' turnin' up. But you go out with a gas-pipe gun an' ketch the little peacockses or somethin'. You kin get one day's leave easy as winkin'. Go along an' get it, an' get peacockses or somethin'."

"Jock," said Mulvaney, turning to Learoyd, who was half asleep under the shadow of the bank. He roused slowly.

"Sitha, Mulvaney, go," said he.

And Mulvaney went; cursing his allies with Irish fluency and barrack-room point.

"Take note," said he, when he had won his holiday, and appeared dressed in his roughest clothes with the only other regimental fowling piece in his hand. "Take note, Jock, an' you Orth'ris, I am goin' in the face av my own will—all for to please you. I misdoubt anythin' will come av permiscuous huntin' afther peacockses in a desolit lan'; an' I know that I will lie down an' die wid thirrrst. Me catch peacockses for you, ye lazy scutts—an' be sacrificed by the peasanthry—Ugh!"

He waved a huge paw and went away.

At twilight, long before the appointed hour, he returned empty-handed, much begrimed with dirt.

"Peacockses?" queried Ortheris from the safe rest of a barrack-room table whereon he was smoking cross-legged, Learoyd fast asleep on a bench.

"Jock," said Mulvaney, without answering, as he stirred up the sleeper. "Jock, can ye fight? Will ye fight?"

Very slowly the meaning of the words communicated itself to the half-roused man. He understood—and again—what might these things mean? Mulvaney was shaking him savagely. Meantime the men in the room howled with delight. There was war in the confederacy at last—war and the breaking of bonds.

Barrack-room etiquette is stringent. On the direct challenge must follow the direct reply. This is more binding than the ties of tried friendship. Once again Mulvaney repeated the question. Learoyd answered by the only means in his power, and so swiftly that the

Irishman had barely time to avoid the blow. The laughter around increased. Learoyd looked bewilderedly at his friend—himself as greatly bewildered. Ortheris dropped from the table because his world was falling.

"Come outside," said Mulvaney, and as the occupants of the barrack-room prepared joyously to follow, he turned and said furiously, "There will be no fight this night—onless any wan av you is wishful to assist. The man that does, follows on."

No man moved. The three passed out into the moonlight, Learoyd fumbling with the buttons of his coat. The parade-ground was deserted except for the scurrying jackals. Mulvaney's impetuous rush carried his companions far into the open ere Learoyd attempted to turn round and continue the discussion.

"Be still now. 'Twas my fault for beginnin' things in the middle av an end, Jock. I should ha' comminst wid an explanation; but Jock, dear, on your sowl are ye fit, think you, for the finest fight that iver was— betther than fightin' me? Considher before you answer."

More than ever puzzled, Learoyd turned round two or three times, felt an arm, kicked tentatively, and answered, "Ah'm fit." He was accustomed to fight blindly at the bidding of the superior mind.

They sat them down, the men looking on from afar, and Mulvaney untangled himself in mighty words.

"Followin' your fools' scheme I wint out into the thrackless desert beyond the barricks. An' there I met a pious Hindu, dhriving a bullock-kyart. I tuk ut for granted he wud be delighted for to convoy me a piece, an' I jumped in"—

"You long, lazy black-haired swine," drawled Ortheris, who would have done the same thing under similar circumstances.

"'Twas the height av policy. That naygurman dhruv miles an' miles—as far as the new railway line they're buildin' now back av the Tavi river. ''Tis a kyart for dhirt only,' says he now an' again timoreously, to get me out av ut. 'Dhirt I am,' sez I, 'an' the dhryest that you iver kyarted. Dhrive on, me son, an' glory be wid you.' At that I wint to slape, an' took no heed till he pulled up on the embankmint av the line where the coolies were pilin' mud. There was a matther av two thousand coolies on that line—you remimber that. Prisintly a bell rang, an' they throops off to a big pay-shed. 'Where's the white man in charge?' sez I to my kyart-dhriver. 'In the shed,' sez he, 'engaged on a riffle.'—'A fwhat?' sez I. 'Riffle,' sez he. 'You take ticket. He take money. You get nothin'.'— 'Oho!' sez I, 'that's fwhat the shuperior an' cultivated man calls a raffle, me misbeguided child av darkness an' sin. Lead on to that raffle, though fwhat the mischief 'tis doin' so far away from uts home—which is the charity-bazar at Christmas, an' the colonel's wife grinnin' behind the tea-table—is more than I know.' Wid that I wint to the shed an' found 'twas pay-day among the coolies. Their wages was on a table forninst a big, fine, red buck av a man—sivun fut high, four fut wide, an' three fut thick, wid a fist on him like a corn-sack. He was payin' the coolies fair an' easy, but

he wud ask each man if he wud raffle that month, an'
each man sez, 'Yes,' av course. Thin he wud deduct
from their wages accordin'. Whin all was paid, he
filled an ould cigar-box full av gun-wads an' scatthered
ut among the coolies. They did not take much joy av
that performince, an' small wondher. A man close to
me picks up a black gun-wad an' sings out, 'I have ut.'
—'Good may ut do you,' sez I. The coolie wint forward to this big, fine, red man, who threw a cloth off
av the most sumpshus, jooled, enamelled an' variously
bedivilled sedan-chair I iver saw."

"Sedan-chair! Put your 'ead in a bag. That was a
palanquin. Don't yer know a palanquin when you see
it?" said Ortheris with great scorn.

"I chuse to call ut sedan chair, an' chair ut shall be,
little man," continued the Irishman. " 'Twas a most
amazin' chair—all lined wid pink silk an' fitted wid
red silk curtains. 'Here ut is,' sez the red man. 'Here
ut is,' sez the coolie, an' he grinned weakly-ways. 'Is
ut any use to you?' sez the red man. 'No,' sez the
coolie; 'I'd like to make a presint av ut to you.'—'I am
graciously pleased to accept that same,' sez the red man;
an' at that all the coolies cried aloud in fwhat was mint
for cheerful notes, an' wint back to their diggin', lavin'
me alone in the shed. The red man saw me, an' his
face grew blue on his big, fat neck. 'Fwhat d'you want
here?' sez he. 'Standin'-room an' no more,' sez I,
'onless it may be fwhat ye niver had, an' that's manners, ye rafflin' ruffian,' for I was not goin' to have the
Service throd upon. 'Out of this,' sez he. 'I'm in
charge av this section av construction.'—'I'm in charge

av mesilf,' sez I, 'an' it's like I will stay a while. D'ye raffle much in these parts?'—'Fwhat's that to you?' sez he. 'Nothin',' sez I, 'but a great dale to you, for begad I'm thinkin' you get the full half av your revenue from that sedan-chair. Is ut always raffled so?' I sez, an' wid that I wint to a coolie to ask questions. Bhoys, that man's name is Dearsley, an' he's been rafflin' that ould sedan-chair monthly this matther av nine months. Ivry coolie on the section takes a ticket—or he gives 'em the go—wanst a month on pay-day. Ivry coolie that wins ut gives ut back to him, for 'tis too big to carry away, an' he'd sack the man that thried to sell ut. That Dearsley has been makin' the rowlin' wealth av Roshus by nefarious rafflin'. Think av the burnin' shame to the sufferin' coolie-man that the army in Injia are bound to protect an' nourish in their bosoms! Two thousand coolies defrauded wanst a month!"

"Dom t' coolies. Has't gotten t' cheer, man?" said Learoyd.

"Hould on. Havin' onearthed this amazin' an' stupenjus fraud committed by the man Dearsley, I hild a council av war; he thryin' all the time to sejuce me into a fight wid opprobrious language. That sedan-chair niver belonged by right to any foreman av coolies. 'Tis a king's chair or a quane's. There's gold on ut an' silk an' all manner av trapesemints. Bhoys, 'tis not for me to countenance any sort av wrong-doin'—me bein' the ould man—but—anyway he has had ut nine months, an' he dare not make throuble av ut was taken from him. Five miles away, or ut may be six"—

There was a long pause, and the jackals howled mer-

rily. Learoyd bared one arm, and contemplated it in
the moonlight. Then he nodded partly to himself and
partly to his friends. Ortheris wriggled with suppressed emotion.

"I thought ye wud see the reasonableness av ut,"
said Mulvaney. "I make bould to say as much to the
man before. He was for a direct front attack—fut,
horse, an' guns—an' all for nothin', seein' that I had no
thransport to convey the machine away. 'I will not
argue wid you,' sez I, 'this day, but subsequintly, Mister
Dearsley, me rafflin' jool, we talk ut out lengthways.
'Tis no good policy to swindle the naygur av his hard-
earned emolumints, an' by presint informashin'"—'twas
the kyart man that tould me—'ye've been perpethrat-
ing that same for nine months. But I'm a just man,'
sez I, 'an' overlookin' the presumpshin that yondher
settee wid the gilt top was not come by honust'—at
that he turned sky-green, so I knew things was more
thrue than tellable—'not come by honust, I'm willin' to
compound the felony for this month's winnin's.'"

"Ah! Ho!" from Learoyd and Ortheris.

"That man Dearsley's rushin' on his fate," continued
Mulvaney, solemnly wagging his head. "All Hell had
no name bad enough for me that tide. Faith, he called
me a robber! Me! that was savin' him from con-
tinuin' in his evil ways widout a remonstrince—an' to
a man av conscience a remonstrince may change the
chune av his life. ' 'Tis not for me to argue,' sez I,
'fwhatever ye are, Mister Dearsley, but, by my hand,
I'll take away the temptation for you that lies in that
sedan-chair.'—'You will have to fight me for ut,' sez

he, 'for well I know you will never dare make report
to any one.'—'Fight I will,' sez I, 'but not this day, for
I'm rejuced for want av nourishment.'—'Ye're an ould
bould hand,' sez he, sizin' me up an' down; 'an' a jool
av a fight we will have. Eat now an' dhrink, an' go
your way.' Wid that he gave me some hump an'
whisky—good whisky—an' we talked av this an' that
the while. 'It goes hard on me now,' sez I, wipin' my
mouth, 'to confiscate that piece av furniture, but justice
is justice.'—'Ye've not got ut yet,' sez he; 'there's the
fight between.'—'There is,' sez I, 'an' a good fight. Ye
shall have the pick av the best quality in my rigimint
for the dinner you have given this day.' Thin I came
hot-foot to you two. Hould your tongue, the both.
'Tis this way. To-morrow we three will go there an'
he shall have his pick betune me an' Jock. Jock's a
deceivin' fighter, for he is all fat to the eye, an' he
moves slow. Now I'm all beef to the look, an' I move
quick. By my reckonin' the Dearsley man won't take
me; so me an' Orth'ris 'll see fair play. Jock, I tell you,
'twill be big fightin'—whipped, wid the cream above
the jam. Afther the business 'twill take a good three
av us—Jock 'll be very hurt—to haul away that sedan-
chair."

"Palanquin." This from Ortheris.

"Fwhatever ut is, we must have ut. 'Tis the only
sellin' piece av property widin' reach that we can get
so cheap. An' fwhat's a fight afther all? He has
robbed the naygur-man, dishonust. We rob him honust for the sake av the whisky he gave me."

"But wot'll we do with the bloomin' article when

we've got it? Them palanquins are as big as 'ouses, an'
uncommon 'ard to sell, as McCleary said when ye stole
the sentry-box from the Curragh."

"Who's goin' to do t' fightin'?" said Learoyd, and
Ortheris subsided. The three returned to barracks
without a word. Mulvaney's last argument clinched
the matter. This palanquin was property, vendible,
and to be attained in the simplest and least embarrassing fashion. It would eventually become beer. Great
was Mulvaney.

Next afternoon a procession of three formed itself
and disappeared into the scrub in the direction of the
new railway line. Learoyd alone was without care, for
Mulvaney dived darkly into the future, and little Ortheris feared the unknown. What befell at that interview in the lonely pay-shed by the side of the half-built
embankment, only a few hundred coolies know, and
their tale is a confusing one, running thus—

"We were at work. Three men in red coats came.
They saw the Sahib—Dearsley Sahib. They made oration; and noticeably the small man among the red-
coats. Dearsley Sahib also made oration and used
many very strong words. Upon this talk they departed
together to an open space, and there the fat man in the
red coat fought with Dearsley Sahib after the custom
of white men—with his hands, making no noise, and
never at all pulling Dearsley Sahib's hair. Such of us
as were not afraid beheld these things for just so long
a time as a man needs to cook the midday meal. The
small man in the red coat had possessed himself of
Dearsley Sahib's watch. No, he did not steal that

watch. He held it in his hand, and at certain seasons made outcry, and the twain ceased their combat, which was like the combat of young bulls in spring. Both men were soon all red, but Dearsley Sahib was much more red than the other. Seeing this, and fearing for his life—because we greatly loved him—some fifty of us made shift to rush upon the red-coats. But a certain man—very black as to the hair, and in no way to be confused with the small man, or the fat man who fought—that man, we affirm, ran upon us, and of us he embraced some ten or fifty in both arms, and beat our heads together, so that our livers turned to water, and we ran away. It is not good to interfere in the fightings of white men. After that Dearsley Sahib fell and did not rise, these men jumped upon his stomach and despoiled him of all his money, and attempted to fire the pay-shed, and departed. It is true that Dearsley Sahib makes no complaint of these latter things having been done? We were senseless with fear, and do not at all remember. There was no palanquin near the pay-shed. What do we know about palanquins? Is it true that Dearsley Sahib does not return to this place, on account of his sickness, for ten days? This is the fault of those bad men in the red coats, who should be severely punished; for Dearsley Sahib is both our father and mother, and we love him much. Yet, if Dearsley Sahib does not return to this place at all, we will speak the truth. There was a palanquin, for the up-keep of which we were forced to pay nine-tenths of our monthly wage. On such mulctings Dearsley Sahib allowed us to make obeisance to him before the palanquin. What could we do? We were poor men. He took a full half of our wages. Will the Government repay us those moneys? Those three men in red coats bore the palanquin upon their shoulders and departed. All the money that Dearsley Sahib had taken from us was in the cushions of that palanquin. Therefore they stole it. Thousands of rupees were there—all our money. It was our bank-box, to fill which we cheerfully contributed to Dearsley Sahib three-sevenths of our monthly wage. Why does the white man look upon us with the eye of disfavor? Before God, there was a palanquin, and now there is no palanquin; and if they send the police here to make inquisition, we can only say that there never has been any palanquin. Why should a palanquin be near these works? We are poor men, and we know nothing."

Such is the simplest version of the simplest story connected with the descent upon Dearsley. From the lips of the coolies I received it. Dearsley himself was in no condition to say anything, and Mulvaney preserved a massive silence, broken only by the occasional licking of the lips. He had seen a fight so gorgeous that even his power of speech was taken from him. I respected that reserve until, three days after the affair, I discovered in a disused stable in my quarters a palanquin of unchastened splendor—evidently in past days the litter of a queen. The pole whereby it swung between the shoulders of the bearers was rich with the painted *papier-maché* of Cashmere. The shoulder-pads were of yellow silk. The panels of the litter itself were ablaze with the loves of all the gods and goddesses of the

Hindu Pantheon—lacquer on cedar. The cedar sliding doors were fitted with hasps of transient Jaipur enamel and ran in grooves shod with silver. The cushions were of brocaded Delhi silk, and the curtains which once hid any glimpse of the beauty of the king's palace were stiff with gold. Closer investigation showed that the entire fabric was everywhere rubbed and discolored by time and wear; but even thus it was sufficiently gorgeous to deserve housing on the threshold of a royal zenana. I found no fault with it, except that it was in my stable. Then, trying to lift it by the silver-shod shoulder-pole, I laughed. The road from Dearsley's pay-shed to the cantonment was a narrow and uneven one, traversed by three very inexperienced palanquin-bearers, one of whom was sorely battered about the head, must have been a path of torment. Still I did not quite recognize the right of the three musketeers to turn me into a "fence" for stolen property.

"I'm askin' you to warehouse ut," said Mulvaney when he was brought to consider the question. "There's no steal in ut. Dearsley tould us we cud have ut if we fought. Jock fought—an', oh, sorr, when the throuble was at uts finest an' Jock was bleedin' like a stuck pig, an' little Orth'ris was shqualin' on one leg chewin' big bites out av Dearsley's watch, I wud ha' given my place at the fight to have had you see wan round. He tuk Jock, as I suspicioned he would, an' Jock was deceptive. Nine roun's they were even matched, an' at the tenth—About that palanquin now. There's not the least throuble in the world, or we wud

not ha' brought ut here. You will ondherstand that the
Queen—God bless her!—does not reckon for a privit
soldier to kape elephints an' palanquins an' sich in barracks. Afther we had dhragged ut down from Dearsley's through that cruel scrub that near broke Orth'-
ris's heart, we set ut in the ravine for a night; an' a
thief av a porcupine an' a civet-cat av a jackal roosted in
ut, as well we knew in the mornin'. I put ut to you,
sorr, is an elegint palanquin, fit for the princess, the
natural abidin' place av all the vermin in cantonmints? We brought ut to you, afther dhark, and put
ut in your shtable. Do not let your conscience prick.
Think av the rejoicin' men in the pay-shed yonder—
lookin' at Dearsley wid his head tied up in a towel—
an' well knowin' that they can dhraw their pay ivry
month widout stoppages for riffles. Indirectly, sorr,
you have rescued from an onprincipled son av a night-
hawk the peasanthry av a numerous village. An' besides, will I let that sedan-chair rot on our hands?
Not I. 'Tis not every day a piece av pure joolry comes
into the market. There's not a king widin' these
forty miles"—he waved his hand round the dusty horizon—"not a king wud not be glad to buy ut. Some
day meself, whin I have leisure, I'll take ut up along
the road an' dishpose av ut."

"How?" said I, for I knew the man was capable of
anything.

"Get into ut, av coorse, and keep wan eye open
through the curtains. Whin I see a likely man av the
native persuasion, I will descind blushin' from my
canopy and say, 'Buy a palanquin, ye black scutt?' I

will have to hire four men to carry me first, though; and that's impossible till next pay-day."

Curiously enough, Learoyd, who had fought for the prize, and in the winning secured the highest pleasure life had to offer him, was altogether disposed to under value it, while Ortheris openly said it would be better to break the thing up. Dearsley, he argued, might be a many-sided man, capable, despite his magnificent fighting qualities, of setting in motion the machinery of the civil law—a thing much abhorred by the soldier. Under any circumstances their fun had come and passed; the next pay-day was close at hand, when there would be beer for all. Wherefore longer conserve the painted palanquin?

"A first-class rifle-shot an' a good little man av your inches you are," said Mulvaney. "But you niver had a head worth a soft-boiled egg. 'Tis me has to lie awake av nights scharnin' an' plottin' for the three av us. Orth'ris, me son, 'tis no matther av a few gallons av beer—no, nor twenty gallons—but tubs an' vats an' firkins in that sedan-chair. Who ut was, an' what ut was, an' how ut got there, we do not know; but I know in my bones that you an' me an' Jock wid his sprained thumb will get a fortune thereby. Lave me alone, an' let me think."

Meantime the palanquin stayed in my stall, the key of which was in Mulvaney's hands.

Pay-day came, and with it beer. It was not in experience to hope that Mulvaney, dried by four weeks' drought, would avoid excess. Next morning he and the palanquin had disappeared. He had taken the precaution of getting three days' leave "to see a friend on the railway," and the colonel, well knowing that the seasonal outburst was near, and hoping it would spend its force beyond the limits of his jurisdiction, cheerfully gave him all he demanded. At this point Mulvaney's history, as recorded in the mess-room, stopped.

Ortheris carried it not much further. "No, 'e wasn't drunk," said the little man loyally, "the liquor was no more than feelin' its way round inside of 'im; but 'e went an' filled that 'ole bloomin' palanquin with bottles 'fore 'e went off. 'E's gone an' 'ired six men to carry 'im, an' I 'ad to 'elp 'im into 'is nupshal couch, 'cause 'e wouldn't 'ear reason. 'E's gone off in 'is shirt an' trousies, swearin' tremenjus—gone down the road in the palanquin, wavin' 'is legs out o' windy."

"Yes," said I, "but where?"

"Now you arx me a question. 'E said 'e was goin' to sell that palanquin, but from observations what happened when I was stuffin' 'im through the door, I fancy 'e's gone to the new embankment to mock at Dearsley. 'Soon as Jock's off duty I'm goin' there to see if 'e's safe —not Mulvaney, but t'other man. My saints, but I pity 'im as 'elps Terence out o' the palanquin when 'e's once fair drunk!"

"He'll come back without harm," I said.

" 'Corse 'e will. On'y question is, what'll 'e be doin' on the road? Killing Dearsley, like as not. 'E shouldn't 'a gone without Jock or me."

Reinforced by Learoyd, Ortheris sought the foreman of the coolie-gang. Dearsley's head was still embellished with towels. Mulvaney, drunk or sober, would have struck no man in that condition, and Dearsley indignantly denied that he would have taken advantage of the intoxicated brave.

"I had my pick o' you two," he explained to Learoyd, "and you got my palanquin—not before I'd made my profit on it. Why'd I do harm when everything's settled? Your man *did* come here—drunk as Davy's sow on a frosty night—came a-purpose to mock me—stuck his head out of the door an' called me a crucified hodman. I made him drunker, an' sent him along. But I never touched him."

To these things Learoyd, slow to perceive the evidences of sincerity, answered only, "if owt comes to Mulvaney 'long o' you, I'll gripple you, clouts or no clouts on your ugly head, an' I'll draw t' throat twisty-ways, man. See there now."

The embassy removed itself, and Dearsley, the battered, laughed alone over his supper that evening.

Three days passed—a fourth and a fifth. The week drew to a close and Mulvaney did not return. He, his royal palanquin, and his six attendants, had vanished into air. A very large and very tipsy soldier, his feet sticking out of the litter of a reigning princess, is not a thing to travel along the ways without comment. Yet no man of all the country round had seen any such wonder. He was, and he was not; and Learoyd suggested the immediate smashment of Dearsley as a sacrifice to his ghost. Ortheris insisted that all was well, and in the light of past experience his hopes seemed reasonable.

"When Mulvaney goes up the road," said he, "'e's

like to go a very longs ways up, specially when 'e's so
blue drunk as 'e is now. But what gits me is 'is not
bein' 'eard of pullin' wool off the niggers somewheres
about. That don't look good. The drink must ha'
died out in 'im by this, unless 'e's broke a bank, an'
then—Why don't 'e come back? 'E didn't ought to
ha' gone off without us."

Even Ortheris's heart sank at the end of the seventh
day, for half the regiment were out scouring the country-side, and Learoyd had been forced to fight two men
who hinted openly that Mulvaney had deserted. To
do him justice, the colonel laughed at the notion, even
when it was put forward by his much-trusted adjutant.

"Mulvaney would as soon think of deserting as you
would," said he. "No; he's either fallen into a mischief among the villagers—and yet that isn't likely, for
he'd blarney himself out of the Pit; or else he is engaged
on urgent private affairs—some stupendous devilment
that we shall hear of at mess after it has been the round
of the barrack-rooms. The worst of it is that I shall
have to give him twenty-eight days' confinement at
least for being absent without leave, just when I most
want him to lick the new batch of recruits into shape.
I never knew a man who could put a polish on young
soldiers as quickly as Mulvaney can. How does he do
it?"

"With blarney and the buckle-end of a belt, sir," said
the adjutant. "He is worth a couple of non-commissioned officers when we are dealing with an Irish draft,
and the London lads seem to adore him. The worst
of it is that if he goes to the cells the other two are

neither to hold nor to bind till he comes out again. I
believe Ortheris preaches mutiny on those occasions,
and I know that the mere presence of Learoyd mourn-
ing for Mulvaney kills all the cheerfulness of his room.
The sergeants tell me that he allows no man to laugh
when he feels unhappy. They are a queer gang."

"For all that, I wish we had a few more of them. I
like a well-conducted regiment, but these pasty-faced,
shifty-eyed, mealy-mouthed young slouchers from the
depot worry me sometimes with their offensive virtue.
They don't seem to have backbone enough to do anything but play cards and prowl round the married
quarters. I believe I'd forgive that old villain on the
spot if he turned up with any sort of explanation that
I could in decency accept."

"Not likely to be much difficulty about that, sir,"
said the adjutant. "Mulvaney's explanations are only
one degree less wonderful than his performances. They
say that when he was in the Black Tyrone, before he
came to us, he was discovered on the banks of the Liffey
trying to sell his colonel's charger to a Donegal dealer
as a perfect lady's hack. Shackbolt commanded the
Tyrone then."

"Shackbolt must have had apoplexy at the thought
of his ramping war-horses answering to that description. He used to buy unbacked devils, and tame them
on some pet theory of starvation. What did Mulvaney
say?"

"That he was a member of the Society for the Pre-
vention of Cruelty to Animals, anxious to 'sell the poor
baste where he would get something to fill out his

dimples.' Shackbolt laughed, but I fancy that was why Mulvaney exchanged to ours."

"I wish he were back," said the colonel; "for I like him and believe he likes me."

That evening, to cheer our souls, Learoyd, Ortheris, and I went into the waste to smoke out a porcupine. All the dogs attended, but even their clamor—and they began to discuss the shortcomings of porcupines before they left cantonments—could not take us out of ourselves. A large, low moon turned the tops of the plumegrass to silver, and the stunted camelthorn bushes and sour tamarisks into the likenesses of trooping devils. The smell of the sun had not left the earth, and little aimless winds blowing across the rose-gardens to the southward brought the scent of dried roses and water. Our fires once started, and the dogs craftily disposed to wait the dash of the porcupine, we climbed to the top of a rain-scarred hillock of earth, and looked across the scrub seamed with cattle paths, white with the long grass, and dotted with spots of level pond-bottom, where the snipe would gather in winter. "This," said Ortheris, with a sigh, as he took in the unkempt desolation of it all, "this is sanguinary. This is unusually sanguinary. Sort o' mad country. Like a grate when the fire's put out by the sun." He shaded his eyes against the moonlight. "An' there's a loony dancin' in the middle of it all. Quite right I'd dance too if I wasn't so downheart."

There pranced a Portent in the face of the moon—a huge and ragged spirit of the waste, that flapped its wings from afar. It had risen out of the earth; it was coming toward us, and its outline was never twice the same. The toga, table-cloth, or dressing-gown, whatever the creature wore, took a hundred shapes. Once it stopped on a neighboring mound and flung all its legs and arms to the winds.

"My, but that scarecrow 'as got 'em bad!" said Ortheris. "Seems like if 'e comes any furder we'll 'ave to argify with 'im."

Learoyd raised himself from the dirt as a bull clears his flanks of the wallow. And as a bull bellows, so he after a short minute at gaze, gave tongue to the stars.

"MULVAANEY! MULVAANEY! A-hoo!"

Oh then it was that we yelled, and the figure dipped into the hollow, till, with a crash of rending grass, the lost one strode up to the light of the fire, and disappeared to the waist in a wave of joyous dogs! Then Learoyd and Ortheris gave greeting, bass and falsetto together, both swallowing a lump in the throat.

"You damned fool!" said they, and severally pounded him with their fists.

"Go easy!" he answered; wrapping a huge arm around each. "I would have you to know that I am a god, to be treated as such—tho', by my faith, I fancy I've got to go to the guardroom just like a privit soldier."

The latter part of the sentence destroyed the suspicions raised by the former. Any one would have been justified in regarding Mulvaney as mad. He was hatless and shoeless, and his shirt and trousers were dropping off him. But he wore one wondrous garment—a gigantic cloak that fell from collar-bone to heel—

of pale pink silk, wrought all over in cunningest needle-
work of hands long since dead, with the loves of the
Hindu gods. The monstrous figures leaped in and out
of the light of the fire as he settled the folds round
him.

Ortheris handled the stuff respectfully for a moment
while I was trying to remember where I had seen it
before. Then he screamed, "What *'ave* you done with
the palanquin? You're wearin' the linin'."

"I am," said the Irishman, "an' by the same token
the 'broidery is scrapin' my hide off. I've lived in this
sumpshus counterpane for four days. Me son, I begin
to ondherstand why the naygur is no use. Widout me
boots, an' me trousies like an openwork stocking on a
gyurl's leg at a dance, I begin to feel like a naygur-
man—all fearful an' timoreous. Give me a pipe an' I'll
tell on."

He lit a pipe, resumed his grip of his two friends,
and rocked to and fro in a gale of laughter.

"Mulvaney," said Ortheris sternly, "'tain't no time
for laughin'. You've given Jock an' me more trouble
than you're worth. You 'ave been absent without leave
an' you'll go into cells for that; an' you 'ave come back
disgustin'ly dressed an' most improper in the linin' o'
that bloomin' palanquin. Instid of which you laugh.
An' *we* thought you was dead all the time."

"Bhoys," said the culprit, still shaking gently, "whin
I've done my tale you may cry if you like, an' little
Orth'ris here can thrample my inside out. Ha' done
an' listen. My performinces have been stupenjus: my
luck has been the blessed luck av the British Army—

an' there's no betther than that. I went out dhrunk an'
dhrinkin' in the palanquin, and I have come back a
pink god. Did any of you go to Dearsley afther my
time was up? He was at the bottom of ut all."

"Ah said so," murmured Learoyd. "To-morrow
ah'll smash t' face in upon his heead."

"Ye will not. Dearsley's a jool av a man. Afther
Ortheris had put me into the palanquin an' the six
bearer-men were gruntin' down the road, I tuk thought
to mock Dearsley for that fight. So I tould thim, 'Go
to the embankmint,' and there, bein' most amazin' full,
I shtuck my head out av the concern an' passed com-
pliments wid Dearsley. I must ha' miscalled him outrageous, for whin I am that way the power av the
tongue comes on me. I can bare remimber tellin' him
that his mouth opened endways like the mouth av a
skate, which was thrue afther Learoyd had handled ut;
an' I clear remimber his takin' no manner nor matter av
offence, but givin' me a big dhrink of beer. 'Twas the
beer did the thrick, for I crawled back into the palanquin, steppin' on me right ear wid me left foot, an'
thin I slept like the dead. Wanst I half-roused, an'
begad the noise in my head was tremenjus—roarin'
and rattlin' an' poundin', such as was quite new to me.
'Mother av Mercy,' thinks I, 'pwhat a concertina I will
have on my shoulders whin I wake!' An' wid that I
curls mysilf up to sleep before ut should get hould on
me. Bhoys, that noise was not dhrink, 'twas the rattle
av a thrain!"

There followed an impressive pause.

"Yes, he had put me on a thrain—put me palanquin

an' all, an' six black assassins av his own coolies that
was in his nefarious confidence, on the flat av a ballast
thruck, and we were rowlin' an' bowlin' along to
Benares. Glory be that I did not wake up thin an' in-
trojuce mysilf to the coolies. As I was sayin', I slept for
the betther part av a day an' a night. But remimber
you, that that man Dearsley had packed me off on wan
av his material-thrains to Benares, all for to make me
overstay my leave an' get me into the cells."

The explanation was an eminently rational one.
Benares lay at least ten hours by rail from the cantonments, and nothing in the world could have saved Mulvaney from arrest as a deserter had he appeared there
in the apparel of his orgies. Dearsley had not forgotten to take revenge. Learoyd, drawing back a little,
began to place soft blows over selected portions of Mulvaney's body. His thoughts were away on the embankment, and they meditated evil for Dearsley. Mulvaney
continued—

"Whin I was full awake the palanquin was set down
in a street, I suspicioned, for I cud hear people passin'
an' talkin'. But I knew well I was far from home.
There is a queer smell upon our cantonments—a smell
av dried earth and brick-kilns wid whiffs av cavalry
stable-litter. This place smelt marigold flowers an' bad
water, an' wanst somethin' alive came an' blew heavy
with his muzzle at the chink av the shutter. 'It's in a
village I am,' thinks I to myself, 'an' the parochial buffalo is investigatin' the palanquin.' But any ways I had
no desire to move. Only lie still whin you're in foreign

parts an' the standin' luck av the British Army will carry ye through. That is an epigram. I made ut.

"Thin a lot av whisperin' divils surrounded the palan-quin. 'Take ut up,' sez wan man. 'But who'll pay us?' sez another. 'The Maharanee's minister, av coorse,' sez the man. 'Oho!' sez I to mysilf, 'I'm a quane in me own right, wid a minister to pay me expenses. I'll be an emperor if I lie still long enough; but this is no vil-lage I've found.' I lay quiet, but I gummed me right eye to a crack av the shutters, an' I saw that the whole street was crammed wid palanquins an' horses, an' a sprinklin' av naked priests all yellow powder an' tigers' tails. But I may tell you, Orth'ris, an' you, Learoyd, that av all the palanquins ours was the most imperial an' magnificent. Now a palanquin means a native lady all the world over, except whin a soldier av the Quane happens to be takin' a ride. 'Women an' priests!' sez I. 'Your father's son is in the right pew this time, Terence. There will be proceedin's.' Six black divils in pink muslin tuk up the palanquin, an' oh! but the rowlin' an' the rockin' made me sick. Thin we got fair jammed among the palanquins—not more than fifty av them—an' we grated an' bumped like Queens-town potato-smacks in a runnin' tide. I cud hear the women gigglin' and squirkin' in their palanquins, but mine was the royal equipage. They made way for ut, an', begad, the pink muslin men o' mine were howlin', 'Room for the Maharanee av Gokral-Seetarun.' Do you know aught av the lady, sorr?"

"Yes," said I. "She is a very estimable old queen of the Central Indian States, and they say she is fat. How on earth could she go to Benares without all the city knowing her palanquin?"

" 'Twas the eternal foolishness av the naygurman. They saw the palanquin lying loneful an' forlornsome, an' the beauty av ut, after Dearsley's men had dhropped ut and gone away, an' they gave ut the best name that occurred to thim. Quite right, too. For aught we know the ould lady was travelin' *incog*—like me. I'm glad to hear she's fat. I was no light weight mysilf, an' my men were mortial anxious to dhrop me under a great big archway promiscuously ornamented wid the most improper carvin's an' cuttin's I iver saw. Begad! they made me blush—like a—like a Maharanee."

"The temple of Prithi-Devi," I murmured, remembering the monstrous horrors of that scriptured archway at Benares.

"Pretty Devilskins, savin' your presence, sorr! There was nothin' pretty about ut, except me. 'Twas all half dhark, an' whin the coolies left they shut a big black gate behind av us, an' half a company av fat yellow priests began pullyhaulin' the palanquins into a dharker place yet—a big stone hall full av pillars, an' gods, an' incense, an' all manner av similar thruck. The gate disconcerted me, for I perceived I wud have to go forward to get out, my retreat bein' cut off. By the same token a good priest makes a bad palanquin-coolie. Begad! they nearly turned me inside out draggin' the palanquin to the temple. Now the disposishin av the forces inside was this way. The Maharanee av Gokral-Seetarun—that was me—lay by the favor av

Providence on the far left flank behind the dhark av a pillar carved with elephints' heads. The remainder av the palanquins was in a big half circle facing in to the biggest, fattest, an' most amazin' she-god that iver I dreamed av. Her head ran up into the black above us, an' her feet stuck out in the light av a little fire av melted butter that a priest was feedin' out av a butter-dish. Thin a man began to sing an' play on somethin' back in the dhark, an' 'twas a queer song. Ut made my hair lift on the back av my neck. Thin the doors av all the palanquins slid back, an' the women bundled out. I saw what I'll niver see again. 'Twas more glori-ous than thransformations at a pantomime, for they was in pink an' blue an' silver an' red an' grass green, wid di'monds an' im'ralds an' great red rubies all over thim. But that was the least part av the glory. O bhoys, they were more lovely than the like av any love-liness in hiven; ay, their little bare feet were better than the white hands av a lord's lady, an' their mouths were like puckered roses, an' their eyes were bigger an' dharker than the eyes av any livin' women I've seen. Ye may laugh, but I'm speakin' truth. I niver saw the like, an' niver I will again."

"Seeing that in all probability you were watching the wives and daughters of most of the kings of India, the chances are that you won't," I said, for it was dawn-ing on me that Mulvaney had stumbled upon a big Queens' Praying at Benares.

"I niver will," he said, mournfully. "That sight doesn't come twist to any man. It made me ashamed to watch. A fat priest knocked at my door. I didn't

think he'd have the insolince to disturb the Maharanee
av Gokral-Seetarun, so I lay still. 'The old cow's
asleep,' sez he to another. 'Let her be,' sez that. ' 'Twill
be long before she has a calf!' I might ha' known before he spoke that all a woman prays for in Injia—an'
for matter o' that in England too—is childher. That
made me more sorry I'd come, me bein', as you well
know, a childless man."

He was silent for a moment, thinking of his little
son, dead many years ago.

"They prayed, an' the butter-fires blazed up an' the
incense turned everything blue, an' between that an'
the fires the women looked as tho' they were all ablaze
an' twinklin'. They took hold av the she-god's knees,
they cried out an' they threw themselves about, an' that
world-without-end-amen music was dhrivin' thim mad.
Mother av Hiven! how they cried, an' the ould she-god
grinnin' above thim all so scornful! The dhrink was
dyin' out in me fast, an' I was thinkin' harder than the
thoughts wud go through my head—thinkin' how to
get out, an' all manner of nonsense as well. The
women were rockin' in rows, their di'mond belts
clickin', an' the tears runnin' out betune their hands,
an' the lights were goin' lower an' dharker. Thin there
was a blaze like lightnin' from ther oof, an' that showed
me the inside av the palanquin, an' at the end where
my foot was, stood the livin' spit an' image o' mysilf
worked on the linin'. This man here, ut was."

He hunted in the folds of his pink cloak, ran a hand
under one, and thrust into the firelight a foot-long em-

broidered presentment of the great god Krishna, playing on a flute. The heavy jowl, the staring eye, and the blue-black moustache of the god made up a far-off resemblance to Mulvaney.

"The blaze was gone in a wink, but the whole schame came to me thin. I believe I was mad too. I slid the off-shutter open an' rowled out into the dhark behind the elephint-head pillar, tucked up my trousies to my knees, slipped off my boots an' tuk a general hould av all the pink linin' av the palanquin. Glory be, ripped out like a woman's dhriss whin you tread on ut at a sergeants' ball, an' a bottle came with ut. I tuk the bottle an' the next minut I was out av the dhark av the pillar, the pink linin' wrapped round me most graceful, the music thunderin' like kettledrums, an' a could draft blowin' round my bare legs. By this hand that did ut, I was Krishna tootlin' on the flute—the god that the rig'mental chaplain talks about. A sweet sight I must ha' looked. I knew my eyes were big, and my face was wax-white, an' at the worst I must ha' looked like a ghost. But they took me for the livin' god. The music stopped, and the women were dead dumb an' I crooked my legs like a shepherd on a china basin, an' I did the ghost-waggle with my feet as I had done ut at the rig'mental theatre many times, an' I slid acrost the width av that temple in front av the she-god tootlin' on the beer bottle."

"Wot did you toot?" demanded Ortheris the practical.

"Me? Oh!" Mulvaney sprang up, suiting the ac-

tion to the word, and sliding gravely in front of us, a
dilapidated but imposing deity in the half light. "I
sang—

> "Only say
> You'll be Mrs. Brallaghan.
> Don't say nay,
> Charmin' Judy Callaghan.

I didn't know me own voice when I sang. An' oh!
'twas pitiful to see the women. The darlin's were
down on their faces. Whin I passed the last wan I
cud see her poor little fingers workin' one in another
as if she wanted to touch my feet. So I dhrew the tail
av this pink overcoat over her head for the greater
honor, an' I slid into the dhark on the other side av the
temple, and fetched up in the arms av a big fat priest.
All I wanted was to get away clear. So I tuk him by
his greasy throat an' shut the speech out av him. 'Out!'
sez I. 'Which way, ye fat heathen?'—'Oh!' sez he.
'Man,' sez I. 'White man, soldier man, common soldier man. Where in the name av confusion is the back
door?' The women in the temple were still on their
faces, an' a young priest was holdin' out his arms above
their heads.

"'This way,' sez my fat friend, duckin' behind a big
bull-god an' divin' into a passage. Thin I remimbered
that I must ha' made the miraculous reputation av that
temple for the next fifty years. 'Not so fast,' I sez, an'
I held out both my hands wid a wink. That ould thief
smiled like a father. I tuk him by the back av the
neck in case he should be wishful to put a knife into
me unbeknownst, an' I ran him up an' down the pas-

sage twice to collect his sensibilities! 'Be quiet,' sez he, in English. 'Now you talk sense,' I sez. 'Fwhat'll you give me for the use av that most iligant palanquin I have no time to take away?'—'Don't tell,' sez he. 'Is ut like?' sez I. 'But ye might give me my railway fare. I'm far from my home an' I've done you a service.' Bhoys, 'tis a good thing to be a priest. The ould man niver throubled himself to dhraw from a bank. As I will prove to you subsequint, he philandered all round the slack av his clothes an' began dribblin' ten-rupee notes, old gold mohurs, and rupees into my hand till I could hould no more."

"You lie!" said Ortheris. "You're mad or sunstrook. A native don't give coin unless you cut it out o' 'im. 'Taint nature."

"Then my lie an' my sunstroke is concealed under that lump av sod yonder," retorted Mulvaney, unruffled, nodding across the scrub. "An' there's a dale more in nature than your squidgy little legs have iver taken you to, Orth'ris, me son. Four hundred an' thirty-four rupees by my reckonin', *an'* a big fat gold necklace that I took from him as a remimbrancer, was our share in that business."

"An' 'e give it you for love?" said Ortheris.

"We were alone in that passage. Maybe I was a trifle too pressin', but considher fwhat I had done for the good av the temple and the iverlastin' joy av those women. 'Twas cheap at the price. I wud ha' taken more if I cud ha' found ut. I turned the ould man upside down at the last, but he was milked dhry. Thin he opened a door in another passage an' I found mysilf up to my knees in Benares river-water, an' bad smellin' ut is. More by token I had come out on the river-line close to the burnin' ghat and contagious to a cracklin' corpse. This was in the heart av the night, for I had been four hours in the temple. There was a crowd av boats tied up, so I tuk wan an' wint across the river. Thin I came home acrost country, lyin' up by day."

"How on earth did you manage?" I said.

"How did Sir Frederick Roberts get from Cabul to Candahar? He marched an' he niver tould how near he was to breakin' down. That's why he is fwhat he is. An' now"—Mulvaney yawned portentously. "Now I will go an' give myself up for absince widout leave. It's eight an' twenty days an' the rough end of the colonel's tongue in orderly room, any way you look at ut. But 'tis cheap at the price."

"Mulvaney," said I, softly. "If there happens to be any sort of excuse that the colonel can in any way accept, I have a notion that you'll get nothing more than the dressing-gown. The new recruits are in, and"—

"Not a word more, sorr. Is ut excuses the old man wants? 'Tis not my way, but he shall have thim. I'll tell him I was engaged in financial operations connected wid a church," and he flapped his way to cantonments and the cells, singing lustily—

> "So they sent a corp'ril's file,
> And they put me in the gyard-room
> For conduck unbecomin' of a soldier."

And when he was lost in the midst of the moonlight we could hear the refrain—

"Bang upon the big drum, bash upon the cymbals,
    As we go marchin' along, boys, oh!
    For although in this campaign
    There's no whisky nor champagne,
    We'll keep our spirits goin' with a song, boys!"

Therewith he surrendered himself to the joyful and almost weeping guard, and was made much of by his fellors. But to the Colonel he said that he had been smitten with sunstroke and had lain insensible on a villager's cot for untold hours; and between laughter and good-will the affair was smoothed over, so that he could, next day, teach the new recruits how to "Fear God, Honor the Queen, Shoot Straight, and Keep Clean."

THE GOD FROM THE MACHINE

Hit a man an' help a woman, an' ye can't be far wrong any-ways.—Maxims of Private Mulvaney.

THE Inexpressibles gave a ball. They borrowed a seven-pounder from the Gunners, and wreathed it with laurels, and made the dancing-floor plate-glass and provided a supper, the like of which had never been eaten before, and set two sentries at the door of the room to hold the trays of programme-cards. My friend, Private Mulvaney, was one of the sentries, because he was the tallest man in the regiment. When the dance was fairly started the sentries were released, and Private Mulvaney went to curry favor with the Mess Sergeant in charge of the supper. Whether the Mess Sergeant gave or Mulvaney took, I cannot say. All that I am certain of is that, at supper-time, I found Mulvaney with Private Ortheris, two-thirds of a ham, a loaf of bread, half a *pâté-de-foie-gras,* and two magnums of champagne, sitting on the roof of my carriage. As I came up I heard him saying—

"Praise be a danst doesn't come as often as Ord'ly-room, or, by this an' that, Orth'ris, me son, I wud be the dishgrace av the rig'mint instid av the brightest jool in uts crown."

"*Hand* the Colonel's pet noosance," said Ortheris.

487

"But wot makes you curse your rations? This 'ere fizzy stuff's good enough."

"Stuff, ye oncivilized pagin! 'Tis champagne we're dhrinkin' now. 'Tisn't that I am set ag'in. 'Tis this quare stuff wid the little bits av black leather in it. I misdoubt I will be distressin'ly sick wid it in the mornin'. Fwhat is ut?"

"Goose liver," I said, climbing on the top of the carriage, for I knew that it was better to sit out with Mulvaney than to dance many dances.

"Goose liver is ut?" said Mulvaney. "Faith, I'm thinkin' thim that makes it wud do betther to cut up the Colonel. He carries a power av liver undher his right arrum whin the days are warm an' the nights chill. He wud give thim tons an' tons av liver. 'Tis he sez so. 'I'm all liver to-day,' sez he; an' wid that he ordhers me ten days C. B. for as moild a dhrink as iver a good sodger took betune his teeth."

"That was when 'e wanted for to wash 'isself in the Fort Ditch," Ortheris explained. "Said there was too much beer in the Barrack waterbutts for a God-fearing man. You was lucky in gettin' orf with wot you did, Mulvaney."

"Say you so? Now I'm pershuaded I was cruel hard trated, seein' fwhat I've done for the likes av him in the days whin my eyes were wider opin than they are now. Man alive, for the Colonel to whip *me* on the peg in that way! Me that have saved the repitation av a ten times better man than him! 'Twas ne-farious— an' that manes a power av evil!"

"Never mind the nefariousness," I said. "Whose reputation did you save?"

"More's the pity, 'twasn't my own, but I tuk more trouble wid ut than av ut was. 'Twas just my way, messin' wid fwhat was no business av mine. Hear now!" He settled himself at ease on the top of the carriage. "I'll tell you all about ut. Av coorse I will name no names, for there's wan that's an orf'cer's lady now, that was in ut, and no more will I name places, for a man is thracked by a place."

"Eyah!" said Ortheris, lazily, "but this is a mixed story wot's comin'."

"Wanst upon a time, as the childer-books say, I was a recruity."

"Was you though?" said Ortheris; "now that's extryordinary!"

"Orth'ris," said Mulvaney, "av you opin thim lips av yours again, I will, savin' your presince, sorr, take you by the slack av your trousers an' heave you."

"I'm mum," said Ortheris. "Wot 'appened when you was a recruity?"

"I was a betther recruity than you iver was or will be, but that's neither here nor there. Thin I became a man, an' the divil of a man I was fifteen years ago. They called me Buck Mulvaney in thim days, an', begad, I tuk a woman's eye. I did that! Ortheris, ye scrub, fwhat are ye sniggerin' at? Do you misdoubt me?"

"Devil a doubt!" said Ortheris; "but I've 'eard summat like that before!"

Mulvaney dismissed the impertinence with a lofty wave of his hand and continued—

"An' the orf'cers av the rig'mint I was in in thim days *was* orf'cers—gran' men, wid a manner on 'em, an' a way wid 'em such as is not made these days— all but wan—wan o' the capt'ns. A bad dhrill, a wake voice, an' a limp leg—thim three things are the signs av a bad man. You bear that in your mind, Orth'ris, me son.

"An' the Colonel av the rig'mint had a daughter— wan av thim lamblike, bleatin', pick-me-up-an'-carry-me-or-I'll-die gurls such as was made for the natural prey av men like the Capt'n, who was iverlastin' payin' coort to her, though the Colonel he said time an' over, 'Kape out av the brute's way, my dear.' But he niver had the heart for to send her away from the throuble, bein' as he was a widower, an' she their wan child."

"Stop a minute, Mulvaney," said I; "how in the world did you come to know these things?"

"How did I come?" said Mulvaney, with a scornful grunt; "bekaze I'm turned durin' the Quane's pleasure to a lump av wood, lookin' out straight forninst me, wid a—a candelabbrum in my hand, for you to pick your cards out av, must I not see nor feel? Av coorse I du! Up my back, an' in my boots, an' in the short hair av the neck—that's where I kape my eyes whin I'm on duty an' the reg'lar wans are fixed. Know! Take my word for it, sorr, ivrything an' a great dale more is known in a rig'mint; or fwhat wud be the use av a Mess Sargint, or a Sargint's wife doin' wet-nurse to the Major's baby? To reshume. He was a

bad dhrill was this Capt'n—a rotten bad dhrill—an'
whin first I ran my eye over him, I sez to myself: 'My
Militia bantam!' I sez, 'My cock av a Gosport dunghill'
—'twas from Portsmouth he came to us—'there's
combs to be cut,' sez I, 'an' by the grace av God, 'tis
Terence Mulvaney will cut thim.'

"So he wint menowderin', and minanderin', an'
blandandhering roun' an' about the Colonel's daughter, an' she, poor innocint, lookin' at him like a Com-
m'ssariat bullock looks at the Comp'ny cook. He'd
a dhirty little scrub av a black moustache, an' he
twisted an' turned ivry wurrd he used as av he found
ut too sweet for to spit out. Eyah! He was a tricky
man an' a liar by natur'. Some are born so. He was
wan. I knew he was over his belt in money borrowed
from natives; besides a lot av other matthers which, in
regard for your presince, sorr, I will oblitherate. A little av fwhat I knew, the Colonel knew, for he wud
have none av him, an' that, I'm thinkin', by fwhat
happened aftherward, the Capt'in knew.

"Wan day, bein' mortial idle, or they wud never ha'
thried ut, the rig'mint gave amshure theatricals—orf'cers
an' orf'cers' ladies. You've seen the likes time an'
again, sorr, an' poor fun 'tis for them that sit in the
back row an' stamp wid their boots for the honor av
the rig'mint. I was told off for to shif' the scenes,
haulin' up this an' draggin' down that. Light work
ut was, wid lashins av beer and the gurl that dhressed
the orf'cers' ladies—but she died in Aggra twelve years
gone, an' my tongue's gettin' the betther av me. They
was actin' a play thing called *Sweethearts,* which you

may ha' heard av, an' the Colonel's daughter she was
a lady's maid. The Capt'n was a boy called Broom—
Spread Broom was his name in the play. Thin I saw
—ut come out in the actin'—fwhat I niver saw before,
an' that was that he was no gentleman. They was too
much together, thim two, a-whishperin' behind the
scenes I shifted, an' some av what they said I heard;
for I was death—blue death an' ivy—on the comb-
cuttin'. He was iverlastin'ly oppressing her to fall in
wid some sneakin' schame av his, an' she was thryin'
to stand out against him, but not as though she was set
in her will. I wonder now in thim days that my ears
did not grow a yard on me head wid list'nin'. But I
looked straight forninst me an' hauled up this an'
dragged down that, such as was my duty, an' the orf'-
cers' ladies sez one to another, thinkin' I was out av
listen-reach: 'Fwhat an obligin' young man is this Cor-
p'ril Mulvaney!' I was a Corp'ril then. I was rejuced
aftherward, but, no matther, I was a Corp'ril wanst.

"Well, this *Sweethearts'* business wint on like most
amshure theatricals, an' barrin' fwhat I suspicioned,
'twasn't till the dhress-rehearsal that I saw for certain
that thim two—he the blackguard, an' she no wiser
than she should ha' been—had put up an evasion."

"A what?" said I.

"E-vasion! Fwhat you call an elopemint. E-vasion
I calls it, bekaze, exceptin' whin 'tis right an' natural
an' proper, 'tis wrong an' dhirty to steal a man's wan
child she not knowin' her own mind. There was a
Sargint in the Comm'ssariat who set my face upon
e-vasions. I'll tell you about that"—

"Stick to the bloomin' Captains, Mulvaney," said Ortheris; "Comm'ssariat Sargints is low."

Mulvaney accepted the amendment and went on:—

"Now I knew that the Colonel was no fool, any more than me, for I was hild the smartest man in the rig'mint, an' the Colonel was the best orf'cer commandin' in Asia; so fwhat he said an' *I* said was a mortial truth. We knew that the Capt'n was bad, but, for reasons which I have already oblitherated, I knew more than me Colonel. I wud ha' rolled out his face wid the butt av my gun before permittin' av him to steal the gurl. Saints knew av he wud ha' married her, and av he didn't she wud be in great tormint, an' the divil av a 'scandal.' But I niver sthruck, niver raised me hand on my shuperior orf'cer; an' that was a merricle now I come to considher it."

"Mulvaney, the dawn's risin'," said Ortheris, "an' we're no nearer 'ome than we was at the beginnin'. Lend me your pouch. Mine's all dust."

Mulvaney pitched his pouch over, and filled his pipe afresh.

"So the dhress-rehearsal came to an end, an', bekaze I was curious, I stayed behind whin the scene-shiftin' was ended, an' I shud ha' been in barricks, lyin' as flat as a toad under a painted cottage thing. They was talkin' in whispers, an' she was shiverin' an' gaspin' like a fresh-hukked fish. 'Are you sure you've got the hang av the manewvers?' sez he, or wurrds to that effec', as the coort-martial sez. 'Sure as death,' sez she, 'but I misdoubt 'tis cruel hard on my father.' 'Damn your father,' sez he, or anyways 'twas fwhat he

thought, 'the arrangement is as clear as mud. Jungi
will drive the carri'ge afther all's over, an' you come to
the station, cool an' aisy, in time for the two o'clock
thrain, where I'll be wid your kit.' 'Faith,' thinks I
to myself, 'thin there's a ayah in the business tu!'

"A powerful bad thing is a ayah. Don't you niver
have any thruck wid wan. Thin he began sootherin'
her, an' all the orf'cers an' orf'cers' ladies left, an' they
put out the lights. To explain the theory av the flight,
as they say at Muskthry, you must understand that
afther this *Sweethearts'* nonsinse was ended, there was
another little bit av a play called *Couples*—some kind
av couple or another. The gurl was actin' in this, but
not the man. I suspicioned he'd go to the station wid
the gurl's kit at the end av the first piece. 'Twas the
kit that flusthered me, for I knew for a Capt'n to go
trapesing about the impire wid the Lord knew what
av a *truso* on his arrum was nefarious, an' wud be
worse than easin' the flag, so far as the talk aftherward
wint."

" 'Old on, Mulvaney. Wot's *truso?*" said Ortheris.

"You're an oncivilized man, me son. Whin a gurl's
married, all her kit an' 'coutrements are *truso,* which
manes weddin'-portion. An' 'tis the same whin she's
runnin' away, even wid the biggest blackguard on the
Arrmy List.

"So I made my plan av campaign. The Colonel's
house was a good two miles away. 'Dennis,' sez I to
my color-sargint, 'av you love me lend me your kyart,
for me heart is bruk an' me feet is sore wid trampin'
to and from this foolishness at the Gaff.' An' Dennis

lent ut, wid a rampin', stampin' red stallion in the shafts. Whin they was all settled down to their *Sweethearts* for the first scene, which was a long wan, I slips outside and into the kyart. Mother av Hivin! but I made that horse walk, an' we came into the Colonel's compound as the divil wint through Athlone—in standin' leps. There was no one there excipt the servints, an' I wint round to the back an' found the girl's ayah.

" 'Ye black brazen Jezebel,' sez I, 'sellin' your masther's honor for five rupees—pack up all the Miss Sahib's kit an' look slippy! *Capt'n Sahib's* order,' sez I. 'Going to the station we are,' I sez, an' wid that I laid my finger to my nose an' looked the schamin' sinner I was.

" '*Bote acchy*,' says she; so I knew she was in the business, an' I piled up all the sweet talk I'd iver learned in the bazars on to this she-bullock, an' prayed av her to put all the quick she knew into the thing. While she packed, I stud outside an' sweated, for I was wanted for to shif' the second scene. I tell you, a young gurl's e-vasion manes as much baggage as a rig'mint on the line av march! 'Saints help Dennis's springs,' thinks I, as I bundled the stuff into the thrap, 'for I'll have no mercy!'

" 'I'm comin' too,' says the ayah.

" 'No, you don't,' sez I, 'later—*pechy*! You *baito* where you are. I'll *pechy* come an' bring you *sart*, along with me, you maraudin' '—niver mind fwhat I called her.

"Thin I wint for the Gaff, an' by the special ordher

av Providence, for I was doin' a good work you will
ondersthand, Dennis's springs hild toight. 'Now, whin
the Capt'n goes for that kit,' thinks I, 'he'll be throubled.' At the end av *Sweethearts* off the Capt'n runs
in his kyart to the Colonel's house, an' I sits down on
the steps and laughs. Wanst an' again I slipped in to
see how the little piece was goin', an' whin ut was
near endin' I stepped out all among the carriages an'
sings out very softly, 'Jungi!' Wid that a carr'ge began
to move, an' I waved to the dhriver. *'Hitherao!'* sez
I, an' he *hitheraoed* till I judged he was at proper distance, an' thin I tuk him, fair an' square betune the
eyes, all I knew for good or bad, an' he dhropped wid
a guggle like the canteen beer-engine whin ut's runnin'
low. Thin I ran to the kyart an' tuk out all the kit
an' piled it into the carr'ge, the sweat runnin' down
my face in dhrops. 'Go home,' sez I, to the *sais;*
'you'll find a man close here. Very sick he is. Take
him away, an' av you iver say wan wurrd about fwhat
you've *dekkoed,* I'll *marrow* you till your own wife
won't *sumjao* who you are!' Thin I heard the stampin' av feet at the ind av the play, an' I ran in to let
down the curtain. Whin they all came out the gurl
thried to hide herself behind wan av the pillars, an'
sez 'Jungi' in a voice that wouldn't ha' scared a hare.
I run over to Jungi's carr'ge an' tuk up the lousy old
horse-blanket on the box, wrapped my head an' the
rest av me in ut, an' dhrove up to where she was.

"'Miss Sahib,' sez I; 'going to the station? *Captain
Sahib's* order!' an' widout a sign she jumped in all
among her own kit.

"I laid to an' dhruv like steam to the Colonel's house before the Colonel was there, an' she screamed an' I thought she was goin' off. Out comes the ayah, saying all sorts av things about the Capt'n havin' come for the kit an' gone to the station.

" 'Take out the luggage, you divil,' sez I, 'or I'll murther you!'

"The lights av the thraps people comin' from the Gaff was showin' across the parade ground, an', by this an' that, the way thim two women worked at the bundles an' thrunks was a caution! I was dyin' to help, but, seein' I didn't want to be known, I sat wid the blanket roun' me an' coughed an' thanked the Saints there was no moon that night.

"Whin all was in the house again, I niver asked for *bukshish* but dhruv tremenjus in the opp'site way from the other carr'ge an' put out my lights. Presintly, I saw a naygur-man wallowin' in the road. I slipped down before I got to him, for I suspicioned Providence was wid me all through that night. 'Twas Jungi, his nose smashed in flat, all dumb sick as you please. Dennis's man must have tilted him out av the thrap. Whin he came to, 'Hutt!' sez I, but he began to howl.

" 'You black lump av dirt,' I sez, 'is this the way you dhrive your *gharri?* That *tikka* has been *owin'* an' *fere-owin'* all over the bloomin' country this whole bloomin' night, an' you as *mut-walla* as Davey's sow. Get up, you hog!' sez I, louder, for I heard the wheels av a thrap in the dark; 'get up an' light your lamps, or you'll be run into!' This was on the road to the Railway Station.

" 'Fwhat the divil's this?' sez the Capt'n's voice in the dhark, an' I could judge he was in a lather av rage.

" '*Gharri* dhriver here, dhrunk, sorr,' sez I; 'I've found his *gharri* sthrayin' about cantonmints, an' now I've found him.'

" 'Oh!' sez the Capt'n; 'fwhat's his name?' I stooped down an' pretended to listen.

" 'He sez his name's Jungi, sorr,' sez I.

" 'Hould my harse,' sez the Capt'n to his man, an' wid that he gets down wid the whip an' lays into Jungi, just mad wid rage an' swearin' like the scutt he was.

"I thought, afther a while, he wud kill the man, so I sez:—'Stop, sorr, or you'll murdher him!' That dhrew all his fire on me, an' he cursed me into Blazes, an' out again. I stud to attenshin an' saluted:—'Sorr,' sez I, 'av ivry man in this wurruld had his rights, I'm thinkin' that more than wan wud be beaten to a jelly for this night's work—that niver came off at all, sorr, as you see?' 'Now,' thinks I to myself, 'Terence Mulvaney, you've cut your own throat, for he'll sthrike, an' you'll knock him down for the good av his sowl an' your own iverlastin' dishgrace!'

"But the Capt'n never said a single wurrd. He choked where he stud, an' thin he went into his thrap widout sayin' good-night, an' I wint back to barricks."

"And then?" said Ortheris and I together.

"That was all," said Mulvaney; "niver another word did I hear av the whole thing. All I know was that there was no e-vasion, an' that was fwhat I wanted.

Now, I put ut to you, sorr, is ten days' C.B. a fit an' a proper tratement for a man who has behaved as me?"

"Well, any'ow," said Ortheris, "tweren't this 'ere Colonel's daughter, an' you *was* blazin' copped when you tried to wash in the Fort Ditch."

"That," said Mulvaney, finishing the champagne, "is a shuparfluous an' impert'nint observation."

THE END

About Rudyard Kipling

Rudyard Kipling is loved by Americans as greatly as in England, where he is regarded as one of that country's finest writers.

In part America can claim him, too, for his wife was an American, and Mowgli and the *Jungle Book* characters were created in Vermont where Kipling lived for a while.

No one has ever known better the India of Kipling's age or has written of it more accurately and excitingly. It is natural that India should fill so many of his books. Kipling was born in Bombay. His father was an art teacher there. As a boy, the author learned Hindustani from his *ayahs* along with his English, and listened eagerly to the stories they told about the jungle animals.

When he was six, he was sent back to England, as he was a delicate boy and the English climate was better for him. Not until he was twelve did he go to school. There he edited the school magazine and had his first verse published in a local newspaper. *Stalky & Co.* gives a picture of these days. He did not go to college, but at eighteen went back to India, where he became a reporter on a Lahore newspaper. His stories and verse established characters which later appeared in a number of his books on India.

In 1889 he returned to England by way of Japan, San Francisco, and New York. In the United States he lived on very little, writing furiously. In 1892 he married an American girl, and one of his best-known books, *Barrack Room Ballads,* was published at the same time.

The Kiplings went to Vermont, where for a time they made their home. It was during this period that the famous *Jungle Books* were written. They began as stories told to his own little girls, the first to hear of Mowgli, the boy who was brought up by wolves; of Baloo, the bear, and Bagheera, the panther.

The Kiplings finally settled in Sussex, where he could be near the English downs that he loved. He wrote of them in *The Brushwood Boy*. By now he was rich and famous, and showered with many prizes and awards. Kipling was the first man writing in the English language to receive the Nobel Prize for literature.